Twinned : Book 3

Tris Lawrence

Schenectady, New York

This book is a work of fiction. The characters and events portrayed are a product of the author's imagination. Any resemblance to real people or events is coincidental.

Into the Split

Edited by Nina Waters
Print manuscript formatting by Hermit Prints
E-book formatting by Nina Waters

Published by Duck Prints Press, LLC
Schenectady, New York
duckprintspress.com

ISBN (ePub Edition): 978-1-962488-49-5
ISBN (PDF Edition): 978-1-962488-50-1
ISBN (Print edition): 978-1-962488-48-8

Tags:
Genre: Modern with Magic
Rating: General Audiences
Trigger Warnings: ableism, death of a parent, death of a sibling, death of a spouse, starvation
Relationships: established relationship, f/f, family, m/m, siblings
Character Features: asexual, bipoc, creature transformation, customer service representative, empathy, gay, lesbian, lucid dreaming, panic attacks, professor, ptsd, student (college), teleportation, weather control
Other Tags: alcohol use (casual), college/university, dimension jumping, dystopia, emotional hurt/comfort, fraternities and sororities, mistakenly believed to be dead, multiverse, new york, post-apocalypse, present tense, restaurant, reunion, third person limited point of view, united states of america

To all those who dare to dream:
may you find your perfect path to travel.

Contents

ARRIVAL

1

After two years of being on their own, mornings have an established routine. Nikolai rises before Seth and spends a few minutes basking in the quiet before he wakes his boyfriend so they can scrounge for food and eat. Showers and baths are a rare luxury, and almost never warm; usually, they change into whatever clothing feels cleaner than what they wore to bed the night before. Then they pack because if they don't get moving, they'll never arrive at their final destination.

"How much farther do we have to go?" Seth shoves his bedroll into his bag, grabbing Nikolai's dirty clothes along with his own to push in on top.

Nikolai digs into his own bag, finding the carefully sealed pouch with the neatly folded, worn map inside. He spreads it out on the table and circles the red dot with his finger. He draws a line from there to where he thinks they are now, then taps the map before repeating the line in reverse.

"About two days," he says. That's his best guess, and after all this time, it seems both too long and not long enough. "That's if we don't run into trouble, like finding an unexpected settlement. As long as we avoid the outskirts of the closest cities, we should be far enough out that whatever people live around here will be the sorts who'd rather stay away from others."

"Until we run into a survivalist with a locker full of loaded shotguns," Seth mutters, "or someone who sees a shadow near us and thinks we're being followed by a Shadow and shoots before checking to see if we're actually a danger to them."

Seth's not wrong: a lot of people panic first and think later.

"Usually you're the positive one," Nikolai points out. Normally, Seth talks about how they can pretend to be nothing more than human, at least for the five minutes it takes to get past someone who isn't actively hunting them. Or how they can avoid houses unless they see one marked as safe, or one that's definitely abandoned. He's not usually defeatist.

Nikolai wonders if it's his fault, because of the new Dreams he's been having.

Seth drops his bag on the floor and sits on the cot. He pushes his patched glasses up his nose. "I'm tired," he says. "We're nineteen. Our adult lives were supposed to be different than this. At least that's what I thought when I was eight. We were supposed to have lives, Nikolai. You and me, together, living some ideal that involved more school than we wanted, drinking too much because that's what college is for, and finding jobs and a home and building a family. We don't even camp because it's fun; we camp to survive. Now I think I'm lucky that humans don't like to camp for fun anymore, because as long as they keep to the protected routes and their cities, and we stick to the rural areas and keep off the roads, we're safe. I can barely remember what it was like before the Split."

"Plus there are sniffers." Sniffers might be an urban legend, but Nikolai's not about to take the chance. He remembers, when he was young and on family road trips, the toll readers hanging low over the highways; he imagines the sniffers are like that, looking for Shadow and Talent instead of charging a fee. Between those and the limited access to fuel, it isn't worth traveling the roads, either by vehicle or on foot. "Besides, we don't know how to drive. We've been literally running for our lives since we were sixteen."

"We weren't always alone."

Nikolai settles on the cot next to Seth, leaning close to him. "No, we weren't," he murmurs.

Their group had experienced some attrition in the early years after the Split, but up until three years ago, they had still been six strong. He shudders at the memory, and there's a soft warmth around him in response, a calming ease. Nikolai closes his eyes and lets himself sink into Seth's emotions; he can feel the shared hurt, sharp around the edges despite the calm. Nikolai whispers the same thing he's said every night since the fire, whether he believes it or not: "It's possible that they've made it to Havenhill without us."

Havenhill.

They've been searching for so long it sounds like a myth.

Seth grasps Nikolai's hand with his own and curls them together, palm to palm and fingers entwined. "Two more days?" he asks.

"Maybe three, if we need to slow down." Something always seems to get in the way. Hunger. Weather. Currently it's nice out, for March, which is good. In the Northeast, it could go either way, and Nikolai doesn't want to end up stuck outside in the middle of a surprise snowstorm.

"Are there any more safe places marked on the map?" Seth asks. "Or are we sleeping outside in the cold tonight?"

Nikolai's spent enough time reviewing the final leg of their trip that he doesn't need to refer to the map to answer. "There's an abandoned campground, but it doesn't look like it has cabins, and it's in the middle of a survivalist complex," he says. "There's an old road that runs past two good places. According to the notes I have, it's still guarded by humans, but it's also the most direct route to Havenhill." He's going based on information that's been passed from Talent to Talent as they each seek a place that supposedly doesn't exist. "We'll need to pass through Unity—the old school there is supposedly abandoned, and we might be able to find a place to rest. We need to skirt around Valiant, though. It's on the border of the Albany spread. There might be protected farms in the Unity area, too, so we'll need to watch out."

"What you're saying is we have to run the gauntlet to get to Havenhill," Seth says flatly.

Nikolai nods. "If we don't want to travel north, almost into Vermont, then yes."

"Fine." Seth unwinds his hand from Nikolai's and pushes himself to standing. "Someone around here is a sympathizer—that food wasn't stale. We should take some of it before we go. Who knows when we'll get another chance."

Nikolai folds up his map, putting it back into the waterproof pouch he'd scavenged, years ago, from another cabin. That gets tucked neatly into his bag—each item has the perfect place, and he's not willing to risk the map by putting his belongings in haphazardly. He's glad that the dirty clothes are in Seth's bag; they'll need to find a place to stop and wash them soon. He feels like the Shadows could smell them coming, if they had a sense of smell. Hell, humans might be able to smell them coming at this point. Even a bath would help, if they can find a swimming hole that's not overwhelmingly cold or a river that has more depth than a trickle over the rocks.

They put the cabin back to rights, leaving it as clean as when they arrived. The available food is a selection of canned and boxed items, some wrapped as if they came from one of the cities, some handmade and packed in old plastic boxes. Nikolai picks out a selection of homemade bars that will be filling without being heavy, then adds a box of granola, a tin of evaporated milk, two cans of beans, and another two of peaches. It's the best they've eaten in a long time.

After the weight is divided between their bags, they head out, walking carefully along the trickling creek rather than following the old, abandoned road nearby.

It's always eerie in places like this, where the houses lie empty all around them. Most of the homes have been abandoned since the residents moved to the cities, inside the protective walls, but neither Nikolai nor Seth trust a house simply because it seems vacant—not after encounters with security alarms that were still active or traps set for unwary Talent who might stumble upon the place.

Humans thought that if they shut out Talents, they could shut out the Shadows as well. They're wrong; the Shadows are more likely to prey on people with Talent, but in a pinch, they'll eat anyone. He wonders how brightly lit they keep the cities to stay safe.

From the few he's skirted close to, he suspects the answer is very, very brightly lit.

The sun peeks through the trees as they walk, warming the air enough that Nikolai strips off his gloves and hat and shoves them into a pocket. By mid-afternoon, it's warm enough that he takes off his outer jacket, too, and pushes it into his bag.

"It's almost enough to make me think spring is coming," Seth comments, pushing his glasses up. They've broken again, and after the last attempt at a repair, they hang awkwardly across the bridge of his nose. Nikolai has a feeling that they aren't the right prescription, either, from the way that Seth usually lets him read the maps and signs.

He wonders if Havenhill has an eye doctor and a way to get new glasses.

"What's that?" Seth touches Nikolai's arm, pointing. There's a place ahead where the gaps between the trees widen and the shallow creek grows into an open, still pool before continuing as a narrow river.

"Looks like a swimming hole"—Nikolai twines his hand with Seth's—"and a bath, I'm thinking." When Seth makes a face, Nikolai squeezes his hand. "We have two choices: either wear our dirtiest pair of underwear in or go in naked. It'll be frigid, but we reek, and it's halfway to warm today as long as we're in the sun. We're washing off, Seth. Who knows when we'll get to bathe next?"

"If Havenhill exists, maybe they have plumbing," Seth mutters, "and hot water. Why did we hate baths when we were kids? We didn't know how good we had it."

"Hey." Nikolai squeezes again, and Seth stops. When Nikolai cups Seth's face with his palm and leans in, Seth comes up to meet him. Their lips brush, light and warm, and Nikolai smiles against Seth's mouth. "When we get to Havenhill, I'll join you in a hot bath for an hour. But we take the opportunities we get, right? Think how nice it'll be to have clean skin."

The stream flows past deserted properties, and for a moment, Nikolai thinks about exploring the house they're closest to. The waterway cuts through what must have been the backyard, and the house's windows are broken, the back door open and off its hinges. It looks as if no one has lived here in a long time. He doubts there are any traps. Anything good is probably gone by now.

The backyard is ringed with trees, hanging heavily over the aging dock that juts into the swimming hole. Nikolai tests the wood carefully; while boards squeak, it seems stable, and the overhang gives them some measure of privacy.

Once in the water, they'll be exposed, but judging by the near silence, no one's left in the area. He leaves his bag on the shore, close to the end of the dock, in case it isn't as stable as he thinks. He sets out his cleanest clothes nearby, for after he dries off, and grabs a couple pairs of his and Seth's underwear and shirts to wash quickly.

A wave of calm slips over him, and when he glances back, Seth's heading for the house. "Do you think that's a good idea?" Nikolai calls quietly.

"I don't feel anyone nearby." Seth speaks normally, unafraid of being heard. "I want to get a blanket or something for after we get out. There's probably something that was too heavy to carry or too big to take to wherever the people went. I'll be careful, in case someone left a surprise behind."

Nikolai has tried to imagine what the interiors of those cities are like now, with the entire population squeezing into such tight confines. It doesn't sound comfortable.

He nods and waves for Seth to go, then finishes quickly washing clothes and laying them on the dock in the sun.

He jumps into the water as he hears Seth returning, the cold shock making him shiver. His teeth chatter when he breaks the surface, and he gets his feet under him. It isn't deep—maybe up to Seth's chin, he thinks, and about mid-shoulder for himself. Nikolai pastes on a grin and tries to keep his teeth from clattering.

"Come on in. The water's fine!"

Seth finishes spreading out what looks like an old patchwork comforter, leaving a holey blanket in a puddle next to it. He crouches at the edge of the dock, leaning down to trail his fingers in the water. "Liar."

"I'll warm you up," Nikolai offers, and Seth grins.

When Seth leaps straight at him, Nikolai doesn't try to get out of the way; instead, he goes beneath the cold water again, this time with Seth in his arms. They break the surface together, and Nikolai kisses Seth, luxuriating in the warmth of his mouth.

For a moment—just this one sweet moment—he pretends they have the future he expected. The one that was supposed to happen, before the Split.

The water is cold, so they don't linger, washing hastily and then getting out and wrapping up in the blankets on the dock. Everything smells musty, and Nikolai tries not to think what might have started growing in the blankets. It is warm enough that they can sit for a while as the sun beats down on them.

They should be moving. But they're always moving. Havenhill is a lure, and Nikolai wants to find it—if it exists—as soon as possible. But relaxing is unusual, and it feels good to simply…sit still. Except for that one cabin they stayed in when it snowed for several days, Nikolai can't remember the last time they've been able to rest and pretend the world is normal.

He tilts his head against Seth's. "Do you think we should get back on the road, or should we stay here tonight?"

Seth shifts slightly, pushing his glasses up his nose.

"What?" Nikolai prompts.

"When I went inside the house, I saw evidence that someone's been through here recently," Seth says. "Not in the last few days, but I don't think it's been long. There were dishes that had been used, and a can of beans eaten but not scavenged despite having been left empty on the counter. I know it looks like a mess from the outside, but there don't seem to be any animals nesting in there. No one's living here now, but this house is getting regular use, and I have no idea if it's Talents or humans using it."

Nikolai grumbles under his breath, shrugging out of the blanket. His underwear's still wet, so he strips out of it to put on dry clothes, then ties the underwear to the outside of his pack. "Fine," he mutters. "So we move on. I'm not sure we'll get to another safe house tonight, though, so be ready to stay outside."

"We've done it before." Seth's expression is clouded as he dresses, and Nikolai knows why. It's winter. That's why they stayed in that one cabin for so long—it wasn't safe to keep going. One surprise snowstorm could kill them.

"You don't feel—?"

Nikolai shakes his head before Seth finishes the question. "No, I don't feel a storm brewing. My family were Weather Witches, not me," he reminds Seth, although it's hardly the first time it's come up.

"Good. Then we should be fi—" Seth cuts off at a loud shout, a sudden rise in voices, and a crash of something breaking roughly through brush and branches. He grabs Nikolai, and Nikolai grabs back.

There's no way that those are good sounds. The only question is what kind of bad they are.

They stand stock-still, listening carefully. "We need to get in the house," he hisses. "We need to hide."

Seth gives him a dark look. "It might be the group who's been using the house, Nik. I didn't explore much. They could have traps in there—a way to capture us, or worse."

They're too far from the cabin they left that morning, too exposed by the water. Nikolai tenses to run but isn't sure where to go—the only real choices are into the potentially dangerous house, into the water, or down the path toward the intruders.

"I'll calm them." Seth pushes his glasses up again and holds them in place. "We've gotten out of worse spots."

"I could—" Nikolai cuts off when Seth grabs his hand and squeezes hard.

"No," Seth says, "you couldn't. Not without attracting the Shadows. And if those are humans hunting us—"

"—then we'll taste better if the Shadows come. I know." It's one of the hardest things about being out in the wild. If something loud is coming, it can't be a Shadow. Those slip up on you when you aren't looking and steal you before you can scream. If it's making noise, it's probably human, which is equally deadly, just in a different way.

And worse, humans tend to hunt in packs.

"Don't move," Seth whispers as calm flows over Nikolai. Seth closes his eyes, shifting his grip to loosen it. "Don't even breathe. And definitely don't think of using your Talent."

The sounds grow louder and more distinct. A woman's voice yells, "Run!"

Another woman grunts, then shouts, "I can't grab all of you at once. Alaric, a little help here!"

"Mac, don't hurt yourself." Male this time, authoritative.

A laugh in response.

The crashing sound again before a dark shape bursts through the trees, wings flapping with a rush of air as it rises.

In its wake come Shadows.

So many Shadows.

"Shit!" Seth shoves at Nikolai; they both leap sideways, out of the path of the dark, swirling shapes. It's as if the Shadows fly upward, scrambling up trees and the side of the house to get to the creature circling overhead. "Nik, that looks like a—"

Dragon.

They don't exist, but that...that's a dragon.

A figure clings to its back, holding on tightly as the dragon dips and swirls over the swimming hole, just out of reach of the trees at the edge. The Shadows flow into the trees, so intent upon the dragon that they don't seem to notice Seth and Nikolai, nor the crowd that crashes along the path that the dragon has created.

The strangers collectively stop and look up. One man in the group has a hand over his brow. "Nikita's holding on, and the Shadows can't reach Alaric," he says. "They only look like they're flying; they can't actually travel through air without some kind of darkness to move through."

"Because we're people," a woman points out. She stands apart from the rest, her arms crossed and jaw set. "Just because some of us are soulless monsters doesn't mean you should treat us like creatures in a zoo."

Seth hisses at the statement, and a different girl turns, dark eyes furrowed in a frown. A blink and she's in front of them, one hand outstretched to grab Seth's collar. Seth pulls back, and Nikolai wraps his arms around him, holding on.

It feels as if his guts twists inside out, then they're abruptly somewhere else, away from the dock and standing in the midst of the strangers, surrounded by Shadows darkening the trees overhead.

"This is bad," Nikolai says. These people obviously aren't human. They keep using their Talent, which is going to attract even more Shadows. And the one...she implied she *is* a Shadow. That makes no sense. She looks normal. His mind whirls, unable to focus.

"That's him!" the girl on the dragon shouts, her words indistinct with distance. "I can see him through the trees. That's Nikolai!"

"We need to take care of this before it gets worse," Seth mutters. "I was wrong. We have to use your Talent. Nik, I need your help. We need to—"

"I know."

They've dealt with Shadows before, but never this many. And there's always a danger to it; any use of Talent could draw more and make the situation even worse. When Seth had said he would calm them, he'd assumed they were facing human hunters. Nikolai doesn't trust this group of Talents, but they must be safer than the Shadows. There's something vaguely familiar about them, but nothing he can hold onto with adrenaline rushing through his veins.

He has no idea how they know his name.

That's a problem for later.

Surviving the Shadows is a problem for now.

Nikolai wraps his arms around Seth, pressing a kiss to his temple, then reaches inward, relaxing into the calm Seth provides until a bright sparkle trips over his skin. Nikolai brings the Dreamscape out, amplifying it until light glitters like diamonds through the trees.

The Shadows wink out like they were never there.

Nikolai catches Seth as he crumples; they both go to the ground when Nikolai's own knees give out.

There's a rush of wind and a low *thump*. "What was that?" an unfamiliar male voice gruffly asks.

"I think that was Nikolai."

"I didn't like it," one of the girls mutters dryly. "On the other hand, I'm still here. Does that prove my humanity to you, Pawel?"

"It proves that you're not easily banished by a bright light." It's the first male voice, drawing closer to the accompaniment of footsteps that crunch on the ground.

Nikolai opens his eyes to see the one who he assumes is Pawel crouching next to him.

"Are you okay?" Pawel asks.

The girl who rode dragon-back pushes forward and leans in over Pawel. "We aren't here to hurt you," she says quickly. "We're here to help. Well. We're not supposed to be here at all, but we are, and as long as we're here, we're going to rescue you."

Nikolai can't help the sharp laugh. "Rescue me? You're the ones who were being chased by Shadows. We would've been fine if you hadn't brought them to us. Don't you know not to use your Talent like that? It attracts them. What I did will only drive them away temporarily. We need to get out of here before more Shadows come."

"Oh, they're aware we're here. They are very aware."

"Mattie."

"Alaric," she retorts, "did you, or did you not, trap me by creating a new ritual and then transforming into a dragon because you knew I would expect you to taste good?" She sighs heavily. "Now I can't even eat properly. I miss it, sometimes. Chocolate is not the same, as delicious as it is."

"You're all hurting my head," Seth says. He nudges his way out of the tight circle of Nikolai's arms, and together they rise.

Nikolai keeps a hand on Seth's side, not wanting to lose contact, not now. "Who are you?" There are seven of them, with no dragon in sight; it's apparently been replaced by someone who must be Alaric.

The girl who'd ridden dragon-back pushes past Pawel, right into Nikolai's personal space. "I'm Nikita. I've been Dreaming about you."

For a brief moment, Nikolai considers sitting down again. He wavers, and this time it's Seth who holds him up, an arm around his back to brace him. "Oh," he says, voice small, because that snaps the familiarity into focus. She's the face in the mirror when he Dreams. These people are her friends. "You like broccoli."

Nikita blinks. "I…I do, actually. And it's one of the few vegetables the campus dining halls do right, without turning it completely into mush. Have you been dreaming that you're me?"

"Sometimes," Nikolai admits. "And it's made me strangely nostalgic for broccoli. When I was little, I hated broccoli."

"This is her," Seth says. Nikolai has told Seth about his Dreams. "You think we can trust her?"

Nikolai looks at the crowd with Nikita, all of them now vaguely familiar, if only half-remembered, from his Dreams. "Probably," he allows, because that's as much as he's confident in saying.

One of the women steps forward, tucking a strand of wavy brown hair behind her ear. She reaches into her bag and brings out a wallet, looking through it until she draws out a piece of paper. She shows it to him; it's a detailed, hand-drawn picture of the cabin they stayed in for so long, the one they had left only days ago.

"I'm Carolyn," she says, "and if this place is still safe, I can get us there."

Nikolai exchanges a look with Seth.

"It's not made to sleep more than two," Seth mutters. "It's also a hike from here, and you don't look like you're equipped for travel. And it'll be pushing us backward several days."

Nikita gestures at the backpacks they carry. "I've seen how you two live, and it's not luxurious. I know what we're getting ourselves into."

"I don't, and I honestly don't want to be here," Mattie says. "However, if I get uncomfortable, I'll just leave. On the other hand, you can trust them, and I promise that I won't eat you because if I did, Alaric would probably eat me."

"With my blessing," Pawel says darkly.

"Can we please—?" There's a wash of calm and acceptance over him; Seth and Nikolai twist to stare at the girl speaking. She reminds Nikolai of Seth; she's obviously an Empath. "Caro, open the gate," the girl says. "We need to go somewhere that isn't the middle of the woods and has a chance of being safe."

"How likely is it that whatever she's about to do will summon Shadows?"

The newcomers exchange looks at Nikolai's question.

Mattie licks her lips, then huffs a drawn-out sigh. "Probable. Everything they do tastes delicious. You go through; I'll stay here. I can deal with them if I'm alone, and I'll come through the shadows to join you provided you leave me a dark corner. They won't follow if they think you're already mine."

"You don't know that it works the same way in this world as in our own," Pawel says.

Mattie shrugs. "Might as well try."

"Then we're decided." Carolyn holds the picture in front of her, and as Nikolai watches, the image of the safe house swells to life size, enveloping them. Mattie carefully steps out of its way as Carolyn gestures. "Go through."

Seth grips Nikolai's hand tightly, and they go together, stepping into the bright image. For a moment, the ground beneath their feet is dirt and leaves, then they stumble onto the rough-hewn wood floor of the cabin.

The others follow in pairs, Carolyn stepping through last with Pawel. There is no sign of Mattie.

Nikolai hurries to light the lanterns, and once he places them, Nikita moves them just enough to leave a corner dark. The darkness there makes Nikolai's skin itch, but he remembers Mattie's words. In the small cabin, Alaric seems bigger than he did before, hulking as he stands near the darkness. They all seem both strange and familiar, and Nikolai isn't sure how to handle this. It's been a long time since he's seen so many Talents gathered together, and he can't remember when he last saw so many different ones in the same place.

Seth sinks onto the cot and pulls his glasses off, rubbing at the bridge of his nose. "We just lost all that time," he mutters. "At this rate, we'll never get to Havenhill. If it even exists."

Nikolai catches Nikita as she throws her arms around him, hugging him hard. "I'm so glad you're alive," she whispers. "I stopped Dreaming, and I thought maybe you were dead. I wanted to find you, and this wasn't an on-purpose mission, but we're here now, and I'm glad we are, because we can help you."

"Help me…what?" Nikolai has no idea what she means, except that it's probably not about getting to Havenhill. He has the feeling she's been getting an entirely different view through the Dreams than he has. He sets her on her feet carefully; as soon as he lets go of her shoulders, she withdraws into the crowd of strangers.

"Help you do whatever it is you're trying to do," Nikita says, as if that's somehow easy.

"Help you stay alive," Pawel says firmly.

Mattie emerges from the shadows, metamorphosing from darkness into human. She crosses her arms, standing close enough to Alaric to touch him but far enough that Nikolai can see the space between them. She looks at Alaric, waiting.

Alaric huffs, a low growl before he rumbles, "We can heal the split."

"The Split isn't something that can be healed," Seth says.

"Alaric."

"We're here for Nikolai!"

"We have to deal with the Shadows."

"Right, like we're a blight."

Nikolai puts his hands up. He can't tell who's said what in the blur of sound, voices merging in the outburst. He doesn't care. "Look, we need to start a little further back. I know you think you're here to help me, but how did you get here? Who are you? Because I'm off-kilter, and any minute now Seth'll start worrying that I catapulted us into a Dream and we're lost there."

Nikita glances at Pawel, who looks back at her. "I mean," she says slowly, "that's possible. If our Talents interact like Dreamwalkers' do."

"They won't, if a Dreamwalker is properly bonded." Seth gestures at the girl with glasses who Nikolai doesn't know a name for yet. "You've got your Empath. Nikolai's got me."

"Wait." Pawel digs in his pockets, brings out a device, frowns at it, then puts it away. "That's useless. I should have brought paper."

"I did. I'll make notes later."

"Thanks, Carolyn."

"Stop." Nikolai presses his hands to his head, pain building quickly. He pushes against his skin as if he can hold everything inside. "I need you to just…stop talking for five minutes, and answer questions. One at a time. Like—" He looks to Seth, then at the other Empath. "Introduce yourselves. Starting with you."

"I'm Heather." She pulls a scrunchy from her hair, wrapping it around her wrist. She reaches up as she talks, combing her fingers through thick curls to pull them back from her round face so she can put the scrunchy back in place. "I think I'm my world's version of your Seth. Sort of." Her smile is fleeting. "Nikita's told me about her Dreams of you both. She's my girlfriend. We're not bonded, whatever you meant by that. We only met a few months ago, when she started school."

Their world's version of Seth. He can see that; she'd reminded him of Seth when she let loose with her Talent before. Now that he looks more closely, he can catalog the physical similarities. The round face shape. Wiry, curly hair, although Heather's is long and Seth tries to keep his short. Glasses. Short build. It makes it easier for Nikolai to place her name with her face, anyway, and to remember that she's their Empath.

"I'm Pawel." Pawel steps forward as he introduces himself, offering a hand and shaking Nikolai's briskly. He's a similar height to Nikolai and doesn't seem much older. His hair is too shaggy to be an on-purpose hairstyle, and his face is covered in scruff. "I'm a professor in Magical Studies at Pine Hills University—"

"There is no—"

"—in our world," Pawel finishes. "I'm aware that your world appears to be vastly different from ours. For one, the Shadows aren't as bold where we come from. For another, Talented and non-Talented people live in peace and interact regularly. Aside from Mattie, these are my students. Mattie is—"

"—a Shadowwalker." She shrugs one shoulder. Nikolai stares at her, trying to see the darkness, imagining that he can see it flickering around her like an outline. "But I'm not soulless," she says, "which makes a difference. You could say I'm the missing link to understanding the Shadows' Talent."

Mac is the dark-skinned girl who grabbed him earlier, a Teleporter who carries herself like a fighter; Alaric is Clan, although Nikolai has never heard of Clan turning into a dragon; and Carolyn claims to be Predictive as well as having some kind of illusion-based traveling Talent.

"We were with Del," Nikita says as if Nikolai will know who that is. "We were brainstorming ways to reach you. There were a bunch of us at Pawel's house—this isn't even everyone. Del did…something…while Carolyn had an illusion open, and then we were just here. In the middle of your woods with Shadows swarming after us."

"You set a beacon for them. What did you think would happen?" Mattie asks.

"There are more of you?" Seth asks.

"They aren't here." Carolyn looks up from the papers in her hand. "I'm sure of it. I reached out to Serina and Kit, but I can't get through. It feels like there's a wall, like when I tried to get directly here without going through the Dreamscape."

Pawel's posture relaxes slightly. "Good. We can hope the influence hasn't spread any further. Seth, Nikolai. Do you have a notebook and pen?"

"Because everyone takes their notes on the run with them?" Seth snarks.

"Yes, but you can't have them," Nikolai tells him, setting a hand on Seth's shoulder to calm him. "What we carry is all we have. I won't give up my resources." Not that he has much; he has one notebook filled with cramped writing from the last two years. Everything else went up in smoke.

Alaric grumbles and sits on one of the two chairs at the old wooden table. It creaks under his weight, and he glares at it. Mac glances at him but appears in a blink next to Pawel, who stands there, one hand out, frowning as if he expected a different answer.

"This isn't home," she says gently. "We need to take stock, yes. We need to understand this world and how to interact with it, and we eventually need to figure out how to get home. Think of it as a military op rather than a field trip."

"I have a point of data," Mattie offers. She looks to Mac, and Nikolai thinks maybe she acknowledges that Mac is in charge, for all that Pawel acts like he is. Mac may be small, but she has that air about her. She knows how things work. Nikolai hasn't trusted anyone at first sight in a while, but at the least, Mac seems practical.

"The Shadows here aren't like those in your world," Mattie says as if she isn't from the same place as them. "If you think those are feral, they have nothing on these. It's as if their souls were ripped apart eons ago, and there's nothing left but their starvation instincts. They don't care that I'm with you. They would happily fight me for your soul, and they will consume me as well. I can't protect you here."

"Are you an Empath?" Seth asks.

Mattie shakes her head. "I told you: I'm a Shadowwalker." She stays near the wall, closer to the shadows than the light. She leans there, her body wreathed in darkness. "I Emerged a long time ago, and I was like your Shadows, only not nearly as hungry. We need to consume souls to stay alive. It's not something we think about; we follow whatever smells best, whatever seems like it will taste best. I didn't think about whether what I ate was alive. I just wanted it to fill me. It never did." She glances at Alaric. "Sorry."

Alaric grunts.

"My Emergence pulled my soul out and shoved it into the Dreamscape," Mattie continues. "Carolyn got it back and put me back together." Her smile is tiny and tight, her arms crossed so hard that she seems to be squeezing herself. "I'm the only sane Shadowwalker I know. The only one with a soul. And I am a clue, apparently. I try to help. No one trusts me."

"Except Rory," Alaric mutters.

"I like Rory," Mattie replies. "No matter how delicious he would be, I won't eat him."

Seth takes off his glasses and rubs futilely at the lenses with his dirty T-shirt while trying not to disturb the fragile repair across the bridge. "So you're saying the Shadows can be fixed."

"Potentially, yes." Pawel makes a motion, and Seth cautiously hands over his glasses. Pawel works as he speaks, stroking his fingers along the plastic of the frames, sparks dancing from his fingertips. "The question is, how do we do it on a global scale? Your light attack was more effective as a deterrent, although I doubt it truly injured them or fixed them. It seemed geared toward scaring them away." He holds out the glasses to Seth, the frames melted back into one smooth piece, the tape removed. "Here."

Seth takes them, staring at them before he puts them back on his face. "I said don't use your Talent," he snaps. "We don't want to attract the Shadows."

Nikolai sinks to sit next to Seth on the cot, and it dips beneath their weight. He reaches out, tangling hands with Seth, relaxing with the calm that always comes when they touch. "What he's saying is thank you, but we really do need to be careful. You come from somewhere where you're free." He gives them a moment to see where he's going before he quietly drops the words "We don't" into their silence.

Pawel gestures, which Nikolai takes to mean that he should go on. The others are silent, watching Pawel.

"Things were—" Nikolai's not sure how to explain. "Normal" isn't the right word, because this is normal now. "Things were different," he says. "Very different. Talent had communities, and while we knew about each other, most humans didn't know about us."

"We're human, too," Nikita protests, quieting as Heather touches her shoulder.

Nikolai looks at Seth, who shrugs. "If I say 'human,' I mean them," Nikolai tries to clarify. "It wasn't like that before. But there's a clear 'before' and 'after'... When we were young, everything was fine. I had Seth, I had two older brothers, our parents were all friends, and there were a lot of Mages. Then the Shadows came, and everything changed."

"They do that," Alaric mutters.

Mattie makes a small noise of assent.

Pawel leans against the table, his arms crossed. The table slides roughly across the floor, and he straightens up, glancing at it like it's offended him. "When you say 'the Shadows came,' what, exactly, do you mean?"

"They attacked," Seth says flatly. "I'd heard about them—we all had. There were stories. There are reasons we do what we do. Empaths and Dreamwalkers are bonded so that no one opens the ways to Shadowwalkers. But they escaped from the Dreamscape, and all I know is that it wasn't Nikolai who called them."

Nikolai's hand clenches around Seth's, because the way Seth says it makes Nikolai think that Seth's thought about this. That he's worked through this, made a decision. That at some point, the idea that Nikolai was the reason everything had fallen apart had occurred to him.

He wonders when. And what changed his mind.

Nikolai swallows hard.

Pawel's gaze narrows. "Go back to what you said about Empaths and Dreamwalkers being bonded."

"Everyone knows that," Seth counters.

Mac snorts softly. She puts a hand on Pawel's shoulder, and Pawel's mouth snaps shut. "He didn't call you an idiot," Mac murmurs, and Pawel looks vaguely embarrassed to have been chastised.

Seth raises his eyebrows.

"Dreamwalkers can be dangerous," Nikolai says.

"No shit," Alaric mumbles.

Nikita swats his shoulder.

"So when we're kids and we first Emerge, our parents seek out an Empath who we're comfortable with. Someone we can bond with instinctively, who can shut down our Talent when needed. Who helps us control our Dreams so that we don't open gateways for Shadows. As soon as my parents realized I was a Dreamwalker, not a Weather Witch, they reached out to every Mage they knew to find Seth's family," Nikolai explains.

"Lemons," Alaric says, nodding to himself as if that makes sense. Carolyn gives him a look, and Alaric gestures at where Nikolai and Seth sit. "We talked about the Clan legends. Lemon trees protect from Shadowwalkers. Nothing smells more like citrus than an Empath. Nothing. All stories have seeds of truth."

"Sometimes they get distorted," Pawel muses. "Yes, I can see it. But what happened when the Shadows arrived?" Apparently, he's not going to be deterred, his gaze still locked on Nikolai, who feels the weight of it keenly.

"They started killing people," Nikolai replies. "Talented people dropped dead in the darkness. I figure the Shadows had actually been here for a while—but no one believed the stories some witnesses told. Then some influential people died, publicly, by drowning in darkness. While humanity can ignore a lot, once it's been witnessed by so many people, recorded for others to see, they couldn't ignore it any longer. That was when everyone learned about Shadows, and it was when humans realized Talent existed. Worse, they realized that being Talented was dangerous, and that being around someone with Talent could be deadly. Humanity and Talents split apart, and we became outlaws."

"You didn't fight back?" Pawel asks.

"Some did," Seth says, his tone flat. "They died. So think about this—because I do, and I was only ten years old when it got really bad—there were Shadows killing us. There were humans killing us. And the government fought against us. Everything was stacked against Talent. Running and hiding was our only option."

Pawel huffs, exhaling slowly. He uncrosses his arms, shakes out his hands. When he lifts them again, there are sparks dancing across his fingertips.

Shit.

Mac reaches out and grips Pawel's hand tightly. "You need to stop," she murmurs, and Pawel follows her gaze to where their fingers interlock. The sparks fade, and Nikolai lets out a breath he hadn't realized he was holding.

"You're going to get us killed," Seth mutters.

"We're here to help you." Nikita crouches in front of them. "I swear, Seth, we're here because I was worried about you both."

"You Dreamed about this, and you didn't think about what your arrival could mean?" Seth counters.

"To be fair, I didn't plan on arriving quite like this," she says.

"I need to take a walk," Pawel says abruptly. He twists from Mac's grip, heading for the door and out. She follows, and a moment later, Alaric moves as well.

"I'll make sure they're safe," he grumbles.

The room seems more spacious now that three of them have left, but even only four strangers are still a lot to deal with. Nikolai pushes to his feet roughly, needing to move, to excise the itch under his skin. He hates how Seth just lets him go.

"You're angry," Nikolai says quietly.

"Furious," Seth agrees. He stays where Nikolai's left him, his body stiff and tense, voice tight. "But there isn't much I can do about it. We need to get some rest, and we need to hope that we aren't eaten by Shadows while we do."

"I'll keep watch," Mattie offers. "I sleep, but it's not the same."

"We'll switch off," Heather says. "Nikita sleeping isn't a good idea right now, at least not without me watching over her."

"She's untethered." It's not a question from Seth, just a defeated statement of fact.

Nikita still crouches, her gaze cast down as they talk over her. She stands slowly; she's almost as tall as Nikolai after she rises. "Is it safe to go outside?" she asks.

"No worse than being inside, as long as we don't use our Talent," Nikolai says.

"I think we can manage that," Nikita agrees. She gives Heather a hug and a kiss, whispering "Trust me" before letting go. "Nikolai and I should discuss what we know and don't know, and how we can help each other. Everyone's overwhelmed, and Heather's probably about ready to explode from wanting to soothe people. Can we go out and talk?"

Ever since these people exploded into their lives, talking is all they've been doing. But Nikolai nods like maybe this conversation will make a difference, will change something. He opens the door and gestures into the cold. "Sure. Let's go."

2

THEY HEAD A little way from the cabin in the opposite direction from where Pawel, Mac, and Alaric stand under the trees. Nikolai can feel the wards around the cabin pressing in on them, trying to keep them there when they're about to stray too far. He stops, and Nikita stops as well, turning to look at him with confusion.

"There are wards," he says, because stepping outside of them magnifies the chances of them being found by Shadows.

"Alaric's Clan," she replies, and when that doesn't mean anything to him, she clarifies, "he has really good hearing."

"I think he's focused on his current conversation, and anyway, I don't care if he listens," Nikolai says. There's a stump nearby, wide and mostly flat. Nikolai perches on the edge, Nikita next to him, their backs to the cabin. While it's possible someone they know could sneak up on them, that isn't as dangerous as the possibility of someone coming out of the woods.

It's so familiar here. Almost like it was home for a while. "Damn it," Nikolai mutters. "This set us back days. I thought we were almost there."

"Where?" Nikita asks, and Nikolai shakes his head, waving away her question.

"Not important right now." He's lying, of course. Havenhill is the third most important thing in his life, after Seth and staying alive. However, he needs a better understanding of what's going on with these intruders who claim to be from another world before he confides in them.

Now that he is able to slow down and think about it—*another world*—it seems impossible.

Nikita huffs, exhaling slowly. "We didn't mean to come here. I mean, yes, I wanted to get to you. Save you. But—"

“What makes you think I need saving?” Nikolai cuts her off. She leans back from him, eyes wide. He spreads his hands. “Seriously, what makes you think that you invading is going to save me.”

She licks her lips. “When I Dream about your life, this world seems so…dark. Bleak. I only wanted to help. I didn’t realize…” She trails off. “You’re furious too.”

“Not as much as Seth, but I might be close once I get my head wrapped around this,” Nikolai admits. It’s too much. Too big. “I thought you were just this weird dream I was having. That worried Seth because we’ve been bonded since we were little and I’ve never had control problems. When I did slip up, they were little blips. But you persisted. I’d close my eyes, and suddenly I was dreaming about this place where things were how I imagine they might have been if I’d grown up without the Split, and I had friends, and hey, so what if I was a girl, because life seemed…right. And familiar. It didn’t even feel new. It felt like how life was supposed to be.”

“Maybe my life and your life would’ve been similar, if the Shadows hadn’t attacked here,” Nikita says. “Maybe you and I are two sides of the same coin. I mean, I can see the parallels. You have a boyfriend, I have a girlfriend. You have older brothers, I have an older sister. Your family sounds like they’re Weather Witches, just like mine. But you knew you were a Dreamwalker when you were young.”

“Very young,” Nikolai agrees. He can’t remember ever being without his Dreams. “You didn’t Emerge when you were a kid?”

“I’m a Weather Witch,” Nikita says. “Like my parents and my sister. I was a little out of control as a kid, but not in ways that were strange or problematic. Then recently, my Talent got weird, and I started falling asleep randomly and creating massive storms while I slept. I didn’t know why I lost control of my weather abilities until I started remembering my Dreams about you.”

“That doesn’t make sense.” Nikolai can’t assimilate the idea of being both.

Nikita smiles wryly. “Pawel has a long list of things that don’t make sense that he’s trying to understand. Like Lineage Talents that Emerge with some other Talent. Carolyn’s a Predictive Mage who can now travel. I Emerged as a Dreamwalker. Alaric's Clan and that dragon form is a new Emergence. And Shadows are Emergent, like Mattie said. Talent is more complicated than we ever knew. Pawel studies that."

Right, they'd mentioned that, along with the name of the university. "Pine Hills University is closed here," he says. It's the abandoned university in Unity where they'd hoped to stop, maybe find a safe place for a night. Every time one of these strangers mentions a detail, it cements the contrast of "there" versus "here," and Nikolai expects they could spend days throwing information at each other. "Nikita, you and your friends need to understand that this isn't your home. If you're from a different world, you should go back there. Be safe in your own place. We're hunted here. The Shadows want to eat us. The humans want to kill us because they think that when we're gone, the Shadows will leave, even though I'm pretty sure that's wrong. But everyone who isn't Talented thinks we're at fault for the plague of Shadows, and they hate Dreamwalkers the most."

"Why?"

He wonders how she can ask that as an unbonded Dreamwalker. She's experienced her Talent going wild and out of control. "Because we break the spaces between here and the Dreamscape," he says. "Because Dreamwalkers let the Shadows in, and Empaths help us keep them out. We're both the killers and the saviors."

"Oh. Oh, that really does explain a lot." Nikita's glance flicks toward the cabin. There's no one outside now, and Nikolai wonders if everything's okay. He doesn't hear shouting, so it can't be that bad.

She lowers her voice, whispering, "Does everyone fall in love with their Empath?"

Nikolai can't help the low snort that slips free. "Not everyone," he tells her, "but it happens a lot. If you've found the right Empath to bond with, you're compatible. You'll be best friends, at least, and some people fall in love if they're attracted to each other. Seth and I were friends for a long time before it changed for us, but when it did change, it seemed so natural. No one was surprised."

Her eyebrows go up. "No one?"

"Conversation for another time." Nikolai doesn't want to go down the rabbit hole of remembering the people he and Seth have lost. "My point is, it isn't fated. And there might be more than one Empath you can click with—but the bond, when it happens, is intense. For us, anyway. Our powers are in sync, and we can work together. I'm not sure I'd be sane without Seth. More than likely I'd be dead, consumed by Shadows long ago."

Nikita nods, and he can almost see the wheels turning as she takes in the information. He has a feeling that while she and her friends are here, they'll have conversations like this often. It's as if they somehow developed a society that's missing some of the most basic information about Talent.

"So," she says, dragging the word out, "where I'm from, we had the Emergence. It's been almost eleven years since then. I was eight when it happened. Pawel was eighteen, almost the same age as my sister. I think he might have known her. They were both students at Pine Hills. Anyway." She inhales roughly. "So," she says again, then stalls.

"When I was eight, we had the Split. There were rumors, like Seth said, but it didn't get bad until we were ten. Something broke, and the Shadows came to hunt us."

"Same time," Nikita murmurs.

"Sounds like." Nikolai isn't sure what that means, but he's learned not to ignore coincidences. "What happened after your Emergence?"

"There was this gymnastics competition on television. One of the girls fell, and she teleported and saved herself from breaking her neck. It was live. So everyone saw magic happen, and there was no way to hide it. And she—she wasn't Lineage. She was Emergent." Nikita's gaze drifts toward the cabin.

Nikolai frowns, remembering how Mac had blinked into being in front of him and Seth. "Wait. Is your teleporter that same—?" He stops when Nikita nods. "Oh. And then?"

"We had to learn how to live with each other," Nikita says. "Some people are scared, and some aren't. It's easier some places than others, and there are all kinds of new laws."

"The humans don't hunt you?"

Nikita shakes her head, stops mid-motion, and shrugs. "Not everyone is happy with integrated spaces for Talented and non-Talented people. We're all still figuring it out. It's getting better all the time, and we've got people like Pawel trying to learn everything there is to know about magic and teach it to others. But—" She stalls again. "Before the Emergence, people would Emerge occasionally, but now it's lots of people, all the time. And now we have Shadows, and people have been dying. Alaric's brother died. Then I started having nightmares about you, and we realized that Mattie's soul was in the Dreamscape, and when Carolyn brought her back, she was better. And the Dreamscape has these paths to all these places. Like, the Dreamscape is a huge place that touches everywhere. My world. Your world. Maybe a million others, I don't know. But your world and mine, they're close. Twins." She swallows. "Like you and me, being twinned versions of each other."

Nikolai doesn't have time to process that right now. He focuses on the last part. "We aren't twins," he points out. "We weren't separated at birth."

"I know." Nikita picks at an invisible thread on her jeans. "But we're similar. And I think I'm my world's version of you, and vice versa. That's why I want to save you. Because your world seems to be going to hell in a handbasket, and you're running, and I didn't want to see you die. Because that'd be like seeing me die."

In a strange way, that makes sense. "I get it," Nikolai says. "When I first started Dreaming about you, I thought you were this escape my brain had made up. It didn't feel like a Dream, but it felt like more than a dream, too." He doesn't know if she can hear the distinction between the words in his voice, but she nods like she can.

"Carolyn has this theory that Dreamwalkers are actually travelers like her and Mac," Nikita says. "That we're meant to go into other worlds, or bring those worlds to us. But we can't control it enough to do it safely."

"So we rip holes between worlds, and the Shadows fall out," Nikolai muses.

Nikita smiles. "Exactly. They're in the Dreamscape. Or in the spaces between the Dreams."

That makes a lot of sense. Everyone knows that an unbound Dreamwalker is a risk, that they can draw the Shadows. If they're making literal holes into the place where Shadows live…Nikolai shudders. "Dreamwalkers are consumed by their Dreams if they aren't bound," he says.

"Where I'm from, Dreamwalkers can't interact with each other, because if they do, entire towns can be swallowed by their Dreams," Nikita admits. "It's messy. I Emerged while at college, and I've been working with another Dreamwalker—one who didn't manifest the Dreaming Talent—and with Heather to figure it all out. I think your world has it right with the Empaths, but our world didn't know that."

Nikolai's amazed that they've only recently started to be invaded by Shadows, but it sounds as if her world took a different path to address the problem of unbound Dreamwalkers. He makes a small noise and tries to assimilate what she's said.

"Nik."

He turns, as does Nikita, when Heather calls. Nikita smiles, and Nikolai has to smile back. She has a point about their similarities, and the name overlap will get confusing if they stick together.

That reminds him. "How are you going to get home?" he asks.

The smile slips away from Nikita's lips. Heather speeds up her approach so she can wrap her arms around Nikita's shoulder and lean in to kiss her temple. Nikolai can't feel it, but he's familiar enough with how Seth calms him to guess what Heather has done to cause Nikita's expression to ease.

"I don't know," Nikita says. "Like I said, we didn't mean to come here. Not yet. We were only at the planning stage. We don't have an 'exit strategy,' as Mac called it."

"It's finally hit Pawel that we are well and truly stuck here," Heather says. "He's tried to use his phone at least a dozen times since you came outside. He's anxious about not being able to reach Conor or Emily."

Nikolai's brow furrows in confusion.

"His son and his neighbor," Nikita says. "Conor's only nine."

"Pawel's a professor and a father and he's our age?" Maybe a little older, Nikolai thinks, but not much.

"All that and he's not even thirty yet, but he is older than us," Heather says. She tugs at Nikita until she stands. Nikita has to hunch over to wrap her arms around Heather, but they embrace in a way that makes Nikolai look away to give them privacy.

Hah. Privacy. That's something they won't have much of going forward.

"It's been a long time since I've traveled with a group," he says, "and you don't know the rules. It's as if you're just starting out."

"Seth went over them while you were out here," Heather says. "Avoid using Talent, although Empathic Talent seems to slide under the radar. Dreamwalkers are dangerous. Don't trust anyone we meet; they might want to kill us. Ration food because we'll be traveling on foot from safe house to safe house. He said something about wanting to talk to you before we get on the road tomorrow morning, and that there's no place close enough to reach if we start out today. He and Alaric had a long conversation about Clan and their appetites, and they decided it would be better for Alaric to shift so he can hunt rather than starving. As long as he's not the dragon, Pawel doesn't think he'll be unique enough to draw the Shadows."

There is so much that Nikolai doesn't know about these people. So many questions he feels he should ask so that everyone will have the information they need. He shouldn't trust them so easily, but another part of him feels as if he knows them. As if he's been with them already. As strange as Nikita's story is, it also sounds right.

Heather nods toward the cabin. "Seth's anxious about how long you've been out here." Her expression is assessing, settled on Nikolai. "You get co-dependent when you're bonded. I can't tell if that's good or bad."

Nikita kisses her cheek, then touches her palm to Heather's face and kisses her lips. "I get the feeling we're seeing what you and I might become," she says softly, and they lean together forehead to forehead.

Heather's breath stutters; Nikolai feels a chill wariness in the air. It's almost like Seth, but not quite, and it's shuttered as quickly as it shows. He's not sure Nikita notices it, but he knows it came from Heather.

They're not in tune yet.

Nikolai pushes to his feet. "I'll go see where we stand and how we're going to manage with so many of us in a small space. We'll see what we can dig up for supplies; you guys aren't dressed for a hard trek. Seth and I will figure all that out, and maybe you two—" He wants to tell them that they need to figure their shit out, understand how to keep Nikita from bringing the Shadows after them, but he doesn't think they need the reminder.

Heather looks scared, and Nikita looks like she wants to wrap herself up in Heather.

Nikolai's pretty sure they get it. He touches Nikita's shoulder, half expecting the world to shift around them when he does, but everything stays as stark and cold and bleak as usual. "Come inside when you're ready."

He leaves them there as he goes to where Seth's waiting for him, still a small bundle of anger but somewhat soothed. Nikolai decides to kiss him, and Seth surges up, grips Nikolai's shoulders, and kisses him back. With everything going on, this, at least, hasn't changed.

He'll always have Seth.

3

Nikolai wakes into darkness when someone moves. A low mutter, an answering soft grunt, and whispered words catch his sleepy attention. As his eyes become accustomed to the low light, he realizes that Mattie and Alaric are speaking, until Alaric turns away and makes his way to the door, stepping over where Carolyn is curled in a tight ball on the floor, then where Heather and Nikita are wrapped around each other. As he passes the bed, he pauses, tense, and glances at Nikolai.

"Sorry," Alaric grunts.

"It's hard to sleep well in the dark with this many Talents," Nikolai whispers. He gently lifts Seth's arm, giving himself space to slide off the narrow bed. The floor is cold under his feet; he finds his shoes with his toes, shoving his feet into them. "I'll walk out with you."

Pawel and Mac are closest to the door, sleeping sitting up with Mac curled against Pawel's chest, Pawel's arm around her shoulders. Mac stirs as they pass, opening one eye and reaching for her side before she spots them. The tension slips from her body as she curls closer to Pawel and falls asleep again.

Alaric eases the door open, and they exit. The sun is barely starting to peek through the trees, the air chill around them. Alaric inhales, exhaling with a puff of condensation.

"It's going to warm up again today," he says, voice low.

"That's good, since we'll be walking for a long while," Nikolai says. The next safe place is small, and it had already been picked over for food. He doubts that whoever maintains it will restock this time of year, and they weren't there long ago.

It rankles, relying on the kindness of the few humans who don't hate

Talent, but it's not as if he can go into the nearest grocery store. Those exist in cities, behind high walls, and the stores in the suburbs were abandoned and looted long ago.

"Where are we going?" Alaric asks, his hands in his pockets, shoulders hunched. He inhales again and slowly straightens, lifting his face to the sky. "I can fly ahead, if you need me to." He glances at Nikolai. "Your boyfriend seems to think that if I only shift through my usual forms, it won't be enough to call the Shadows. Dragon's still new to me anyway. Eagle's easy."

Nikolai can't remember the last time he met anyone Clan, and he's not sure of the right vocabulary. He hopes Alaric won't take offense at the way he asks. "What kind of Clan are you?"

Alaric snorts. "My family tends toward mammals. I'm—unique. I only have a few forms, and they're not all one sort. Eagle. Hound. Bear. Lizard." He shrugs. "Dragon."

Nikolai wonders if that sort of uniqueness will be enough to change the way the Shadows sense him, but decides to let it be. "We'll be traveling along a small river that runs during the winter: it's too quick to ice over and not shallow enough to dry out. It should be good fishing for the bear."

"I'll keep that in mind. Used to swim in the river when I was a kid." Alaric stretches, twists in place as he tilts his head, and sniffs at the air. "Where are we, anyway?"

The question stuns Nikolai into silence for a long moment. Then he gives a dry laugh. "I can't believe you're the first person to ask that. I assumed we were all from the same place. Nikita says she thinks our worlds are twinned or something, so I— You know what, I should assume instead that you don't know anything about this world's geography. So. From my perspective, we're east of the Hudson River, traveling north and east, heading toward what used to be the Vermont border. There're rumors about a safe place where a large group of Talent live together."

Alaric's gaze narrows abruptly, his hands falling as he leans in close enough to Nikolai that Nikolai takes a step back.

"What?" Nikolai asks.

"Nik?" Seth calls, voice faint from inside the cabin.

"Coming," Nikolai calls back. He lowers his voice and gestures at the cabin. "We should go in."

"Wait." Alaric wraps one hand around Nikolai's wrist, the grip solid and strong, holding him in place. "Where are we going?"

These people are Talent, like Nikolai and Seth. They need to be safe too. "It's called Havenhill," Nikolai says, "and it might not exist."

"Havenhill," Alaric murmurs, a grin lighting his expression. "Well, if it's near the Vermont border, I grew up around there in my world, and from what you said, the geography sounds similar. Might be able to help us navigate. How far away are we?"

"Still south of the Albany city walls, so we'll have to skirt around them—they keep expanding and taking in abandoned towns," Nikolai says. He tugs, and Alaric lets go. "We need to eat and get on the road. Traveling with this many people will slow us down, and it took us days to get as far from here as we were when you found us. We're at least a week out of Havenhill, maybe more, and finding safe places on the way that are large enough for all of us to sleep will be tricky."

For a moment Nikolai thinks Alaric's going to hunt or stay outside, but after a heartbeat, Alaric is close behind, following Nikolai into the cabin.

Everyone is awake. Mac and Pawel still sit on the floor, backs against the wall. Heather is in a chair, while Carolyn and Nikita are working her hair into two thick braids. Mattie leans against the wall in the one corner not lit by the rising sun, shadows wreathing her features in darkness. In this light, she looks like a Shadowwalker mimicking humanity. It's chilling.

Nikolai isn't comfortable with the way she watches them.

Seth digs through the cabinets, dropping freeze-dried food packets and a box of granola bars onto the small oak table. "Someone restocked this one," he says. "I'm pretty sure this came out of some survivalist's pre-Split basement, but I'll take it."

Mac scrambles to her feet and appears next to Seth. She reaches to touch his shoulder, stabilizing him when he startles. "Sorry, they're all used to me, and I forgot you're not."

"The worst part was we got used to her doing it when we didn't know she could," Alaric mutters. "She'd blink everywhere, and we just thought she was fast, or had moved when we weren't looking."

"The human mind is capable of creating excuses for almost any situation," Pawel says, his voice hoarse and rough. "That's how Talented people survived living side by side with those without Talent for so long, in both our worlds. It's only when we can no longer be ignored that we are noticed and believed." He pushes to his feet. "I'll be back."

The door bangs behind him as he exits.

"On it," Alaric says, and heads out as well.

"He's worried about Conor," Mac says, and all the world-jumpers go quiet. Heather nods, making a small, worried noise. Nikita keeps braiding, while Carolyn stops and watches the door.

"We need to get moving," Seth says as he divides the pile of food on the table.

It's more than Nikolai was expecting, including at least a dozen freeze-dried meals in faded brown packaging and two boxes of more recent granola bars. There's a jar of some kind of sugary drink mix that's hard when Nikolai opens it, but they can make it work. They'll have to share canteens regardless.

Seth opens cans. "These are too heavy to carry along with what we grabbed yesterday morning, so we'll eat them cold here. You can either take your favorite, or let me mix it all up into cold soup. I don't have a preference."

There are five cans and nine people.

"Mix it," Nikolai says. "We'll deal with it. It'll be hard to eat as it is. Not like we're set up for fine dining." He has a vague memory of sitting at the kitchen table when he was young, his feet kicking, unable to reach the ground. He remembers someone telling him why there were three forks and two spoons, and why he had multiple glasses to drink out of. He thinks it might have been a holiday, but he's not sure, and he can't remember who was speaking.

He remembers good food, though, and feeling loved.

Life before the Split was very different.

Nikolai unearths four spoons while Seth stirs together tinned pasta, beans, tomatoes, and broth into a large pot. There's no fire, and there's only one bowl. "We'll share."

Mattie motions for the others to eat first. "I'm fine. I'll take care of myself later."

"We don't want you getting hungry," Mac says.

"I'm not going to eat you," Mattie counters. "I'll find something. That food isn't appealing, and there's no point in me taking something you need more than me."

The door slams open with another *bang*.

"Where are we going?" Pawel asks before he's fully back inside the cabin, Alaric trailing behind him.

Seth glances at Nikolai, who digs for his map. Seth makes space on the table for Nikolai to lay it out, and Nikolai points at the red circle. "There," Nikolai says. "That's where we think Havenhill is, according to rumor."

"I told you," Alaric says as Pawel leans in close to the map. Everyone crowds around until Nikolai nudges them back.

"I think you're right. We moved in space, yes, but not as far as I'd worried," Pawel says. "That's definitely the right area for Haverhill."

"Havenhill," Nikolai corrects him. "It was supposedly established by Alia Davis as a safe haven for all kinds of Talent. According to the rumors, it's safe from humans and Shadows. No one can find it if they're not Talented."

"It's also possible the rumors have no basis in reality, but it's the best idea we have right now," Seth grumbles. "We need someplace to live. We can't keep running. If there is a community that has figured out how to hide, I want us to be there."

"Bedrock," Mattie murmurs.

"I wouldn't be surprised if there's another haven farther north in Vermont, although they are very close to Burlington," Pawel muses, drawing a finger along the map. "On the other hand, Burlington is too far away to walk to, and why aren't we driving?" He shifts gears mid-sentence, straightening to look at Nikolai and Seth.

"Because the highways are gated and controlled, we don't have access to any kind of a vehicle, and it's impossible to get fuel," Seth says. "Everything's controlled by the humans. If it was left behind when they went behind their walls, it either belongs to a survivalist now or it's been sitting, dead and abandoned, for years."

"I know which way to go," Alaric says. He points to the map. "I grew up in the area you circled. I've never tried to walk there—it'll take a fucking long time to get there by foot—but I've flown enough times that I can scout for us. Maybe find us shortcuts if you think they're safe."

"We've been traveling based on known safe houses," Nikolai explains. "Most of them are still there and maintained."

"Fine, then we need to get on the road." Alaric carefully folds up the map and hands it back to Nikolai. "Let's scrounge around for things to get everyone outfitted."

"What, what if there's an easier way?" Mac asks, looking at Carolyn.

"I have Kit's art of the Berman place," Carolyn says. She pulls out a piece of paper, staring at it fiercely. "I can try—"

"Could you please stop trying to summon the Shadows!" Seth snaps. He pushes forward, getting in their faces, jabbing a finger at them. "Don't use your Talent. Every time you do something that would appeal to their hunger, you risk bringing them to us, and I don't want to have to fight them off a second time. Did you see how many of them came when you crash-landed here? That was bad. Don't let it happen again."

"If we're fast enough, we'll be in Havenhill before the Shadows notice—"

"And the Shadows might follow us to Havenhill," Seth points out. "You could make the one place that's safe for Talent not safe after all."

"This isn't our world," Nikita says softly. "We have to remember that. You probably can't go places you remember because they aren't actually the same places, Carolyn. Of course Kit's drawing of that place won't work—he drew Alaric's home Haverhill, not Havenhill. We can't jump home because it's on the either side of the Dreamscape, and we don't know anywhere here yet. We need to play by these rules."

"Eat," Seth orders. "Eat and do whatever you need to do to feel awake and ready to go, then we'll hit the road."

"Alaric can scout," Nikolai agrees. "We'll stick together otherwise. No teleporting or whatever you do. We need to avoid attention." It's sort of a plan—the best they've got. It'll take time—probably more than when he and Seth traveled on their own—but at least they'll get there alive.

4

It doesn't take long to get everyone cleaned up and ready to move out. They take the blankets from the cabin, and Nikolai hopes that, someday, he can make it back to replace them for future travelers. The morning's warmth faded abruptly with the arrival of a chill breeze, and temperatures have dropped back to those typical for March. Without winter coats, these newcomers won't survive long.

As Nikolai finishes shoving the food into the bottom of his bag, there's a touch to his back. He turns to find Mattie stepping away quickly. Her smile flickers and is gone.

"You taste like him," she says. "That's not to say I plan on sipping from your life, just that you taste like lemon, not Dreams, and that isn't what I expected."

Nikolai blinks. He has no idea how to respond. "I'm not going to travel with you."

Mattie points behind herself to the shadows lingering in the corner. "It's too bright to be comfortable, and while I could handle it, I have my own ways of getting around. If they notice I'm gone, tell them I'm not in trouble, and I'm not causing trouble. I promise I will be back." She pauses, then offers, "I'll bring food, if I can."

"I can't tell you not to go. But do you really want—?"

"I'm not like your Shadows," Mattie says firmly. "But I am like them. I'll be fine. They won't want to swallow me down—I'd give them indigestion. They want bright life, not more darkness." When she smiles, her teeth are sharp and gleaming. "Besides, I make your skin crawl. You won't miss me."

Nikolai feels like he should disagree, but she slips away before he can. The darkness wraps around her, enfolding her, and when she turns sideways into it, the shadows swallow her and she disappears.

He's still staring at the darkness, the bag held loosely in his hands, when Seth comes into the cabin. "Nik, are you ready to go?"

He looks up, nods. "Yeah. Just—" He grabs the box of crackers that Carolyn had found while they were pulling out blankets, shoves it into his bag, then zips the bag up and throws it over his shoulders. "I'm ready."

When they get outside, everyone is waiting. Mac and Carolyn each have a blanket around their shoulders, while Nikita and Heather are sharing one. Pawel bounces on his toes, and Alaric is nowhere to be seen.

"Alaric's gone ahead, so now that you're—" Pawel cuts off. "Where's Mattie?"

Nikolai doesn't wait for the conversation, striking out down the same path they left by days before. He whistles once and points, assuming that Alaric will hear and see him. "She left," he says as soon as Pawel catches up. "She's neither causing trouble nor in it, so we should let her be."

Pawel makes a noise that Nikolai interprets as distrustful of Mattie. Nikolai shrugs because there was absolutely nothing he could have done to stop her leaving.

The trip is both easier and more difficult this time. Nikolai knows the path laid out by the map, but Alaric swoops down periodically throughout the day to offer alternatives. Each time, they consult the map, considering what Seth and Nikolai know of this world versus what Alaric has seen. Three times they follow Alaric's advice, but several times, Nikolai forces them to turn away and shift their path. He's not sure if they're making better time overall, but the path is less treacherous.

The others walk without complaint, despite how their feet must hurt and their hands must be cold. Pawel jogs through the day, constantly moving, bouncing forward then back to rejoin the group. Mac teases him, and at one point, they playfully fight along the path until Seth shushes them. Quiet is good; noise can bring unwanted attention.

As the afternoon sun draws close to the horizon, Alaric drops out of the sky, reforming into his human form as his feet touch the ground. It was strange the first time he'd done it, early that morning, but by now, Nikolai is used to it.

"There's a road over there," Alaric says, pointing away from the river. "It'll be easier than sticking close to the riverbank, and it doesn't smell like it's traveled regularly."

Nikolai brings out the map, and he and Seth look closely until they find their spot. The road is a rural highway, far enough away from the cities and the main roads that it might be safe, if Alaric's assessment is correct. "You'll need to keep watch and let us know if we have to hide," Nikolai says. "If someone has a car, they're human." He trusts that Alaric can smell the fumes of people and vehicles, but "not often" doesn't mean "never."

They pick their way through the trees, and once they reach the road, Alaric takes flight. He's visible now that they're out of the trees, wheeling overhead.

Pawel pauses to look at him, his hand shadowing his eyes. "If it's this clear, it's going to be cold tonight," he mutters. "Are we close to someplace safe for the night?"

Seth's lips press together tightly, and he gives a small shake of his head.

Nikita makes a displeased sound, and Carolyn huddles under her blanket.

"We've moved away from our original path," Nikolai reminds them. "The road will be easier, yes, but it's also farther from the places where Seth and I stayed when we traveled this way. I don't think the nearest safe house would be much use anyway. It wasn't much more than a lean-to that kept out the wind, nowhere near big enough for all of us."

"The sun'll go down soon," Seth says curtly. "I know you're tired, but we need to keep going. If we spot a house off the road, we'll need to scout it to figure out if it's occupied by survivalists or abandoned, and if it's abandoned, if it'd be safe to stay there."

"If it's been abandoned, why wouldn't it be safe?" Nikita asks.

"Traps. Some people thought that if they couldn't have the home they worked their whole life for, they wouldn't let anyone else to have it either." Nikolai remembers the first time his family found someplace like that, years ago. His mother had tried to keep him from reading the vicious words that had been painted on the walls. His father had lost a hand. "We have to be cautious."

Heather wraps an arm around Nikita, drawing her closer. "We will be."

"Let's move," Seth says.

So they do.

As the sun drops lower, the air chills quickly. They pause at the end of a dirt road, an old, rusted mailbox hanging off a wood post nearby. Nikolai whistles sharply, and Alaric drops out of the sky, shifting again as he lands. Alaric glances at the road. "Thinking of stopping?"

Carolyn huddles in her blanket, shivering, and Heather and Nikita are so close together that they have trouble walking. Mac shrugs out of her blanket and hands it to Pawel, fixing it around his shoulders. "I'll go with you," she says. "Running, not teleporting, I promise. I'm another pair of hands, and a lethal pair if needed."

"Watch out for traps," Seth warns.

Alaric grins, snarling under his breath. "I'll sniff them out." A hound replaces him, and he lopes off, Mac keeping pace easily at his side.

"What do we do now?" Heather asks.

"Move off the road and wait," Seth says.

There isn't really anything to do but wait.

Pawel gives the blanket to the girls, who each wrap themselves in one then huddle together. Faint flickers of electricity trail across his checks, and Nikolai watches the shadows around them nervously. Pawel picks a flat stretch alongside the road and moves through sets of footwork—punches and kicks in a style that Nikolai doesn't recognize. Doing so seems to calm Pawel, and the light dancing over his skin fades away as his face turns rosy from effort.

Pawel stops mid-kick, lowering his foot and shading his eyes to look down the road. Nikolai feels it then, the faint rumble that implies something is coming.

"Hide!" Seth shouts. They scramble down the embankment, running for the trees. Nikolai's feet are half numb and awkward from the cold; he stumbles but Seth catches him, dragging him to his feet.

When Nikita stumbles as well, Pawel grabs her, hoisting her up in a bridal carry. He's skinny and strong, but she still slows him down to a walk.

"Put her down and let her move on her own," Seth yells from the edge of the trees as Carolyn joins them there.

Pawel tries setting Nikita down, but she shakes her head—"I twisted my ankle," she says—and he lifts her again as cars come into view.

There's nothing they can do. They've been spotted, and the vehicles slow abruptly, stopping at the end of the dirt road. Nikita slides from Pawel's arms, leaning against him as she stands on one foot.

Something taps Nikolai's shoulder. He jerks sideways, turning to see Mattie emerging from the darkness fostered by the trees.

"They're friends," Mattie says.

All three vehicles are old, covered in rust, painted to blend in under the trees. There are numerous dents on the car bodies, but the engines rumble quietly once they are stopped. They're well-kept.

The passenger door of the front van opens, and a woman climbs out. She's tall and tanned, her dark hair pulled back. She smiles sharply, then drops to her knees and transforms into a roaring lion.

There's an answering, baying howl in the distance.

She stands again to speak as a woman and calls out, "I am Alia, and I am here to take you to Havenhill. Get in, and we'll be there not long after nightfall. We have beds, and food, and you will be safe."

Havenhill. These cars—these people—they're from Havenhill.

Seth grips Nikolai's hand, holding on tight. "It can't be this ea—"

"She's Talented," Nikolai cuts him off. That's why she changed shape, to prove that she's not human. It gives them every reason to trust her, even though parts of him scream to be wary. He has so many questions, from how do they have cars to how they found them.

"Bedrock," Mattie says firmly. "I told you, but no one listens. Are you going to get in the van or not? I'll take the shadows back and meet you there."

She's gone before Nikolai can blink.

Another low howl, long and mournful and coming closer, then Mac is there, appearing by the mailbox. She takes two steps back, shouting, "Alaric!"

Pawel lifts Nikita, carrying her toward the van. "Thank you," he says to Alia, then calls back over his shoulder, "We can trust them. Let's move."

The hound skids to a stop, paws raking through the dirt, then Alaric transforms. “Mom?” he asks, voice breaking and raw.

Alia looks at him, frowning. “No,” she says. She turns away to pull the side door of the van open, and the back doors of the other two cars open as well. “Get in if you’re coming with us. We shouldn’t linger.”

From the journal of Alia Davis.

May 5th, two years into the new world

The deed is as good as done.

It isn't perfect, not yet, but we will find our way to survive. We have worked hard to create this space, to make it safe from the outside world, and to encourage those of Talent who wish to find us to do so.

I have written each day of our progress forward, but for those who may read this decades later, as I have read the records left by my own family, I am certain that this summary will become the much-dog-eared page at the end of our efforts and the beginning of our new lives.

The borders are finally set. I could never have accomplished these protections on my own, without Val and the strength of the Mages she brought here. We are one community now, more than Clan or Mage. We are Talent, and we must forge new bonds if we are to survive.

Haverhill has been forgotten as a town, wiped from the map as if it never existed. The humans have left, and we have appropriated their homes for our own. There were many discussions along the way about this, about whether this was right or good. We killed no one; we only made this place feel as if it were dangerous, as if they should consider leaving for their own safety, and they did, fleeing to hide behind the walls that have grown up around Albany and Troy.

It took little more than a nudge to quietly convince them to leave.

We were surprised when some people stayed, but then, I have written of the Allens and of the extended Malcolm family before. We were pleased to discover that other Talents were already among us and equally pleased to welcome them to our midst, Emergent and Lineage alike.

We all require Haven, after all.

We have extended the borders of what used to be Clan territory to include the entire town, and as time goes by and humanity recedes from the wilderness, we will expand those borders. We reside in the north, but we have brought in those with a Talent for growth, and citrus flourishes at our border. We will plant new orchards, new borders, as we claim fresh land. The wards created by Val and the others keep us safe.

The humans forget us.

The Shadows are repelled.

And my people…our people… We are safe.

It has taken us more than a year to establish our new home. We are working to forge our world and be independent. We need to find ways to move among the humans when needed, to get supplies we cannot create on our own. We need to establish electricity and return our facilities to working order so that we can withdraw from the human's networks. Even humans will notice if a place that does not exist still relies upon what remains of their electrical grid.

We will make our way and continue our withdrawal. We will send out ambassadors to find those who have been lost. We will create safe routes and spaces to lead those of all kinds of Talent to us. The humans create their walls to force us out, so we must make our own walls, of magic and will. We thus have we created a Haven.

Havenhill.

The present we have is not the future that I expected. My father is gone, and I lead now. But I don't lead alone, and I am stronger for it.

HAVENHILL

5

THEY SPLIT THE group across all three vehicles. Pawel helps Nikita into the van and is about to follow her when Mac and Carolyn claim him, rerouting him to the second vehicle in line. Nikita waits, perched on the seat in the middle, until Heather climbs in and helps her get settled in the back row.

"We should get in," Seth says.

For the first time in years, Nikolai gets into a car. He settles into a seat in the middle row, Seth next to him. When the van rumbles to life, Nikolai reaches across to hold Seth's hand, tangling their fingers tightly together.

"You don't like cars?" Nikita asks.

"I haven't been in one since I was ten," Nikolai mutters. "It's been a while. And this one seems old."

"We have people who are good with cars," Alia says. Nikolai isn't sure if that's code for "Talented with cars" or if they are mechanics. "They keep us running."

The woman driving the car snorts softly. "Keep the cars running. Get us fuel. Deal with every little tinkering thing that needs to be done."

"Val," Alia warns.

"Alia," Val mocks, fondness in her tone. She puts her hand on the console between them, palm up, and after a moment Alia puts her hand atop it. Val curls their fingers together, and Alia exhales.

"It'll be fine, Alia," Val murmurs, her voice barely audible over the rumble of the engine.

"Do you have Healers?" Heather asks. Val and Alia don't respond, so she raises her voices and asks again, "Do you have Healers?"

Alia glances back, and Nikolai follows her gaze. Nikita's foot is propped on Heather's lap, and she sits sideways so she can lean against the side of the van. Nikita's expression is twisted and pained, her lips pressed together as Heather works to get Nikita's shoe off.

"We have Healers," Val says conversationally; Alia makes a small noise, her nostrils flaring.

"Good," Heather murmurs, pushing up the leg of Nikita's jeans and sliding her fingers along her skin. She tugs the shoe free, then the sock; the ankle is already purpling and swollen. "Nik's hurt, and I think she's needs more help than I can give her."

Alia's nostrils flare. "I can smell her pain."

"That figures," Nikita says. Her voice is purposefully light and cheerful. Nikolai doesn't know her well, but the tone is at odds with the lines around her mouth and eyes and the way she grips Heather's hand tightly. "I mean," Nikita continues, "Alaric smells everything about everything. Right? And he's your…I mean, he's Clan, like you."

"We have a lot to talk about," Alia says. She pauses, looking down to where Val runs her thumb along the side of her hand. "We will wait until we reach Havenhill. There's no point in discussing everything multiple times. I want to have everyone involved in one place."

"Havenhill is real," Seth says.

Alia's expression eases with a smile. "Yes," she says gently. "It is. And all Talents are welcome. We will even find a place for Mattie, although I am concerned about trusting someone who walks through shadows."

"She's not your typical Shadowwalker," Nikita volunteers, then falls silent at a look from Alia. "Fine. Yes. When everyone's together, I get it."

"I'm pretty sure they won't stop talking, no matter how frustrated it makes you, my dear wife, and there's no trouble in repeating some of the basics." Val lets go of Alia's hand, lifting her fingers to wave. "I'm Val Munroe, and this is my wife Alia Davis, the founder of Havenhill. We've built a safe place for Talent, and I'm aware that it's widely believed to be a legend. That's intentional. The more effort we put into making the humans forget our home ever existed, the harder it is for Talent to find us. That last bit is a side effect, but it keeps us safe. If we hear of anyone seeking refuge, we try to bring them home. Like you."

Val points at the space in front of Alia, and Alia opens a hatch and withdraws something. “And now, some in-flight entertainment for the passengers,” Val announces. She takes a slender silver disk, slides it into a slot, and music starts to play.

“I still have more—” Nikita cuts off as Alia twists a dial and the music grows louder.

The song is vaguely familiar, but it’s been so long since he’s heard anything like it that listening to it now feels like slipping into a dream. If Seth’s hand weren’t solid in his own, he’d wonder if he’d wandered during his sleep. But no, this is reality, with the van rumbling beneath him and the music playing loudly. Val taps on the steering wheel with her fingertips, matching the song’s rhythm and singing along as she drives.

There’s a soft wave of warmth from Seth. “Sleep,” he says, his voice low beneath the music. “I’ve got you.”

Nikolai dozes, mind whirling with imagery, some like memories, others alien and strange yet somehow familiar. It’s easy to let himself float, sifting through different scenes and places, filing away the emotions to be cataloged later. He dimly registers occasional conversation around him, and he half wakens when he hears Val’s voice.

“Open the wards, Ethan.”

“Yes, Mom.”

Nikolai falls deeper into sleep then, walking a path in his dreams. Beside him is Nikita. A woman around their age, with dark skin and many tiny braids, skips on his other side. When Nikolai hesitates, she skips away down the path, then veers off and between trees.

“Don’t go off the path,” Nikita says seriously.

“Wake up.”

Nikolai jolts when Seth tugs on his hand. There’s a whimper from the back seat, and Nikita stretches with another soft groan.

The van rumbles to a stop; a squeal of brakes announces the other cars stopping as well.

“We are here.” Alia opens the door and climbs out as Val does the same.

One of the side doors slides open; Seth gets out while Nikolai helps Heather maneuver Nikita to the ground. They gather in front of a house that is larger than any single home Nikolai can remember seeing. It stretches three stories high, with a covered porch and heavy columns holding up the roof. The front of the house is a typical width, but to the right and left, there are diagonal buildings that seem to be attached, as if it's grown over the years. He wonders if the space between them in the back is also part of the house or if it's open land.

Alaric steps toward the building, but he stops when Alia moves to stand in front of him, her hand on his chest to keep him back. "No," she says, and Alaric rocks back on his heels.

Mac takes his hand when Alaric whines his annoyance.

"It looks exactly like his home," Carolyn murmurs. Nikolai isn't sure who she's speaking to, but the quiet words are audible even without Clan hearing.

"Welcome to Havenhill," Val says. She stands with one arm around Alia's back, fingers resting possessively against her hip. Three more strangers have emerged from the other cars, and more come out from inside the house.

So many new faces at once is overwhelming. Nikolai clings to Seth, relying on the calm that washes over him.

"I am Alia Davis, and Havenhill is our home," Alia says. "We are open to all who are Talented and need a safe haven. When Mattie arrived, her story was unusual, but we could not deny those in need." She glances at one of the men who came from the house—he looks as if he might be about the same age as Nikolai.

"She's inside," he replies to the unspoken question, and Alia nods.

"Allowances have been made to permit a Shadow within the borders of Havenhill." Alia looks at Pawel; his mouth is open as if to speak, but he snaps it shut under her gaze. "We will discuss the particulars of Havenhill and your expected behavior later; for now, let us begin with introductions, then Ethan can take you inside to get settled."

She runs through the introductions too quickly for Nikolai to get more than quick mental notes to help him attach names to faces. The Asian woman wearing shorts and no jacket in March, who drove the sedan for Alaric, is named Sakura. Amaranth is a tall woman with curly hair pulled back from her face with a knit headband and laugh lines crinkling around her eyes. Jefferson is short and broad-shouldered, black leather gloves on his hands and an expression on his face that remains pinched despite his smile of welcome. Ethan's voice, he recognizes from earlier; his eyes light up when he grins a hello. Val introduces him as her son, and introduces the last woman there, Marybelle, as Ethan's cousin and Val's foster daughter.

From the way Alaric looks around, gaze narrowed and nostrils flared, Nikolai is certain that there are more people here, that these are only the ones in human form. When a cat walks up to him, meows loudly, then twists to rub against his ankles, Nikolai isn't sure if they are a person or an actual cat, and Alaric's expression doesn't help him figure it out.

Nikolai steps carefully around the cat when Ethan motions for them to follow.

"Mattie's waiting in the suite we're giving you short-term," Ethan says. He repeats their names back to them as he points at them each in turn, frowning when Pawel scoops Nikita up to carry in his arms. "You've been injured."

"I'll get Genevieve," Jefferson says with a deep bass rumble before heading toward the left wing of the house. "We'll meet you in their rooms."

"Come on." Ethan motions and waits for them to keep up. He moves slowly, making allowances for Pawel and Nikita.

When Alaric barges ahead, Marybelle shoots a look at Ethan. He nods quickly, and she races after Alaric, who strides determinedly through the door and the halls. Mac disappears and reappears by Alaric's side, keeping up.

"We couldn't believe it when your friend stepped out of the shadows and started talking to us," Ethan says. "We've never met a Shadowwalker like her before."

"Neither have we," Carolyn says. "I'm pretty sure there isn't one. She used to be as bad as the rest of them until we put her soul back into her body. She killed Alaric's brother."

"Alaric is the big one…?"

Pawel jerks his chin at the space ahead of them. "The one who took off like he knows the place. He does, in our world."

Ethan opens his mouth, then shakes his head. "I'll wait until we're upstairs," he says. "We've got three bedrooms, a small sitting room, and a private washroom set up for you guys. There's a shared bath on the hall… Are any of you Clan?"

"Alaric," Pawel says.

"Right. So. Let him know that there's a bath—"

"He probably knows," Carolyn cuts him off.

Ethan pauses at the base of the stairs, turning to look at them. "Every time you say that, you make it more difficult to not ask questions until we're upstairs." He grins. "But Mom raised me to be patient. Or at least, Alia expects me to be, so I try."

There are people everywhere Nikolai looks. They watch as the group treads the path—children who peer curiously and adults who try to pretend disinterest. Nikolai grips Seth's hand and is relieved when Seth squeezes tightly in return. He exhales, trying to map this place in his mind as Ethan leads them into what Nikolai thinks might be the right-hand wing of the house. They go up to the third floor and down to the end of the hall.

He can hear voices as they approach, Ethan pointing out occupied rooms and the bath as they go. Nikolai peeks through the open door, spotting a huge, filled tub, with shower nozzles set into the wall along the side. Public bath. Okay.

Seth smirks and brings Nikolai's hand up to kiss his fingertips, and Nikolai fights the flush that warms his cheeks.

When they arrive, Alia is in the room; she must have taken a different path to arrive before them. Mattie sits on a chair in the corner, slouched in the shadows, her legs crossed at the knees and hands folded in her lap. Marybelle is off to one side, eyes wide, while Alaric stands with his feet set and arms crossed.

"I want to be sure you understand," Alia says, her tone firm, "that our trust in your Shadowwalker friend relies upon our trust in you to have no harm in your hearts. Should we discover differently, you will be dealt with."

Alaric growls under his breath.

Alia glances at him, then looks away. "Ethan, Marybelle: please ensure they eat tonight. We will welcome them properly at another time. I am certain they need rest, and that good food and beds will be a luxury."

What Alia describes sounds like bliss, even if they are still crammed into a space too small for their numbers. Even if he is forced to share space with these seven strangers. Seth wraps his arms around Nikolai, and Nikolai enfolds him in return and kisses the top of Seth's head. He wants to stay like this and forget that these other people are here, that everything is so new. He wants to luxuriate in the idea that they can stop running.

They've finally found Havenhill.

6

Alia leaves moments before Jefferson arrives, a woman who looks too much like him to be anything but related in tow. He releases her, gesturing with one gloved hand to where Nikita sits on the bed in one of the three bedrooms, her foot up on a pillow that Heather has tucked in place.

"I'm Genevieve," the woman says as she steps forward, both hands up, fingers slightly spread. "Do I have your permission to touch you?"

Her hair is cut bluntly around her face, squaring it, but there are crinkled lines around her soft, kind eyes. She smiles slightly, and Nikita nods.

"I'm hoping you're a doctor," Nikita says.

"Better," Genevieve says. "I'm a Healer."

Jefferson stands nearby, his arms crossed. Genevieve sits on the edge of the bed, placing a hand on Nikita's ankle and closing her eyes as she runs her finger over the swollen, bruised skin. She makes a small noise.

Nikita's breath catches with a shrill sound. "I was running, and turned my ankle in a hole, I think," she says, voice strained.

"It's your ankle and your foot, both," Genevieve says. "A small fracture in the fifth metatarsal and a crack in the fibula. I can heal those, and ease your trauma, but you will still need to rest. We can give you a compression wrap and ice. Keep it elevated. This will only jump-start your healing."

"I always thought Healers were able to do miracles," Alaric mutters.

Genevieve glances at him, amusement pursing her lips. "Healing the break in a bone isn't a miracle?"

"We covered this in class," Pawel says, his tone shifting to what sounds like that of a well-memorized lecture. "Healers are able to repair the body, but the trauma has still been sustained. They are unable to repair mental damage, and while repairing damage to nerves and tissue is possible, they cannot destroy the results of the trauma. Bruising, blood loss, swelling: that will all remain. The body will still need to recover."

Genevieve makes a small noise as she bends back to her inspection of Nikita's ankle. Her fingers move with more purpose now, stroking along the skin, pressing in enough that the shift in blood flow is visible in the color of Nikita's skin. "What, exactly, do you teach?" she asks.

"Please don't get him started," Mac says, adding, "and you, Pawel, don't start. This isn't a lecture hall; this is life."

Pawel makes a disgruntled noise and walks away, stopping at the window, which is as far as he can get from the crowd. "I'm aware, Mac. Believe me, I'm well aware that this is real life. Remember, my son is in another world. Alone."

"He was with Emily when you left," Mac says quietly. "She'll take care of him."

"But I'm not there," Pawel snaps. He goes silent, lips pressed together as he leans on the windowsill, his forehead against the glass. Mac joins him there, her hand on his back.

"You'll be fine," Genevieve says, slowly withdrawing. She holds out a hand, and Jefferson is there, one hand under her elbow, the other at her side, helping her rise. He withdraws as soon as she's steady. "Either Jefferson or I will be back with some ice and a wrap. I didn't stop for supplies because Jefferson implied it was an emergency. He doesn't like to see anyone in pain."

"Ironic, isn't it," Jefferson says, deadpan.

Heather climbs onto the bed next to Nikita, curling in close. Nikolai is uncomfortable with the visible level of emotion between them. He slowly backs out of the bedroom as Jefferson and Genevieve leave. Seth follows close behind. Mattie is still sitting on the sofa in the living room, but the other newcomers stay with Heather and Nikita.

"They come from a different world," Seth grumbles. "They don't know what it's like here—what it's like to finally be in Havenhill after we've looked for it for years."

The door crashes open, a cart visible. "It's not an easy place to find." Ethan follows the cart and continues speaking. "Mom made sure of that, because that's what Alia wanted. People have to really want to know about this place, and have to come here for sanctuary, not to do harm. I mean. We took over an entire town."

Jefferson and Genevieve slip out the door around Ethan, Marybelle, and what looks like dinner.

And oh, what a dinner, better than Nikolai's seen in years.

Between Ethan and Marybelle, they have three carts and multiple shelves worth of food. Seth grips Nikolai's hand, and Nikolai itches to grab one of the carts and eat as fast as he can.

As Alaric and the others step out of the bedroom, Nikolai moves between them and the food and holds his hands out.

"We need to ration," he says.

"Actually, you don't," Ethan says gently, "but let us get everything laid out first. Then, if some of you aren't used to starving, let the starving people eat first." His gaze falls on Nikolai and Seth. "And you, eat slowly. Don't binge. Don't do more than your stomachs can handle. There's plenty more food than this, and I'll leave you with snacks tonight. Most of our newcomers eat until they can't fit another thing in their stomach for the first week or so here. We understand."

Marybelle works quickly, taking trays of food and setting them on a sideboard near the windows in the sitting room. She has a stack of plates and silverware, and when she runs out of serving space, she arranges the rest on the top of the carts. Steam rises from some platters: roasted meat in sauce, hot vegetables, and an entire tray of crispy roast chicken. There are cold breads and jams, and what looks like butter. Nothing tinned, nothing years old.

Nikolai's stomach rumbles, and Seth's stomach answers.

"We eat seasonally," Marybelle says, her voice delicate and high-pitched. Her smile wavers as she gestures for them to take plates. "Whatever's current gets eaten, and we live by the flow of the year around us. We do have ways to get things out of season, but it's better we focus those efforts on acquiring things other than food. Alia's community was already almost self-sufficient before the Split, and Aunt Val's from a farming community as well. Everyone who lives here helps."

“I can spin, dye, weave, and knit while we’re here,” Alaric rumbles, voice low.

“I’ll put you in touch with the right people,” Ethan offers. His attention swivels back to Nikolai, and he continues as if he and Marybell have given similar welcome spiels many times. “People don’t usually stay here as guests for more than a day or two. You can walk around. You might want to have someone with you, at first, until you get used to the layout. We’ll set up a tour, maybe a car tour because of your friend with the broken foot. Eventually we’ll get you moved into your own place, either here or in town.”

Nikolai nods; that’s more than enough for now. He places a chicken leg on his plate, then hesitates. Marybelle points out different dishes; he adds more food to his plate as each catches his attention: a heaping spoonful of macaroni and cheese; a spoonful of sweet squash; a pile of mixed steamed vegetables that includes broccoli, exactly like he’d been dreaming about; and another pile of roasted root vegetables. He takes a slab of ham, and a slab of beef.

All the food he’s taken fills two plates. He sets them on the coffee table and steps away long enough to get butter for the bread.

Spreading the cold butter on his warm bread brings back memories from a decade ago, of feeling so small at a large table, reaching for more butter so he can spread it thickly, and his father stopping him with a quiet touch. He’s careful now, spreading sparingly, but the taste is still a sweet explosion on his tongue. Beside him, Seth is devouring macaroni and cheese; he licks his lips when he finishes it, then turns to Nikolai. He grins and leans in for a kiss, and Nikolai can taste the rich sauce on his lips. Seth withdraws, but Nikolai doesn’t let him go too far, reaching a hand to the nape of his neck so they can lean forehead to forehead.

“We’re safe now,” Nikolai murmurs. “We aren’t going to starve again.”

“Goal achieved. We can go home now,” Mattie says.

Nikolai realizes that the others have settled down with their own plates while he and Seth were distracted by the bounty of food.

“Nikolai’s safe, yes, but we don’t know that we’ve done enough for him to *continue* to be safe,” Nikita points out. “This world is overrun with

Shadows." She rests with her foot propped on an ottoman. Heather sits on the edge, holding a plate for them to share.

"It's safe here," Ethan says.

"We haven't healed the split," Alaric mumbles around a mouthful of bread. He sets down the slice and looks through small jars Nikolai hadn't noticed. He stops with one in his hand, opening it to dump jam thickly onto the bread.

"Don't waste that," Seth snaps.

Alaric rights the jar, looking to Ethan.

"It's fine," Ethan says, his gaze shifting from Alaric to Seth. His smile slips away, becoming serious. "We're working through last year's preserves, and we have plenty. Not many people love strawberry rhubarb as much as I do." He pauses and adds, "You won't go hungry here."

Alaric grunts and adds more jam to his bread.

"Never had it," Seth says. Nikolai doesn't think he has ever had rhubarb either, although he remembers the sweetness of plain strawberry jam from his childhood.

Alaric hands Seth the jar and a spoon. "'T's my favorite," he mutters, taking a big bite of slathered bread. "We make the best here—" He stops, growling under his breath.

Ethan takes Alaric by the shoulders, nudging him to the coffee table; Alaric sits, his shoulders hunched, leaning over the plate on the coffee table. He shrugs Ethan's touch away and doesn't say more.

Nikolai returns to one of his plates and tries to eat slow enough to savor the tastes, but all he wants to do is fill his belly. Everything tastes so good, so different from shelf-stale, cold tinned food.

Seth spreads the jam on his bread and offers Nikolai a bite. It's the sweetness he remembers with a tart after-bite that Nikolai doesn't recognize. Seth makes a face after trying it and hands it off to Nikolai, scooping half the macaroni and cheese from Nikolai's plate in exchange.

Nikolai knows they could get up and get more of either food, but sharing with Seth feels right.

"Tell us about it," Ethan says, pointing to himself and Marybelle. "Your friend Mattie didn't explain a lot, and we'd like to know where you're from.

Tell us how you got here."

"We're from here," Seth mutters, getting up and returning with two slices of bread. He drops one on Nikolai's plate, pushing the butter toward him.

"I'd like to know how we're getting home," Carolyn says.

Pawel's response is cut off by Mac putting a hand over his mouth.

Carolyn's mouth quirks up on one side, her smile without humor.

Nikolai tunes them out. He's heard this story, and he doesn't care to hear it again right now. He cares about the sweet-and-spicy way the squash melts on his tongue, thick and smooth. He cares about the tang of the jam, and the creaminess of the cheese over macaroni. He spears a piece of broccoli and drags it through the cheese sauce in the way he remembers doing as a child, and for a moment, he can close his eyes and imagine that nothing's changed, that his brothers are across the table while Seth sits next to him. That his parents and Seth's are there, chiding them for eating too quickly, reminding them to eat their vegetables.

Nikolai cleans his plate to the sound of remembered voices admonishing him that there are starving children. He understands now, knows what it means to wonder where your next meal will come from.

His belly aches when it's full, and he hopes he can keep what he's eaten down. He doesn't want to waste this bounty. Seth tilts toward him, and Nikolai raises his arm, tucking Seth in against his side.

Now that Nikolai's sated, he tunes back in to the conversation.

Plates are empty, and the sideboard is still laden with food. It takes effort not to get another plate just because he can, because he never knows when food will be available again. He twitches, and Seth pokes him.

They're safe here, safe and fed. Nikolai needs to remember that.

"So I grew up here," Alaric says, gesturing with a fork. "Never had Mages, though. My father doesn't believe anyone but Clan's worth much." He hesitates, then says slowly, "Theobald Herne."

Ethan's brow furrows, and he shrugs and shakes his head. "Never heard of him. Alia's in charge here, her and my mother Val. They've been partners since we came here, not long after the Split."

Alaric makes a small, thoughtful noise.

"You said we could walk outside?" Seth stretches slowly, tugging his shirt down when it rides up. He nudges his glasses up his nose, then looks between Marybelle and Ethan. "We're not used to sitting still, and we're definitely not used to eating like this. It'd be good to get out."

"I'll get someone to meet you." Marybelle jumps up and runs out the door, letting it slam with a *thunk* behind her.

Nikolai stands slowly, feeling the pull of heavy food in his gut. A part of him regrets the meal, worries that he'll be too heavy if something happens. He won't be able to run or fight. Seth grips his hand as if he knows what Nikolai is thinking, and calm washes over him.

Nikolai closes his eyes, breathes in and out slowly. When he opens them again, everyone is watching him. Heat rises to his cheeks. "Could you just—? If there's a way we could have more food when we get back... I didn't get to taste everything, and it's all amazing. The bread—the butter..." He tries to find words, but they fail him. He falls back on lessons learned as a child, and offers a simple "Thank you."

"There's a fridge under the—"

"You have electricity?" Seth interrupts Ethan, crouching to see the small box refrigerator that looks as if it might be as old as they are.

"Wind, solar, and water," Ethan says. "We're independent, as much as we can be. I'll put the butter and jam in the fridge, and leave you the bread. It makes a good snack. I'll make a couple plates of the real food, too. It'll be just as good cold."

Nikolai hesitates, eyes still on the food. And it's so comfortable here...

Ethan waves him to the door. "Go. Walk."

This time Seth is the one who hesitates.

"Come on," Nikolai says, adding, "just you and me," when it looks like Alaric is rising to maybe follow them. Nikolai grabs Seth's hand and heads out the door. A walk will do them good, and the peace of exploring safe place will do them even better.

7

Nikolai ignores the people and animals scattered everywhere, and he's thankful that they seem to ignore him in return. He stays linked with Seth, unwilling to give up that small connection to the familiar as they follow the path back to the central stairs and down. Nikolai shortens his stride to match Seth's, which works until they reach the stairs. Nikolai is a full step below Seth before he realizes that Seth still stands at the top.

"What?" Nikolai asks, turning back.

Like this, they are eye to eye, with Seth just a bit taller. It makes it easy for Seth to put his arms over Nikolai's shoulders, leaning in as he smiles. "Stop worrying," Seth murmurs, his breath a warm wash over Nikolai's skin. "This place is safe. I can feel it. I've never felt as secure anywhere in my life. Even before. There are…I don't know if there are wards here, but it feels secure. They mean us no harm."

"I didn't think they did. I just—" This is his Seth again, the one who is positive in the face of adversity, Nikolai's rock in a stream to cling to when the current threatens to pull him away. "It's hard to stop worrying. We've been running for so long. It's hard to let go."

"It is for everyone when they first arrive," a voice calls from below.

Amaranth stands on the landing, her hair pulled into a bushy ponytail at the nape of her neck. She's bundled up, a scarf wrapped around her throat and a heavy wool poncho over a sweater, gloves covering her hands. "Come on down. I've got cold-weather gear for you, since it sounded like we'd be heading outside. Seems to be the thing to do after getting here. Everyone wants to know what the place is like and how far out is safe."

They follow her down the stairs to the door, taking the borrowed coats, mittens, and hats to gird themselves against the chill. Nikolai hates how the temperatures change so abruptly and starkly this time of year.

"Ethan said something about taking over a town," Seth says as they step outside.

"He's not wrong," Amaranth says.

She beckons, and they follow her down the steps into what looks like an old gravel driveway that is no longer maintained. There's a horse tied to a hitching rail on one side, and on the other, the van and cars along with two trucks. "This commune used to be one part of a small town, the kind that had a downtown and a bunch of little stores and a few box stores on the way between it and the nearest bigger town. Now there's a school in the center, neighborhoods all around, and a big town square."

She starts walking, and it's easier to follow than to ask where they're going. Nikolai's relieved they aren't getting into another car, or worse, expected to ride the horse. "How do you take over a town?"

"Magic." She sets a strong pace, but they're used to walking and can keep up. "Val arrived not long after the Split, and she set up wards around the town. Made it so people who weren't Talented wanted to leave, and so people who were Talented were drawn in. We grew quickly in those early days, but the beacon attracted the Shadows, too, so we had to do away with it. Pity; since it did help. Talented travelers get lost coming here now. We've become a hidden community, and we have to rely on word of mouth to get information out."

"How do you ward a place this big?" Seth asks.

Amaranth stops so quickly that Seth has to rock back on his heels to avoid running into her. She grins. "I'd worry about why you're asking, but Alia thinks you smell fine. In case you're worried, you're also not our first bonded pair; we won't throw anyone out for being a Dreamwalker."

"That's good, since Nikita is one as well," Nikolai says. He gets the feeling that hiding anything here is a bad idea. "Heather is her Empath." Amaranth makes a small noise, a gesture as if to say go on. Nikolai's gaze drops. "We don't actually know them that well."

"We got that impression from Mattie, so don't worry. It's fine. Alia will deal with anyone who works against the community." Amaranth pats Seth's shoulder. "We're all good."

They walk down the long drive, both sides lined by thick trees. Amaranth veers onto a side road Nikolai hadn't spotted and stops. "If you keep going this way, you reach the groves. The outer grove is beyond the main road; you probably didn't even notice it. Definitely a car or horse ride away, or a good run for the Clan folk. The first grove is closest to here, a line of lemon trees around the original Clan property."

"Lemons won't grow in the Northeast," Nikolai protests.

Amaranth holds her hands up, wiggling her fingers. "That's one of the reasons they keep me around. Val brought me in during the early days, when we could still travel fairly easily. I brought seedlings with me from Florida. Plants are my innate ability. I can grow anything, anywhere, and keep it safe from frost. We planted these as soon as we knew Shadows were the problem."

"Do they stop them?" Nikolai remembers myths about lemons and Shadows, but for him, protection has always been about having Seth by his side.

"They helped us create a border," she says. "There are several groves, several iterations of the border as we've pushed out. And we'd like to keep growing, to create our own little forgotten nation here. When I got here, there were about three hundred Clan, and Val brought in twenty-five mages—about half her commune—and a few Talented folk from town who'd chosen to stay. Later, the rest of Val's Mages came, as did many of my old community. Since then, people have drifted in. It takes a lot of work to maintain this community. We have our own natural power and our own electrical grid. We have mechanics and engineers. We're self-sufficient. You're welcome to stay here as long as you'd like. We welcome any and all Talent with open arms, as long as they mean no harm."

Her gaze drifts away, and Nikolai takes a guess what she's thinking about. "I haven't known her long, but Mattie hasn't attacked us," he says. "We've been attacked by many Shadows over the years. She seems different. How do you keep the Shadows away?"

"That's part of what the shield does," Amaranth says with a smirk. "They attack the borders all the time, which makes humans less likely to try to get here. It helps keep us hidden. So. Let's go to the first grove, then we can walk some of the boundary so you can see how far you can go without worrying about going outside the main wards." She sets a pace more leisurely than the earlier rush when they left the house. "If you want to travel into town, you'll need to get someone to take you in a car or carriage. It can be walked, but you don't want to spend that much time in the places where the wards are weaker. We have social gatherings there, as well as at the house. You should get to know people. Make some friends."

"Give us time," Seth says, glancing at Nikolai.

"We can introduce you to other newer arrivals, people who may have been through things similar to what you've endured to get here, if you want to talk about it," Amaranth offers gently. "I've been here since I was a teenager. My family let me go on this long road trip by myself. I was scared as hell on the way."

"Are they here now?" Nikolai asks.

"My family?" Amaranth asks. When Nikolai nods, she continues, "Yes, actually. My parents live in a house in town. My grandfather passed away on the trip here, and my grandmother lives with my parents. I'm an only child, but I have cousins here too."

Seth makes a small noise, and Nikolai leans closer to him.

"We don't," Nikolai says, his voice carefully flat, "have family. Not anymore. We had to make our way here alone." Nikolai shudders. "We're all each other has, now. So you're talking about meeting people and making friends, but I'm not sure we're ready to develop new relationships. I mean, yes, I know we can't be reclusive. You want us to be part of this community, and we have to do our part. We *will* do our part. But we'd been alone for two years when that group dropped out of some weird world rift and into our lives. A day later, we're here. It's an adjustment."

He says "we," but he means himself. He's not ready. Seth's hand on his back is soothing, drawing slow circles, stroking calm into Nikolai's skin.

"You ready to talk about your family?" Amaranth asks. She lets the question hang, doesn't dig at it while they keep walking.

It gives Nikolai time to think, to work through the prospect of saying more.

Seth's fingers curl into the fabric at the base of Nikolai's back, sliding under his jacket. Nikolai breathes through the memories, heat and smoke and flame still vivid in his mind. "Everyone here has a story like ours," he says, because he knows that has to be true.

"Some worse than others," Amaranth agrees. "But this one is still yours, and it will always be a part of your history. It's a burden you can share, if you want. But no one will make you."

Nikolai carefully unwinds from Seth. He strips his mitten off and shoves it into a pocket, then tangles his fingers with Seth's, skin to skin. The touch eases him, makes it easier to center his mind and stay focused in the here and now.

"I'm willing to share," he says quietly.

"I'm willing, too, if you do the talking," Seth says.

Nikolai squeezes his hand in assent. "We grew up south of here, in northern New Jersey," he says. He looks at the trees, holds onto Seth as his anchor, looks everywhere but at Amaranth while he speaks. "I had two older brothers—Mikhail and Josef. I'm much younger—they were ten and eight when I was born, and I got the feeling, growing up, that they weren't excited to have a brand-new baby brother. Then my Talent Emerged. I was a Dreamwalker in a family of Weather Witches. My parents made arrangements, and we were lucky; I found Seth, and we were instant best friends. Our Talents intertwined, and the bond grew swiftly. His family moved up to Jersey, and childhood was awesome. Before the Split."

He glances sideways. Seth's jaw is set tight, adding definition to his round features.

"The Split happened, and at first, things weren't bad where we lived," he says. "No one knew we were Talented. No one got panicky right away. Then the Shadows descended on New York City. That was bad, and it was nearby, so the humans noticed. When the first city wall went up, we knew we couldn't stay where we were and pretend everything was fine. So both our families packed up to move. Mikhail was pissed off. He and Josef were in college, and they thought they'd be safe because no one knew they were Weather Witches. Mom and Dad insisted they come home. Said it wasn't safe for them to be among the humans. They were right. Josef was jumped in his dorm, and he ran; Mikhail had to find him, and they met up with us on the road. And by then—we'd run into Shadows. Seth's parents were dead."

Nikolai rushes, not giving Seth time to dwell on the memories. Nikolai doesn't want to remember the details, either, even though he recalls what happened with a bright, sparkling clarity. It had been the first time he and Seth combined their Talents against the Shadows. They were only ten years old, and they saved Nikolai's parents and themselves.

Unfortunately, they were too late to save Seth's family.

"By then, a lot of humans had fled into New York City, so a lot of places around the city were...well, they weren't exactly emptying out, but we could find abandoned places to move into. Start over and pretend to be human. It didn't work, though, because people kept leaving. There weren't any resources, and people wondered why we stayed out and risked our lives among the Talents and the Shadows. I figure that's why someone decided we were dangerous; a couple years ago, humans set fire to our house. Seth and I ran."

Nikolai grips Seth's hand tightly, focusing on that single point anchoring them together. He looks ahead as they walk, trying to memorize this path so they can walk it again. "We'd heard about Havenhill. There was this family who'd stayed with us while we were still trying to set down roots—I don't know if they made it here or not. I don't think they did." Nikolai remembers the conversation he'd overheard when the fire was set, the implications about what had happened to Erica and her family. "The fire wasn't long after they left us. But while they were with us, they told Dad about Havenhill, and they helped him work out a route to get there...here," he says, realizing that's in the past. That they aren't traveling any more.

"You've found a safe place," Amaranth says. They've curved back to the main road—or onto another road that's as large, Nikolai can't be sure. When she gestures, he sees the way the trees thin into a field planted with a grove of low fruit trees. "This is the first grove. The wards are hung on those trees; these are the most solid of the lines of wards. Stay inside that line and you'll be safe."

Seth slips his hand free from Nikolai and goes to one of the trees, reaching up to touch the branches. The leaves are curled as if seeking to avoid the chill in the air, and Nikolai can't think how they survive here. "It's too cold," he says.

Amaranth wiggles her fingers again. "I told you—it's magic. Seriously. We use some weather witchery, and my natural Talent for plants, and we keep them going. We also have lemons and lemonade year-round, which is wonderful. There are a few other citrus trees mixed in, so we have oranges and grapefruit as well, but the lemons form the primary border."

Seth is still touching the tree, running his fingers along the branch. "Amazing," he whispers.

"You two take some time. I'm going to—" Amaranth gestures to one side.

Nikolai waves her away, then wraps his arms around Seth from behind, chin on his shoulder. "You look like you can't believe it," he murmurs.

"Lemon trees in the Northeast. A literal border made of lemons to keep us safe from Shadows," Seth says. "It seems too good to be true, and I keep thinking you're going to tell me we're about to freeze to death and we're drifting into a brilliant Dream."

"It's hard to believe we're really safe." Nikolai exhales slowly, closes his eyes, and tries to let his guard down. There's a faint scent of lemon in the air, and he enjoys the crisp breeze which isn't overpoweringly cold right now. "Everything's seemed off-kilter since those people showed up."

"But they got us here," Seth points out.

"They got us here," Nikolai agrees. He nudges Seth until they both stand beneath the lemon tree, the branches surrounding them with the biting citrus scent. "We're safe," Nikolai says, and Seth pushes up, meeting him for a kiss.

8

AMARANTH LETS THEM be for a while. When Nikolai glances over at her, she's bent close to something held in her hand, speaking into it. By the time he looks back to Seth again, he has stopped at the edge of the grove, standing under the branches of a tree. He has his hand on the trunk and is staring out.

"What is it?" Nikolai asks. He slips in behind Seth, dropping one hand to the middle of his back; Seth flinches under his touch, and Nikolai pulls away.

"It's okay." Seth says. "You startled me." He drifts closer, and Nikolai answers by sliding his arm around Seth's middle and drawing him in. Seth raises a hand and gestures, careful not to go beyond the line created by the trunks of the trees. "Look. You can see them out there, in the darkness."

It's late enough that the overhang from the leaves creates deep pockets of shadow that almost seem to move. "Can they get this close?" Nikolai whispers. "This is the first grove. I got the impression there were more, and while this is the safest area, it's safe all the way to the outermost grove."

Seth shrugs; Nikolai feels it against his side rather than seeing. "Maybe I'm hallucinating," he says. "It's possible I'm anxious. Or it's possible that with this many Talent in one place, they can't quite keep them out, and that's why we need to stay within the first grove. We arrived with a crowd not long ago. Maybe the Shadows have followed us here."

There's a low rumble in the distance, coming from outside the grove. Nikolai's gaze narrows, and he tugs at Seth, pulling him back. "Something's coming." His hand falls to Seth's, and he feels the wash of calm over him, the indication that if he wants to—if they need to respond to a threat—their Talents are linked.

Amaranth shoves something in her pocket as she approaches. "You don't need to worry," she calls out. "That's just the Jeep."

Nikolai remembers Jeeps from years ago—shiny and bright, bulling along through snow with all-wheel drive and over-confident drivers.

The vehicle that comes into view is not that.

It's old and battered, the creamy white of its paint stained by rust along the bottom of the door panels, the hood a dark, matte gray. It has a hard top in that same white, preventing Nikolai from seeing the driver. Amaranth waves one hand eagerly as the Jeep cuts off the road and toward the grove, swerving through an opening between the trees.

It comes to a stop just inside the border. Nikolai knows the occupants must be friendly, but he feels a trickle of anxiety from Seth and feeds him back his own.

The Jeep's doors creak open.

Amaranth holds her hands up, and both doors are yanked shut again with a creak and *thump*. She turns to face Nikolai and Seth, her hands still in the air in a placating gesture. "So. After hearing your story, I thought—I want you to meet my boyfriend. And his brother." Her voice is tight, and a little hopeful, lilting up at the end like she's asking a question. When she gestures, the doors to the Jeep creak open again, and two men spill out. They're both tall and skinny, light-haired and bearded over sharply cut features. It's easy to see that they're related from the similarities, not only in looks but in the way they move, as if they've traveled together for a long time. The differences become more obvious as they walk; one moves with a heavy limp, and the other shortens his stride to stay with him.

"They live on the edge of town," Amaranth continues. "They got here maybe a year ago, and Josef—he wasn't my boyfriend then—was injured. I stayed with them while he healed. Genevieve could fix the break, but he needed to recover from the infection that had set in. He's lucky to be alive."

The two stop; the one without a limp grabs the arm of the other, leaning in to say something before taking off toward them at a run.

Seth shoves Nikolai behind him, a wave of *don't come near us* stopping the newcomers in their tracks. It's awkward to hide behind Seth, considering Nikolai is so much taller than him, but he appreciates the sentiment.

"Nikolai," the stranger says. The other approaches quickly to catch up to where the first has stopped.

Wait. Nikolai knows that voice, and Amaranth said "Josef," so that means…

His heart thumps loudly, and he pushes past Seth. "Mikhail?" He only has to take a few steps before he's caught up in a hard hug that squeezes the breath out of him, his brother's familiar voice murmuring words that are impossible to hear through the buzzing in Nikolai's mind. Another moment, and there are more arms around him, and Josef's voice, and someone is crying. Maybe all of them. Nikolai's cheeks are wet, and his chest aches, and when he draws back, Mikhail's eyes are rimmed in red.

Josef pulls Nikolai in, framing his face with his hands, and kisses him soundly, once on each cheek. "We thought you two were dead."

"God, I'm glad I guessed that right," Amaranth mutters. "If they hadn't been your family, this would've been awkward."

"Where the hell did you find our brother?" Mikhail asks.

Nikolai doesn't want to step away. He burrows close as if he's nine instead of nineteen, dragging Seth into the mix because he's family, too. They're all family.

Wait.

"What about—?"

Josef doesn't let Nikolai finish the question, shaking his head in negation. "Burned in the fire," he says quietly. "We thought you two had as well, even though we never found your bodies. We barely found Mom. Dad helped us get out, but it got into his lungs, and he never recovered. Neither did I, really; I still have trouble breathing some days. And when I wasn't able to run away, the Shadows came damned close to taking us out. I was hurt badly, and Mikhail refused to leave me. If Alia hadn't sent out a mission to ransack the houses where we were hiding, I would've died."

"Even as it was, it was closer than I care to think," Mikhail says. He slides his hands to Nikolai's shoulders, looking at him. "You've gotten tall in the last couple of years." His gaze slide to Seth, and he grins. "You haven't."

Seth pushes his glasses up with his middle finger; it's a familiar gesture, although his smile eases it. "You do remember my dad, right? I was always going to be short. Don't worry, I've still got Talent to make up for it."

"I remember how big you are emotionally," Mikhail says.

When Seth takes his hand, Nikolai has to close his eyes against the onslaught of emotions. He knows Seth is filtering them while still letting Nikolai feel the relief, the joy at finding family, and the sorrow at imparting dark news. Tears spring to Nikolai's eyes again, and he brings up his free hand to rub them away.

"You can stay with us," Mikhail offers. "The house isn't big, but you'll want a place to stay other than Alia's. It's not bad to start out there, but it's easier once you have a place of your own."

Nikolai glances at Amaranth, not sure how that works. "I don't want to put you out."

"It's complicated," Seth says at the same time.

Josef laughs when they speak in stereo. "How complicated could it be?" he asks. "You're family."

"I live in Alia's house," Amaranth says. "You wouldn't be putting me out. There are times I stay with Josef, yes, but they have an extra room. It's filled with crap, and they could use the excuse to clear it out."

"It's filled with research and weather-pattern logs," Mikhail counters. "It's an office. But yes, we could easily set it up so you can sleep there. You two may want your own place eventually, but it's a place to get started."

Too much. Too fast.

It's hard to move from being on the run, to knowing that they're safe, to being dumped into the deep end of potential stability. Nikolai knows that this is good, that it's not a reason to worry, but his chest goes so tight that he can't catch his breath. Seth wraps his arms around him, drawing him off to one side, gentle waves of calm battering against the furious crests of panic. In the background, he can hear low voices; he catches pieces of what Amaranth is telling his brothers. The names of the people who arrived with him stand out starkly, each one a thrum against his skin.

He shouldn't feel responsible for the strangers from another world, but he does.

"We should get back," Nikolai says. "Find out how the others are doing."

"I don't think Nikita is going anywhere," Seth points out. "I assume she's the one you're most worried about."

It's true. Seeing her is like looking in a mirror.

"They're still new arrivals." Amaranth's voice rises, loud enough to hear clearly. "And yes, you can take him home when he's ready, but right now, we should go back to the house and let them settle in. You remember what it's like."

"Our friend is injured," Seth says as if they're all standing together in one conversation. It's odd to hear Seth refer to Nikita as a friend. "Things really are more complicated than you think."

"Amaranth was saying." Mikhail is there, one hand on Nikolai's shoulder, the other on Seth's. "We'll drive you back to the house. It's late, and you're probably exhausted. We'll come by the house tomorrow to meet these other people you arrived with. It sounds like a hell of a story."

"We barely know them, but—" Nikolai cuts off, uncertain how to finish.

"It's complicated," Mikhail finishes for him.

After all this time, Nikolai just wants to sink into having an older brother again. There's finally someone else to be responsible, someone else who can be the adult. He smiles slightly at Mikhail. "It's complicated," he agrees, pushing his hair out of his face. "It'll take some time to uncomplicate it. Not to mention that Nikita seems determined to rescue me."

"I think you've already been rescued," Mikhail says.

Nikolai laughs, a short, sharp bark. "According to our experiences, yes. Her world is like ours was before the Split. She thinks we're still in dire trouble."

"Aren't we?" Seth says. That's a sobering thought. Even though they're here, and they're safe, it might not mean long-term safety. There could still be a blade hanging over them, and Nikita is more aware of it than they are.

To Nikolai, being in Havenhill feels like bliss. He shakes his head, determined not to let go of the good feeling of finally being safe. "No, we're not, and she'll figure that out eventually. This isn't like her home. This is the best we can get here, and I'll take it." This time when he smiles at Mikhail, looking past him to see Josef and Amaranth standing together, there's honest pleasure in his expression. He squeezes Seth's hand, holding on tight. "We have so much more today than we had yesterday. I'm glad of that."

9

The next morning, Nikolai is so used to being on the move that he packs as soon as he's awake. He remembers, then, the promise of hot water in the bathroom. As soon as he twists the tap, he knows that this is pure luxury. He calls for Seth, and they stand under the high spigot together until their skin is shriveled and pruny. Decadently, they linger over soft touches and kisses, helping wash each other with sweet-smelling soap. There are soft, clean towels and clothes on the bed when they are finally done; someone must have come in while they showered. He doesn't mind, accepting the towels and the clean clothes as the gifts they seem meant to be.

Holding the clothes in his hands, Nikolai is able to accept the truth: they aren't going anywhere today. He doesn't need to pack.

They take their time getting dressed, then they pull all the dirty clothes from their bags, spreading them out across the bed. They don't possess much, and what they do have is in terrible shape.

When Ethan arrives, he puts everything in a basket and leaves it outside the door. "Someone will clean it for you," he says. "We'll make sure you get new if you need it, and repair what's ripped. You have time. You're not going anywhere. You're home." They sound like words he's said a hundred times before, to other new arrivals struggling to acclimate.

It hasn't even been a day since they arrived. Nikolai suspects it will take several mornings like this to fully assimilate.

"Everyone else woke up a while ago and went to breakfast," Ethan says. He brings them down to a room off the kitchens. There are several long tables, enough to fit three or four times as many people as are present. While it's a crowd for breakfast, at least they're all people Nikolai has already met—those he arrived with and some who brought them in or met them here.

Mikhail rises from his seat at a table laden with food and gestures to the waiting empty chairs and plates; Nikolai immediately veers to join him. As Nikolai sits, Mikhail leans close to him. "We're going on a tour of Havenhill. You and Seth will be with me in the Jeep," he says.

Nikolai's stomach rumbles despite how much he ate the night before. He nods, willing to go along. A tour of another part of their new home seems logical, and he's happy to let Mikhail be the adult in his stead. Besides, there is food to focus on. He reaches for the platter of bacon on the table, drags it close enough to pick up several slices for himself and Seth, and adds them to plates Seth has already filled with sweet pancakes and fresh fruit. He can't remember when he last had meat that wasn't caught fresh, cooked gamey and tough and bland without seasonings over an open flame. Salt and fat explode in flavor on his tongue.

"Where's Josef?" he asks around a mouthful.

"He and Amaranth are working on cleaning out the office so you two can sleep there if you want to stay with us," Mikhail says. He's done eating, his plate pushed away, and he watches with a small, indulgent smile as Nikolai reaches for another stack of pancakes.

There's fresh butter again—sweet, creamy, and slightly salty—and Nikolai slathers it on thickly. He doesn't need the maple syrup, but he's amazed by the presence of the sweet treat even though he knows that these are resources that should be easy to create in a self-sufficient commune.

"Seems like someone may not want to join the tour," Mikhail adds, nodding toward where Val sits with Pawel.

"Yes," Val says firmly, her voice rising as she looks at Pawel. "You will come with us. You can spend time in the library tonight; we'll be back long before dinner. You need to see Havenhill, see what we do here. You don't have to know right now, but eventually you will need to make a decision about how you will contribute to our community."

Pawel opens his mouth, but nothing comes out. Mac's hand curls over his wrist, dark skin against pale where she touches him. Pawel closes his mouth and sits back, pulling away from Mac to cross his arms.

"We're happy to help as long as we're here," Heather says with a smile.

The sense of calm is faint, and Nikolai doesn't think he'd feel it if he weren't so in tune with Seth's use of Empathy.

There's a low growl; Alaric drops his fork and knife on the table. "Let's go look, then," he mutters. He glares daggers at Heather, but she ignores him.

Nikolai is torn between wishing he understood the undercurrents these people brought with them and being glad that he doesn't.

It's easier to breathe after they've separated into groups and entered four separate vehicles to caravan through Havenhill. Genevieve sits in the front of the Jeep, chatting with Mikhail, and Seth and Nikolai are in the back. It rattles alarmingly when it starts up, shaking as they roll out behind the minivan, the sedan, and a truck Nikolai doesn't remember seeing yesterday.

Seth's hand finds his, and that makes everything easier. Riding in a vehicle is still strange to Nikolai. The world passes by so quickly outside the window, and he sits, glued to the view, as they drive down the long road and past the lemon trees that mark the first grove. Nikolai can see small houses in the distance with winding drives leading to them, some in the woods off the private road and others along the main road. Looking carefully, he can recognize lines of citrus trees, and he guesses that they are the different groves that have sprung up as Havenhill has grown.

"You'll be safe here," Genevieve says, and Nikolai wonders if she's mistaken his silence for nerves.

"We hope so," Seth says quietly. "We've been trying to get here for years. We don't plan on leaving."

"You won't need to," Mikhail assures them.

They travel slowly through the town, like a parade. Nikolai sees other cars occasionally parked in driveways or on lawns—nowhere near as many as he remembers from his childhood, but more than he's seen since then. He spots people, as well, from older folks out working on their houses to small children playing. When they drive by the school, there are lights on, and Mikhail slows down.

"All of the kids go to school until they're sixteen, then they have a choice whether to continue or not," he says. "It's a bit more 'one-room schoolhouse' than when I was in school, but we do work with tougher subjects on request, using textbooks we've scrounged up. It's hard to teach engineering without calculus, so we're always glad when kids are willing to learn. We need to train engineers; we can't be independent without them."

Nikolai blinks, shaking his head. He has no idea what calculus is.

Mikhail makes a small, displeased noise. "I forget how young you were when everything fell apart."

"That only means you're old now," Seth retorts, a small smile tilting his lips.

"Feels like it sometimes," Mikhail admits.

The caravan turns left at the next crossroads, but Mikhail turns right, heading up a small incline behind the school. There are houses in a neatly arranged neighborhood here, and when Mikhail makes another turn, Nikolai sees Amaranth and Josef on the porch of a blue house, waving. Mikhail stops in front of the house rather than pulling into the gravel drive. Genevieve rolls down the window, and Amaranth comes close to lean on the sill.

Seth unbuckles his seat belt and slides closer to Nikolai. "You okay?"

Nikolai lifts his arm, helping Seth tuck himself in close by his side. He lowers his head so he can press his face against Seth's curls and inhale the scent of the shampoo they both used that morning. "We smell so clean," he murmurs, even though it doesn't answer Seth's question.

Seth twists, reaching up to touch Nikolai's face. "It's hard to believe we're here," he says.

A rich crackle echoes inside the Jeep, and Nikolai sits upright, pressing back into the seat. He half expects to see lightning despite the clear skies.

Mikhail doesn't seem bothered, reaching for something on the floor. He passes it to Genevieve, and Nikolai realizes that it's a radio as a voice comes from it with another crackle and hiss.

"We're meeting at the Benford house." It's Val's voice, Nikolai thinks, distorted by the radio. "Mikhail, catch up with us there or let us know that you're dropping out of the tour."

Mikhail glances back, and Nikolai looks to Seth, who shrugs.

"We'll be there," Genevieve says into the radio, then sets it down on the floor again. Amaranth backs up, and she and Josef wave as Genevieve puts the window up and they head out.

They were given a choice, but Nikolai wasn't actually allowed a say. He exhales, leaning his head against Seth's. "I feel like everything's happening around me." As if they're expected to settle in and move on. As if this new normal is easy to accept.

"It took a long time before I was able to feel comfortable here." Mikhail speaks as if Nikolai meant him to hear, and Nikolai bites his tongue rather than snap.

Seth's squeeze of his hand is a welcome anchor.

Nikolai isn't sure why they went by Josef and Mikhail's place if they were only going to leave again. It was easy to go with the flow in the beginning, but now he feels adrift, as if he's being dragged around like a child with no opinions.

If he asks the right questions, maybe he can regain some of the control that he's lost.

"What's the Benford house?"

"It's a large house on the outer edge of the first grove," Genevieve says, turning to speak as Mikhail drives. "It's been abandoned since early in the Split, which means it's available if your friends want to move into it. There's another small house nearby, if there isn't enough room in the one place."

"Why was it abandoned?" Seth asks. He carefully moves back into his own seat and buckles the seat belt. Nikolai feels the loss of his warmth keenly.

Genevieve looks toward Mikhail, whose fingers tighten on the wheel, and Seth exhales as a wave of gentle calm washes through the car.

"I'm fine," Mikhail says. "I wasn't here when it happened, so I really shouldn't find it as disturbing as I do. It's only a story now. You might as well tell it."

"I wasn't here either," Genevieve admits. She turns to look between the seats at them both, propping her chin on her hand. "It happened not long after the Split, before the world turned upside down, so most folks were still living their lives. Rumor has it that it was the event that inspired Alia to create the first grove."

Mikhail makes a small noise. When she glances at him again, he waves his fingers as if to tell her to keep going. "The Benford family was big: a mom and dad, a set of grandparents, three or four kids, maybe more. The grandparents had their own home—the other, smaller place nearby. The thing is, the Benfords were happy and involved with the rest of the Clan community. Everything was good," Genevieve says. "Then one day, they just weren't anymore."

"What do you mean?"

"When Alia went to investigate, they had apparently disappeared in the middle of dinner," she says. "There was a cake in the oven, plates on the table, food half eaten. Clothes in the wash, music playing upstairs. The house was full of life, but the family...wasn't there."

"Shadows?" Nikolai asks. He can imagine them sneaking in through the darkest corners of the rooms, taking those they came to take, then stealing away again unseen. No wonder Mikhail finds it chilling. Anyone who's been chased by Shadows would.

Genevieve nods. "Probably Shadows, yes. Clan being the way Clan is, they've shunned the place. Don't want anything to do with it, and no one has been willing to move in. Even when Val arrived with her folks, they said it felt off. It's been offered to new community members arriving in Havenhill over the years, but everyone's found a reason to reject it, and some would rather build a new tiny cottage than take it."

"It's a legend by now," Mikhail says. "The place kids dare each other to go into because they think it's haunted. But Val's right: it'd be perfect for your friends. The small house stays empty even though it doesn't feel as wrong as the Benford place because it feels like the two belong together. Everyone acts as if both of them need to be lived in to be right. And no one wants the Benford place." He glances at Genevieve, and she nods agreement.

The Jeep bumps along the road back toward the main house, then they veer to the left, down a narrow road. It's clear driving at first, but after a time, the road goes from gravel to mud with fresh ruts down the center. The trees hang, overgrown, branches brushing against the top of the Jeep as they pass.

"It's been a while," Genevieve says. "No one else built out this way, either, even though it's inside the first grove. It's safe."

Nikolai feels the sense of some impending danger hanging over head as the Jeep bumps down the road. He looks up into the leaves. They cast dappled shadows over everything, determined to bring darkness within the grove.

Seth reaches for him, and Nikolai takes his hand gratefully. He understands why no one wants to come here. It weighs on his shoulders, and if it were up to him, he'd say to turn back. But he's tangled with these strangers from another world, and he should at least hear them out, even if he fears that living here would be a bad idea.

10

The other vehicles are there when they arrive at the house, the truck still rumbling with Jefferson in the driver's seat. Sakura leans against the door, talking to him through the window. Everyone else stands in small knots. Carolyn is with Heather and Nikita, though Nikita still stands gingerly on her recently injured ankle; Heather's hand is on Carolyn's shoulder as if she needs steadying more than Nikita does. Mac and Pawel huddle with Alia and Val, speaking in hushed voices. Nikolai guesses that the conversation is urgent based on the way Pawel gestures broadly. Alaric is by the door to the house, his hand on the knob as he looks up, Ethan and Marybelle close behind him. Mattie's shadowy form is nowhere to be seen.

They all glance over as Nikolai carefully climbs down from the Jeep. He reaches, and Seth takes his hand, his touch calming in this sea of uncertainty and change. There's an undercurrent of something here, a depth to the Benford house that threatens to drag Nikolai beneath dark waves.

"I'm going in," Alaric rumbles, twisting the knob and letting go as the door pulls away from him, opening inward.

Mattie stands in the shadows inside, leaning into the doorway. "I'm not here," she announces, "but I can feel the pull into the Dreamlands. There was someone here, once upon a time, but she's long gone, and the connection to her feels broken. You couldn't bring her back from here, Carolyn; this isn't her home anymore."

Alaric growls and pushes past her, Ethan and Marybelle following.

"It's the truth," Mattie calls after him. "Is it any surprise that events would happen the same here as at home?"

"But not exactly the same," Carolyn says. "It wasn't you."

"It wasn't me," Mattie agrees. She pulls the door open and gestures inside. "This isn't my house, either. It's larger; there were more people in this family. My grandparents never lived nearby. The house isn't to blame for what happened. It can't hurt anyone."

"If anyone would know, it's Mattie," Carolyn says. She touches Heather's hand, then shrugs out from under her touch and follows Mattie inside.

With Heather's support, Nikita heads in as well. That draws Nikolai forward, while Seth trails along behind him, their hands tightly clutched together.

"I don't like it," Seth mutters, and Nikolai squeezes his hand in response. Nikolai isn't sure how he feels, other than that he doesn't want to let Nikita go inside alone.

"The question is simple," Val says as they pass. "You need to tell us what you bring to Havenhill. What can you do for our community? Everyone plays a part."

"We're not staying," Pawel says sharply. "You haven't been listening to a word I've said."

"Your husband seems very upset," Alia says.

Mac abruptly appears between Nikolai and the door. She has her hands up, wiping the air in front of her. "My what? Oh God, no, no, we're not even involved." She looks at Nikolai, and at the door, and offers a wry smile. "Sorry. Wasn't thinking." She disappears with a soft *pop*, reappearing next to Pawel and thwacking him lightly on the back of the head. "We're just friends. Give him time to come to terms with this."

"Conor—" Pawel's voice goes inaudible as Nikolai steps into the house and Seth pulls the door shut behind them.

Carolyn is the only one in the room, and she stands half turned, staring at the door. She raises her gaze to meet Nikolai's, her brows furrowed and mouth in a wry twist. "He's a single father. I don't blame him for worrying."

"It's at least partly his fault you're here," Seth says. Nikolai tightens his grip, trying to silently warn Seth to stop, but Seth continues. "Maybe you should have thought before you jumped from one world to another."

Carolyn flinches. "It wasn't entirely on purpose."

Nikolai can hear Nikita's voice from the upper floor. "I'm going upstairs," he says. He wants to talk to her before making any decisions. It would be easy to stay with Josef and Mikhail: they're family, and that would be the uncomplicated choice. But Nikita came here for him, and he feels partly at fault for that, as if his existence pulled her and her friends here.

Seth lets go and waves him off. He pushes his glasses up his nose, then crosses his arms.

Nikolai recognizes that stance—Seth is settling in for an argument. Nikolai hopes Carolyn can read body language well enough to realize what she's in for.

He leaves them to it and goes upstairs.

The house is stale, like many Nikolai stayed in along the route to Havenhill. The stench of burnt food lingers in the air, and he wonders why no one has aired the place out. There are pictures on the wall, dust heavy on the frames. He touches the first one near the base of the stairs. There are two adults and four children in the photo. Two of the children are too young to guess at gender, an infant and a toddler, but the other two look like a boy and a girl, maybe in their early teens. The girl stands with the toddler on her hip, helping the child wave, while the boy is turned toward the baby, making faces. As Nikolai goes up the stairs, the pictures along the wall spell out more of their lives. The children preferred avian forms, ducklings and chicks playing together, and one image shows a pair of fledgling sparrows.

At the top of the stairs, a door sits open to show a bathroom. To the right is a bedroom, the smell of must strong. He follows Nikita's voice past another bedroom to the end of a hall, where there are two rooms across from each other, another bathroom between them. Nikita kneels in one of the rooms, an old wooden toy car in her hands.

Off to one side, Alaric tugs a window open, and the fresh breeze is cold and sweet.

"I think this is the farthest I've seen anyone come into the house," Ethan says. "It feels different than the last time I was here."

Nikita looks to Heather, who shrugs. "It might be us," Nikita says. "You have two Dreamwalkers, a Shadow, and two Empaths in here. I wouldn't be surprised if we've set up some kind of strange resonance."

"We could try a cleansing," Marybelle suggests. "You have enough people to do a good ritual. A strong ritual, too." She grins at Alaric, who grumbles under her breath. "Yes, even you. We know how to leverage Clan with Mages here. We do it all the time."

Alaric stares at her for a long moment. "No," he says firmly, and in another breath, he disappears, replaced by an eagle who sits on the sill briefly before flying away.

"I'll talk to him," Ethan offers, his footsteps thundering down the stairs as he heads out.

It's quiet once they're gone. Marybelle moves around the room, pulling open drawers, unpacking clothes clearly meant for a teenage girl. She piles them on the bed in careful stacks.

Nikita winces, rubbing her knee before she switches to sitting instead of kneeling on the floor. Heather crouches next to her.

"What?" Heather asks.

Nikita shakes her head, touching Heather's knee as if to say she's okay. She looks up at Nikolai. "Why did you come here? I thought you'd stay with your brothers. I mean, I'm glad you found them. And you found Havenhill. And this community seems safe. I just—"

"I'm here because you are," he says. He can't blame her for asking; he's as confused as she is and can't really say anything more. He folds slowly, kneeling on the floor in front of Nikita. "You came to this world for me, right?" She nods. "And I'm safe now, but you don't seem satisfied. Alaric keeps talking about—"

"—healing the split," Nikita says. "I don't know how to do that, or if it can be done, but it feels like the right answer. It's like, if I don't do it, and I get home, I'm going to keep Dreaming of you, and you'll keep Dreaming of me, and our worlds will still be twinned. But if we fix things—"

"—the worlds can separate, maybe. Or at least we can." Nikolai huffs because it sounds ridiculous. "Two worlds being held together by the split seems wrong. Shouldn't it have torn us apart?" That's a disturbing image. Is he talking about the worlds being torn apart or themselves? He suppresses a shudder.

"Apparently not," Nikita mumbles. "Unless we're talking emotionally. In which case, I was a mess before I got here."

"If you're going to stay, you'll need to decide where you're living, and you'll need jobs," Marybelle says, still folding clothes. All the drawers are open and empty. "Even Pawel. Everyone who is able to work works here. We take care of our community. That's how we survive."

"I'll talk to them." Nikita pushes to her feet carefully. "I want to try something, maybe before you cleanse this place, but it'd probably be fine to wait until after. I want to see if we can combine our Talent"—she gestures between herself and Nikolai—"and if that's enough for us to get through to the Dreamscape. Or to my home. We might not be leaving yet, but I want to know we have a way out when we need it."

Seth's not going to like that idea any more than Nikolai does. He tables the thought for another time; Nikita doesn't need an answer right now.

"It might take some time for Seth and me to figure out what we can do to help here, but we'll do something," he assures Marybelle. "We know a lot about survival, but not a lot about building a community. We've spent half our lives hiding."

"We'll work it out," Marybelle agrees cheerfully. "So you're going to live here? We should tell Alia and Aunt Val."

"And the other house," Nikolai adds. "Seth and I—I think we'd like to stay there." There might be an argument later, because if this feels oppressive to Nikolai, it's likely worse for Seth. But Mikhail had said that the smaller houses wasn't as bad, and Nikolai feels wrong choosing to live somewhere far from Nikita.

Marybelle glances at him, her eyes wide. "What about your brothers? We thought you'd stay with them."

Nikita smirks.

Nikolai doesn't need to be a Telepath to know what Nikita's thinking. The idea of losing their privacy, the one good thing about their life on the road, pricks at his skin uncomfortably. "We're used to being on our own," he says. He wants to be with his brothers, but he also wants to have time to build his life with Seth, to adjust to being in Havenhill, and to understand these people from another world. "Being around so many people feels strange."

"We get it." Heather's response is gentle. She rises and tugs until Nikita comes closer to her, then settles her hand against Nikita's hip as they lean into each other.

Nikolai misses Seth keenly.

Yeah, they definitely get it.

By the time they get downstairs, the crowd has gathered again outside the house. The truck is gone, as are Sakura, Jefferson, Pawel, and Mattie. Alaric comes around the building's side with Ethan, stopping when Mac appears in front of him, grabs his shoulders, and pulls him down to whisper something in his ear. His brow furrows, then he shakes her off and walks to where Alia and Val stand.

"I can spin, dye, weave, and knit," he announces. "I can provide yarn and fabric if you can provide the raw materials, and I can teach people my methods if you use different ones. I can also coach football if your kids play."

Val slides an arm around Alia's shoulder, her hand squeezing lightly to head Alia off before she can speak. "Thank you for volunteering," Val says. "I know it's awkward—"

"—for both of us," Alia snaps. "This is—"

She cuts off when Val turns and kisses her. "It'll work out," Val promises.

Alia goes silent, her lips pursed.

"Wait." Alaric gestures between them, his eyes going wide then narrowing rapidly. "You two…"

"Please don't say you're offended, because if you are, this fledgling friendship is over," Ethan says.

"I'm not offended. I have Chri—" Alaric bites off the word, continuing with, "a boyfriend, but…back home, Mom's—" Alaric cuts off. "She…and my dad. They… My mother doesn't…."

"I am not your mother," Alia says, each word quiet but sharp. "You need to come to terms with that. She and I may outwardly appear to be the same person, but given that I never had children, and your mother is obviously in a different position than I am, we are nothing alike."

"It's disconcerting," Alaric mutters.

"Imagine how I feel every time you call me 'mother,'" Alia retorts. "'Disconcerting' is one word for it."

"I'm Predictive," Carolyn blurts out.

Alia and Alaric fall silent. Alaric takes a step away, his stance looser as he distances himself from the discussion. then he shakes himself like a dog, shoulders relaxing. Ethan leans in to speak softly to him, and Alaric grumbles in reply.

"I'm a sociology and psychology major, and I've got a grounding in classics," Carolyn continues in a rush. "I can teach mythology to kids, although I don't know if the mythology and history of my world are different from yours. I'm also a researcher, and I've been trying to learn more about how Talent works, how we classify it, and how it functions within societies. I'd love the chance to look around and talk to people. Study your community, if you don't mind, and in return, you'd get access to everything I can write down about what I know. If you have researchers, I can work with them so we can share knowledge."

"I'm a bio-chem-physics joint major," Mac says. "I don't know how that fits in yet, but I'm sure you've got a job somewhere that'll work. Water testing. Helping Healers. Anything. I'm flexible."

"Nikolai says he'll help, too," Marybelle pipes up, her soft, light tone carrying easily above the end of Mac's words. "He doesn't know how yet, but he'll learn. Seth'll learn."

"Everyone will help," Alia says firmly, "and we will accept you in Havenhill."

11

The remains of Monday and the entirety of Tuesday are spent cleaning both houses from top to bottom. They remove the personal belongings of the Benford family, keeping the furniture that is in usable condition. Tables and couches are kept, but beds are replaced with ones that smell fresh and are adequate for the number of occupants. Alia requests that the houses be placed on Havenhill's electrical grid, and by late Tuesday night, lights are on and refrigerators hum. The water runs dark at first, but once they let it go for an hour, it's clear, the pump functioning perfectly to pull water up from the well.

On Wednesday, they bring over fresh linens from the main house, then go into town to trade services for goods so that they can have food. They need to be out of the houses while the Mages take care of the cleansing ritual. They stop at the school, and Nikolai and Seth find a potential place to fit in within Havenhill: tutoring teenagers in survivalist skills. In return, those teens will work as a group to teach them the basic history, math, and science that they've missed during their years on the road.

Seth finds the school library and stuffs his backpack full of books to borrow.

Alaric proves popular with the younger children, letting them climb on his hound's back, giving them rides around the playground.

Mac sits on a bench, grinning as she watches. "He's so gruff," she says, "but so good with kids. I've seen it before, but every time it makes me smile."

"It seems like he's the one with the most to offer here," Nikolai replies. He feels inadequate, without any skills to help keep Havenhill going. He knows he and Seth will learn, but he's anxious to do something now to pay the community back for the safety they provide.

Mac pulls her feet up to sit cross-legged. "He was raised to live like this, in an independent society partly cut off from the world. His home isn't as big, and they do have access to stores, and they go out into the human community for education. But in the end, they go back and live in their commune. So Alaric fits in because this is what he always thought he'd be doing."

"It's easy for him." Nikolai envies that.

Mac nods. "It's harder for the rest of us. We all have to shift our paradigms. For my friends and me, it's realizing that we might be stuck here. And for you, it's moving from running to finding a way to live again." She turns her smile toward them. "For what it's worth, I'm glad you've found a home. Nikita's been a wreck worrying about you ever since she started remembering the Dreams. I'm glad we came to help you."

"Even if it means never getting home again?"

Mac makes a face, drawing her knees up to hug them tight to her chest. "I'm still coming to terms with that, and I can admit that I'm not thrilled about trading my life for yours. But I'm not going to say your life isn't worth it. I was a soldier, once upon a time. I had an entire life built around doing things I didn't like to make sure other people survived."

There's a darkness in the way the vowels lengthen and her tone goes soft; Nikolai knows she's not telling the whole story. Nikolai gets it. He knows what it's like to have his life ripped away unexpectedly and not be sure he'll get it back. He's gotten lucky. He's found Mikhail and Josef, and he thinks he's on his way to finding his happy ending. "You'll get home," he says confidently. She has to believe that, much like Nikolai held on to the belief in Havenhill.

"Mm." Mac slowly relaxes, letting her knees fall down. She leans back, hands behind her head, still watching Alaric and the kids. "If you had the chance to come with us when we leave, would you?"

"It would depend," Nikolai says. He doesn't want to give a gut-instinct answer, because he assumes she's not asking out of idle curiosity. "If Seth would come with me. If I'd have a way back. If you need me to come with you for a reason, or if it's simply Nikita trying to save me again, because

I think that's misguided. This is my home. I don't know what to do with my life yet, but my life is here, with Seth and my family. I'll figure it out."

"Mm," is all Mac says in reply, which doesn't help.

"Nikolai!"

He turns at Nikita's shout. He stretches out a hand, and Mac takes it, coming to her feet easily beside him. Nearby, Alaric returns to human form and the kids rush off toward the school.

"What?"

Nikita runs to meet him, her gait uneven but her ankle mostly recovered from her injury thanks to Genevieve's healing. Heather and Carolyn trail behind her at a brisk walk. "Marybelle radioed to say they're done with the cleansing rituals. She said Alia and Val are waiting for us at the houses, along with Pawel. We want to try that thing we talked about, and we need you and Seth."

"Do I even want to know what we're doing?" Mac asks dryly. She fishes a bandana from her pocket, tying it around her curls to pull them back from her face. "Because after the last time—"

"Exactly. After the last time." Nikita leans into Heather's touch and gestures between herself and Nikolai. "I think both of us need to be involved in the ritual to send us home."

Mac glances at Nikolai; this must be why she was asking. He knew Nikita wanted to try to reach the Dreamscape together. He wasn't prepared to do so right now.

"What if I don't want to go with you." His voice is flat. It's not a question.

"We're not planning on going anywhere today." Nikita swipes that thought away with a flick of her fingers. "Alaric won't be there, and we can't go anywhere without him anyway. We want to try a ritual to see if we could reach the other side."

"It's not like we meant to go through the first time," Alaric mutters. "You hadn't planned a ritual, because if you had, I wouldn't have been there."

"Huh? Oh." Nikita sags against Heather. "I think that had more to do with me and Del."

"And you think you can get back without Del?"

There's a small pause before Nikita disengages from Heather's hold, hands on her hip as she stands taller. Despite being as tall as Nikolai, she still seems small next to Alaric. "We have to at least try. I mean, I figured—don't you miss Chris?"

Alaric takes a step back, and for a moment, it looks as if he's been struck. His gaze drops, and he growls low under his breath. "Meet you at the cars," he mutters.

"That was rude," Mac says.

"I didn't mean— They're…whatever it is they are." Nikita watches Alaric walk away. "I'm sorry!" she calls after him.

Alaric doesn't respond as he shifts into the hound and lopes away.

Nikolai is positive he missed something, but he's more worried about this ritual Nikita is proposing. "Why do you think you need me involved in your ritual? You got here without my help."

"We had Del," Carolyn says, "who isn't exactly a Dreamwalker, but she's…something. Several of us are 'something,' which is what's so complicated. I've been researching how different traveling Talents can be linked—teleporters like Mac and Dreamwalkers like you seem to be at opposite ends of a spectrum, and then strange intermediary Talents like me, Del, and Nikita fall between those two poles. Even the Shadows might be linked."

"That clears up nothing," Nikolai admits. These people are so intertwined socially that they keep assuming he's one of them simply because he's been on the other side of Nikita's Dreams. And while they all seem familiar, in that dreamlike way, he doesn't know them or have any idea what Carolyn's talking about.

"What's wrong?" Seth joins them, his calm a familiar wash over Nikolai's skin. He places his hand against the small of Nikolai's back; Nikolai relaxes into it.

"I'm so confused that I don't even know if I can explain." Nikolai glances at where the cars are parked and Alaric's hound lies in the sun, one paw over his nose. The backs of two cars are open while Mikhail, Amaranth, and Josef load crates into them. "How did getting food go?"

"We have staples for both houses and some fresh foods. Plenty of preserves. Last year's canning and frozen foods come cheaper than current, so we went with those for the most part," Seth says. He nudges his glasses up his nose. "It's all better than what we had on the road, and we've got plenty of ingredients. Also, Amaranth and Josef picked out a few basic cookbooks so we can learn how to cook for real."

"The houses are cleansed and everything, and Pawel's waiting for us to get back," Nikita says. She takes a step toward the cars, pausing when Heather stops her with a hand. She licks her lips and looks at Nikolai. "Maybe we can make better sense of the ritual when we're there. When all of us can talk."

"Things are getting complicated and weird," Nikolai says, trying to forestall Seth's questions.

Seth's response is a disgruntled noise, but he lets it go until they're in the Jeep, just the two of them and Mikhail. Then, he says, "Give me the rundown."

So Nikolai does, to the best of his ability.

Seth doesn't seem any less confused than he does. "Do you think there's a risk to us?" he asks.

"I'm not one for traditional ritual, but it sounds to me like there is," Mikhail says. "I'll be blunt: I don't want to lose you." He pulls up at the new house and parks next to the other cars. He turns around before they can get out of the Jeep. "Be careful, Nik," he continues, "and don't do anything that'll call attention to Havenhill. This is a safe place, and nobody wants the wards broken. Trying to bridge between the worlds might need to be done outside the groves."

Nikolai makes a sound of agreement. That's valid. but none of the newcomers have listened to logic thus far. He doubts they'll start now.

Seth leans over the seat, his shoulder pressed to Nikolai's. "When do we get to learn to drive?"

"I can take you out late tomorrow morning," Mikhail offers. "We've got a meeting early so that the Weather Witches can look at the patterns that are building and see what we need for this week, but after that, I'm free. Josef and Amaranth need the Jeep to ride the borders first thing in the morning anyway. Eventually we'll need to look at getting you a car; someone in your group needs transportation."

Seth runs his hand along the back of the seat. "I like your Jeep. It feels…comfortable. It has a good aura."

"It's not human."

Seth rolls his eyes and elbows Nikolai. "I'm not saying it is. But sometimes objects resonate, and this Jeep is old enough that it does."

"Josef's always saying it's got personality," Mikhail says dryly. "So you might be right. I'll teach you to drive in the Jeep, but I'm not giving it to you. We'll find you something of your own." He points at where Pawel stands in front of the main house, arms crossed, glaring between Alia and Val and the arriving cars. "I think someone's waiting for you." A moment's hesitation, then, "Be careful. I want you to be here when I bring the Jeep over tomorrow to teach you to drive."

"We will be," Nikolai answers with conviction, refusing to consider the alternative. He has no plans to leave, and if the ritual risks that, he won't help.

Mikhail gets out long enough to pull Nikolai in for a rough hug and one more whisper of "Be careful" before he heads out, the Jeep rattling down the road.

Ethan and Alaric come out of the main house. Ethan waves cheerily. "Everyone's stuff has been put in their respective houses and rooms. Seth, Nikolai—we washed what we could of your clothes, and replaced what we couldn't. Alaric's agreed to work with our textiles group to pay that off. Everyone needs clothes anyway, since your friends arrived with only the shirts on their backs."

"It's too much," Nikolai says. They already owe Havenhill so much.

"It's what we do for all new arrivals," Alia assures him. "We have been taking in newcomers for a decade, Nikolai. You are welcome, and you will find your place here."

"Havenhill is a place for strays," Val adds. "Don't worry."

"I don't want to be here," Alaric grumbles, turning to leave. He makes it two steps before he turns back. "Not Havenhill; I'm grateful for that," he mutters. "Thanks for taking us in. I don't want to be around for your ritual. It reeks."

"You should stay. It took time for Alia to get used to the feel of magic on her skin and the scent of it in her nose, but most Clan are fine with it now. We're one community."

"I'm getting used to it. One of my best friends is a Mage," Alaric says, "but I still don't like it. I can feel it crawling all over me when Rory's designing rituals. I'm not sticking around; don't leave without me."

"This is a fact-finding ritual," Pawel says, arms still crossed and stance tight. "No one is going through."

"That's what you said the last time," Alaric points out, "and look where we are."

"If we do go through, we'll know how we did it and we'll come back for you," Nikita says quickly. "No one will be left behind."

Nikolai doesn't find that reassuring. They assume that nothing will go wrong yet still recognize that it went wrong before and are making plans in case it does again. He reaches blindly for Seth's hand and grips it.

"I want all the people with Talent related to traveling involved," Carolyn says. She points to the space in front of her. "That means Nikita, with Heather to anchor her, and Nikolai, with Seth. Me. Mac. Mattie."

"Sakura and I will hold the wards," Val says.

Nikolai hadn't noticed Sakura until Val mentioned her. She stands at the edge of the clearing in front of the house, close to the edge of the grove. Same as on the first day they met, she's dressed in a T-shirt and shorts, with mid-calf boots on her feet. Her feet are spread, her arms loose by her side, and her gaze narrows when she hears her name. She nods once.

"Alaric, come with me," Ethan says, gesturing toward the edge of the grove, past Sakura, where a path leads through the trees. "Let me show you around the grounds some more, so you can see how this place is different from where you grew up. It might help settle the beast under your skin." He flashes a quick grin. "A little help settling can't be a bad thing, right?"

Ethan tilts his head, and Alaric growls softly at the line of throat exposed.

"Ethan," Val says quietly.

Ethan shifts into a more neutral posture. "It's just a walk," he assures Alaric. "We'll get you away from the magic, then you can relax. Right?"

Nikolai isn't sure which Alaric's more nervous about: the feel of the magic or that he might be left behind. "No one's going anywhere," Nikolai says, his hand tight in Seth's. "We need to stay here. We belong here." He tries to sound confident despite his own concerns.

Alaric huffs and takes a step back, ducking his head. He exhales, long and slow, then stands up straight and crosses his arms. He stands for a moment, staring at Pawel, then drops to all fours to become a bear and lumbers away.

"I've got him," Ethan says, following after.

"And we've got this," Nikita says cheerfully.

Nikolai doesn't contradict her. Someone has to believe things will work out for the best.

12

"THE WARDS ARE tight, and nothing dangerous is close, other than her." Sakura speaks as if each word is sliding out along a magical current. Her gaze is unfocused; both hands hang by her sides, fingers spread. She curls one hand, and a soft *zing* slithers over Nikolai's skin.

Seth's grip tightens.

Sakura's gaze drifts to where Mattie sits on the steps, darkness wrapped like a haze around her in the daylight.

Nikolai doesn't remember Mattie arriving. She's silent, her lips twisted sour and pursed, elbows on her bent knees. She glares at Sakura, who looks away again, staring at a spot in the air.

"Val, if you want to join me, we'll be fine. There are no holes," Sakura says.

Val kisses Alia's cheek and joins Sakura.

"It's time." Alia gestures to Pawel, who hesitates before joining her by the stairs of the house. Pawel's fingers stretch and flick, as if he's trying to sink his fingers into the rise of magic around him. He only lowers his hand when Val covers it, nudging him down.

As they approach, Mattie rises and circles away from Alia, her gaze dark and wary. "Bedrock," Mattie murmurs. "The other is not nearly as progressive as you, nor is she as strong. Yet. She will be." Mattie cocks her head, frowning. "She hates me, and yet she's safer to be around. Interesting."

"How much do you remember of the other worlds you've seen?" Carolyn asks. She reaches for Mattie's arm; there's a small pause before her fingers close around Mattie's wrist to grip her tightly.

Mattie's expression twists, but she doesn't flinch away. "Very little, other than yours," Mattie admits. "It's not so much memories I can recall as ones that slides in and take me unaware. Déjà vu. I couldn't send you to seek another person who might be bedrock, but I'll know one when I see them, if I've met them before." She tilts her head. "Or killed them." Her gaze drifts to where Alia watches her carefully. "I wouldn't do that again. It does something to a world when one of the underpinnings is removed."

"Every path leads to a world, and every world is overrun by Shadows in its own way, some worse than others," Pawel mutters. "There are lynchpins."

Carolyn raises a finger to her lips. "Shh. You're observing, not teaching. Consider this a silent research position."

"What, exactly, are we doing?" Seth pushes his glasses up his nose with his free hand, holding them there with the tip of his middle finger. "We didn't grow up with ritual magic, and we weren't interested in trying to learn while we were trying to stay alive. Not attracting attention from the Shadows was a much higher priority."

"The only ritual Mages here are Pawel, Sakura, and Val," Carolyn points out. "This isn't so much a ritual as a...combining of forces. The rest of us have Talent linked to traveling or to the Dreamscape. We punched through it from our home to here. I want to try to punch a hole back without going through it. I've already tried a few things on my own that didn't work."

"Can we sit down for this? I want to be comfortable." Nikita lowers herself to the ground, sitting with her back against Heather's chest and Heather's arms around her center. She cranes her head back to kiss Heather's cheek.

Seth grins and tugs at Nikolai, and yes, that does sound like a good idea. They take up a position opposite Nikita, Nikolai's toes almost touching hers. Seth sits with his knees bent with Nikolai in the space between his legs. Seth leans forward and wraps his arms around Nikolai's center, his head a weight against Nikolai's shoulder, his body warm and welcome.

The warmth seeps through Nikolai, the closeness making his body taut with sudden hunger. Nikolai shifts to get comfortable, working to push those thoughts down.

"We'll have a house to ourselves," Seth murmurs against Nikolai's neck. Of course Seth knows what he's feeling.

From the bright flush on Heather's skin and how she buries her face against Nikita's neck, Nikolai isn't the only one affected by the closeness of the moment. "Remind me of that later, and don't distract me now," he mutters. Seth laughs in a whisper of warmth against his skin.

Carolyn coughs and points to the space around their feet. "Mac. Mattie. If you guys could hold onto them and onto me, I'll try to open up a connection home. I've already tried traveling here and it's—it's not what I'm used to. None of my pictures are of anything here, and I tried art from here, but it just feels like art. So I think I need art from home for my traveling to work, but I need that art to be of someplace here. Or I need to make my own art."

Nikolai lets the words wash over him as if they mean something. They do to her, he's certain. "What do you want us to do?"

"You and Nikita are Dreamwalkers, which means if you let loose, you should be able to interact—"

"No," Seth cuts her off. "That's how you rip holes in the world and let Shadows in."

Carolyn crouches in front of them. "How else are we going to get home?" she asks. "There isn't a door, so I want to make one, or find a way... a path. Or something. I don't want to let the Shadows out of the split, which is part of why Mattie's here. If we don't do this, I don't go home. Pawel never sees his son again. I never see my twin. Alaric never sees his family. Trying to keep from tearing a hole is where you and Heather come in. You keep everything under control."

Nikolai isn't sure her words have clarified anything, but Seth's hands slide under his shirt, stopping just above the waistband of his pants, and fingers press against his bare skin. "So you want us to do something like when we got rid of the Shadows," Seth says, pressing the words into Nikolai's shoulder as he speaks. "You want Nik to bring Dreams to life."

"To help me bring my illusions to life, yes," Carolyn says. She rocks back on her heels, still crouched, arms across her knees. "Do you think you can do that?"

Nikolai doesn't want to. But Nikita is watching him, and he may not be an Empath, but he sees the tension as she waits for his response.

Fine, he can try.

Nikolai nods, and feels Seth do the same behind him.

"Then let's get started." Carolyn kneels, her wallet in her hands. She shuffles through her small stack of papers, picking one to place on top. She waits until Mattie and Mac are arranged, touching the shoulders of Nikita and Nikolai and reaching for Carolyn to complete the circle. When she smiles, it's drawn tight with lines around her mouth. "These are pictures of people from home. I'll try to reach my twin first."

She stares at the picture, her brow furrowed in concentration.

Nikolai can't feel anything; he's not even sure there is something to feel.

After a few minutes she sighs and lowers her hands.

"Nothing," she says. "I can't even make an illusion. There's no connection from here to Kit." She shuffles to the next picture in her stack and stares at it.

She continues until Nikolai's stiff, his legs cramped from how he's sitting, his shoulder aching from reaching for Carolyn. Nikita makes a pained sound, and they all change position. Now, Nikita, Nikolai, and Carolyn forming a triangle at the center, Heather and Seth behind their respective partners. Mac and Mattie are at the spaces between Nikita and Nikolai. Carolyn shuffles through more papers, the lines around her eyes furrowing deeper in her frustration.

She makes a low noise and lowers the stack as her head drops. She presses fingertips to her brow, massaging. "I have a headache. I tried Kit, Serina, the library, Sam, my room, Rory, Pawel's living room—which is where we started—and this random picture of Nate that Kit added to my pictures at some point. None of them connect. It's just art. Really good art, but nothing more."

She holds up a piece of paper. The image is almost photographic: a picture of a dark-skinned girl with an impish grin and heavy braids around her face. She has one hand raised as if she's reaching out of the page.

Nikolai recognizes her from the Dream.

"I've got Del left," Carolyn says.

"Why didn't you start with her?" Pawel asks. "She was with us when—"

"Because the idea of matching mind-to-mind with Del is terrifying," Carolyn says. "Sometimes she's in the Dreamscape, which could help, but if she's in there, and no one is with her, she might not be sane. When we've been there together, we've been able to act as her anchor. If she came with us but got stuck in the Dreamscape on the way through…well, she could still be there."

Nikolai glances at Nikita. Her tongue peeks out until she catches her lower lip in her teeth, chewing lightly. She meets his gaze and nods, and Nikolai hopes this means that the brief Dream he had in the van was shared and that Nikita remembers it as well.

"Is Del another Dreamwalker?" Seth asks.

"Not exactly, but she's somewhere on that side of things." Carolyn sets aside the other pictures, cradling the one of Del in her lap as she stares down at it.

Nikolai could swear the picture winks at him. He pulls back and almost lets go of Carolyn.

The image slowly rises from the page, forming into a girl crouched in the space between them. She's incorporeal, one foot planted squarely where Nikolai's knee is, the other somewhere around Nikita's crotch. She looks at Carolyn and smiles, then draws a line down Carolyn's cheek with one fingertip. Her lips move, then her brow furrows with a pouting scowl.

"Hang on," Carolyn mutters. She screws her eyes tightly shut, and Nikolai feels a tug against his skin. He twitches, letting his power bleed out as if this is a Dream he has control over.

The girl—Del, he supposes—turns to him, her head cocked. "Oh. There are more of you," she says. "And fewer at the same time. Did you lose the dragon?"

Nikita exhales roughly, and Del's Dream snaps into being around them—a forest, full of dark trees and darker recesses beyond. The house is still here, intermingled with the forest, the two occupying the same space. Del is insubstantial, as is the new world that's come to them. When Nikolai leans forward, Del's fingers skate across his forehead, then down his nose, barely tickling as her touch presses into his space.

Carolyn's eyes flicker open. "This is as far as I can take us."

"What did you think you could do, open a doorway home?" Del tsks. "That won't work, not unless you slip between and slide through the split. And that's dangerous, unless you have a guide." Her gaze drifts to Mattie.

"The right guide, not one who's broken beyond repair."

"I'm not broken. Supposedly, I'm fixed," Mattie says mildly.

"Depends on who you ask," Del replies. Her gaze drifts to where Val and Sakura sit with Pawel, and her head cocks, brow furrowing, then she smiles, the lines disappearing from her face. "I have someone for you," she says, pointing at Pawel.

He blinks, and Val leans to murmur something to Sakura. Pawel points at his own chest and speaks, slowly, as if he's not sure Del will hear him. "You have something for me?"

She laughs, a bright, joyful sound that has a sharp edge. She wags her finger at him. "That's not what I said." Her attention shifts abruptly, dismissing him as she pops to her feet. She spins around with her arms spread wide, stopping to face Carolyn.

The ease in her expression fades, twisting into concern. "Kit worries about you," she whispers, "and Sam worries about me. But you need help getting home. When you find your way into the Dreamscape, I'll be here, and we can get out together. Come find your path to my meadow. But be careful—the Shadows are moving, and the split is growing. If it breaks apart entirely, you could be lost. You need to find her." A small smile. "Isn't it handy that I found her first, and now she wants to find you, too? But be careful. She's hungry. And she's not a vegetarian."

"What, does whoever-she-is eat people?" Seth asks. He cuts off abruptly with a small hiss, fingers going tight where they rest against Nikolai's hips. "Oh, is she—"

"—in the split?" Del asks. "Yes."

Carolyn raises one hand to her head, and the image around them wavers and reality once again becomes more solid than the Dream. Nikolai tries to grab onto the Dream; Nikita makes a small sound, and pain thuds behind Nikolai's eyes. He closes them involuntarily.

Seth exhales.

"She's gone. I think I'm going to puke." Carolyn pushes roughly to her feet, stumbling a few steps before Pawel catches her. They barely make it to the side of the house before Carolyn is on her knees, retching.

Nikolai doesn't blame her. The thud behind his eyes travels up and back, wrapping around his head and squeezing hard. He brings his knees up and lowers his head, breathing into the dark space his position makes. Seth's hand on his back and the soft calm he exudes is the only thing that makes the pain bearable.

"That went well," Mattie mutters.

"I hope that was sarcasm," Seth says. He rubs small circles across Nikolai's shoulders, and Nikolai presses back into the touch, unwilling to raise his head or open his eyes.

"I'll get Genevieve," Sakura says. There are footsteps, then none. "I'm sorry it sounds like you're stuck here for the time being. I know what it feels like to not be able to go home again. Even if it's safe here—even if the people are great—it took a long time for it to feel like home. But, speaking from experience, your life will be better if you put in the effort to settle in. Don't fight it."

Footsteps again, then the rumble of the truck, fading as Sakura drives away.

There's quiet for a moment.

"Oh, that's nice," Mattie says.

"I've never seen magic work like that," Mac adds.

"It's a variation on calling fog," Val says. "You should be able to open your eyes now; it's darker."

Nikolai looks up cautiously, blinking into the dim light. It isn't exactly foggy, but there is a thin layer of darkness over everything.

Mattie stands and stretches. "This is my kind of place, now," she says.

"We've learned how to combine our skills," Val says. "We aren't Weather Witches, but we can learn from them and have created rituals to mimic certain abilities."

"People here are better at that than most Talents at home," Pawel says. He offers a hand to Carolyn and helps her rise. "I'd be interested in observing your ritual development and discussing how you've chosen to adapt to these new techniques."

Nikolai stands slowly, still leaning into Seth's touch. They all gather close enough to see clearly through the dim light. "I need to go lie down," Nikolai says. Without the light, it doesn't feel as much like someone is shoving spikes into his eyes, but his head still aches, and he can feel his pulse in his ears.

"You're not the only one." Nikita shades her eyes, pressing her fingers to her temple.

"We have plenty of time." Pawel's voice is low, his words carefully chosen. "We need to think about what Del said. We're going to be here for a while. I hope that Del will pass the news that we are alive and well back to our families and friends at home, and that she is able to stay sane in the Dreamscape long enough to help us. For now, we will settle in and work toward a plan for our return."

His smile is strained as he turns to Alia, one hand out. "Thank you for your hospitality. It seems we will continue to impose upon you. I would appreciate being able to utilize your resources for research, and in return, I would be more than happy to provide any information for your historians that I can."

Alia clasps his hand. "You are welcome in Havenhill, Pawel. May it feel like home."

It sounds like a blessing, and Nikolai chooses to take it as such.

The others look worried. Nikita curls close to Heather, her head tilted to lean against hers. Mac budges up to Pawel's other side, and together she and Carolyn nudge him toward the house.

Nikolai finally feels like he can breathe. The other options have been taken away, and nothing hangs over him. He doesn't have to worry about suddenly being whisked away, and he can finally enjoy their safety.

"Come on," Seth says. "Let's go home."

Nikolai would follow Seth anywhere, but this may be the best thing Seth has ever suggested. "Let's go home," Nikolai echoes, and follows as Seth leads.

Letters written by Mikhail and Josef Petersen.

Dear Mom & Dad,

Stop worrying. I'll be fine. This is a school, not some backwater suburb where no one understands what it's like to be different. People here aren't scared. Most of them don't believe the stories that are coming out of the cities. I think it's an exaggeration, honestly. Have you seen any Shadows yet? They're a nightmare story that's supposed to scare kids.

I don't know why non-Talented people are suddenly hearing about them. It's like finding out someone took one of our legends and made it into a horror movie, and next thing you know, everyone believes the bogeyman is real.

If you're afraid that people out there are hating Talents, then the safest place for me and Josef is where we are. At school, lost in a crowd, looking like anyone else. We'll be okay, I promise. If people are panicking, I don't want to travel. We'll come home for the holidays, when everyone's forgotten about this. It'll fade in the winter, just like the memory of every other summer blockbuster.

I love you. I'll call Josef, too, I promise. We wanted to get together soon anyway.

Stay safe. Hug Nik for me.

Love,
Mikhail

Mom & Dad,

Mikhail and I got together for a movie over the weekend. We met up at the theater and got dinner after. I met his girlfriend, which I am not supposed to tell you about, so I won't tell you that they've been dating for three weeks and I think she's much more into him than he is into her. I'm sure you'll hear about her if that changes.

Mikhail was angry about you telling us to come home. I think things at school are better for him than they are for me. Not that anything's happened! Not yet. His school is very traditional but also very progressive. There's a lot of money at that campus, and it's set apart from the rest of town. It's like its own little world. But it's like you go there and you disappear. And they had some good student communities on campus.

But where I am…there have been some fights on campus. There are signs up on the walls about "taking back the world for humanity." Some of it is really subtle, like the signs that say "I will walk in the dark by your side, and I will protect you from the shadows" which could be about being a good Samaritan. But it's not like that. Not here.

There was this girl on my hall. She's a Mage. I really liked her—we hit it off during orientation. I had looked over and she was playing with water—making it move around, then freezing it, then subliming it. That's her natural ability. So I made it rain, just a little cloud right over her hands, and we started talking. There's no formal community here for Talents, and it was nice finding a person I could be myself around.

Someone found out about her. She got threats left on her door and others slipped under the door into her room. After the news broke about the wall going up around New York, someone left her a big bag of dog shit, and she wouldn't show me the letter that came with it, but she cried.

A few days later she withdrew and went back home to somewhere outside of Boston. She won't answer my texts. I hope she's okay.

You're right. It's not nice everywhere. But this is where I am right now, and I want to stay as long as I can. Let us know if you're leaving. Tell us where you're going and we will meet you there when we can. The world isn't ending, and we'll all be okay.

Love,
Josef

Dear Mom & Dad,

You've got to be kidding me. You can't do this! I'm only a junior, and I'll be fine until I graduate. Everything's good here! I keep my head down, I get great grades, and I'm one of the top engineers in my class. I've got a girlfriend, too. I know Josef told you about her. Her name's Karen, and she's really pretty, with these big green eyes and dark curly hair. Her family's kind of conservative, but she isn't. She's also a biomedical engineer, and she's planning on going to medical school. We've been together two months, and I really like her. She says she loves me, but I don't know about that. Love is a weird thing, right?

I don't want to leave school. I'm an adult, so if you cut me off, I'll get financial aid and my own loans and everything will be fine.

Yes, I did hear about the city. I know they're building a wall, and I heard they're going to do the same around Philly and Boston and Trenton. I think everyone is overreacting. I mean, I know you're not the only ones. My friend Sage took a leave of absence from school last week. She said she's going home to help with her grandmother, but I know she's Clan. They've always been weirder than anyone else about the Shadows, haven't they?

How is Nik? He and Seth are still close, right? Like, he won't go into a Dream and pull Shadows to you? You're safe, aren't you?

Tell me where you're going, and I'll be there to visit, but I'm coming back to school.

Love,
Mikhail

Mom & Dad,

I'm sorry that this email is going to be really short, but I'm on a bus on the way to meet Mikhail. I'm trying to play it cool, but I feel like I'm having a panic attack right now.

Someone lit my project on fire.

I don't mean a pyrotechnic thing from a Mage. It wasn't an accident. It was arson. The rag was soaked in gasoline and tossed on top of it. It wasn't a big project—I'm only a first year. There was another architecture major who was working on her senior design project. It was spray painted with slurs about Clan then set on fire. One of my classmates was working on his project when it happened, and he got caught in the fire. I don't think he's Talented, but I don't think whoever did it cares.

I don't know how they found out. I didn't talk to anyone but my friend from Boston who left early in the semester. I'm a freshman. I'm not out in public as Talented, but I'm scared.

They left a note that said if they found me, they'd kill me.

They've hurt people.

I called Mikhail and he's meeting me at the movie theater, and we're going to see a movie like everything is normal and get dinner after. Then we're hitting the road to try to meet up with you.

Love,
Josef

Dear Mom & Dad,

You were right. I was wrong. We'll meet you as soon as we can.

Love,
Mikhail

AVALANCHE

13

The rumble of the approaching Jeep is familiar. Nikolai pulls aside the curtain and looks out to confirm he's right as Mikhail parks in front of their small house.

Seth comes down the stairs, his hair still wet, shirt sticking to his skin. He must have rushed to get dressed so quickly after his shower. "Time to go?"

Nikolai opens his arms, and Seth drifts closer. By the time Mikhail knocks and opens the door, Nikolai has Seth wrapped close. Nikolai presses a kiss to Seth's temple, then noses at his cheek until Seth looks up so Nikolai can kiss him.

They had a good evening and a quiet morning, safe for the first time in what feels like forever. Nikolai doesn't want to think about going beyond the borders of Havenhill.

Mikhail coughs. "I thought I was taking you both out for a driving lesson."

Seth's calm wraps Nikolai in warmth as he cups Nikolai's face and slides a thumb along his cheek.

They'll be okay.

Nikolai takes his hand, entwining their fingers.

As long as they're together, they'll be okay.

"We're ready when you are," Seth says.

Nikolai hands Seth a jacket, then shrugs into one of his own. They have new mittens and hats as well. Nikolai remains amazed at the generosity of the people of Havenhill. Even knowing that they'll pay for these items going forward, it is a sweet luxury to be given brand-new protection against the elements.

Mikhail hands them each a pair of soft gloves. “Easier than mittens for driving. It’s cold, and the Jeep takes some time to heat up. The drive from home wasn’t long enough. However, it’s trying hard to be spring out there, so you might not need anything on your hands after a bit. Who’s going first?”

Nikolai nudges Seth forward. “I remember Seth talking about driving all the time when we were kids and thought we’d be getting licenses at sixteen. He should get the first shot.”

Seth follows Mikhail outside, climbing into the driver’s seat of the Jeep and paying close attention as Mikhail helps him adjust the seat and mirrors. It’s strange to sit behind Seth instead of next to him.

“Do you remember Mom’s minivan?” Mikhail asks. “Or that little red car I had when I went to college?”

Nikolai nods. “When we were leaving to meet up with you, she showed Seth and I how the car started, the basics of putting it in drive, and how to use the brake and gas and the emergency brake.” He’s amazed at how even his voice sounds when he’s shaking on the inside. He’s not prepared to talk about the past. It’s a chill rush through him, squeezing at his heart. His breath shudders, and when he glances at Mikhail, he can see the tense line of his jaw.

Mikhail exhales. “Yeah. Okay, I can see why she’d do that. Anyway. The point I actually wanted to make is that this Jeep is nothing like that.”

“Helpful,” Seth mutters dryly.

Nikolai leans over the seat, watching as Mikhail gets Seth settled with his feet on the pedals—three, instead of two. Mikhail makes him put the car in neutral and shift through the manual gears several times before they start to move.

Nikolai laughs when the car jerks backward then immediately turns off.

“Don’t worry, you’ll suck just as much,” Mikhail says confidently.

“Thanks,” Nikolai grumbles, his laughter fading.

Nikolai watches avidly, hoping that, by observing, he’ll get past the first pitfalls that Seth falls prey to. The car jerks and stalls several times before Seth manages to get it backed up and turned around to head down the dirt road. Pawel, Mac, and Alaric stand on the steps of their house as the

Jeep creeps by. They stay carefully out of the way until Seth passes them, then move into the road. Nikolai watches out the back window as Mac and Alaric do some kind of complicated fighting dance with each other. Pawel's gaze lingers on the Jeep until he turns his attention back to the other two.

"Okay, keep accelerating," Mikhail says. Seth presses on the gas until the Jeep rumbles loudly and feels as if it might shake apart. "Now, push down on the clutch, shift into second, then switch from clutch to gas slowly—" The Jeep shudders to an abrupt halt, and Mikhail repeats, "Slowly."

"That was slow." Seth drags his hands through his hair. Nikolai struggles to keep a straight face, and Seth turns to glare at him. "I feel you laughing at me. This is going to be you in twenty minutes. Remember that."

"Remembering it doesn't make it less funny," Nikolai admits. "Feel free to laugh when it's my turn." He doesn't mind. He'll fail at first, but it's easy to sink into the joy of acting his age for once. He can be awkward and confused about something as normal as driving. It makes it a little easier to pretend that life in Havenhill matches the expectations they'd had growing up, before the Split.

He sits back, crosses his arms, and braces his knees against the back of Seth's seat. He tries to stay quiet, but a low laugh slips out every time Seth stalls the car and when Seth throws his hands in the air, not sure if he's supposed to be steering, shifting, or doing something else entirely.

It takes time, but Seth starts to get the hang of it. They slowly make their way down the main drive without stalling once, and Seth manages to get into fourth gear on the road into town.

When Seth parks the Jeep in front of Mikhail's house, he brakes too hard and it jerks, but he manages to shut it off before it stalls.

"Not bad," Mikhail says. He clasps Seth's shoulder, and there's a low wave of appreciation mixed with sorrow around them.

Nikolai imagines Seth's dad teaching them to drive instead, his dark eyes serious. He wonders if Seth remembers how easily irritated his father was with failure, or if he remembers only the good things.

Nikolai doesn't think it matters. They're here and now, and it's better to leave the past as past.

He switches places with Seth, pausing outside the Jeep as Seth squeezes his hand and presses a kiss to his cheek. Sitting in the driver's seat is even more daunting than he'd expected it to be while he was watching. He needs to hold the steering wheel, handle the shift, and deal with three pedals with only two feet. He tests pressing the pedals down and runs through the gears while he has the car in neutral with the emergency brake on to keep it from rolling.

"Yeah," he mutters under his breath. "This has to be hysterical to any outside watcher. This is ridiculous. It's like they meant to torture us. Couldn't we learn on a less complicated car?"

"You could," Mikhail agrees. He reaches across to help Nikolai position his hands again, nudging his knee until his right foot is on the brake instead of the gas. "But then you couldn't drive the Jeep. Believe me, any other car will be easy after you learn this."

Hah. Right.

Nikolai is positive that Seth must be laughing, but he doesn't have a spare bit of brain left for hearing him. He can't deal with anything other than figuring out how to get his hands and feet in the right places at the right times to move this metal monster forward without killing anyone around them (or themselves). He inches down the street, relieved not to stall but uncertain how to accelerate past second gear. They approach an intersection where he knows he'll have to turn, and he panics, slams on the brakes, and the car shudders to a stop and stalls.

In the back seat, Seth cackles.

Nikolai raises one hand, middle finger extended, then quickly gets that hand back on the wheel. Mikhail reaches across to twist the key and start the car again. Seth's amusement lingers, but he leans forward, one hand on Nikolai's shoulder to calm him. Nikolai sinks into the touch, narrowing his focus to his hands and feet and the road in front of him. By the time he manages to go five minutes without stalling, his fingers are cramped around the steering wheel.

He slows down as they travel through the center of town, intending to turn toward Mikhail's home, but Mikhail shakes his head. "We're going outside the wards."

Nikolai takes his feet off the pedals and Jeep coasts, guttering into a stall.

"What?"

"What about the scanners?" Seth asks. "You're not planning on taking us on the highway, are you?"

Mikhail shakes his head, motioning for Nikolai to start the car again. "We're not getting on a highway," he says. "Not a major one. There's an old state route that heads northeast toward the Vermont border and southwest toward Albany. It's not traveled often, but we use it when we need to get places quickly. You should practice how to drive somewhere other than in a neighborhood."

Nikolai's fingers tighten on the wheel. "It won't be safe."

"It'll be safe." Mikhail's voice is slow and even. "Nikolai, I just got you back. I'm not going to put us in danger for a driving lesson. Start the car. We'll drive to that main road, then go down it toward Albany. We won't get anywhere near the walls."

"The walls are outside of Troy." Seth pushes his glasses up his nose, holding them in place. "They're closer than you think."

"I know exactly where the walls are," Mikhail counters. "I've seen them."

Nikolai's chest is tight. "You've seen them? You've been close enough to—" He cuts off, closing his eyes. Seth grips his shoulder, fingers digging in, and Nikolai focuses on that. "Why would you do that?"

"Someone needs to," Mikhail says. "We take turns. We need to know where their borders are to keep ourselves safe. We can't cut ourselves off and expect that will be enough. So yes, we know exactly how far the Albany walls reach. We know where the surrounding communities are, as well. That's why I know that where we are going is safe." He pauses, waiting for Nikolai to open his eyes. "Start the car and drive."

Nikolai's fingers shake as he twists the key and the Jeep rumbles to life. He inches forward, driving at a snail's pace until he reaches the corner that would take him back to his new home.

Mikhail touches the steering wheel and points forward.

They're doing this.

Nikolai hates the way his hands still shake, the way his pulse pounds in his ears. Even Seth's hand on his shoulder isn't enough to keep him calm. He accelerates when Mikhail tells him to, managing to get into fifth gear on a semi-straight patch of road. They drive past houses abandoned long ago, fallen into disrepair with broken windows and peeling paint, overgrown trees resting heavily upon their roofs.

"We're outside of Havenhill now," Mikhail says.

"You're not going to spook me," Nikolai mutters. "Not any more than I already am. I can't panic more without curling into a tiny ball and screaming."

"I don't want you to do that while you're driving."

Nikolai risks a glance at Mikhail; he's not laughing.

Okay, so they're both being serious.

Nikolai huffs. "I mean it. So talk to me. Please."

"If you think we need to know something, tell us," Seth adds.

"You'll come to a big intersection up here," Mikhail says. "Slow down so you can turn right onto the other road. If you go left, you'd head for Vermont, and straight takes you to Unity. Almost everything around here is abandoned. We've scouted in Unity, and the university is empty. People at the school in Valiant turned it into a compound, and we don't go there."

"Could they be Talents?" Seth asks.

"It's not worth the risk."

Mikhail points down the road, and Nikolai accelerates again, gaining speed until he feels like he's racing, the car barely under his control. The steering wheel quivers under his fingertips, and the Jeep judders beneath his feet. Nikolai's heart races, and he grips the steering wheel tightly as he navigates.

Mikhail doesn't tell him to turn, so Nikolai keeps driving over the gentle curves and slopes of the road.

They pass an abandoned golf course, and a sign carved into a tree says it isn't safe for Talents to shelter there. He touches the gas, accelerating until they're past. The dilapidated antique store only a mile or so later has a subtle sign indicating safety.

Nikolai almost slows and turns in to see if anyone is there who needs help. He eases back on the gas, but Mikhail shakes his head, putting his hand on the shift before Nikolai can reach for it. "We check all the known nearby safe houses regularly," he says. "Don't worry. Alia takes care of anyone in need."

Seth sits twisted in his seat, face out of view of Nikolai's mirror, his nose pressed against the window's glass. "What do scanners look like?" he asks.

Mikhail is quiet.

Seth sits back. "Mikhail?"

"We don't know," Mikhail admits. "Val and Ethan think they're an urban legend. Something made up to scare—"

Nikolai slams on the brakes, trying to simultaneously stop, downshift, and steer into the parking lot of some kind of abandoned shop. The car jerks to a stop and sits there, half on the road and half off.

"What?" he says.

"The scanners—"

"No," Nikolai says. His hands are shaking too hard to turn the key, so he gives up, trying to shift into first gear and failing as the gears stick. "I'm not going farther. No. If there's a chance there could be something out here to find us—if there's a risk—I'm not doing it. Maybe you feel safe, Mikhail, but I've spent the last two years running. I want proof that it's safe, not a belief that all the bad things are urban legends." He glares at his brother, trying to will him to understand how Nikolai feels hot and cold all at once, how he's shivering with the sensation. "We're going back to Havenhill. And I'm not leaving again unless I absolutely have to."

"Put one foot on the clutch, the other on the brake—"

Nikolai shakes his head, undoing his seat belt. "You drive back." He gets out and climbs into the back with Seth, tangling their hands together and holding on.

Mikhail takes the driver's seat. He turns around in the empty lot and drives down the road the way they came. Nikolai's breath slowly evens, matching Seth's as Seth holds him. Small drips from Seth's curls are still drying after his morning shower, and Nikolai closes his eyes and focuses on that sensation rather than on how they are in the middle of this open road, exposed to humans and Shadows.

"I'm sorry," Mikhail says when they make the turn toward Havenhill. "I promise, you're safe. If you're going to be a part of the community, you need to—"

"Later," Seth says, his hand curled around the back of Nikolai's head.

Nikolai inhales, and Seth exhales when he does. "Later," Nikolai echoes. He's not ready for this, not yet.

Mikhail points out the groves as they drive back in along the main road, heading for Nikolai and Seth's new home.

As they approach the larger house, Pawel comes out and waves to them.

Mikhail slows, cranking down the window.

"Driving lessons?" Pawel calls out.

This seems as good a time as any to get the hell out of the car. Nikolai yanks the door open and tumbles out, and Seth follows him. Mikhail stays where he is, the Jeep still running.

"Driving lessons," Seth confirms. "We drove through the main town, then out past the borders."

Pawel's gaze narrows thoughtfully. He opens his mouth, then closes it. He touches the hood of the Jeep. "It's seen better days," he murmurs. "Jeeps are good vehicles, though. Dependable, right up until they aren't."

"Did you have one?" Mikhail leans his elbow on the open window, watching Pawel.

"Learned to drive a Jeep even older than this one," Pawel admits, tone soft and nostalgic. "A 1980 CJ-5. It was my mom's car before she died, and my dad saved it and gave it to me when I got my permit. I drove it through high school—took it everywhere, including my first visit to PHU before I applied. It died before I ever got there, though. Broke down the summer after my senior year, and my boyfriend had to rescue me from the side of the road in his Porsche. Never heard the end of it." He smiles slightly, shaking his head. "I had to get this intensely practical used car when I left for PHU, and I didn't get a good car until Chelsea was pregnant with Conor and we needed something safe."

He tells the story as if they should know who these people are. Nikolai vaguely remembers a mention of Conor, but the rest are a mystery to him.

"What did you think of your first lesson?" Pawel asks like it's nothing. Like there's nothing out there other than the excitement of their first time behind the wheel.

"Terrifying," Seth says flatly. "We were worried about scanners. It was too open, too exposed."

"Scanners?"

"They might be an urban legend," Mikhail says. "Rumor has it the government tracks travel to see if the travelers are human or Talent."

Pawel's eyes widen and he steps back. "That would mean they have a way to tell the difference. If someone has created technology able to do that from a distance, that means..." He trails off, gaze on something in the distance. Then he turns without another word and walks away, into the house.

"It's easy to tell he's not from around here," Mikhail comments. He taps the side of the door. "Get in. I'll drive you to your house."

Nikolai touches Seth's hand, grateful when Seth holds on in return. "We'll walk," he decides. "It's not far, and I've had enough driving for today."

Mikhail waits, the Jeep still idling, as Nikolai and Seth walk away. Nikolai doesn't look back, but he hears the tires spin against the ground when Mikhail turns the Jeep around to leave.

Nikolai exhales, trying to let his tension go. He's glad that Seth doesn't force him to explain what he's feeling. Seth slides an arm behind Nikolai's back and they walk together until they're home.

Home.

It's only a house, but as Nikolai stands in the small entryway, he can see signs that they live here—things that were left in place earlier that day rather than packed up, evidence that shows that this is a place they can come back to.

This house can become an anchor for their new lives.

"Better?" Seth asks. He takes his glasses off, exhaling over them to mist the lenses before he wipes them clean with the bottom of his shirt.

Nikolai takes the glasses from Seth's hand, walks them both into the living room, and leaves the glasses on a table. He sits on the couch, pulling Seth to straddle him as he reaches up to hold him. Kiss him. Fall into the sensation of being quiet and here and safe.

"Yeah," Nikolai murmurs against Seth's lips. "Better. And getting even more better all the time."

14

ON SATURDAY MORNING, a sweet scent lingers in the air, infusing the house and recalling lingering memories of childhood weekends. Nikolai leans out an open window to inhale the scent. It's crisp outside, starting to warm as the sun rises above the trees. This scent has been in the air all week, but not as thick as it is now.

Seth is in the kitchen, hair pulled back from his face with a bandanna, a deep frown furrowing his brow as he works at the stove. A pile of lumpy, misshapen pancakes rests on a plate, and the table is set. Seth glances up, grinning when he sees Nikolai.

"You were still sleeping, and I was craving pancakes because of the sugaring, so Mac came over and showed me how to make them," he says, waving the spatula at Nikolai. He points at the table. "Sit down. I've got that milk we picked up, and I'll have eggs in a minute. I didn't burn anything, but some of the earlier pancakes are a complete mess."

Breakfast. In their very own house. A breakfast pulled from childhood memories of pancakes and eggs, with a small pitcher of maple syrup next to a round tin of softening fresh butter. Nikolai's stomach rumbles, and he reaches for the pancakes as soon as Seth sets them on the table.

Seth sits after finishing up a pan of scrambled eggs, and they both tuck in.

Nikolai wonders how long it'll take before every meal stops feeling like a last chance. Someday it'll be routine, but not yet. The pancakes might be lumpy and the eggs dry, but they are real and fresh and they aren't from a tin. Every meal is better than the last, and every day it's easier to believe that the next meal will be waiting when he's hungry again.

"Mac said that she and Pawel and some of the others are helping with the sugaring festival. We should go." Seth gestures with his fork toward the window.

It takes Nikolai a moment to place what Seth is talking about, then he remembers that, during dinner last night at Josef and Mikhail's house, Amaranth had been excited about a celebration taking place today, and Sakura and she had been making plans for some kind of… Nikolai doesn't remember, exactly, but he knows they had something to do.

"Sounds fun," he says. It also seems like a luxury to be able to celebrate food and the spring bounty. He wonders if they were asked to help and he forgot, or if they've been let off the hook because they're so new. He supposes it doesn't matter, but he feels like he needs to do more here. Something to pay the people here back for the safety they provide.

Seth touches his arm. "You okay?"

Nikolai nods, catching Seth's hand in his own. "Yeah." It's not entirely true, and Seth probably knows that, but it's close enough. The discomfort will fade once they've better integrated into the community.

They finish every last scrap of breakfast, eating until Nikolai's stomach is overfull. Cleaning up doesn't take long, then they make the long walk to the central house.

The sweet scent grows stronger as they approach. They spot the fire burning first: a long pit, with grates above holding more pots than Nikolai can easily count. Someone stands at every pot, stirring periodically, and as Nikolai and Seth pass, they see people change places, relief coming in to give the stirring people breaks.

Amaranth spots them, and she and Sakura both wave. Amaranth leans in to speak to Sakura, then runs to join them. "We've got more people than fires; I can take a break and show you around the celebration" she says cheerfully, walking by Nikolai's side. "With so many maple trees in the area, it'd be a waste not to pull the community together to get as much sweet from that sap as we can. There will be another push for the group that crystallizes the syrup into sugar, but that doesn't happen today."

As they draw closer to the big house, tables and small stands line the narrow road. The set-up reminds Nikolai of a market or a festival. He hears shouts and cheering. He spots a booth with children lined up, holding cups of ice or snow, while someone ladles something atop each cup. Another booth has children waiting patiently to get their faces painted.

Alaric sits surrounded by kids, a pile of rough fluff in a basket by his side. He has two wide combs—one in each hand—and there's some fluff on the tines of the comb. He scrapes them against each other, and the children mimic his motions with smaller combs.

"It's not just the sugar," Amaranth says as they walk over to Alaric. "We're celebrating everything about spring. The melting snow. The sheering of the sheep. Baby animals—some of them have been brought over so the kids can see them and pet them. Anyone who has anything they can share is here to help."

Alaric sets aside his combs and touches one teenager on the head; that teen takes his place on the chair. "Did you have anything yet?" There's a bright, excited light in Alaric's eyes, a flare to his nostrils that makes Nikolai think that this is more familiar to Alaric than it is to himself.

"We just had breakfast," Seth says. His fingers tangle with Nikolai's. "We're helping use up last year's syrup, I think."

"There'll be time today to try the treats. They're doing spun syrup on the other side," Amaranth says. "You should take a look around, see what everyone's brought to the festival."

They start walking again, and Nikolai tries to look in every direction at once, but it's too much to take in.

He spots Carolyn under a small awning, sitting at a table with bright cards spread out in front of her. She speaks earnestly to a woman who sits across from her while Nikita and Heather rest, curled together, on the grass nearby. Nikita waves, but she doesn't get up.

They stop at a fire tended by Ethan and Marybelle, long iron pokers sticking out of the flames in pairs. They take out one pair, and they turn out to be the long handles to a pair of flat presses, which, when opened, drop something that smells like grilled bread onto a plate. Marybelle cuts it into four pieces and hands pieces to anyone waiting while Ethan butters bread and slathers it with jelly before putting the sandwich between the plates and back in the fire.

Nikolai's stomach grumbles, and even though he just ate, he takes an entire grilled peach-jelly sandwich to share with Seth. It burns the roof of his mouth, but Seth's lips taste sweet when they kiss after eating it.

Ethan winks at Alaric, who growls in response.

"Stop it," Marybelle says, elbowing Ethan sharply in the side.

Ethan pulls another sandwich out and cuts it for Alaric and Amaranth. He leans on the table, into Alaric's space, as he points. "There's a booth over there with sausage and bacon, and your friends are just past that, in front of the porch, doing something that involves a lot of teleporting, kicking, yelling, and throwing each other. It's an entertaining show, so they've got a good crowd watching."

"If you want a break to walk over with them, I can take over here." Amaranth doesn't wait for an answer, pushing Marybelle and Ethan toward Alaric with both hands. "Go. Be kids. Have fun."

"We promised Aunt Val—" Marybelle cuts off mid-protest when Ethan tugs at her hand.

"Don't argue. Escape while Amaranth's offering." He grins, then bows. "Please, let us be your guide."

Nikolai goes with the flow as they move down the road. The shouts are audible, sharp sounds that seem to be little more than explosive noises. He leans close to Seth, asking quietly, "What do you think they're doing?"

"Some kind of theatrical martial arts," Seth murmurs. "I talked to Mac this morning. Or maybe it's practical martial arts, I don't know. They're putting on a show, so how real can it be?"

There's a large crowd gathered, with maybe thirty kids sitting in front of a small stage and several adults lingering around the edges. Pawel spots Alaric and gestures for him to come over, and Nikolai takes a seat to get comfortable as Alaric joins the show.

Pawel is smaller than Alaric, and Mac is smaller yet, but they both easily place him into holds he can't get out of, and Mac flips him over her hip as she ducks a punch. Seth rumbles with laughter, and Nikolai gets the impression that Alaric's glares and loud growls are only for show.

Alaric gets a break when Pawel grabs a small stack of boards. Alaric looks at the boards in confusion, but they have a hasty, quiet conversation, then Alaric nods, moves away, and holds one of the boards over his head. Mac positions herself on the opposite side of their makeshift stage, and Pawel is in the middle, crouched with his hands together, fingers interlocked. Mac shouts, then runs, stepping into Pawel's hands and tumbling in the air as he tosses her up. She blinks out of existence, then reappears to kick through the board above Alaric's head, one foot pushed out as the board snaps.

It's impressive.

The kids scream, begging for her to do it again. Between Mac and Pawel, they work their way through a small stack of boards, the broken ones placed in a wheelbarrow and carted toward the fires once they're done.

Pawel raises a hand and bows. "Thank you. Mac and I will be teaching self-defense and martial arts after school on Mondays and Thursdays. Everyone is welcome."

The crowd disperses slowly, kids gathering around Alaric to see the last few board pieces, touching them as if to confirm that they are solid.

Nikita and Heather are approaching.

Nikolai is comfortable on the ground. He has a feeling that if he stays where he is, everyone will come to him. He tilts his head, and Seth puts an arm around his shoulder, kissing his temple.

"It feels good to forget about everything," Seth murmurs.

It's bright enough outside that Nikolai can't imagine any Shadow other than Mattie being able to tolerate it. It smells like spring, the air warm and sweet. He makes a small noise of agreement and leans into Seth, letting him take his weight.

Once the stage is cleared, two women bring out chairs and violins. The music they play is quick and light. Small children use the audience space to dance, so Nikolai and Seth inch out of the way without getting up.

"It's always like this," Marybelle says. "This is one of my favorite festivals. Harvest is good, too. We feast then. But sugaring is a chance to gather the syrup and to celebrate the end of winter. It's been dark for so long, and now we're finally getting some light."

"And new life in this place," Ethan says, nudging his cousin. "It seems like most people who come to Havenhill are either older or families with small children. New people our age aren't typical."

"There were the Simmons," Marybelle points out.

"They didn't stay," Ethan mutters.

Marybelle makes a soft sound.

Nikolai can't think why anyone wouldn't stay.

"We're here for good," Seth says. "I know the others want to return home, but here? This is it for us."

"We will go home." Mac lowers herself to crouch next to Ethan, who startles at her sudden appearance. "We've got a break and figured we'd all hang out. How'd the pancakes go this morning, Seth?"

"Lumpy but appreciated," Nikolai responds.

"I make them all the time for my Sisters," Mac says. "They're the best pancake recipe, right, Heather?"

Heather, Nikita, Pawel, and Alaric join them. Nikolai and Seth shift to open the circle enough to give them space.

"Pancakes that I don't make myself or go to the cafeteria for are always the best," Heather agrees. Her cheeks are flushed, her lips plump and bitten. Nikita's ponytail hangs ragged, and she leans into Heather, wrapping her arms around Heather's waist and nuzzling close.

"I haven't had these pancakes," she confides, "but half the time when I'm staying with Heather, I'm also fucking up the weather or making chaos. Maybe once things calm down and we get home, Mac will make pancakes while I'm there. If she thinks I deserve the pancakes, that is."

"Speaking of," Pawel says, the words dropping flatly between them. He sits up, gesturing for Heather and Nikita to take a seat. It's interesting how the others obey him; Pawel doesn't look like he's all that much older than they are, but he acts like he expects people to listen.

Once everyone is seated, Pawel leans forward, motioning to Nikolai and Seth. "I want to hear more about the scanners you mentioned. How widespread and commonplace is that technology, and how long have they been in use?"

"You think we know?" Seth grumbles. "We're not human. We're being hunted; we aren't the hunters."

"I've never seen one in person." Ethan's voice is dry with disbelief. "I'm not sure they exist, but according to rumor, they came into use a few years after the Split. People were able to travel at first, but the government wanted to track us once they realized that the Shadows preferred to kill Talents."

"That means they've identified some technological method of scanning a person and recognizing them as Talented," Pawel muses. "There must be physiological evidence of Talent. I'd say DNA, but a DNA scanner wouldn't work from a distance. Still. It seems that this world has developed a much higher understanding of the physiology of Talent than ours has."

"I wonder what Sera would say about this. She's got tech inside her, right?" Alaric touches the side of his head. "I wonder if that changes how she sees Talent. Or maybe the government has someone like Rory's mom. She knows who has Talent, right?"

"Technopaths," Pawel says slowly. His gaze sharpens, shifting to where Marybelle and Ethan sit. "You have those among the Talents here, I assume."

"No idea what you're talking about," Ethan tells him.

"Sera's got a cellphone in her brain," Alaric repeats, tapping the side of his head again. "She's online all the time. She's got a printer, too. She prints new tattoos on her body. Changes them when she's bored." He sits back, looking to Mac. "If Sera were here, bet she'd be able to tap into whatever communication grid is out there. If there are any Talents like her around, they might still have a global network we could access."

"If you can find one of them to ask," Ethan says. He spreads his hands. "Our technology might be different than yours, and you're talking about tech I barely remember."

"It'd be worth finding out," replies Alaric. "There might be other places like Havenhill. You might be able to reach out to them without the Shadows or your human hunters finding out."

"It's not a bad idea." Pawel taps a finger against his chin, thoughtful.

"What about the military?" Mac rolls to her feet, stepping backward. Nikolai isn't sure if she's bouncing on her toes or teleporting in place; she wavers when he looks at her. "What you're talking about—creating scanners to find Talents. That sounds like something you use a Talent to do. Our military started pulling in Talents before the Emergence. They probably did the same here before the Split."

Nikolai opens his mouth, then closes it. That had never occurred to him. "I have no idea."

"Seth? Ethan? Marybelle?" Mac asks.

"I know history, but I don't know anything current, and we can't drive to Albany and ask," Ethan says.

"Alia might know." Mac turns on her heel, then turns back, one hand raised like she's going to speak. Instead she shakes her head and quickly walks off.

Alaric rises. "I'll stick with her," he says, forestalling Pawel.

"I'm still not sure about healing the split," Pawel murmurs, "but I'm beginning to think that you brought us here for this very reason, Nikita. We bring a new perspective to this world, and the friendships we make here bring a new perspective to ours. We can learn from each other, and that may be far more important than saving each other."

Pawel calls this learning, but Nikolai's merely confused. He's never heard of a Technopath before. But if there's a way to bring Talents together around the world, that sounds like a good thing.

That they may have been hunted even before the Shadows came? That can only be bad.

15

Nikolai and Seth meander slowly through the crowd, Nikita and Heather trailing after them. Out of the corner of his eye, Nikolai sees Heather kiss Nikita, then head in a different direction. His attention remains on Seth and those around them, and on the chaos of different small stalls and demonstrations.

Nikita grabs Nikolai's hand, tugging him a few steps away from Seth. "Come with me."

He doesn't reach out to grab onto Seth, but it's close. Seth's his anchor, and he knows that he's Seth's. If Nikolai feels at sea in this crowd, Seth likely feels worse, overwhelmed by external emotions.

Seth nudges his glasses up his nose. "It's okay. I'm going to…" His voice trails off and he points past the house, into an area of the festival they haven't explored yet.

"You sure?"

Seth grins, nodding. "I'm sure. It'll be quieter over there. Fewer people, more animals, from what I've heard. Unless some of the animals are actually people, which around here is a possibility."

It feels wrong to walk away.

Nikolai shakes off Nikita's hand so he can frame Seth's face with his hands and kiss him slowly. "I'll see you at the house later."

Seth tilts his head into Nikolai's touch. "Be safe," he responds.

It's as if there's a string stretching out as they head in opposite directions. It tugs in his heart and his gut, and he does his best to shove down the way it twists inside of him.

"You two are a little co-dependent, aren't you." Nikita doesn't say it like a question. "We're all here, right? He'll be fine and you'll be fine. No one's going to let anyone get in trouble, and it's way too light for Shadows."

"It's not that." Nikolai places a hand flat on his chest, then draws it out slowly to point at Seth. "For the past two years—since my parents died, and we thought my brothers died with them—we've been stuck together like glue. We do everything together because we've been all we have. And we're bonded. You know what that's like."

"Not exactly the same," Nikita points out.

"I think it's more the same than you think," Nikolai counters. He ticks points off on his fingers as he speaks, matching her pace while they walk. "You can't sleep easily without her, right? And you're more comfortable when you know where she is. If you're in the same room, you sit together, touching. She settles you simply by being nearby, and if she and Seth are both doing something Empathic, you can tell which Talent influence is Heather's." Nikita nods along with every statement. "You see my point. You're new to each other so the bond is still settling. Seth and I have been together for years. I can't remember him being that far out of my sight since…since before the fire. Even when we weren't in each other's sight, we knew where we each were. It was never far. We…" He stumbles, and admits, "We're co-dependent, yes, and we need to learn how to be independent again. But it's not easy. It'll take time."

"Where I'm taking you might help with that." Nikita stops, and Nikolai stops right behind her. They've arrived at Carolyn's booth. She has no one with her, and she sits idly shuffling her cards while looking through a journal she has in front of her.

"I think you should get a reading from Carolyn."

Nikolai has no idea what that means.

"She's Predictive. She'll—" Nikita cuts off, her head tilted. "It's not telling your future or fortunes. It's like, she'll give you a reading about how your life is now and what some of your possible paths are going forward. It'll give you things to think about related to your current choices. Okay?"

Nikolai's never met someone who is Predictive. It sounds more like storybook magic than Talent. But what has he got to lose? "Sure. Okay."

He lets Nikita push him into the seat at Carolyn's table.

Carolyn stops shuffling and looks up, blinking at Nikolai.

"Hey."

"Hey." Nikolai looks at the cards under her hand, then the closed notebook. "Nikita says—"

"—you should give him a reading." Nikita sits on the grass with her knees bent and arms around her legs. "It'd be interesting to see what comes up, given everything."

"Is this reading for him or for you?" Carolyn mutters dryly. She pushes the notebook to the side and shuffles the deck a few more times before handing it to Nikolai. "Go ahead and shuffle it, then cut it and give it back to me."

"Him," Nikita says. She holds one hand up, scrubbing the air in front of her. "This has nothing to do with me."

That's a lie. He and Nikita are entangled in ways they don't understand. He gets the feeling their futures are entangled as well, even if he doesn't know how yet.

The cards feel large to his hands. It's been years since he last played cards, and those were smaller. And fewer. These are awkward, and he drops them twice, scooping them up and patting them back into a neat pile before he tries to shuffle them again. The motion comes back to him, something he learned as a child before everything went wrong, and he realizes he's still shuffling because it feels like a tiny piece of the past that he has reclaimed.

He sets the deck down, cuts it in the middle, and pushes the stack toward Carolyn. She lays down cards on the table: two crossed, then four cards around those, then another four to their right, in a column.

Nikita comes to her knees and leans up to look at them curiously.

The pictures are interesting, but they don't mean anything to Nikolai.

Carolyn examines the cards, running her fingers over them in the same order that she laid them down. She pauses occasionally and backtracks before moving forward. Her lips move, but there's no sound.

Nikolai sits back and waits.

"Okay. So. These two cards represent your current situation and something that goes against that situation. Usually these two cards are in opposition, but not always." Carolyn taps the first card, an upside-down picture of six glasses. "You've got all these pent-up emotions about the past, but you're starting to move on from those. You've got a chance to start over, and you're trying to pay attention to the future rather than lingering over what's happened." Her fingers move to the card that lies across it, an image of a man walking from one circle to another. "The thing is, life isn't as settled as you want it to be. There are complications, and magical changes, because of—" She frowns. "Usually, I don't try to interpret a reading based on life, but this one is so obvious to me, I have to say something. This is a card about balancing two things that are in flux, and I think the big interruption is Nikita and our world impinging on you while you and Seth are trying to settle here in Havenhill."

It's funny how the card almost looks like he's moving from one world to another. "It could mean any kind of transition or move," Nikolai says.

"That's why I usually don't try to tie readings into my knowledge of a person's life," Carolyn says. "I'll tell the story the cards tell and leave it to you to figure out what you get from it. Using that approach, I'd say you're settled and trying to move on, but because of something twinned—some kind of balance between two objects in flux—you're being pushed out of sync." She inhales roughly, shakes her head, and moves her finger to the next card. "Right. Let's keep going."

The card is upside-down again, showing a man and woman standing in a cage made of swords thrust into the ground.

"This is usually a dark card," Carolyn says, "but because it's reversed, it's positive in this case. You've been in a mental prison, but if you focus on inner dialogue and listen to yourself, you can take steps to move beyond your fears. And beneath that card, you have the Moon, which represents your toolbox to escape whatever mental block has you trapped. The Moon represents instinct and intuition, love and being able to lose yourself and be emotional. So trust those instincts and move beyond your fear."

She touches the next two cards, those surrounding the crossed cards to the left and right. "These are your recent past and near future. Behind you is Justice, reversed, which indicates you were in a place of chaos and prejudice. Ahead of you is the Ten of Swords, also reversed. This is another card that's more positive when it's reversed. You're going to hit rock bottom and start going back up. Trust in yourself to move beyond your fears. Take things one step at a time. Even when you're at the lowest point you can imagine, it's not that bad because moving forward means you're climbing up. It'll get better."

That's positive? Nikolai supposes it is, in that the message is about being able to get better. But the idea of hitting rock bottom doesn't sound good, especially when she refers to it as something that will happen in the future.

He bites his tongue rather than put voice to the thought.

Carolyn moves on to the four cards in a neat line to the right. "This is you. You're balanced neatly on those six swords. You've found your path, your way through. You think you're going in the right direction. Your family and friends are positive, too. The Ace of Cups is a great card, about joy and fulfillment and being able to relax into a safety net of having those you love around you."

Right. That one is obvious.

"The thing to remember is that having your anchor and being stable emotionally means you can have new beginnings in other directions, too," Carolyn continues. The next-to-last card, when she touches it, is meaningless to Nikolai. A woman stares out at him, yin and yang on her forehead, alpha and omega written before her.

"Balance," he says, pointing to the symbols. "Are all your cards about balance?"

Carolyn presses her lips together in a thin imitation of a smile. "No, not all of my cards. Only the ones in your reading. Almost every card that talks about balance is on the table right now."

Oh.

"That's chilling."

"I'm Predictive." Carolyn taps the woman's face. "And yes, this card is also about balance. She represents your hopes and fears. She's a reminder to rely on your instinct and intuition to use your Talent effectively. Your heart knows more than your mind, which ties back to your romantic and emotional connections." A flush stains her cheeks. "The High Priestess also refers to your sexual connections."

Nikita snickers.

"Seth has my heart and my body," Nikolai says plainly.

Carolyn shrugs, the color high on her cheeks. "Not my area of expertise. I don't know if it's relevant to your reading. It's something for you to think about."

"What about this one?" he tries to redirect the conversation by tapping the last card. It shows a man wielding a wand and fighting off other wands, again upside-down.

"That's the final outcome," Carolyn says. She rubs at one cheek like she can scrub away her flush. "It's a warning. You can be a role model, but you're resisting. Be careful and guard against being indecisive. Do what needs to be done; don't let yourself rest and become unmotivated because things are easy. Everything is in your hands, and you can either fight the battle or let them win."

When Nikolai considers everything she's said, it makes a coherent story. He's in Havenhill. His life was shit, and it's gotten better. He's got Seth, and he's got his family, and currently he's got Nikita, barging in to disrupt everything. He has a choice between sinking into the safety of living in Havenhill or figuring out how to do something dangerous, such as helping Nikita heal the split.

He's tempted to say he's been set up, but the way Carolyn's brow furrows deeply as she runs her fingers over the final card, her lips pursed, makes him think that the fall of the cards is as much a surprise to her as it is to him.

"Carolyn's really good at this," Nikita says. "I didn't bring you over because I thought she'd be like 'listen to Nik, she knows what she's doing' or something. I don't know what I'm doing at all. But I thought the cards might say something interesting to you."

Nikolai huffs, crossing his arms. "I don't have to like what they said," he grumbles. He'll talk to Seth about this tonight because he doesn't want to think that anything is pushing them into doing something they don't want to do. But Carolyn's reading implies they may be shoved out of their comfort zone whether they want to go there or not.

Carolyn sweeps the cards into a stack, shuffling them roughly. "I need to write that down," she says. "Go get ice cream."

"What?" Nikolai barely manages to speak before Nikita is on her feet, pulling Nikolai with her.

"Ice cream! I forgot they said they were making it. It'll be brilliant. Fresh milk, the winter preserves, such good flavors." Nikita pulls, and Nikolai has to follow or lose his balance. "It's the perfect thing after being raked over the emotional coals, right?"

"I haven't had ice cream since I was ten," Nikolai says. "Maybe younger."

Nikita grins, and yeah. She has definitely barged into his life and upset the careful balance. He's managed to get everything properly put together and here's this person from another world, knocking it all over.

Carolyn's reading was uncomfortably accurate.

"Then it's time for you to have it again," she says, and it takes Nikolai a moment to remember that she's talking about ice cream. "Come on, let's find Seth and Heather, then we'll get ice cream together. Like the cards said—it's time to forge ahead and move on."

Trying new things. Rediscovering old things. Recreating his life, and trying to find balance. Stepping from his past life into the future. Nikolai can do that. No fears involved at all.

16

A FEW DAYS after the sugaring, Nikolai asks Alaric if there's a lake nearby, and Alaric is more than happy to show them where to find one. A chill remains in the morning air, but it warms more quickly than before. It's going to be a perfect spring day; summer heat will come soon enough.

Alaric leads the way as a hound, padding along a path with his nose to the ground. Nikolai walks hand in hand with Seth, fingers tangled and relaxed. They have towels—actual towels—looped over their arms, along with shorts they were given specifically to use as swim trunks. It's a luxury to be able to swim for fun, rather than doing it to wash their underwear.

"We have showers," Nikita points out. She and Heather trail behind, Nikita wrapped in a thick, heavy wool jacket, and Heather still wearing a hat and mittens. "We don't need to go bathe in the lake."

"Alaric said it's a swimming hole," Seth counters, "and the point isn't bathing. Although a day warm enough to submerge in a lake was always good when we were on the road. You interrupted our last one."

Nikolai squeezes his hand. "There aren't many things I look back on happily from the last few years, but swimming is one of them. It'll be cold, but it'll be worth it."

The rush of water sounds in the distance.

Alaric barks sharply and takes off running.

Nikita wraps her arms around her middle. "I still think you're nuts."

"You said you want to know more about the life you've been Dreaming," Nikolai points out. He gestures down the path. "This was part of my life, and there's no better way to learn about it than to live it. Trust us, okay? It'll be worth it," he repeats.

She's not convinced—he can tell by the way her nose wrinkles and her lips purse—but she and Heather still follow.

The afternoon sun beats down on them as the path widens at the edge of a swimming hole. A small waterfall—a few feet high—empties into it on one side, and the river ambles off on the other side. The pool is twice as wide as it is long, as if something dug deep long ago. Old leaves flow quickly along the far side, showing where the current runs, but the closer part of the pool lies quiet, water gently lapping at the rocky beach. Alaric is already in the water.

Heather strips off her mittens and shoves them into the pockets of her sweater. She crouches near the water, picks up a rock, inspects it, then drops it ands selects a different one. She turns it around several times in her fingers and stares out over the water.

Alaric paddles by, barking, and she waves for him to keep going.

As soon as Alaric is out of the way, she pulls her hand back, then flicks her wrist. The stone flies out and strikes the water, skipping off the surface for several hops before it *plunks* and sinks.

She straightens up. "Only seven. I'm out of practice." She shoves her hands in her pockets as she turns. "We used to go camping in the summers. My parents are both teachers, so they had summer off, and we'd hit the road as soon as schools were closed. I learned how to skip rocks, and my dad had to swim in every lake or river we saw, no matter how cold it was. He'd insist it would be invigorating, and Mom would laugh all afternoon when he complained afterward about being cold." She grins. "So don't mind me if I don't go in; I'm just here to laugh when you comment on the cold later because you're too stubborn to back down now."

That may be the most Heather's said at one time since arriving. It's definitely the first time she hasn't tried to be a calming influence.

Seth tilts his head. "I'm beginning to think I might like you."

"Nikita thinks you are me," Heather counters.

"Teach me how to do that." He gestures from the rocks to the pool as he crouches. "What kind of rock am I looking for?"

"Flat. Light, although sometimes the heavy ones go farther if you have excellent technique. Try that one." Heather points, and Seth picks up the rock she indicates. "Did you change your mind about going in?"

"Because you're teasing us? Definitely not." Seth bites his lip as he mimics the throw Heather made; the rock flies out and kerplops in the river. "We have time to play and swim, so I want to know how you do that."

"Hey." Nikolai touches Seth's shoulder to get his attention, then leans down to kiss the top of his head. "Join me when you're ready. I'm going in."

Seth waves him off, but it still feels strange to walk away. Nikolai is trying to relax, to allow them both freedom now that life is more than the two of them. He can't resist watching, however. Seth leans toward where Heather crouches; she shows him how to hold the rock and the motion of the throw without letting go.

Nikita follows Nikolai to the edge of the water. She shivers dramatically when he strips down to his swim trunks.

"I still think you're nuts," she says.

Nikolai steps to the edge, letting the frigid water lap against his toes. Running water is always cold, and at this time of year, the river must be filled with snowmelt from the mountains. He shudders at the thought of that chill enveloping him, but he doesn't want to give Nikita the satisfaction of being proved right, so he takes several more quick steps forward.

The rocks under his feet seem to simply disappear as the river floor drops abruptly, and he loses his footing and slides down, abruptly submerged.

He comes up sputtering and shaking his head to get his hair out of his face. Alaric swims by, splashing him, and Nikolai instinctively sends a wash of water back at him. Alaric barks and rolls over in the water, belly up for a moment before he paddles away again.

"How is it?" Seth calls from where he crouches, another rock in his hand. He brings his hand back and flicks forward to let the rock fly, and this one skims the water twice before dropping beneath the surface. Heather squeezes Seth's shoulder, and even from this distance Nikolai can feel Heather's approval and Seth's pleasure at learning the new trick.

Nikolai drops beneath the surface again, letting himself sink until his toes graze the rocks at the bottom. He swims into the center, then pushes to the point where he can feel the pull of the current. He surfaces, then, and pushes his hair back. "Not bad," he calls back. "The current's frigid, and the shallow edges are cold. When you get in the center, there's some warmth at the deepest part. Come on in, Seth!"

"In a minute," Seth agrees. He tries skipping another rock.

Nikolai rolls onto his back, arms and legs spread out, letting the warmth of the spring sun beat down on him. He closes his eyes, floating in the quietest and warmest part of the pool, disturbed by small currents as Alaric swims nearby.

It's easy to lose track of time.

When he catches himself drifting into cooler water, he rights himself so he can swim back.

Alaric has climbed out and lies on his side on the ground, panting and relaxing in the sun. One ear twitches, and he whines in his sleep. Seth treads water in the middle of the pool. He's shivering as if he got in only moments ago, and Nikolai wonders if Seth swimming closer was the current he felt.

Doesn't matter.

Nikolai's happy to meet him in the middle and wrap his arms around him, kissing him slowly. They linger over the kiss, and Nikolai holds Seth close when they finally part.

Seth gets a hand on top of his head and shoves him under the water.

"Oh, so that's what we're doing?" Nikolai asks when he surfaces. He pushes through the water, chasing Seth as they play tag, taking turns dunking each other. They splash, and when Nikita yells from the small beach—"Watch out!"—they splash toward her and Heather instead of each other.

It's fun but exhausting, and eventually they return to the shore, slogging across mud and wet rocks once the water goes shallow.

Nikolai falls onto the towel, stretching out. Nikita tosses a second towel at him, and he uses it to wipe his face. "Thank you," he says.

"You're welcome," Alaric rumbles; he's changed to his human form again. "In my world, I spend a lot of time here with my twin and my best friend. Spring and fall are good for swimming, even if it's cold."

"*Still* think you're nuts," Nikita says.

They end up stretched out across a set of towels. Seth's head is on Nikolai's stomach, and Nikolai combs his fingers through Seth's thick curls. Nikita lies with her head on Alaric's lap and her feet on Nikolai's calves, Heather curled in close to her.

Nikita twitches, tapping at Nikolai with her toes. "Do you ever imagine what'd be like if we were actually twins?"

"Why would I?" He closes his eyes, the sun making the insides of his eyelids red; he throws an arm across his face to block it out. "We aren't from the same world. We aren't twins; presumably, we're essentially the same person. Right?"

"Metaphysically, I guess so," Nikita agrees. "I was thinking, though… My sister Tammy is so much older than me? She's Pawel's age. She's a grown-up, graduated ages ago, and she had a baby recently with her husband. She's an adult doing adultier things than I am. And when I was a kid—when the Emergence happened—she already seemed like an adult to me then even though she was only a senior in high school. I was ten years old. I couldn't play with her. We were like 'only children' who happened to live in the same house. So I keep thinking, what if you and I had grown up together. Like twins."

"It doesn't matter because you can't go back in time and change it," Seth points out practically.

"That sounds lonely," Nikolai says. He sits up, dislodging Seth just enough to frame Seth's face with his hands and press their foreheads together.

Seth grins and kisses him, then rolls away, grabbing a bag he brought.

"It was," Nikita admits. "Being at PHU is like having the family I didn't have while growing up."

"We are in really different places," Nikolai murmurs. He takes the muffin Seth hands him, biting into the maple sweetness. "I had family even though Mikhail and Josef are older than me. I've been friends with Seth since long before the Split, so probably since before your Emergence, too. We've always had each other, so I never got the chance to be lonely. That's a terrible feeling for a Dreamwalker to have."

Heather coughs, and Alaric grumbles.

Nikita rolls onto her side and stares across the water.

"You were lonely enough that you punched through reality to get to me," Nikolai says quietly.

No one says a word, but he's sure that's what they were all thinking.

He rolls to his feet, staying in a crouch, fingers drifting over the damp sand and rocks. "You don't get to take me home to be the twin you never had," he tells her.

Alaric sits up abruptly. "Pawel's coming," he says.

Nikita turns and looks at Nikolai. "I'm not trying to kidnap you," she whispers.

"If they mentioned swimming, they'll be right here." Ethan leads the way. "Hey, Alaric. I figured you would know about this place."

Alaric mutters wordlessly.

"Coming down to swim?" Seth asks. He offers the small fabric sack he holds in his hands, and Pawel takes a muffin from it while Ethan waves him off.

"Too cold," Ethan says, crouching next to Seth and Nikolai.

"Right?" Nikita asks.

Pawel idly eats the muffin while looking out over the water. "It's beautiful, isn't it?" He pauses for another bite before adding, "We bring news."

"What kind of news?" Alaric asks.

"We found two Technopaths in Havenhill," Pawel says. "Amerika and Shamir. We talked. I had wondered if Technopaths could connect with each other inside and outside of Havenhill. And it turns out they can. Amerika was surprised to discover that the network is still there. Shamir was less surprised, and he was instrumental in determining that Technopaths around the world have built their own space within the human networks." He crouches, idly picking up a rock and turning it over in his fingers. He shifts his stance and throws the rock out, skipping it easily across the river.

"Wait." Seth holds both hands up. "Go back. You said around the world."

Pawel stays crouched, elbows braced against his knees. "You sound surprised."

"Sometimes I've wondered if the Shadow invasion is a local phenomenon. That if we went far enough north or south, things would change," Seth admits. "If this started because a Dreamwalker—"

"I didn't start this," Nikita interrupts.

Seth gives her a dark look. "I didn't say you did. This started a long time before you went looking for Nikolai. My point is, Dreamwalkers created the breaks between here and where the Shadows lie. If it's all over the world, there must have been a lot of Dreamwalkers involved. And a big Split."

Nikolai isn't surprised. It's always felt like the whole world was involved; the Split would have to be huge. He can't imagine there are places where life is still normal. The Shadows are everywhere.

"It's global," Pawel says quietly. "We know that for certain now, and Shamir and Amerika will learn more. They are creating links to other Technopaths and finding ways into trusted networks so that Havenhill can become a part of the outside world again."

"Alia must love that," Alaric mutters.

"She's not thrilled," Ethan admits. "Mom's been talking to her, and if anyone can turn her around, it's Mom. They work best together. Alia tempers Mom's enthusiasm. Mom makes sure Alia keeps pushing our limits as a community."

The sun drifts behind a cloud, and shadows spread across the beach. Nikolai suppresses a shiver; it's cooling off quickly, and it's time to get dressed. He grabs his discarded clothes and pulls them on.

"Are you only trying to get news from elsewhere, or is there something we want this Technopath network to do?" Heather asks. "Isn't it a risk to put Havenhill back on the map?"

"Shamir says humans can't get into Technopath spaces," Ethan says. "He used to work in computer security before the Split, and he said the protections in place on the Technopath network are magical, not technological."

Pawel rises, walking toward the path and the tree line surrounding the beach.

"It's getting colder. Let's go back," Nikita says. She pushes to standing and pulls Heather up so she can lean against her. Heather's arms wrap around her.

The shadows drift closer, thicker than the clouds in the sky above. Nikolai's skin pricks, and he reaches for Seth without thinking, grateful when Seth's fingers cling to his. "I don't think this is—"

"Yeah," Ethan agrees quickly. "Someone grab Pawel."

Pawel is already halfway to the trees. There, shadows dart and move, twisting around the tree trunks in a way that seems sentient. As if Shadows have come within the wards, but they aren't attacking, instead staying out of reach as Pawel slowly approaches.

Alaric becomes the hound and bounds forward, knocking into Pawel's knees. Pawel stumbles, gaze dropping as he falls to his hands and knees.

The sky brightens, and Mattie emerges from the trees as the shadows drift away in the blooming sunlight.

Nikolai's skin is too tight, waiting for something more to happen.

"They can't get in," Mattie calls out, "but they want to." She looks at Pawel and smiles softly. "She wants to."

Pawel stays where he is, one hand in the sand, fingers dug in. His shoulders are curled and tense. "We should go back," he says.

Nikolai glances at Seth, and Seth nods. Nikolai is thankful as always for the way Seth reads his mind and knows what he wants to do. "You go back," Nikolai says. "Seth and I need to do something first."

Pawel's expression twists sour. "We should stay with you."

"We were fine on our own before you barged into our lives; we'll be fine here, now, inside of Havenhill's wards," Seth insists. He shoos them toward the path. "Go. It'll be easier if we're on our own."

"Oh, it's that kind of thing," Nikita says cheerfully.

Alaric looks at her doubtfully, but his ears go pink.

Heather laughs, the sound strained. Ethan grabs Pawel's arm and pulls.

"We should leave them alone," Mattie murmurs, her voice low and sibilant. "They want privacy, and they'll be safe here." She looks back at them. "There's nothing but light left around them."

Seth waits until they are out of sight. "You saw them, right?" he asks.

"I did." Writhing in the trees, like the remnants of that dream Nikolai shared with Nikita in Del's Dreamlands. Seth saw it too; it was real. The Shadows were here, so close to the center of Havenhill. It's impossible, but he knows what they saw, and he knows what they need to do.

Nikolai clings to Seth's hands, then he calls the brightness of Dreams to wrap around them.

Together, they let the light sparkle and spread over the area.

This is Havenhill, and there is no way in hell that they're letting the Shadows in.

17

Nikolai vaguely remembers dinner parties, but he's never considered attending one. After the Split, his family had shied away from befriending other families, and once he and Seth were on their own, gatherings were impossible. But now he's walking up to the larger Benford house with Seth, carrying a pan still warm from the oven, meeting a large mixed group of people in order to eat together.

As far as he knows, that's a dinner party.

Heather throws open the door and motions them inside. "We decided on buffet-style because we couldn't fit enough tables together for a formal dinner. There are so many of us we barely fit in the house. We figured it'd be easier to pick and choose, eat when we can and what we want. Find a seat or stand anywhere you want. There's a lot of food. You'll find something you like."

"Clan's good at that," Ethan says cheerily from behind her. "I think Alaric's already eaten three plates full, and we're barely set up."

Alaric's growl rumbles from somewhere else in the house, but he doesn't deny it.

"It's kugel," Seth says, holding the pan out. "Sweet." He looks down at the towel-wrapped pan. "It's not exactly like Bubbe made since we don't have normal sugar or cinnamon, but I think she'd understand. I used dried apples instead of raisins, to go with the maple and black walnut. I haven't tasted it yet, but I think it'll be good."

"I can't believe you remember how to make something that you haven't had in years," Heather says. She gestures to a table laden with desserts. Seth slides the pan next to a dish that looks like corn pudding. "I can't remember how to make something I had a recipe for last week. We let Alaric and

Mac tell us what to do. They're better in a kitchen than any of us. Everyone attending brought dishes too. Even Alia and Val are here."

From what Nikolai can see, "everyone" is a good description. It's not everyone in Havenhill, nor even everyone he's met, but it's a large crowd. He can't see Alaric, but he can hear him from where he guesses the kitchen is, arguing with Mac. Nikita sits with Carolyn and Pawel. Josef is squeezed into a single chair with Amaranth, and he grins when he spots Nikolai, waving for him to come closer. Nikolai would, but every seat is taken, to the point that Jefferson is standing, gesturing with gloved hands while speaking to an older man Nikolai doesn't recognize.

Nikolai stalls, not sure where to go. The house seemed big when Nikita and her friends had moved in. Now it feels closed and small.

Nikita slides off the couch, and Sakura takes her seat. Nikita approaches quickly, hooking her arm around Nikolai's and drawing him into the next room, an empty dining room off the kitchen. "We're serving in the entryway because there's room, and then people can eat either in the living room or in here, but no one else has come in here yet." She nudges out one of the chairs.

Nikolai takes the offered seat, and Seth sits on his lap. Nikolai wraps his arms around him, pressing his face against the back of his neck and inhaling to center himself.

"I didn't realize there would be this many people here," Seth says. "I don't think I made enough kugel."

Nikita waves his comment away. "Don't worry about it. We have enough food to feed a small army. Potluck dinners always have more than enough food but never enough of any single dish."

Nikolai will take her word for it.

Ethan and Heather drift in, along with the man Nikolai saw talking to Jefferson.

"I heard someone mention kugel," the man says, holding out a hand to Seth. "My name is Shamir."

"Seth." Seth shakes Shamir's hand firmly. "I didn't have cinnamon." It comes out apologetic.

"We'll have it someday," Shamir says with a small grin as he takes a seat. "It's been an age since I've had a kugel—either sweet or savory. My bubbe favored savory, but my wife liked sweet, and we had that for every holiday before the Split. Now that I'm reconnected to the rest of the world, I'm doing research and working with Amaranth to see if we can introduce certain spices to our greenhouse, cinnamon included."

"Then your wife can make you a more traditional—" Seth's voice falls away at the shift in Shamir's expression. "Oh. I'm sorry."

Shamir spreads his hands and shrugs. Nikolai can't interpret that response, but it stalls the conversation, leaving an awkward silence.

"So," Ethan says, leaning on the table where he sits. "This party got bigger than expected, and Mom tried to convince Alia to move it to the main house. But Alia insisted that your friends wanted it to be here, and that it was important to them, so here we are. Squeezed in."

"Considering who's here, we'll be talking magic later, I'm sure," Nikita says. "It feels like Pawel's assembled a crack team of Talent rather than a potluck housewarming."

"It'll still be a fun evening," Ethan says. "We'll make sure of it."

"I think your Pawel has an ulterior motive." Shamir leans back in his chair. He's not a tall man, but he's broad-shouldered, and Nikolai thinks this is how Seth may look when he's older. Tight curls cropped close and graying. No glasses, but there are similarities between their features, in the roundness of their faces.

"Pawel wants to go home," Nikita says. "He's torn between learning more about this world and trying to push through and leave."

Seth nudges his glasses up his nose. "Please use different words. 'Push through' sounds like he'll be breaking down walls and letting more Shadows in."

"That would be very bad, considering what I've been learning," Shamir says. He raises a hand, starting to speak, but pauses as a clap echoes from the other room.

Alia's voice is clear despite the barrier. "Eat first, talk after. Be social first, research after." There's a pause, and Nikolai imagines her looking at Pawel as she says those words. "Enjoy what Havenhill has to offer and enjoy the time with our family and friends."

"Let's do as Alia says," Shamir murmurs, pushing back his chair. "Come. Eat. There will be plenty of time to talk once we're sated."

The crowd is dense, but it's worth braving it to get the food. Nikolai fills his plate and eats quietly, sitting on one half of a chair while Seth sits on the other side of it. They balance carefully to eat at the table along with eight others. The group changes regularly, people drifting away and others taking their places.

Nikolai gets up for more food and loses his spot, so he sits outside on the front steps with a roll stuffed with roast beef and a bright, sharp horseradish sauce. When he makes his way back inside, Pawel stands with Alia and Val in the entryway, gesturing with his empty plate.

"You keep saying eat first—"

"Because this is a dinner among friends and family," Alia says mildly. "I know you want to discuss your options. Your world. Your findings. You want to open Havenhill to the world at large. But this is, first and foremost, a meal to welcome newcomers to Havenhill, to unite them with our community. Your welcome continues."

"Why are we still celebrating our arrival? We've been here almost two weeks," Pawel protests. He reaches to the side and sets the plate on a table without looking at it. Both hands go into his hair, fingers threading through the strands and pulling at it roughly. "We've been here for almost two weeks," he repeats. "And my son has been home without me. I need to push this, Alia. We need to do whatever we're here to do."

"Or you need to realize that this is your home now, because if you destroy the veil between the worlds, what else will come out?" Alia's voice rumbles, elevating to a roar by the end.

Pawel takes a step back, his hands dropping. "I will not allow Shadows—"

"You say that now," she says, taking a step closer. "*You* say that, but *we* know what happens when the barrier between Dreams and reality is torn. That is how the Shadows come into this world. And you want to destroy that barrier on purpose. Do you realize what probably followed you here?"

Nikolai remembers the thick wave of Shadows that had chased these people when they first arrived, the way they swarmed like a solid wall of darkness, trying to capture them.

He'd thought they were attracted by the blatant use of Talent.

Maybe they'd come through with them from the split.

Nikolai swallows hard, exhaling roughly.

Pawel shakes his head. "It wasn't like that."

Alia raises an eyebrow. "Put yourself in my position, and tell me—if you were home, and you saw this risk to those you protect, would you allow a small group to put everyone in danger?"

"If I knew it would work, then it wouldn't be a risk," Pawel insists. "That's why we need to understand the details. That's why we need to have these conversations."

"And we will." Alia pauses, glancing at Val, who has a hand on her arm. "Not yet. Allow yourself time to acclimate, Pawel, to understand where you are so that you can understand your resources. You cannot know anything will work if you do not take the time to learn your options."

Pawel makes a strangled sound, throwing his arms wide. He stalks past Nikolai and yanks the door open, exiting and slamming it in his wake.

"He's like a child," Alia murmurs.

"He's stressed," Mac replies quietly. "Tell me. If you had a small child, wouldn't you move heaven and earth to be with them? Isn't that what you do here, when you reunite families? That's all he wants. But he also feels responsible for all of us. It's a lot."

"And I'm responsible for everyone in Havenhill," Alia says firmly.

"The problem is, the risk already exists," Shamir says. He glances at a woman who stands across the room. She's small and sturdily built, her features dark aside from pale-blue eyes. She makes a face at Shamir's words and walks over to stand by his side.

"He's not wrong," she says, her tone as low and serious as his. "Shamir and I have been putting out feelers into the network, trying to reach other Technopaths around the world. Some, like us, have recently returned to the network, and some have been out there all along, creating a…" She glances at Shamir.

He smiles slightly. "I hesitate to call it a shadow community. Consider it something like the Underweb. Not the dark web that existed for illegal activity before the Split. A separate but connected online space, created in and around the existing network and entirely for Talented use. Technopaths have created private network access to their spaces, and Amerika's pulling together old technology here that might be able to do that for us."

"Creating a link between Havenhill and the world that can be followed," Alia says sharply.

"Only by Talents," Amerika replies, "and only by people we trust. We're taking this slow, trying not to expose more than we have to. At this point, no one can trace where we are, and we haven't announced ourselves to the world. We're working together to make sure we present a united front and don't contradict each other. But yes, we are trying to link to other communities. We can't survive alone."

Alia lifts one eyebrow as if to argue.

"The Shadow infestation is growing." Shamir speaks quickly to forestall further argument. Or maybe to get the point out before they can go off on a tangent. Nikolai can think of a few tangents to explore. Like the idea Mac brought up about the human government using Talented people to track other Talents. Restricting something to Talents-only might not keep the humans out as well as they think.

"What about—?" Nikolai is interrupted by Mattie.

"Please don't call it that," she says loudly, tone quieting when Nikolai falls silent. "We aren't an infestation. We aren't cockroaches or carpenter ants. We're people, beneath the mindless hunger that our Emergence creates. The Shadow incursion is an invasion."

"Invasion implies intelligence," Val says.

"Exactly," Mattie replies.

"Focusing on news from our own country," Shamir says, raising both his hands. "Boston and Los Angeles have been consumed." He gestures first with his right hand, then his left, then slowly brings them together. "Combined with the information that this attack is being intelligently directed, that implies they'll be working from both coasts toward the middle. I haven't had time to dig past that, but I have yet to meet a Talent from Florida in the Underweb, so I suspect the Shadows are using a southern route as well."

"How do you know about Boston and LA?" Nikita asks.

"Both cities have gone dark, according to Talents who live near them," Amerika explains. "Los Angeles was one of the largest and brightest walled spaces. Even from a distance, it was obvious when it went dark."

Nikolai shudders. He may not be a fan of human settlements, but he knows that the bright lights, the intensity of the daylight even in the depths of night, is what keeps the Shadows at bay. "If it's dark, it has to be dead." He nods at Shamir, agreeing with his words. "Consumed."

Even Mattie is sobered by the news.

"It'll take time to learn more," Amerika says. "That's why it's important to create links to other communities of Talent. We are the only people we can trust, and we need to be able to get this information. We're safe here, now, but without more information, we can't be sure we'll stay safe."

Alia's brows are furrowed, her lips pressed thinly together, and Nikolai swears he hears a soft growl that fades when Val slides an arm around her wife's back and tugs her closer.

"Safely," Alia snaps. "We only do what we can without revealing Havenhill's location, without exposing us to further risk."

"Is it possible that there are Talents who are allied with humans?" Nikolai asks. He needs to put the question out there, though he regrets it when Alia gives him a sharp look. "Mac mentioned the possibility when we explained the highway scanners to him."

"It's a slim possibility," Amerika allows, "and even slimmer that one would be a Technopath and know about this private network. But that's why we're not giving out personal information. We're being careful. I think the benefit outweighs the risk, especially if the Shadows are making an effort to destroy human strongholds. They must be looking for us."

"Then we need to stop the Shadow invasion," Nikita adds. "What?" she continues when no one responds. She spreads her hands, stepping forward until Heather's hand on her arm gently stops her. "Isn't that why we came here? To help you find a way out from under the darkness. We need to make sure you survive."

"And you'd do that by punching a hole through the Dreams to let more Shadows through," Alia says dryly.

"Just like that, we've come full circle," Seth murmurs, standing close enough to Nikolai to keep the words between them alone. Nikolai slips an arm around his shoulders, drawing him closer; he exhales when Seth's lips brush his cheek.

"We'd do it by healing the split," Nikita protests. "It's a huge, gaping wound between our worlds, and Shadows are festering there. The worse it gets, the more Shadows there are, and the worse the invasion becomes. They're breeding."

"How do you know that?" Alia growls.

Nikita takes a step back into Heather's grasp. "I don't," she admits, "but it seems like a logical conclusion given what we've seen. We need to find out for sure, and the only way to do that is to go into the Dreamscape and—"

"No," Alia cuts her off. "Again, you want to put Havenhill and our people at risk. I have never denied sanctuary to any Talent, but you are pushing the limits of what I'll allow."

"Nikita, we have to be careful," Alaric rumbles. "The split might just exist. It might not be healable."

"And if more of those things that killed your brother get into our world?" Nikita protests, despite a soft "*Hey*" from Mattie. "This world and ours are tied together. Twinned. We need to remember that because being here lets us see what our world could become."

"The Technopaths have a private connection," Seth says slowly, "because they are able to access a place that humans can't. That's also what Dreamwalkers can do."

Nikolai can see the idea forming in Seth's mind. He doesn't like it. He clings to Seth, silently willing him to be the practical one of their partnership, the way he has always been.

Heather's eyes light up, a wave of excitement crashing through the room. "We could create a network of Dreamwalkers in the Dreamscape." She voices the idea Nikolai does not want to hear. "No one but Dreamwalkers could access it, and you could reach out to find others all over the world. Safely."

She points between Seth and Nikolai, and Seth nods quickly.

Nikolai's stomach sinks; he holds on to Seth more tightly, seeking his anchor. Seth's excitement doesn't reassure him.

"You crossed through the Dreamscape to get here," Seth builds on the thought. "We saw your friend there. This could link the worlds. We could talk to Dreamwalkers from—"

"It will endanger us," Alia snaps. "It will expose us to rifts and holes, and allow more Shadows through."

"She's right." Nikolai is barely able to get the words out.

"Or we could patch those holes," Seth counters. His hand is warm around Nikolai's, squeezing reassuringly. "If we work together. What if that's what we've been doing wrong all along? What if the solution is to fix the entry into our world from the other side, but because we avoid going into the Dreamscape, we haven't been able to see that?"

"It's dangerous." Nikolai regrets eating so much, his stomach roiling with nerves.

"It is," Seth agrees, "but you wouldn't be doing it alone. We'd have an entire network of Dreamwalkers and their Empaths to anchor them. You and I bring a bit of the Dreamscape here when we scare off the Shadows. Maybe we need to do that on a global scale."

Nikolai glances at Nikita, who's smiling like the sun. "Or a multi-global scale," Nikolai echoes. "It's a terrible idea, but it just might work." He exhales, trying to breathe out the anxiety and inhale the confidence and security that Seth exudes. "I don't like it," he says, because someone has to be the voice of reason. "But I'm in."

"We don't need to heal the split," Nikita says, clapping her hands together. "We only need to heal the breaches into our worlds."

Alia stands stiffly, lips pursed, but she remains silent. When Val tugs, Alia follows her into the living room; their departure releases the tension that holds their group in the entryway.

Seth tucks his hand into Nikolai's and together they go to the dessert table and fill a plate to share. It looks delicious. Nikolai hopes his stomach will settle enough for him to enjoy it. They end up back in the dining room, and conversation slips into more mundane topics. Alaric growls loudly to punctuate a story, something about a bear and football, and Mac leans in with her hand on his shoulder. Seth bumps against Nikolai's hip, the two of them sharing a single chair again, while Nikita perches on Heather's knees on the next chair.

Nikita glances at Nikolai, smiles, and whispers "Dreamwalkers unite" as she offers her pinky. She wiggles it, and Nikolai carefully links his own pinky with hers. Nikita beams.

He's going to miss them, he realizes with a sudden, aching certainty. These strangers from another world will go home, and someone else will become his neighbor in Havenhill, and he will actually miss them.

"Do you think the network could reach between our worlds?" Nikolai whispers, leaning his elbows on the table as he tilts toward Nikita.

She leans closer to him. "I'm positive it can," she whispers back. "We lived each other's Dreams, right? We reached across worlds to find each other. We can't be the only ones who can do that, and if we encourage everyone to meet in the middle, it should be easier. Like Del in her forest."

They'll be able to meet up again, then, after Nikita is gone. After everything's done and everyone's safe and they're each where they belong in separated worlds. At the least, he and Nikita can see each other. They aren't siblings, but they are tied together, and Nikolai wants to continue their friendship.

This is the good in the Dreamwalker network. When the split is healed, the Dreamscape will be a safe space. Nikolai pushes himself to see this as a good idea, not a terrible one that he is forced to accept.

The front door opens and closes with a *bang*, and Alaric stops mid-word to growl softly. He rises, hands on the table, stopping only at Mac's touch to his back. "If you say 'what is it, Lassie,' I swear I will…" Alaric's low grumble fades when Mac laughs.

"Corbin says that to you, right?" she asks, laughing harder when Alaric mutters under his breath.

"It smells like death swept in." Alaric pushes away from her touch and away from the table, stalking out of the dining room.

Everyone else rises and follows him. As much as Nikolai doesn't want to meet anything that smells like death, he goes as well.

Pawel stands in the entryway, combing his fingers through his hair, then slowly peeling off his jacket. He looks up as people converge on him, Alia and Val joining from the living room. His eyes are wide, pupils dilated.

"It's getting dark outside," he says, and Nikolai hears something else in his words.

Mattie makes a small noise, and Pawel looks away from her.

"Pawel," Heather says, too gently not to be using her empathy.

"You stink," Alaric says, nostrils flaring.

Mac inhales roughly, shaking her head. "I smell wet earth, like right after the rain."

"Decomposition," Alia corrects, moving past Pawel to the door. She has one hand on it when Pawel slides in next to her, holding it against her attempt to open it. "Pawel," she warns.

"I wouldn't." His voice is flat. "There was a face in the darkness."

"Shadow," Alaric says suddenly. "Not death. It smells like Shadows."

"We don't smell," Mattie says sharply. When Alaric looks at her, she crosses her arms, adding, "We do not stink." Her lips are pursed; she seems to be fighting a smile.

"Matter of opinion," Alaric rumbles. "It smells like the Berman house back home. That layer of thick, dark magic, like something died ages ago and is waiting to take us with it."

"I don't like the sound of this." Alia turns and, at her gesture, Val motions for those in the living room to join them. "Sakura. Val. We need to check the wards. We are within the first grove. The Shadows should not be able to reach us here."

"I'll check on the groves," Amaranth offers. "Josef, ride with me?"

Josef leverages himself up. "Always."

Nikolai feels a sharp strike of guilt. His brothers have been here all evening, and he has barely acknowledged them. "Come back after?" he asks. "To mine and Seth's place. We didn't get to spend any time together."

"I'll go with them and make sure everyone gets back safely," Mikhail offers. "If I drive, you two can focus on the grove."

The party breaks up quickly, and in the chaos, Nikita pulls Nikolai to one side, staying perfectly still and silent. They are within earshot when Pawel drags Mattie into the kitchen.

"What are you doing?" Pawel asks, voice low and dark. "Every time I mention—"

"I'm not doing anything," Mattie says, "and neither are you. But you're here, and that's enough. I need to go."

"Mattie—damn it!" Something breaks in the kitchen, and a moment later, there's a low murmur of voices as if Mac has appeared there as well.

"We'll get this cleaned up. Pawel, stop. You've already cut—"

"I'm fine. I don't need you to mother me."

"We're friends."

Nikolai isn't certain what he's overheard—it sounds as if Mattie thinks the Shadows are drawn to Pawel. He meets Nikita's gaze, and she smiles weakly. "Maybe it's him" she says softly. "Or maybe it's us. It wouldn't be the first time I've interacted with another Dreamwalker and that's brought the Shadows."

All the hope in Nikolai's heart drains out. "It's time to head home," he replies, because it's the only thing he can think to do right now. Walk home with Seth, back to solidity and walls and safety. Away from Nikita and back to a place where it's just them, exactly the way it's been for the last two years.

18

Nikolai is unsurprised when research confirms that the wards are weakest around the two Benford houses. He sits on the steps as people gather. Mikhail arrives with Josef and Amaranth in the Jeep. Sakura comes with two people Nikolai doesn't recognize in her little sedan. Val and Alia walk to the house, Alia in leonine form until she shifts to become her human self upon arrival.

"We'll do heavy ritual work around both houses today to shore up the wards," Val says. "There may be localized bursts of uncomfortable changes in the weather. We have enough people for the ritual work, so for anyone not participating, I'd recommend leaving. Things might get messy."

"Alaric's already gone," Nikolai says. He'd seen the hound lope into the woods, Mac trailing after him. "Seth's inside, but we can head out. I wanted to see my brothers."

They'd spent most of the evening together discussing the incursion of Shadows into Havenhill.

The theory behind shoring up the wards went over Nikolai's head, but the ritual work seemed valid given what little he knows; Josef had outlined their plans to redo the wards from the inside out, in widening arcs around this pair of houses. Nikolai will need to learn how to integrate his Talent with traditional ritual in the future. He's impressed by how much Josef and Mikhail have learned in their time here.

"Does your Mage plan on staying?" Val looks past Nikolai, her voice raised as a small smirk tilts her lips. "He seems like he'd be interested in seeing how the wards are constructed."

The door opens, and Pawel emerges with Seth close behind. "I am," Pawel says, "but I also don't want to be blamed if something goes wrong.

I don't know if my magic will blend well with yours, and I'm not familiar with your ritual construction. We've caused enough trouble already, and you need to be secure in your ability to protect your people. It's better if I get out of your hair."

Val nods, her smile widening and reaching her eyes. "Good thoughts. Is there anyone left inside?"

Pawel shakes his head. "Nik, Heather, and Carolyn left early this morning. Carolyn wants to explore how her Talent can interact with this world, and the others are going along to keep her company and out of trouble. Mattie's not around, and Mac and Alaric are planning on training. I was thinking I could take Seth and Nikolai out for a driving lesson in the Jeep, if Mikhail and Josef don't mind."

"Treat her well," Mikhail says.

Pawel puts a hand over his heart. "As if she were my own." He accepts the keys that Mikhail offers.

Nikolai lingers on the steps, moving one down when Seth nudges him. Seth stays on the top step and rests his hands atop Nikolai's shoulders, leaning in forehead to forehead. "Hey," Seth murmurs, and the world narrows to just the two of them.

Nikolai smiles, tilting his head to let Seth feel that smile against his own lips. "Hey," he murmurs back. "You ready for another driving lesson?"

"Yes," Seth answers, following quickly with, "and no. Pawel says he knows the area, but I'm wary of the wards."

Nikolai thinks about scanners, and how they have no idea how the humans track and hunt them. Between that and the weakened wards, his brain is screaming that he needs to stay safe. "Same," he murmurs, kissing Seth instead of saying more. Unfortunately, it's not as if they have a choice. They have to leave the house. Driving lessons are a good distraction, and they need them. It doesn't mean they have to rush, however. Nikolai takes comfort in Seth's closeness, lingering over the taste of his lips.

He pulls back when Pawel coughs loudly.

Pawel dangles Mikhail's keys, shaking his hand to rattle them. "Who's going first?" Pawel asks, and when Seth raises a hand, Pawel tosses him the keys.

Nikolai opens the back door of the Jeep, but Pawel stops him and points to the front. "Go ahead," Pawel says. "I can instruct as well from the back seat as from the front, and I don't think the old laws about having a licensed driver in the passenger seat apply here."

Seth buckles himself in and adjusts the seat and mirrors while Nikolai climbs in. By the time Nikolai's ready, the Jeep is rumbling and Seth has it in reverse, one foot on the clutch as he waits. Seth's tongue pokes out as he focuses on pressing down the gas carefully and easing up on the clutch. The Jeep lurches backwards but doesn't stall, and he manages to stop it before he backs into Sakura's sedan. He switches to first gear and slowly moves forward.

"Not bad," Nikolai says.

Seth darts a quick glare at him. "Laugh at me and I will laugh harder at you when it's your turn again."

Pawel leans his elbows on the seat between them, stretching the seatbelt that straps him into the middle of the back. "Mikhail gave me directions for a planned route, but I only caught about half of them. I've been to Haverhill a couple times and worked to become familiar with the area in case we needed to go back." He points at the dirt road ahead of them. "Keep going this way until we get to the main house, then turn onto the main approach. There are some side roads we can use to turn around and drive back, or we can drive into town."

"I'm good with going into town." Seth inches along cautiously, the Jeep rocking when he shifts from first gear into second, then again into third. It bumps over the uneven ground, moving faster than Nikolai feels comfortable with. Seth stomps on the brake when he realizes they're approaching the house far too rapidly; he stalls out before making the corner but gets started again quickly.

Seth drives slowly, his shoulders relaxing as the ride becomes smoother. The less he has to focus on shifting, the more tension drops from him. Nikolai spots the second grove on the way to town, then the third grove after they pass through the closest set of homes. The farther they go, the more land he sees, farms with freshly plowed fields lying between houses. He spots what he thinks is the fourth grove, or it might be the final one.

They must be close to the edges of town at this point. It's strange to think that the boundaries of Havenhill end, and they can keep going. There are no walls, no lights to keep the Shadows out.

Only magic.

Seth pulls over on the side of the road. The Jeep stops with only a small jerk and shudder; Seth manages to shut the car off before it stalls. He pulls the keys out and hands them across. "Ready?"

Nikolai closes his hand around the keys, tugging to pull Seth closer. He wants to kiss him, but he's aware of Pawel leaning over the seats, watching them.

Pawel clears his throat. "Maybe I shouldn't teach you two to drive. At the rate you're going, you'll soon be learning the joys of parking."

Nikolai frowns. "What?"

"Parking the car in a remote place so you can—" Pawel cuts off, closes his eyes, and shakes his head. "Never mind."

"We've had no lack of privacy for the last few years," Seth says. "But I do remember Mikhail taking his girlfriend out for a drive after Nikolai and I caught them making out in the family room when Mikhail was in high school." Seth shrugs, and Nikolai blinks because he hadn't thought anything of it at the time.

"We don't need to do that," Nikolai says. "We have a house." He takes the keys and slides out of his seat. Once he's swapped places with Seth and settled in the driver's seat, his nerves come back. He touches the wheel and remembers driving down that small highway toward Albany while Mikhail reassured him that everything would be fine. Except it wouldn't be. It couldn't be.

This time he sits on a long road with only a few houses dotting the landscape that stretches out ahead of him.

Maybe this way is safe.

"If you turn down that next road, it should take us back to Havenhill," Pawel says, leaning in to point off to the left through the front window.

"You think we're outside the wards?" Seth asks.

Pawel shakes his head. "I think we're still inside the outer grove, but not by much. Those are actively farmed fields." Pawel points to the fields, where it looks as if tall grass or hay has been cut down in the recent past. "I'd guess these are the wheat or oat fields. Some kind of grains, to make the breads we've eaten. They'd need a lot of space for those to grow, and they don't need to rely on magic to produce them. Grain and flour can be stored. It makes sense to grow them on the outskirts, where land is plentiful."

Nikolai turns down the road, which is narrow and made of stone instead of pavement. The Jeep rumbles along the rough surface, but he's pleased to make the turn without stalling. It's weird to shift, press the clutch, and turn all at once, but it's getting easier. He'll get the hang of it eventually.

The sun goes behind a cloud, and shadows stretch across the field, mixing with narrow streaks of light where the sun tries to shine through. Pawel sits back, gaze drifting to the fields instead of the road ahead.

Seth's hand covers Nikolai's on the gear shift. "Keep going straight," he says, and Nikolai nods.

The field ends, giving way to forest. Nikolai looks for lemon trees but doesn't see any.

Pawel moves quickly in the back seat, turning to look from one side to the other.

"What?" Seth asks.

"I thought I saw something moving," Pawel says.

"In the shadows?"

Pawel hesitates, and Nikolai's fingers tighten on the steering wheel.

"Between the trees," Pawel responds, and he doesn't mention shadows again.

Nikolai slows the car, and Pawel leans forward again. There's a sharp sting in Nikolai's shoulder when Pawel's fingers brush against him, and Pawel quickly leans away. "Sorry," Pawel says. "My magic's just under my skin."

"You remember what we said about using Talent and calling Shadows, right?" Seth's words sting more sharply than Pawel's magic. "I can feel your anxiety. You need to calm down."

"Want me to stop?" Nikolai asks.

"Turn left when you see a road," Pawel says, his voice tight. "That'll circle us back toward the center of the groves."

Nikolai spots a driveway heading off to the right, up a hill with a house sitting at the top. It's dark despite the cloudy day, and it doesn't feel inviting. There are no marks here, no sign that people have passed through or that people might live here. There are only houses, distant from each other, with trees crowded in around.

Nikolai passes three driveways before Seth touches his hand then points. "There, that break is a road, I think."

"Shit," Pawel whispers, and the world flickers dark around them. Then sun breaks through, and Pawel grabs Nikolai's shoulder, squeezing hard and sending sparks prickling through him. "We're definitely outside the wards. Turn around."

"Nik." Anxiety is thick in the air around them. Seth's fear rises until it could choke Nikolai, as if he didn't already have enough of his own.

There are Shadows here. So many Shadows, bearing down on them, racing as if flying low along the ground, running toward the Jeep.

One swarms up to the windshield, presses its face against the glass, and shrieks, "Go back!"

"Oh my God." Pawel scrambles backwards, half standing in the back seat. "Turn around, Nikolai. Turn around now."

Turn around.

Turn the car on this narrow road, with Seth's fear choking him and Pawel clutching at his chest in the back seat.

Nikolai swings the wheel, twists the car to the left, and feels one tire drop lower than the other, into a small ditch on the side of the road. He shoves his left foot down, hoping the Jeep is solid enough and that he doesn't put the clutch through the floor. He slams the gear shift into reverse. He shoves his right foot down, the engine revving rough with both the clutch and gas pedals down. He pulls his foot off the clutch, and the Jeep leaps backwards. He twists the wheel again, popping out of the ditch. The Jeep rolls into another ditch and stalls when he slams on the brakes, barely shy of a tree.

His heart hammers in his chest. That same Shadow—he has no idea how he can recognize it as different from any of the others—is behind them, face pressed against the rear window.

"Go!" it shrieks, the word echoing inside his heart as much as in his ears.

Nikolai puts the Jeep in first gear, twists the key, and revs the engine hard. It leaps forward, bumping down the road. He has no care for shifting kindly; he pushes the Jeep as hard as he can to get into second gear, then third. The Jeep's rumbling finally evens out when he reaches fourth gear, the engine whining low.

Pawel slumps on the seat and turns around, staring behind them.

Nikolai glances in the rearview mirror.

The Shadows are following.

"We're inside the grove," Pawel mumbles. "We're inside the outer wards. I felt them snap back around us, and the Shadows are still following us."

Following them. Fuck, one is clinging to the back of the car, shifting in and out of view as Nikolai struggles to drive the Jeep in a straight line along the road at this speed.

"One is holding on," Nikolai yells.

"Yes," Pawel says. "Yes, she is. God, Rory was right. They're people. Just like Mattie said. They're real people, *were* real people before they Emerged. They have faces. Names. They were people once, and it's her. It's Chelsea."

"Pawel," the Shadow whispers, a soft hiss in the air around them. "Run."

Seth's anxiety eases, forced calm suffusing the atmosphere. Seth sets his hand on top of Nikolai's, covering it. A low exhale pushes through Nikolai's body, rushing out of his lungs. Tears leak from the corners of his eyes. His body shakes.

"Run, fast," the Shadow whispers. "Run from the Shadows." She clings resolutely to the Jeep, and Nikolai thinks that he could get rid of her if he could stop driving long enough to bring the light of Dreams out.

But if he stops, the Shadows will catch them.

"What do I do?" he asks, taking a corner far too quickly, the Jeep's tires squealing.

"I think she's trying to help us," Pawel says. "Chelsea says run, so we run, and we hope that when we reach the strongest ward at the first grove, the rest of them can't follow."

Nikolai's chest aches, a sharp metallic tang at the back of his throat, his lungs ready to burst, desperate for a full breath. They race through town, and he's thankful not to see anyone outside.

When he spots the road that turns toward the big house, he slams on the pedals. The Jeep gutters but doesn't stall as he pushes both brake and clutch down hard enough that it hurts. Seth's hand is over his, both of them clutching the gear shift; Seth's touch is a tiny island of calm in the panic that has Nikolai's heart hammering in his chest.

"Go," Seth says, and Nikolai jams his foot down on the gas, letting go of the clutch so fast that the Jeep lurches forward, shaking and almost stalling again. It makes horrifying noises as he shifts through second and third and finally lets it stay in fourth even though he's pretty sure he's going too fast down the twisting road.

In the back seat, Pawel makes a strangled sound.

Seth twists in his seat to look back.

Nikolai risks a glance in the rearview mirror.

The Shadow clings to the back of the car, fingers pressed against the seams of the window. Its mouth moves in a whisper Nikolai can't hear, but he swears it has an expression. Pleading. The other Shadows are in the distance, the car moving faster than they can flow. Pawel's expression twists in pain, one hand pressed to his temple.

"What happened?"

"I felt us crash through the wards," Pawel bites out. "I think with Chelsea—I think we broke something, bringing her through. I felt it." The words are tight, forced out. When he exhales, his entire body shudders.

He opens his window a crack, and the Shadow flows in and wraps itself around Pawel. It looks almost human, with soft features and long hair, one hand pressed over Pawel's heart.

Nikolai has to watch where he's going. He can't watch them. His fingers are white with his tight grip on the steering wheel, his eyes aching from staring forward. "Pawel. Are you safe?"

A short, tight laugh. "As safe as I'm going to be right now, I think."

"I came through for you," the Shadow hisses.

"Chelsea."

"Yessss..."

Not it. *She*. And she has a name.

Nikolai doesn't know what to do with that realization. All he can do is drive. He can't look at the animals running alongside the road, in the trees. He can't think about how there are Shadows here, within the wards, and it's Nikolai's fault.

Nikolai brought Shadows into Havenhill.

The tires skid on gravel, and he slams on the brakes. He keeps the Jeep from sliding off the road, but it stalls, and when Nikolai twists the key, the starter fires but doesn't turn over.

In the back seat, Chelsea whispers.

Pawel gasps for breath.

Seth's half out of his seat, twisting to look at Pawel. "Turn the Jeep off," he says. "Turn the key off and take it out."

The crowd of Shadows is still chasing them, getting closer now that they've stopped.

Nikolai's fingers shake, but he does what Seth says, the keys banging against his palm as soon as he has them free.

"One foot on the clutch, one on the brake. Put the Jeep in in first," Seth says, his voice careful and low, a calming counterpoint to the panicked inhalations from Pawel. Nikolai follows directions as quickly and precisely as he can. "Put the key in and try again."

The starter kicks over this time, and Nikolai doesn't wait to see if it's steady. He jams the gas pedal down, forcing the Jeep forward as quickly as possible. The rear end fishtails as he takes the next curve, then the Jeep roars down the road, outpacing the Shadows once again.

Except for the one in the back seat, clinging to Pawel as if he's her lifeline.

"Will she hurt you?" Nikolai asks.

"No," the Shadow replies. "I would never."

"I've got him," Seth says. "You drive."

Seth reaches across the space between the front and back, lays a hand on Pawel's shoulder, and shudders. Nikolai reaches blindly for him, but Seth knocks his hand away. "You drive, Nik. Damn you, Shadow, let me do this," Seth mutters. "Pawel. I need you to breathe."

The steering wheel shakes beneath Nikolai's hands. He grips tightly to keep the Jeep going forward when it wants to slide or stall. A truck pulls in behind him, between the Jeep and the Shadows. Nikolai slows down enough to make the final turn toward the big house. They are inside the first grove. The Shadows should be gone. But Chelsea is still in the back seat, as if the wards have been thrown wide and granted her entrance.

Something on the floor crackles. Nikolai hears his name, but he doesn't know how to respond. He forges ahead until he sees the Benford house with Sakura's sedan parked out front. The Jeep squeals when he pushes hard on the brakes, stalling in place. Pawel pushes the back door open and spills out like a baby deer finding footing for the first time.

"What have you done?" Alia roars. Nikolai hears the lion in her voice. He's stuck in his seat, his fingers tight around the steering wheel, uncertain if he should get out or drive away again.

The truck pulls in behind him, blocking any way out. Jefferson and three people Nikolai doesn't recognize climb down as soon as it's stopped.

"We need to push them back!" Val calls out, rallying the newcomers and Sakura to her side. Ethan and Marybelle run up, Ethan standing beside Val as she leans back against him.

"Nikolai," Seth says, and he doesn't need to say more than that. Now that they're stopped, now that they're still, Nikolai knows what he needs to do. He reaches across to grip Seth tightly and closes his eyes. The Dreamscape is there, just out of reach; Nikolai dives into it, permitting it to swallow him. When he surfaces, guided by Seth's hand on his, he brings the light with him, and it bursts outward like a thousand sparkling diamonds in the air.

The Shadows scream and stop before the wall of bright light. Even with his eyes closed, Nikolai can see that brightness and feel the Shadows beyond. He can feel the Dreamscape calling to him, begging him to fall in or become consumed by it. Doing so would bring safety, and the Shadows would be gone.

"That's good, that helps!" Ethan yells.

"We need to rebuild the ward now, thicker than it was before," Val calls out.

Nikolai has no idea what they are doing; he keeps his eyes pressed tightly closed. The Dreamscape washes over his skin. He sees things in a different way through the Dreamscape, but the Shadows roiling as they try to approach are a blot against the light. He doesn't dare open his eyes; if he does, reality and the Dream may come into contact with each other, and that would be catastrophic.

So he holds everything in place until he hears a shout and the Shadows are pushed back, out of range. Two engines roar, and doors slam before the sedan and truck peel out.

Calm washes over him, wrapping around him like a warm blanket.

"Come back," Seth murmurs.

Nikolai's eyes flicker open as the brightness fades. The clearing in front of the house is filled with dust that slowly drifts away. The Jeep is the only car left, and Alia stands with Pawel and Mattie outside the still-open back door.

All other Shadows are gone, including Chelsea.

Seth squeezes Nikolai's hand, then lets go so he can open his door and carefully climb out. Nikolai gets out as well, his legs shaky; he wobbles, clinging to the door, until he feels strong enough to join Seth on the other side.

Alia's eyes are bright, her breathing rough.

Nikolai is surprised that she's silent.

"It was a mistake," Pawel says quietly, and Alia roars—entirely animal and inhuman—in response.

Nikolai takes a step back, the Jeep solid against his back.

"The ward's closed," Mattie says, shrugging. "The Shadows are gone."

"We have to fix the other wards," Alia snaps. "All of them. Every single grove was broken through, every single ward laid open to bring Shadows into Havenhill. Why did you do that? How did you do that?"

"It was an accident," Pawel repeats.

Nikolai takes a cautious step forward, one hand out; Alia's sharp gaze snaps to pierce him through, and he stops mid-step. He swallows with a throat far too dry to say another word.

"Why did you lead them back here?" she asks.

Nikolai swallows again, licking his lips. "I didn't know where else to go," he says hoarsely. "It happened so fast. We were driving. Practicing, out on the roads by the farmlands, where Mikhail had told Pawel to take us. We must have gone outside the outer wards."

"We did that the other day, and it was fine," Seth adds quickly, stepping up to press against Nikolai's side, entwining their hands. "There wasn't any reason to think today would be different. Mikhail said we were safe here."

"Do you think I'll blame Mikhail?" Alia asks.

Nikolai shakes her head.

"You'll blame me," Pawel mutters. "Me, and my excessive magical Talent. The fact that I come from another world. I think you'll blame me for calling them here."

"Would I be right?"

Pawel looks her in the eye. "I don't know. And I don't know if there is any way to tell for sure. But Chelsea is a Shadow, and she found me, so it is a possibility."

Mattie smiles slightly.

"You brought it back here," Alia snaps. When she steps closer, her hands have claws, her teeth are sharp, and Nikolai wishes there were someplace else he could go.

"Her," Pawel counters. "The Shadows are people who have Emerged."

"I wanted to be someplace safe," Nikolai blurts out, capturing Alia's attention again. "Havenhill is safe, and I knew you had wards, and each time, I thought—if we could get through the next ward, they wouldn't be able to follow us. But they kept coming. No matter how many wards—no matter how close we came to the center of Havenhill—they *just kept coming.*"

"So you broke the wards and brought Shadows within our borders," Alia says, lip curled in a snarl.

Nikolai can't deny it. He drops his gaze, closing his eyes. He feels her gaze still upon him. "Yes."

"Go inside," Alia says, pointing at the house. "All of you, go inside. Do not leave. Your friends will be here soon, and we will discuss this after the wards have been reset and Havenhill is safe again."

There is a part of Nikolai that wants to talk to Pawel about what happened—*how* it happened—but Seth steers him down the hall and into a small bathroom, closing the door behind them. Seth grabs a towel and wets it, then presses it to Nikolai's face. It is blessedly cold.

Nikolai hadn't even realized the headache was blooming until Seth tried to help. "Fuck," Nikolai mutters, sinking to sit on the closed toilet. Seth's fingers are warm against the nape of his neck.

"Figured that would happen," Seth murmurs. "You pushed too hard. Too much, too soon, too fast. Let me help."

Nikolai turns sideways and leans against the wall, his head tilting back to keep the cloth in place over his eyes. Seth's hands frame his face, warm and comforting as calm seeps into him.

Ease.

Care.

Love.

The tension slowly seeps from Nikolai's shoulders, and he lets them fall; they'd crept up around his ears. He exhales softly and reaches up, tugging Seth close until their lips meet.

"I love you," he murmurs.

"You love how well I know you," Seth teases.

"That too." Nikolai can admit that. He sits upright, the cloth falling from his face. He catches it and lays it carefully on the side of the sink. The light is too bright, but the headache has faded into the background before it could fully take hold. It'll be back, but for the moment, he's all right. "We should go back out. I think—" He hesitates. "I think Alia is lumping us in with the others. She's right to be angry. I was the one driving the car. I could've headed away from Havenhill."

"And we'd be dead, sucked dry by the Shadows," Seth says. He steps back and gives Nikolai space to rise and wash his face. "You did the right thing. We needed a safe place to mount the defense, and this is the only safe place we knew. We couldn't fight out in the open, not with that many of them swarming us that fast. We had no reason to think the wards would fail. The Shadows shouldn't have been able to follow us."

Nikolai knows this is true, but Alia's also right. He shouldn't have brought them into Havenhill. He willingly broke the wards.

When they reach the living room, the others are already there. Alaric is a hound, his paw over his nose as he lies on the floor at Mac's feet while she sits on the couch. Carolyn has her cards in her hands, shuffling through them. Nikita and Heather are curled together in one chair. Mattie is nearly invisible in the corner, half blended with the shadows. Pawel paces back and forth, muttering to himself, threading his fingers through his hair until the strands stand up.

Pawel stops and turns as Nikolai and Seth enter. He rubs one hand against the scruff of his beard. "You saw her," he says quickly. "You heard her."

"They heard her," Mattie replies before Nikolai can. "*You* heard her. That's all that matters."

The front door opens, and Alaric looks up, tail thumping against the floor. Pawel goes completely still when Alia stalks into the living room, Val close behind. Val's skin is pale and gray, her hair teased out of the ponytail that had held it when she left, strands frayed and scattered around her face.

"The wards at the first and second grove are solid again," Val says. "Sakura is leading the initiative to repair the remaining wards, and they will hopefully be fixed by tonight. We can't afford to lose any of Havenhill."

"I'm sorry," Nikolai says.

Alia ignores him, her attention entirely on Pawel. "You will leave," she says flatly. "I have never refused sanctuary to anyone before, but I have never met a group such as yourselves. You flout all caution. You brought Shadows into Havenhill. You put my people at risk, and you cannot stay here."

"They don't have anywhere to go," Nikolai says. Everything in his own life has been turned upside down since Nikita and her friends arrived, but if Alia sends them out into this world, they'll die. They don't understand life after the Split.

"Then you go home." Alia's gaze darkens, and she exchanges a look with Val. "Our Mages will work with you to make sure you don't destroy our wards when you go. But whatever it takes, you go home. I can't have you in Havenhill. I don't know why you came here, and I don't trust that you can safely return home, but it has to happen. And it will happen as soon as possible, because you being here puts my people in danger. By tomorrow at the latest, you will go."

As told by Victor (last name unknown).

That night I dreamed.

I went to bed in our room with Marilyn by my side. I woke in the Dreamscape.

I felt her still, though she wasn't with me in the Dream. I could feel her arms around me, the way she kept me safe and solid and tethered to reality. I couldn't go too far, and I wouldn't be lost, as long as she held me.

So I walked through the Dreamscape.

They say we can't see the forest for the trees, and in our Dreams, it feels as if the trees have become so overgrown that they've blocked the view of the forest entirely. The path had narrowed since the last time I was there, the darkness around the path's edges deepening. Since the Split, the Dreamscape grows darker each time I find myself there; I think the Shadows might encroach within that darkness. I know that the path is safe, but the spaces between drift barely out of reach and dangerously close.

I followed the path, its familiar tread under my feet until I came to a point where the roads diverged. One path was my usual way, a wider trail with enough light to drive the Shadows away. The other was a smaller pathway that looped back, mirroring the way I'd just traveled.

I rolled over in my sleep, wrapping my arm around Marilyn's waist and burying my face at her throat to inhale her scent. She murmured something, and calm washed over me as I took my first step upon the untrod path.

I expected the path to open from its narrow start. Perhaps it would merge with another way and become more stable. I thought that it would be suitable to lead me to another Dreamwalker. But it remained small and narrow, thick with dirt and lacking in footprints. Abandoned.

I could see my own path in the distance, beyond the shadows, a faint light in the darkness.

But this path beneath my feet resonated with me as well. Whatever else it might be, it was somehow also mine.

It finally opened into a small space with heavy trees leaning over me. The canopy shaded the clearing, leaving it full of dappled shadows and faint inklings of light.

A boy, perhaps 8 or 9 years old, played at the center. He knelt in the dirt, pushing a stick through it to draw lines. There was a truck by his knee and a wooden horse by his hand.

He didn't notice my arrival, and I didn't want to startle him. I coughed quietly. He fell back on his heels, coming to his feet as he shifted and changed, until a teenager stood before me with a face as familiar as my own.

"Luke," I said, and he smiled, swift and bright, his teeth still cast in the braces we both had back then.

"Victor." He wrapped his arms around me, pulled me in, and clapped his hand on my shoulders. "I've been trying to find you. I knew you had to be here, and that, if the paths converged, someday you might find mine."

He was solid in my arms, sixteen again and as real as anything in the Dreamscape could be.

I hadn't seen my twin in a decade, not since he was consumed by darkness in our room one night. Not since I watched the Shadows sweep in to make him one of them, and when darkness finally receded, he was gone.

He was one of the first to disappear after the Split.

I had no idea—

"How are you here?" I pushed at his shoulders, and he stepped back and gave me space, turning from me as the tiny clearing became a living room: two low, ratty chairs and an old television crackling with the sound of a video game.

He sank into the chair on the left, leaving the other for me as he always had. "How's Marilyn?" he asked, picking up a remote and tossing it onto the empty chair, then motioning for me to sit.

"We have kids."

He looked at me then, his brow furrowed as if the statement made no sense to him. He gestured again, so I picked up the remote and sank into the chair. It fit like a glove, like it had molded to my shape, and when I looked at my hands, I had no ring and no lines. I was a teen again as well.

We played games—ones I hadn't touched in years. I had no video games now. I could barely remember this life from before the Split, and he lived it with me in the Dream as if it happened only yesterday. He told me a story about Tommy down the street, something I remembered vaguely from the week before we lost him.

"Have you been here ever since you—?" I didn't know how to put it, and he went silent. He stared at me, waiting for me to finish, his head tilted and brow furrowed. I tried again. "Have you been here since you disappeared out of our room?"

"How could I disappear?" he asked. "I haven't disappeared if I've been here all along."

He set the remote down, and music played on in the background. He leaned toward me, and behind him darkness loomed, thick and deep. "Be careful, Victor," he whispered. "Don't fall into the split."

Marilyn cried out, and the sound yanked me from the Dream. I woke into a room that was too cold and too dark, the chill deep in my bones. I rolled over to turn on the light, and it burst into being as my door slammed open. Allison rushed in, climbing into bed with us.

"I heard Mom scream," she said, burrowing between the two of us. She made space, and Marilyn pulled Jacob from his bassinet, bringing him into the bed with us as well.

Marilyn met my gaze above Allison's head. She mouthed words to me, and I didn't need to hear her to know that she asked, "Are you all right?"

I touched Marilyn's head, running my thumb along her cheek as I nodded. "We're all fine," I assured Allison. I opened my arms, and they all came closer. We huddled, in the bed, in the too-cold room. I didn't reach for the light, and no one asked me to turn it off.

"It was only a nightmare," I said.

"Bad dreams can't hurt you," Allison echoed the words I had given to her often over the last few years. I wondered if this was a warning for her. If we needed to find her Empath so she wouldn't be swallowed by Dreams.

Or maybe I truly met Luke in the Dreamscape, and the Shadows stole him away when we were sixteen.

I didn't know what to think anymore.

Into the Dream

19

NIKOLAI SITS BENEATH a lemon tree, his eyes closed as he focuses on breathing soft and slow. The ground is hard and cold, the trunk narrow and rough against his back. The sharp scent of citrus in the crisp spring air is a comfort. This is the first grove. It's warded. It's stable. It should be safe.

No thanks to him.

"Nikita, he wants—" Seth's voice cuts off.

Nikolai opens his eyes, exhaling at the intrusion.

Nikita barges between two trees and drops into a crouch in front of Nikolai. "I know, but this is important. I need to talk to both of you about coming back to our world with us."

Nikolai meets Seth's gaze. Seth sinks to kneel next to Nikolai, his hand stealing over Nikolai's to hold on to it. His lips are pressed thin, and he shakes his head. "You know what I think," Seth mutters. "It's a bad idea."

"I swear I will get you home after." Nikita switches from crouching to kneeling, inching closer to Nikolai. "We're twinned. Our worlds are twinned. I think the only way we can heal the split is by working together. And maybe there are other twinned people who'd be able to help us. Look at Alia! But Alia won't come with us, and besides, Mattie says she's 'bedrock' so if she leaves it'll make things worse. But you and me—when we're together, we're representative of our twinned worlds. We can make a difference."

"We need to stay here," Seth says firmly. "Someone has to be here to help create the network of Dreamwalkers."

"There are other Dreamwalkers in Havenhill," Nikita counters. "If you come with us, you could help us bridge between the two worlds." She's so close to Nikolai that he can feel every huff of her breath as she speaks. "In the Dreamscape, the way into my world and the way into your world are different. They're close together, and I think Del can find them both. But won't it be easier to stay together now than to try to find each other again after we go? You'll have a link back here and can be our liaison. We must be able to—"

"It's dangerous." Nikolai pushes the words out, interrupting her. He looks up at her, blinking. She does look like him, if the mirror were slightly cracked and off-center. "Not only physically dangerous. It could change our lives forever. We might never get back. Our family's here. This is our home."

She leans back, sitting on her heels, and a small smile lifts one corner of her mouth. "But you see why I'm asking you to come."

His heart aches, a physical twist in his chest. He nods once. "Yeah. I think I do." He can see it, even if he doesn't understand it. "If I go with you, we will be the only Dreamwalkers who know how to go from one world to another. Dreamwalkers in both worlds can reach the same Dreamscape. We can meet with them there, and we can work together to figure out how to heal the split. And…" There is one important thing that he and Seth understand that Nikita still doesn't get. "You need Seth and me to show your world the importance of bonding Dreamwalkers and Empaths."

Nikita worries at her lower lip. "Do you think us lacking that is why the split started spilling into my world?" she asks.

Nikolai shakes his head. "Probably not only that. Your Emergence and the Split sound like they happened at the same time. Your Dreamwalkers have never been bound properly, so the Split would have happened earlier if that was the reason. And our world is in worse shape—we have more Shadows. There must have been something more in both worlds."

He has no idea what that "something more" was, but they need to find out.

"So it's settled." Nikita leans forward and gives him a quick hug before bouncing to her feet. "I need to talk to everyone, and we need to figure out exactly how this is going to work."

"Since you don't know how you got here in the first place?" Seth says dryly.

Nikita makes a face but doesn't deny it. "Be at our house tomorrow morning," she says. "We're going then." She runs off, not waiting for him to reply.

"It's not like Alia left them any choice," Seth says.

Nikolai kisses the top of Seth's head. "Did you feel like she was talking to us, too, when she ordered them to leave?" Tension steals into Seth's body, leaving him tilted stiffly against Nikolai's shoulder. Nikolai touches his face, sliding a thumb along his cheek. "It's not only that Nikita wants us to go with her, nor is she only considering how we can help her. All of this is my fault. I brought a Shadow through the wards." Breath shudders in his chest. Heat makes his eyes ache. "I don't want to go, Seth. I don't want to leave my brothers—they're all the family we have left. I want to stay here, safe. I want to live in our own house and have a chance at a peaceful life together. But I'm the one who made it unsa—" He cuts off.

Since Nikita arrived, it feels as if they've been heading for this moment.

Nikolai wonders if he ever had a choice.

"Mikhail and Josef could come with us." Seth's tone is doubtful.

His brothers have connections with the community in Havenhill. They won't leave. But Nikolai and Seth haven't put down roots yet. If they follow the newcomers, they will hardly be missed.

"We need to find them. Talk to them before we go." If they go. Nikolai heard the rumble of the Jeep leaving not long ago. He's impressed it still runs; he felt as if he stripped the gears trying to get home, and the way the engine roared hadn't filled him with confidence. But the Jeep had rumbled to life when it was started, and the sound faded when it left. Nikolai assumes both his brothers were in it at the time.

Hands clasped, he and Seth walk to the main Benford house. It's funny how, in the last week, no one's stopped calling the two houses by the name of the family that disappeared. Now that they won't be staying, that will never change.

Nikolai wonders if they'll maintain the smaller house for him and Seth, for when they return.

He wonders if Alia will let them return.

He exhales in a soft rush, and Seth stops before they head up the steps.

"Are you sure?"

About leaving? No, but probably yes. "Going into the house won't make us disappear," Nikolai replies. "Let's see if anyone knows where my brothers went."

The door opens before they get there, Ethan pushing through with a radio in his hand. It crackles as Marybelle's sweet, high voice comes through. "…at the house. Now. Aunt Val is in a mood."

"Yeah, I saw." Ethan stops, one hand pushing his hair back, the other holding the radio before his face as he looks at Nikolai and Seth. "Did you say someone was looking for Nikolai?"

"Mikhail's here. They drove over to talk with Alia."

Ethan nods. "Okay." He touches something on the side of the radio and the crackling stops. He slides it into a pocket of his light jacket, then crosses his arms. "You up for a trip to the main house? Apparently Mom and Alia are holding court."

"Depends. Are they going to yell at us again?" Seth edges closer to Nikolai.

Ethan winces. "Maybe. They're worried as much as angry. Any one of us would've done the same thing if we were chased by Shadows. In fact, it's happened, and the wards held. No one's ever carried a Shadow through the wards before."

Maybe it was because Pawel was in the car and the Shadow knew him, or maybe it was because of Nikolai and Seth. Nikolai has no idea. Neither does Alia, which is why everyone's so pissed off about it. And scared.

"We should talk to her about what'll happen when we come back," Seth murmurs.

"We'll go with you." Nikolai makes room for Ethan to descend.

The path they follow is familiar, winding through the trees on a path parallel to the main road to the big house. Nikolai spots the Jeep parked outside when they arrive, near Jefferson's truck and Sakura's sedan.

Everyone's here.

This is going to be great.

Marybelle meets them at the entrance and leads them to a large open room with tables around the edges and scattered chairs. "We have meetings here, and dances, and all our holidays," she explains.

It's perfect for celebrations, but the air feels sober and heavy now. Val sits in a large, comfortable chair near a table at the other end of the room, her feet bare and drawn up, tucked in next to one hip. She tilts to one side, eyes closed and head pillowed against the back of the chair. Alia's hand rests on her head, fingers idly combing through her hair.

Alia has claimed one end of the table, and others are scattered around it, chairs angled to face her. There's food out—a heavy loaf of bread, already cut, with meats and cheeses and jams, a bowl of nuts with a nutcracker nearby.

Nikolai's stomach rumbles, and Alia stops speaking.

She presses her lips together in a thin line and motions for them to approach.

Nikolai wonders if this is how peasants felt approaching a king, begging for a breadcrumb. Alia's been reserved since they arrived, but she had been welcoming. Until now.

Ethan pulls out a chair and drops into a seat next to Sakura. "Pawel's working on a ritual. Alaric's whining but he won't leave the house because he's afraid of being left behind. Carolyn's drawing something. Heather's trying to keep everyone calm, and so's Mac. I don't know where Mattie is." He slides a glance at his mother. "Pawel promises she'll leave with them."

"What about that other Shadow that clung to him?" Alia asks stiffly.

"She's gone." Ethan's words have a sense of finality to them, and Nikolai wonders how Pawel feels about that. He knew her, after all. He knew that Shadow, somehow.

Mikhail nudges a chair out with his foot, and Nikolai leans on the back of it without sitting. Seth presses in close, and they create a united front, awkwardly shifting from foot to foot.

"We're going with them," Nikolai says. He looks straight at Alia, waiting for her to look at him. When Nikolai had said they had no place to go, Alia had replied that they could leave. She'd implied that he and Seth were a part of the group, and he supposes that, in her eyes, they are. She turns now, her gaze calm and her jaw set as Nikolai continues speaking. "Seth and I will go with them to their world, and we will work with a

Dreamwalker network that you'll set up here, and with your Technopaths. We will find a way to stop the Shadows from spilling through the cracks. We'll find a way to seal this world—our home—off from the split, and then we'll come back. And we hope, when we get back, there will be a place for us in Havenhill." His throat is dry, his lungs empty as he blurts everything out in one breath, rushing so no one interrupts him and so he doesn't lose his nerve. He rocks to one side when Amaranth stands and throws her arms around them both, pulling them in for a rough hug.

"Of course you're coming back," she says. She lets go long enough to reach for Josef, pulling him with her into the hug. "We're here."

Mikhail joins the group hug.

But Alia has yet to answer.

They draw apart, and Josef sinks back into a chair, the corners of his mouth white with pain. Nikolai wonders how much he strained himself while they were rushing to fix the wards.

"Amerika and Shamir are working on the Technopath network," Val says, her voice rough and husky. Her eyes don't open when she speaks; Alia's fingers go still on her head. "It will be valuable for many reasons, but most importantly, we need to know if the Shadows are coming here. And we need to let others know what has happened, see if we can pool our resources and understand why those Shadows were able to break through. It might be because of the visitors from another world, or it might be because of the rise in the number of Talent here. Our wards might not be strong enough to hide us anymore. We don't know, and the Technopaths can help us learn."

"And the Dreamwalkers?" Seth asks.

Val huffs slightly. "Harder, but we'll find a way. It will take time. We need to be cautious, and we don't want to create more breaks in our wards. Talk to Ethan about that thing you two do together to scare off the Shadows. Our Dreamwalkers need to know how to do that."

"Shadows can't exist where there's that much light," Nikolai says. "I bring a bright part of the Dreamscape here, and Seth…" He glances over; he isn't sure how to explain how they amplify the light. "He keeps me from losing control at the exact moment when I let myself lose control." It's hard to explain that joy of reaching into the Dreamscape and pulling it out, letting it slip into reality but knowing that it won't become real, that it won't break the walls down. He can create Dreams in the midst of reality. "It feels awful after. If I didn't have Seth, I'd go into the Dreamscape or bring it here. Or my head would explode. We don't do it lightly."

Seth huffs. "'Lightly,'" he mutters. "It's all light, Nikolai."

"You should explain it to our Dreamwalkers," Ethan says. "Anya already agreed to reach out to other Dreamwalkers, if she can. She and Damon know it won't be easy, but they're a stable bonded pair, like you two. They can learn to do your light trick, too."

"We'll need that network to get back, I think," Seth says. "We want to make sure we can return safely, without breaking anything between here and there—"

"You think you will make things worse when you leave?" Alia asks, half-way to standing, both hands on the table.

Seth looks at her, licks his lips, and pushes his glasses up his nose. "What Nikita and her friends are about to do requires a great deal of raw power, and by having us help, we might be able to provide some finesse. We know more about working with Dreams than they do, but it's still risky. Sending all of them home will cause some damage. But if we create a network on both sides, we should be able to move back and forth more easily. You could wait to send them back until the network is established..."

The gears are almost visible as they turn in Alia's mind, as her thoughts twists through the options. The risk of the Shadows already threatening around them versus the possibility that the transfer could be smoother and not create new risks. She shakes her head.

"They go now," she says firmly.

Val reaches out blindly, pats Alia's side and then her hip.

Alia looks to Val and her expression softens. She reaches out to touch her hair again and slowly sits. "You'll be welcome back," she says, not looking at them. "Your home will be waiting for you if you can return."

Not when. If.

"We'll teach your Dreamwalkers what we can tonight, before we go," Nikolai says. "And we'll fix this. We'll do everything we can to make sure Havenhill stays safe."

20

NIKOLAI KNOWS THIS is a Dream.

He remembers falling asleep with Seth beside him. They were tangled, warm under multiple layers of blankets despite their lack of clothes. Nikolai had curled behind Seth, letting their ankles cross as he held him, resting his hand against Seth's heart. The solid *thump-thump* had lulled Nikolai to sleep.

Now he stands on a forest path, dressed in his new clothes, the heavy wool sweater far too warm and prickling at his skin. He pulls it off, leaving himself in only a T-shirt, and now he's cold and shivering.

The trees rise high around him, the tops leaning toward each other to cast shadows over the path. There's a thin ray of light, and he follows it like a beacon drawing him forward. Beyond the trees are more trees, and he catches glimpses of movement.

There are Shadows in the Dreamscape. He can't step off this path.

Nikolai exhales and pulls the sweater back on. It leaves him sweating and chilled at the same time; the cold is inside his heart, not external. He shoves his hands in his pockets and walks faster, as if that'll chase away the chill.

He spots more light in the distance, and he almost runs the last of the path, emerging into a field of high grass and tiny flowers. He spots a woman spinning happily with her hands spread wide, her face raised toward the sun as her braids swing around her.

He wonders if the childish innocence is an act, or if the Dreamscape pulls her inner child free.

"Del!" He thinks that's her name, and he calls it loudly.

She slows then stops, facing him. "I was expecting Nikita," she calls back. Time slips, and she stands in front of him, both hands on his shoulders as she looks behind him.

"She's not here." Nikolai nudges her back, putting space between them. "Do you want me to take her a message?"

Del's lips press thin. "Yes. And no. I don't know why she's not here. She has to be here eventually; it's the only way through. And aren't you stable? I thought you didn't like to do this." She gestures between Nikolai and herself, then sweeps her hand in a circular gesture indicating their surroundings.

The Shadows move in the distance, two of them emerging into the light.

Nikolai takes a step toward the path. "We have company," he says.

Del turns, shading her hand over her eyes. "Oh. Them. It's okay, we're all going to talk."

"You seem different." Nikolai can't quantify it exactly, but she seems more coherent. More direct, perhaps, speaking in words instead of riddles.

"I'm spending a lot of energy to be here, and if it weren't for Sam and Shawn, I don't think it would work," Del says. "I need to focus, and that's hard for me here. The Dreams want to take over, and I want to give in. I can't let that happen. But I couldn't bring them with me here, so I'm with them in the real world. And they are ensuring that, while I'm Dreaming, I'm not lost to the Dream. That's why we can speak as if this were real."

They are anchoring her, in the same way that Seth anchors Nikolai. For now, at least, she's stable.

Del glances at the two figures who approach: one Shadow and Mattie.

"This may be the last chance I get," Del says. "You need to know what to do. My friends need to know how to get home. I'm running dry, and the split is crumbling." She turns away from him, walking into the field. "Come with me. We shouldn't stay near the edges."

He follows. There are no time skips; in fact, it seems to take longer than it should, the field stretching out around them. By the time they reach the center, Mattie and the other Shadow are waiting. Mattie has flickering obsidian around her edges. The other Shadow looks uncomfortable, her face twisted in pain barely visible amongst her darkness.

"I can't make it dark here," Del says. "They'd eat us, and we need my field to stay safe."

"I know." The Shadow's voice is a wistful hiss of sound. "But it hurts."

"Sit."

They all do, the tall grass rising around them. The sun beats down from above, but they are hidden and cool in an almost-darkness, and the Shadow lies down, sighing.

"This," she whispers.

"You're Chelsea," Nikolai says.

"You're the driver," Chelsea replies. "I can taste you in the air. You're stronger here, but not as bright as she is. Del would warm me from the inside, make me feel human for a breath of time."

"No," Del replies calmly. "No eating friends. You said you'd help, and I need you to."

"I'm hungry," Chelsea whispers. She hisses softly when Mattie lays a hand on her shoulder.

"I know," Mattie says reassuringly. "You'd do anything for a bright soul, and believe me, these are some of the brightest. Such beautiful Talents…they are so strong and effervescent, but you can't have them. We'll help Del, and after that, maybe you'll be able to have chocolate."

Chelsea seems…almost human. Aware, unlike other Shadows Nikolai's encountered. Although he's never stopped for a conversation—that had been the furthest thing from his mind. But she's not as human as Mattie.

Del turns, leaning up to peer above the grass. She has one hand placed to push herself off, and she looks as if she might dart away.

"Del," Nikolai asks, and she sits down abruptly, blinking at him.

"Sorry. That happens," she says. "It's hard not to let myself slip into the Dream."

"Then we need to make this quick," Nikolai says. Whatever "this" is.

He waits for one of them to start, but no one else speaks.

Fine.

"The Shadows came into Havenhill." He picks a piece of long grass and twists it around his finger. "She"—he nods at Chelsea—"clung to Pawel, and when I drove through the wards, her being there broke them and the Shadows followed us in."

"Sorry," Chelsea whispers.

"She"—Del tilts her head in Chelsea's direction—"is your way out. She'll lead you through the split."

"I could do it," Mattie insists.

"Would he remember me then?" Chelsea wonders. "Would I remember him?"

"Pfft." Del flicks her fingers at Mattie. "For my purposes, you're useless."

"You don't sound worried about the Shadows in Havenhill." Nikolai tries to pull the conversation back to something that not only makes sense but is important to him. "Or in my world in general. The Technopaths say that the coasts are falling to the Shadows, that they've consumed entire cities."

Del leans forward, hands on her knees. "That's interesting. They're getting bolder in my world as well. I've seen reports on the news—footage of darkness that comes to life, and when it fades, someone's dead. They think it's magic gone awry, and they're scared."

"The humans already know that you exist," Nikolai says slowly. "That was your Emergence, right?"

"They know some people are Talented and some aren't." Del makes a face, brow furrowing and eyes scrunching. "The Shadows targeting people with Talent makes everyone think it's something to do with using Talent. The popular theory is that magical Talent is consuming the victims. There's a ritual, something goes wrong, people end up dead. The thing is..." Del lets the words hang as she leans back, tilting her head to stare at the sky.

Nikolai waits.

"The thing is...?" he eventually prompts.

Her voice is lighter when she replies, soft and lazy. "It's getting so much harder to cross," she says. "They're in the way, you know. So many of them, and when I push through, I can feel them coming to me. Drawn to my energy."

"You would taste delicious," Chelsea agrees.

"And here—did you see them?" Del asks, her attention shifting to Nikolai. Her mouth twists up. It isn't a smile, but there's something in her eyes, some light that dances as if she's distracted and ready to jump away. To run. He's worried he's going to lose her any second.

"I saw them," he says.

"My field is safe, and I could dance here all the time. It's easy when I'm here, and it calls to me, begs me to make it light. But the Shadows, they're getting darker, creeping closer. They're trying to block the way." She rolls to her feet abruptly as she spreads her hands and spins in place. "They want to block the way between here and there. They want to control the way in and out, ensure that only they can use that path. They want your world and mine to fall to them."

"What will they do when they run out of food?" Nikolai asks.

"Leave," Chelsea murmurs. "Find a new food source. I've been to other worlds. I've eaten the best. I've seen bedrock, and I've seen darkness. I've seen light shining so bright that I had to have it for myself. Some fade because they don't want to eat anything else. But the strong move on. We hunger, and we search for something sweet."

That is a desperately chilling thought. No matter who Chelsea is, Nikolai doesn't think he'll ever be able to forget that she said that. He doesn't want to stay here with her, not when she's watching him, her head tilted like an animal waiting for her prey to run so she can chase.

"What do we do?" Nikolai asks. If Del has a message for Nikita, then he needs her to deliver it to him before she forgets. "We need to cross back to your world, and no one is sure how they left there in the first place."

Del drops like someone has cut her strings, arms and legs folding delicately as she hits the ground. "Wait. What?" she asks. "'We'?"

Nikolai licks his lips; his nails bite his palms as his fists go tight. "We," he confirms. "They have to leave, and Seth and I are going with them."

"Interesting." Del rearranges herself until she's kneeling in front of him, hands on her knees as she leans in close. "That'll be easier. Two are better than one, after all. Reach for me. I'll be here."

Nikolai thinks of the way she almost darted off a moment ago. "Will you be?"

Her brow furrows, pain lining the edges of her eyes. She twists, looking away from him for several breaths. Her tension slowly eases, and she turns her attention on him again. "I can't leave. Don't take long. Tell them we have all the pieces and have Carolyn start the path. With Chelsea, I'm certain that you and Nikita can walk it."

"If you have more Dreamwalkers on the other side, it might help," Nikolai says. "We've been talking about creating a Dreamwalker network, similar to the Technopath netwo—"

"Not in one place," Del says curtly. "That's a good way to destroy—"

"Not if they're under control." Nikolai knows this will work. "Nikita and I are fine. We have our anchors. That's all we need."

"Your world has its issues, and so does ours," Del mutters darkly. "The inability of Dreamwalkers to collaborate is one of them. You know what happened when Nikita and I were in the same room"

They opened up a path to Nikolai's world and threw Nikita and her friends through.

"We'll figure out a way to create the network later. When we're not in a rush. With control, things could change." Nikolai pushes himself to standing, his knees somehow stiff even though this isn't reality. His body aches when he takes a step. He can't move farther from Del nor closer to the trees. "I need to go back."

"You need to take yourself back," Del says. She lies down, spreading her arms out as if she's making a snow angel among the grass.

Mattie and Chelsea are gone. He has no memory of them walking away; it's as if they were never there.

Del closes her eyes. "Wake up," she says.

Pain shoots through his side, and he does.

He flails out, smacking his hand into something hard and soft—Seth and his glasses—and his hand is caught and held tight.

"Nik," Seth says hoarsely. "I thought you were—I thought I'd lost you."

Light filters through the curtains, and Nikolai realizes it's long past dawn. Past when they should have been awake. There's a pounding downstairs, and he thinks it might be someone at the door. "I'm here," he reassures Seth. "I'm okay. I Dreamed."

"I could tell," Seth says. He doesn't let go of Nikolai as he turns away. "We should…"

Nikolai kisses Seth's fingers, then carefully unwinds his hand. "Get the door. I need to write down what Del said before I forget. Nikita needs to hear it. This is how we can get through; they need us to do it."

21

It's strange to pack again. It hasn't been quite two weeks since they arrived, but Havenhill has become home, and Nikolai is loathe to leave it. There's an all-too-real chance that he will never see it again.

Nikolai specifically leaves things out of his bag. He leaves his new coat and hat and mittens, instead wearing his heavy sweater. He packs one change of clothes; he'll need different clothes there anyway. The clothes in his Dreams of Nikita's life were nothing like this homespun.

The map to Havenhill, still wrapped in its waterproof bag, is on top of the bureau in the bedroom. It is a symbol for him, a signpost. Every belonging left here, he will return to.

He makes his way downstairs slowly, aware of the way the murmur of voices slows then stops as he approaches.

Mikhail turns to look at him, brow furrowed. "You okay, Nikolai?"

No, he's not.

The thought of leaving his brothers twists in his gut with brutal strength. Nikolai blinks back dampness from the corners of his eyes and nods quickly as he lies, "I'm ready to go."

Mikhail meets him at the bottom of the stairs, wrapping his arms around him and yanking him into a swift, hard hug. Josef hangs back, leaning heavily on his cane, Amaranth budged up against his shoulder to prop him up.

"You don't have to go if you don't want to," Mikhail mutters. "Their world isn't your problem."

"The Shadows are a problem for both worlds, and our best chance to solve that is to work with them," Nikolai mumbles. He doesn't want to let go. He doesn't want to give up his brother yet. "They have to leave, and based on what Del said, they can't get home without me."

"How are you getting back on your own after you're done?" Mikhail holds Nikolai's shoulders, nudging him back to look at him seriously. "You need to find a way back."

"I will." Nikolai's heart sinks as he says the words; he hates lying to his brother. He gets hugs from Josef and Amaranth.

Amaranth pulls the tiniest lemon he's ever seen from her pocket and places it in his palm. "For luck," she says quietly.

Nikolai raises it and inhales the sharp, sweet-tart scent. He tucks it into his bag. "Thanks."

Seth is by his side when the goodbyes are done. Nikolai wraps an arm around him, leaning on him more than he should. "I'll keep him safe," Seth promises, and Mikhail nods.

"We need to go," Mikhail says.

Nikolai wants to race after them, beg them not to get in the Jeep and drive away, but he stands perfectly still and watches them go.

There's a chance the ritual will pull through anyone nearby. His brothers and Amaranth are needed here.

Knowing that doesn't make it any easier to let them go.

"It hurts," he mumbles, and Seth squeezes him, leaning in to kiss his shoulder.

"I know."

They smell bacon and eggs and pancakes before they reach the Benford house. As soon as they get inside, Nikita hands him a plate, and Nikolai gives her a notebook containing his notes on his meeting with Del; Pawel promptly steals it from her. Seth and Nikolai are left to eat in peace while the others go over Nikolai's quickly written notes. He hopes they make sense.

"We need to go soon," he says. "Del's waiting."

Carolyn shuffles through the papers in her hands. "Okay," she says, drawing the word out slowly. "Okay."

The food tastes delicious but sits heavily in Nikolai's gut. He manages a slice of bacon and part of a sweet pancake but sets the plate aside after that. He isn't trained in ritual—he has to trust that they will create one that will work.

Trusting anything involving the Dreamscape is difficult.

Nikita joins him, opening his bag to tuck the notebook inside. "Thank you," she says. "We can do this, you and me. We'll bring the Dreamscape here while Carolyn reaches out to Del."

No.

On the other side of the room, Pawel speaks to Mac in hushed tones, his hands moving in huge, awkwardly graceful arcs to emphasize his words.

Nikolai watches them; doing so gives him time to get his reaction under control. "You want me to bring the Dreamscape here?" he asks, trying to keep his tone even. He shakes his head. "We can't break the wards around Havenhill again."

"They'll come in after and make sure the wards are solid," Alaric rumbles. "Ethan told me they've got that covered."

"We don't want a direct hole into the Dreamscape," Nikolai protests. "What if the Shadows spill out into the heart of Havenhill?"

"We have to go from here to the Dreamscape somehow," Nikita points out. She jabs a finger toward where Carolyn sits with her hands cradled around a paper at which she stares. "She can travel. She'll open up the path, and you and I will make it wide enough for us to go through. 'Bring it here' isn't the right way to say it—we're making a bridge so we can walk from here to there. But we need to make it solid so we can cross. We'll anchor it on this side so we can all get to Del."

"Is that what happened when you came here?" Seth asks.

Nikita makes a face. "We still don't know what happened when we came here. This is our interpretation of what Del told Nikolai."

That doesn't fill Nikolai with confidence.

Pawel breaks off from Mac. "Let's get started." His call to order is loud and sharp. "Unfortunately, we don't have someone with us who knows how to balance this ritual, so we'll have to do our best."

"Pawel." Mac touches his shoulder. "We understand. Tell us what you need us to do."

Pawel exhales, his shoulders relaxing and his speech slowing. "Carolyn, bring your chair here. I want you in the middle." He gestures to the entryway. "Alaric, I know you dislike magic, and that's why we need you at the center of the ritual. Stay close to Carolyn, and Mac will stay close to you. Please try to avoid becoming the dragon unless we are outside."

Alaric grunts but goes where directed, Mac by his side; she takes hold of his hand. There are tight lines around Alaric's eyes, and Mac stands on her toes, murmuring something to him.

Alaric flushes, pulling away to cross his arms, and she rolls her eyes.

"Look at me," she orders, and they move so that Alaric is facing her, staring at her while Mac grips his wrists tightly.

Alaric shudders and closes his eyes, breath rasping.

Pawel moves Mattie into position behind Carolyn, then has Nikita and Nikolai form a triangle with Carolyn. Heather stays with Nikita, and Seth with Nikolai. Pawel stands between the two pairs, his hands on Nikolai's and Nikita's shoulders.

It's cramped and tight and they are too close together.

When the Dreamscape comes, it could swallow them all.

That's probably what Pawel wants.

Nikolai reaches for Nikita, gripping her hand tightly; he doesn't know if Pawel wants them linked, but Nikolai does. The solidity of Seth behind him and Nikita in front of him serves to anchor him.

"I'm reaching out to Del," Carolyn says, her voice tight. "Nikolai, Nikita—bring the Dreamscape here as soon as I've got her."

It happens too fast.

There's a flicker in the air, and Del is there, standing in their midst, a dark Shadow behind her. Pawel makes an aborted movement. Nikolai reaches for the Dreamscape, wrapping it around them. Seth is a line of strength behind him, and even with that anchor, Nikolai reaches with his free hand, needing to hold on.

Del grins, and the field is suddenly solid around them, the house gone.

"Alaric, Mattie, Carolyn, Pawel, Nikita, Heather, Seth, Nikolai, me, Del, and—" Mac stops her headcount, staring at the dark blot in the light drifting behind Del.

"Chelsea," Pawel says.

"I'm sorry," Del murmurs, and the field ripples around them. "There's no other way."

Del remains in the middle of the field, but their group is now at the edge, the thickening darkness barely out of reach.

Chelsea stands between them and the bright light.

Then Del is gone.

"Don't slip," Chelsea whispers. "Hold hands, and don't let go."

She reaches for Pawel, and they form a chain. Nikolai has Nikita on one side and Seth on the other, and while he can feel them, he can't see them. The line tugs him from the path and into the darkness.

Don't leave the path.

The words echo through his mind over and over, once for each step he takes forward. The darkness has weight and chills him to the bone. Unseen *things* whisper across his skin, words almost audible in his ears. He trips over his steps, chasing after Nikita, moving too fast as they crash between unseen trees.

Carolyn yells out; he can't tell if she's ahead or behind. "Why are we leaving Del's meadow?"

"The way through the Dreamscape is blocked." Mattie's voice is even despite the rushed pace. "We're going through the split."

Light filters through the canopy overhead, flickering on the edges of his vision. Nikolai sees people doing ordinary tasks—flashes of images that he has no time to process.

He spots a young woman sitting at a desk, her features indistinct, her laugh ringing bright. The mad rush slows, almost stopping. Pawel whispers, "Chelsea."

"No. You can't. We'll be lost," the Shadow whispers, words wrapping around them. "Here," she says, and the images disappear, darkness swallowing them. "Now. Go through."

Nikolai stumbles, shoved forward. He loses his grasp of Seth and Nikita, crying out and falling to his knees. He blinks in sudden bright light, sunshine spilling through glass, a wooden floor hard beneath him. He takes a deep breath, struggling to parse where he is.

This is not the Dreamscape.

He doesn't understand how they did it. Why it worked. This is reality, and they are all here.

Pawel lies face down, sprawled in an uncomfortable-looking way. He pushes to his hands and knees, rocking back until he's kneeling. He looks around, eyes wide. "We're home," he says, shifting to get his feet under him. "I'll be back." The door slams after he rushes through, the sound a *thud* behind Nikolai's eyes.

Nikolai sits up more carefully, staying on the ground while his head spins. Seth rubs the back of his neck, pressing fingers against the base of his skull, and Nikolai hangs his head to give Seth better access. It feels good, but the headache is blooming.

"I feel like I've been run over by a truck," Nikita mutters, one hand on her head. "Ow."

Something clatters against the windows.

Hail.

"Nik," Heather murmurs. Calm spreads throughout the room, and the clattering eases.

"I think I'm allowed one tiny weather tantrum after that," Nikita mumbles.

Nikolai understands the thought, even if that's not how his own Talent reacts.

Mac crouches in front of him, one hand out. "Welcome to our world," she says. "This is Pawel's house. Bathroom's that way, kitchen's down there, and if you need to rest, there are rooms at the top of the stairs. There are two that look lived in—don't take those. Pawel went next door to get Conor from his neighbor; he'll be back soon." Mac stands. "Pawel has pain-killers somewhere. I'll get those for you." She heads in the direction she'd pointed out as the kitchen.

"Nikita," Nikolai says.

Nikita crawls closer to Nikolai until she sits on the floor in front of him, Heather behind her. "Hm?"

"Now that we're here, be honest," Nikolai says, keeping his voice low. They aren't alone, but he wants this to be between her and him. "I don't know how we got here—it was all Chelsea. Can you get us back to Havenhill?"

She wrinkles her nose. "We'll get you home, if that's what you want."

It's not what she says, it's the way she says it. She thinks he's going to change his mind.

She doesn't understand.

"I don't want to be rescued." He enunciates each word carefully. "I didn't need to be pulled out of my home. You think I needed to be saved; you're wrong. When we're done, I want to be with my family. I'm here to help deal with the Shadows. When that's done, I'm going home."

Nikita bites her lip. "Right."

"You thought I would eventually decide to stay," he says. "You don't want me to go." When her gaze drops, he adds softly, "Be honest."

"I thought we'd figure it out later." She speaks to the floor, flinching when Heather comes up behind her to put a hand on her shoulder. "If you couldn't get back home, at least you'd be safe here. If I left you there, it'd be like abandoning myself to die!"

Something here pricks at his Talent, picking at his senses until he wants to sink into the sensation. Seth wraps his arms around Nikolai from behind, resting his chin on Nikolai's shoulder. Seth's presence makes the itch recede.

Nikolai inhales roughly and closes his eyes.

"When everything's done, we're going home," Seth says, his voice rumbling in Nikolai's ear.

"I know," Heather replies. "We all know."

Nikolai needs that to be the truth.

Letter written by Erica (last name unknown).

Dear Jessie,

You are my big sister. I've always looked up to you, believed that you walked on water and could do anything. When I was younger, I told you everything. Then things changed, and we grew apart. Now I want you to know the truth. You deserve that.

I think it began when I was five and you were ten. Do you remember that year? We moved across the country, then a month later, we moved halfway around the world. Our entire lives felt like pure chaos. That was when I started to Dream.

I didn't realize at first that it was a Talent. How could I? We didn't know Talent existed. Dad called me his creative boy, and Mom...well...we know Mom never did do well with storytelling, did she?

Me, I loved that every night when I went to sleep, no matter where we were in the world, I had a safe place to be. It was the same, and I was always...me. I wasn't alone.

Dad said Ethan was an invisible friend. He thought I had made him up. But when I went to sleep, Ethan was waiting for me in the same small room. We could do whatever we wanted, eat whatever made us happy. We had toys and costumes, and we acted out elaborate stories. He was the first person to call me by my name. We'd play for hours, until it was time to wake up.

As the years passed, I grew, and so did Ethan. Our meetings in the Dreamscape moved from that single room to a small, cozy house. I spoke of him as if he was real because to me, he was. You'd left for college; I was about to start high school. Ethan was all I had.

Mom had me talk to a therapist, who theorized I was creating a safe person to talk to and a safe space in my mind. The therapist thought it was a healthy coping mechanism. Mom thought I was lying, making things up because I wanted to sleep longer.

And I did. The older I got, the more my mind and heart wanted to stay in the Dreamscape. Ethan and I would prolong our nights as long as we could, staying together until I absolutely had to fall out of bed, into my clothes, and out the door to catch the bus.

When the Emergence happened, we found out about Talent, and I saw the lightbulb go off for Dad. He asked me questions—thousands of questions—and he researched. He made me tell him, in detail, about my life in the Dreamscape. I told him about talking all night with Ethan, about the face in my mirror while I was there, and about our picnics, our games, the forest outside our small home. And Dad realized that I was a Dreamwalker.

He knew I was potentially dangerous, too. If the Dreams escaped from my head, they could hurt people.

I saw a new therapist. I don't know how much you know about this. Dad tried not to talk about it, and I sure as hell didn't want to. You were at college, and my life was so *complicated.* Dad was thrilled because magic existed! Mom was…Mom. She denied my magic and my gender alike.

They divorced when I was sixteen. You went home to Mom for holidays, and I stayed with Dad. It worked out for the best.

You're a lot like Mom, aren't you? You prefer things that you can touch and feel. Things that are real. I love the things I can imagine, and believe me, I can imagine an awful lot. I've spent most of my life Dreaming, after all.

One time when Ethan and I were exploring the forest, we found two trees. He was drawn to one, and I was drawn to the other. The trunks were thick and strong. They grew up separately, but high amongst the branches, they intertwined.

Ethan pointed up as he took my hand, then showed me our tangled fingers. "Just like us," he said.

And they were.

We realized those were our trees, that they were gateways to ourselves. To our minds, to our worlds. The Dreamscape was a haven for us, and we had found each other because our worlds were closely tied.

I relish sleep, Jessie. It is my blissful place. I love to know that when I close my eyes, I will be with Ethan and we will be happy. I miss him desperately when I wake and spend my day longing to return.

Mom asked why I'm still single. That's why, Jessie. Ethan isn't here. He *can't* be here. We can only meet in the Dreamscape.

I would stay there if I could, but my body needs sustenance. I need to live in order to Dream. I can't pull the Dreamscape here; I've tried. We've both tried. Our tiny home in the Dreamscape is the only place where we are able to intersect, and we will both protect it with our lives.

Every chance we get, we Dream.

I love you, Jessie. You are my sister, and in so many ways you are luckier and better than I could ever hope to be. But I have Ethan, and he loves me, too. If only in our Dreams.

Your loving sister,
Erica

Out of the Woods

22

Nikolai has no energy to stand after their trip through the Dreamscape, so he stays on the floor with Nikita. The others appear to be recovering.

"I need to go." Alaric's announcement and departure are abrupt, the door slamming in his wake.

Carolyn stands with something cradled in her hand. "My phone's dead. It's been two weeks, and I didn't have a charger. I need one. I need to call Kit. Or I could walk to"—she looks at the door—"the kitchen. Pawel has a charger in the kitchen. If anyone needs me, I'll be—" She follows the same path that Mac took a few minutes ago.

"I'll make sure they're okay." Heather nuzzles close, kisses Nikita's cheek, then pushes away. "Besides, Pawel might have a landline we can use while our phones charge. Yell if you need me." She finger-combs her hair as she walks, pulling it back into a ponytail.

"Pawel will be back soon," Nikita says.

Nikolai isn't sure if that's meant as a warning or as reassurance. "Great. We can't go anywhere anyway. We don't have anywhere *to* go, and half of what Heather and Carolyn said sounded like nonsense." Seth nods, and Nikolai's glad he's not the only one feeling off balance.

From the other room, Carolyn's voice yells "Kit!"

"No one knew we were leaving," Nikita murmurs.

"We didn't know we were leaving," Mattie says. She sits on the back of a couch, one foot propped on the arm, the other on the seat. A slender pillar of darkness hovers close behind her. Her features are vaguely feminine, and she radiates discomfort.

"How do you stand the hunger?" Chelsea whispers. Her voice shivers through Nikolai. Chelsea leans toward him as if she can taste his fear.

"It gets easier," Mattie says, patting the darkness near where Chelsea's arm should be. "You'll remember how delicious they are, but you'll find other things to eat."

The front door bangs open, and Pawel stands in the doorway, shoulders hunched.

"Chelsea," he says.

"Pawel," she whispers.

The silence is strained.

Pawel turns away, still hunched tight, a hand over his face.

When Nikolai blinks, the Shadow is gone.

Mattie rises and drifts into a corner, slipping into darkness to disappear as well.

"They're gone," he says.

Pawel's shoulders relax and his head drops forward. "I don't know how to handle this. It's probably for the best that my dad came out to pick up Conor. I wouldn't even know how to explain that that's his—" He cuts off abruptly.

Silence again. There's a soft undercurrent of wrongness that prickles against Nikolai's skin. He shudders, and Seth's fingers tighten over his knee. Nikolai covers Seth's hand with his own and clings to him.

"Nikolai needs a place to stay." Nikita drops words like little bombs into the quiet, and Nikolai flinches.

"I—"

"We do," Seth says firmly. "You dragged us here, and we need somewhere to live while we're here."

"I can accommodate you." Pawel turns away from them, takes two steps, then turns back. "I have a spare room, and you're welcome to use it for as long as you'd like. I'll get you some clothes; we can find something for you to borrow for now." Hands on his hips, he looks them both over, his mouth pressed thinly. Nikolai can almost see his mind processing, ticking over a problem to solve. "Where are—?" He turns in place, as if expecting someone to step out of the woodwork.

Of course, Mattie could do that.

"Alaric left. Carolyn, Mac, and Heather are in the kitchen using your phone charger and making calls," Nikita says. "Do you need to call your dad?"

Pawel licks his lips and exhales roughly. He pushes his hands through his hair, pressing the heels of his palms against his eyes. "Probably. Soon. Emily's letting him know I'm back. I told her that I had things to take care of here. I don't want to leave Nikolai and Seth at loose ends."

Seth rises, offering a hand to Nikolai. When Nikolai stays seated, Seth asks, "You good?"

Nikolai nods. He's lying, but they need Pawel to not spin out of control. So Nikolai can pretend to be fine.

"Good, then let me take care of this." Seth grabs Pawel's shoulders and looks up at him. "Listen to me."

Pawel blinks.

Mac appears behind Seth. "Maybe you shouldn't—"

"Calm down," Seth says. "One breath at a time. One thing at a time. Because right now, I am in a world completely different than the one I left, and I need the person who is supposedly the adult in charge to not be freaking out more than I am."

That doesn't make Nikolai feel better. Everything about this place feels not quite right, from the way the air feels on his skin—as if he can sense Nikita's Talent nudging into his—to the way this room looks like any other room from his memory, only twisted sideways and a little to the left. Like, there's a large flat thing that reminds him of a television, but it's as thin as a painting and hangs on a wall. Nikolai can't get his bearings.

"It's like being in a Dream," he mutters. Like everything is real and not real at the same time. He's seen these things before through Nikita's eyes, which makes them familiar, but he can't shake the idea that he might actually be asleep. Maybe their plan to transport between the worlds didn't work. Maybe they haven't emerged from the Dreamscape after all.

Maybe they're trapped. Maybe he's falling entirely into a Dream.

Nikolai's chest is tight. He curls in on himself, his arms wrapped around his knees. The floor is cold, and he should get up. Everyone else has gotten up. Moved on. Even Seth. But Nikolai can't stop feeling wrong wrong *wrong wrong wrong*. Breath hitches, and he struggles to drag in another.

His head falls, making a dark, warm space for him with his forehead resting against his knees.

When he manages to exhale, the warmth washes back at him.

Something ticks sharply against the windows, slow at first, then faster...then fading.

"Nik!"

Was that Heather? Seth? Both of them? Nikolai isn't sure, but there are hands on his shoulders, and Seth wraps around him, familiar and strong. Nikolai can't stop shivering despite the warmth of the room. He's hot and cold down to his bones, and it's all too much. He hiccups around a strained breath.

Someone's talking. Angry. Hushed. Worried.

Too much. It's all too much.

His fingers are pried loose, and Nikolai clings to the familiar shape of Seth's hand. He pulls it in, pressing it to his heart. An exhale shudders loose.

"Breathe," Seth whispers, and Nikolai manages to take one slow breath, then another. He's in a safe, dark place, circled around himself, with Seth wrapped around him to protect him.

"I think there may be a fundamental metaphysical difference between our world and Nikolai's," Pawel muses, his words the only clarity in the darkness. "Is his Talent interacting with yours, Nikita?"

Oh.

Nikolai raises his head. It feels like it's been replaced by a bowling ball, a stodgy weight atop his neck. "What?"

Seth's hands on his shoulders settle him under his skin, keep the prickle to a dull itch.

Nikita is on the other side of the room, curled in the corner of the couch, Heather next to her. Her posture radiates sorrow. She raises her head and blinks at Nikolai.

"We're the same person," she protests. "It shouldn't interact. Besides, I can be around Del now. Mostly. Sort of."

"While we were in Nikolai's world, you didn't have any difficulties," Pawel replies. "However, if this world has a different—" He waves his hand, expression twisting in frustration. "I don't know how to explain it. Nikolai's world knows far more about Dreamwalkers, and there's nothing in the base magic of the world that's unsettled with respect to Dreamwalkers. But in our own world, we never learned that—all we learned is that if two Dreamwalkers are too close to each other, their Talents interact. Instead of teaching our Dreamwalkers how to control their Talent, we separated them, to the point where the genetics of Dreamwalker lines altered. We made a fundamental change to how that magic works, and it's been going on for generations. You two"—he gestures between them—"either need to be separated, or need to learn how to work with that interaction and settle yourselves."

"The news is already talking about the freak snowstorm." Carolyn taps at something in her hands. "It's not like the ice storm, Nik. You haven't hit the entire Eastern seaboard. But the storm came out of nowhere, essentially blown into existence here in Unity. It reaches as far as Valiant. We're going to go viral. Again."

Nikolai doesn't understand, so he focuses on the one thing she said that makes sense. "You've done this before?" he says.

Nikita flushes. "I told you when I first arrived in your world. When I was Dreaming about you, my Weather Witch Talent went out of control. This time, I think the storm was caused by your panic attack. But we can't be separated if we want to get rid of the Shadows and heal the split, right?"

Nikolai pushes to his feet, keeping Seth's hand clasped in his, unwilling to release that tether to the familiar. "It's not only you; it's this place, too. Everything here is almost normal but not quite, like a memory, or a promise of how things could be if I kept Dreaming instead of living in reality." He takes a low, shuddering breath. "Your world moved on from the point where ours broke a decade ago. It feels unreal."

"And a Dreamwalker feeling unreal is a Dreamwalker who thinks he's trapped in a Dream," Pawel muses.

Nikolai's shoulders are tense. "Exactly."

"We can work with that." Mac is behind Pawel, her hand on his back, between his shoulders. "You have an air mattress, right? And the couch pulls out. Slumber party tonight. We'll crash on your floor and watch movies and show them the Hollywood idealized version of our world. We can catch up on the news we missed the last couple of weeks and help Nikolai and Seth get a crash course in what our world is like."

"I need to leave. I'm sorry," Carolyn says. "I've been talking to Kit and Serina, and I need to see them both. Serina's got work in the morning, so I'll come back then."

Nikolai doesn't care, even though he struggles to conceive of this group as composed of independent individuals. For the last two weeks, these people have been attached to him and to each other, constantly nearby. Considering them separating adds to the moment's surreality.

"Go ahead," Pawel says. "If you feel like stopping back later, please do. We'll be here. Kit and Serina are welcome to join us."

Nikita unfolds from the couch and meets Nikolai in the center of the room, wrapping her arms around him, holding on, and resting her head on his shoulder. Nikolai's surprised when the itch under his skin eases at her touch; she sighs as if she feels the same thing.

"I think the snow's stopping," Heather says.

"Good," Nikita mumbles. "It's totally unfair for it to snow in April. Especially when it's my fault."

She steps back, and the itch stays quiet. Nikolai can breathe. He'll need time to feel stable in this world, to understand how it differs from his own. He never expected that something as fundamental as his innate Talent could be affected like this.

Seth's fingers, still tangled with his, are perfectly real, and he squeezes to say *thank you.*

"Pawel, you set this room up, and I'll give Seth and Nikolai a tour," Mac says. She motions for them to follow her as she heads for the stairs.

Seth waits until they've reached the landing before asking quietly, "Are you sure you two aren't…?" as he points back to where Pawel is talking to Nikita and Heather. He doesn't bother to finish the question, voice fading as Mac laughs.

"We aren't," she says firmly. "We've been friends for a long time. It's probably inappropriate that one of my best friends is also my advisor and a professor. I'm older than most of my class year, and he's young for a professor, so we're closer in age than we would be otherwise. He was there for me freshman year when I needed a friend. We've both lost someone." She glances down the stairs again. "I don't know what it means for him to have Chelsea here, on top of everything else. I had no idea she…I don't think he knew, either."

"That she'd become a Shadow?" Seth asks, and Mac nods.

"There are some extra blankets and pillows in the closet up here; we can bring those down when we go. The room at the end of the hall is Pawel's. He's got his own bathroom in there, so you don't have to worry about sharing until Conor's back." She makes a face, and Seth's brow furrows. Nikolai wonders what emotion he's not catching.

Mac stops at the first room along the hall. A blackboard hangs on the door with a list of tasks, some crossed off. "Conor's room," she says. "Bathroom's here across the hall, and the guest room—which doubles as Conor's playroom—is between Conor and Pawel." She nudges the door open, makes a face, and quickly closes it. "Might be for the best that you'll be staying downstairs tonight. That room needs a little help before it'll be ready for you. Unless you feel like stepping on Legos. Did you have Legos?"

Nikolai grins and holds up his hand with his fingertips close together but not touching. "Small plastic bricks to build with? Yes, we did." He's tempted to go into that room so he can rediscover that piece of childhood, but these are Conor's toys, and it wouldn't be right to use them without asking. He might not appreciate a stranger touching them.

"We found a house when we were first on our own," Seth says. "Most of the clothes were cleared out, but they'd left books and toys behind. They had a huge train set, and while we stayed there, we built a rail that went around their entire downstairs. Then Nikolai built plastic planes and buses to travel around it."

They had still been grieving then. It had felt good to act as if they were six instead of sixteen.

Tears prick the corners of Nikolai's eyes, the memory of his parents sudden and bright. "I'd forgotten about that," he says.

Seth leans into him, a welcome pressure along his shoulder. "I'm not surprised."

They collect pillows and blankets, dropping them in the living room. Mac takes them around downstairs, showing them where to find food in the kitchen and how to go out to the fenced backyard. She demonstrates how to work the coffee maker as she puts a pot on, then she also starts water boiling in an electric teapot.

Nikolai touches the small appliances, vaguely remembering how most of them work. "I haven't seen a working electric stove in a long time," he admits. "Even Havenhill was using wood. We had one like this when I was a kid, but we only used flames after the Split. Electricity didn't make it out of the cities once the walls went up. All the abandoned houses were cut off. Havenhill had the first working electricity I've seen in ages."

"You've got a lot to relearn," Mac says. "Get down mugs, then pick hot chocolate or coffee."

Nikolai looks at the cabinets, waiting until Mac points before he opens one and starts pulling down mugs.

"Chocolate," Seth says decisively. "Definitely and always chocolate."

Mac grins. "Smart guy."

Voices call out as the front door slams from across the house. The electric teapot hisses while Mac tears open packets and shakes powder into mugs. She pours in hot water, and the smell of chocolate fills the room.

"If you're making tea—oh, it's chocolate. We brought dinner."

Nikolai turns as Mac disappears from beside the counter and reappears in front of the tall, broad, dark-skinned man in the doorway. Mac hugs him hard, and he bends down, his dreadlocks swinging over her shoulders as she buries her face against his shoulder.

"Yeah, Mac, I missed you, too. We were all worried," he murmurs.

"Bet you missed Alaric more," she says. She steps back, gesturing at Nikolai and Seth. "We brought back new friends. Nikolai, Seth, this is Chris. He's Alaric's—" She stops at the rising growl from the other room. "He's Alaric's," she says again and stops as if that's explanation enough.

"I called over to Minnisale's," Chris explains. "Had them make some catering trays, then we drove over with Rory to pick it up. Rory's, uh..." His voice trails off, and he shrugs. "It's been a rough couple of weeks. I think Rory and Kit were the worst off out of all of us. It's a good thing they had each other."

Seth has already claimed one mug of hot chocolate, and Nikolai grabs another. He ignores the conversation as he blows on the liquid carefully then takes a sip, luxuriating in the taste.

"You get plates," Mac directs, and Chris moves past Nikolai to get to the cabinets. "I'll bring out the drinks, and then we're having an evening of games and movies and food." She hesitates. "It's just you and Alaric and Rory, right? I don't think Seth and Nikolai are ready for Thorne."

Chris laughs softly. "He's aware you're all back and safe, and no, he's not here."

Nikolai keeps sipping at the chocolate, unwilling to leave the quiet of the kitchen yet.

"Why don't we take these out, and I'll come back for silverware and to make these guys another cup of cocoa," Mac says, ushering Chris out the door.

They don't come back right away, and Seth sets his mug down on the counter. "We're really here," he says.

"Yeah," Nikolai replies, still wrestling with wrapping his head around it. "We're really here. This isn't a Dream. And there are more people out there than those we've already met, and there's even more of this world outside the house, and Seth, I don't know—"

Seth cuts him off by surging up and lightly brushing his lips against Nikolai's. "No more panicking. We'll get through this together. Whatever it takes."

Right. No matter what, they've got each other. "Whatever it takes," Nikolai echoes. When he kisses Seth again, he tastes like chocolate. Nikolai smiles. He could get used to this.

23

THE DOORBELL RINGS in the morning, startling Nikolai from sleep. He is too warm to want to move, but his heart pounds at the half-remembered unfamiliar sound. Pawel pushes himself out of the recliner, stepping over sleepy people on his way to the door, then opens it.

"Del."

"I slept in my car and it's cold, so I've decided it's late enough to wake you all up." Del pushes through the door. She's the same person Nikolai remembers from the Dreamscape, but this Del is real and solid, her tone matter-of-fact and body language taut instead of loose with Dreaming.

It's good seeing her like this. His heart slows, and the grip of Seth's hand on his thigh eases.

Del sweeps the room with her gaze, brow furrowing. "Carolyn?"

"With Serina," Pawel says. He threads his way through the room again, heading for the kitchen. "I'm making coffee."

Del bites her lip, nodding as her gaze falls on Nikolai. "You made it through. Cool."

"Maybe not cool if we can't get back," Seth mutters.

"You're the anchor." Del drops onto the couch, sliding under Nikita's outstretched feet.

"Do you see how much better I am?" Nikita mumbles. "A couple months ago this would've resulted in a surprise ice storm. Del's a Dreamwalker. She doesn't have an Empath. She has...she has a Sam and a Shawn, and Shawn's kind of a dick."

"But he's my dick," Del wiggles her eyebrows. "I left him home because I didn't want him and Carolyn to get awkward. He's still dealing with her truth bombs, even though he deserved them."

Nikolai's lost, but everyone else seems to understand, so he stays silent.

Nikita yawns and sits up, untangling herself from Heather. Mac is in the other chair, curled into a small ball. Alaric, Rory, and Chris have created some kind of a tangled pile on the floor, with Alaric behind Chris and Rory half on top of Alaric.

"God," Nikita mumbles. "I'm glad it's Sunday. It *is* Sunday, right? I can't imagine going back to classes like none of that happened. I have been to a whole other *world*, and my professors are going to be annoyed that I haven't turned in two week's worth of assignments and missed a ton of notes."

"I haven't been in school consistently since I was 8 or 9," Nikolai says. "So. Everything you're saying is alien to me. Even the small school in Havenhill was weird."

"We need food," Rory says. He shifts off Alaric, sitting with his knees bent and arms looped around his legs, his shoulders hunched. His frame is narrow and long, and he seems like he's trying to make himself appear smaller than he is. "We shouldn't make any major decisions—or have major discussions—if we haven't eaten properly."

"There was really good food in Havenhill," Alaric says. "Like home." He leverages his way to his feet, pulling Chris with him. Together, they're big enough to feel like they fill the room. "We're going to shower." He makes a disgruntled noise. "Should've brought a change of clothes over."

Pawel returns as Alaric and Chris disappear up the staircase together. He sighs. "There isn't enough food in the house for this crowd."

"Teas Please," Nikita says, and everyone nods as if what she's said makes sense.

"Can they handle this large of a group on a Sunday?" Rory asks. "I've heard that Nate thinks we've got someone whose Talent is to make sure our table is always available when we need it, but that doesn't guarantee us space."

"I'll call in a reservation," Heather offers, holding up a slender metallic device. "Carolyn says that Serina left for work this morning, so you know she'll hold it for us if we give her enough warning."

"I…" Pawel pulls a similar thing out of his pocket and stares at it. "I shouldn't. I should hit the road, pick up Conor, and bring him home."

These tiny, slim things…they're phones and computers that fit in a pocket. After an evening's immersion in this world, he's starting to find his feet, but he still feels like he's floundering in the deep end.

Mac appears next to Pawel, snatches the phone from his hand, then reappears on the other side of the room. She taps the screen, and the sound of ringing fills the room.

"Mac," Pawel says quietly.

"Hello?" A man's voice, low and deep.

"Mr. Szczek. This is Mac Palmer, from PHU. We've met. I work with your son in the taekwondo club," Mac says. She blips to a different place in the room as Pawel stalks toward her. "Pawel's fine, but he's conflicted."

"Call me John." There's the faintest hint of an accent when John speaks, but Nikolai can't identify it. "Let me get Conor."

Shuffling sounds come from the speaker. Pawel stops in the middle of the room with his arms crossed. He holds out one hand, and Mac shakes her head.

"You won't be able to settle down until you talk to them both," she says. "So talk to them. If you go home, you're going to worry about what we're getting up to. If you stay here, you're going to worry about Conor. You need to find a way to stop worrying and focus, Pawel, because you're already worn thin."

"Hi, Dad!" A boy's voice calls out. "Emma's dads are picking me up soon. I'm going to her place. She has four not-brothers and not-sisters, and her dads are really awesome. Her parents disappeared, too, just like you did. Or not just like, since I'm pretty sure you went somewhere kind of on purpose, and they didn't. Can we help her find them after you're done saving the world or whatever?"

A low chuckle from John underlines Conor's words.

Nikolai can't imagine being that calm about a disappearing—and returning—parent. He clenches his hand tight, easing when Seth covers his hand with his palm.

"What Conor's trying to say is: we understand that you're working on something world-shattering," John translates, voice full of pride and affection. "Pawel, he's fine here with me, and I'm fine having him here. Le—"

"Emma's dads said I could visit any time I want if Dziadziu needs a break!" Conor yells. "I can even stay over, although they don't have a lot of room. I think they need a new house, especially if they want more kids. Emma says they take them in from all over, Talented kids who have problems. Jennie's the baby, and she's pretty cute. Emma's the newest. I think she likes it there even though she sometimes says she doesn't. I miss Alan. Can you tell him I said hi? I think he and Emma would really like each other."

"Do you talk faster when you can't see me?" Pawel says dryly. "Slow down. Can I trust Emma's dads?"

Silence for a moment, then John says in carefully measured words, "One works with me. The other's a lawyer. They're good people. They've got five foster kids, all Talents who don't have anywhere else to go."

"I've got a really good teacher and I'm not doing any magic at school. I hear the car. Gotta go. Love you, Dad!" Footsteps fade as Conor runs away, and a door slams in the distance.

"Does he even miss me?" Pawel mutters, pushing at his hair.

"Yes, he does." John's voice is sober. "But he's excited by everything, and he has a whole new Talented family for friends. Do you remember that time when you stayed with—?"

"Okay, yeah, not going there." Pawel cuts him off, fingers pressed to the bridge of his nose. "But I get your point. It's possible to be upset and happy at the same time, and Conor's found that balance. Are you sure—?"

"Save the world. That's what you're doing, right?" John says.

Pawel glances at the others. Nikita shrugs, and Nikolai echoes the motion. He has no idea what's going on, but that seems like a decent summary. Get rid of the Shadows. Heal the split. Save the world.

"We're trying," Pawel replies. His hand falls limply to his side, and he closes his eyes, exhaling. "I think we've got a chance of putting something back to rights, if we can figure out how."

"Will you be less stressed after?" John asks. Pawel nods, and John continues as if he could see him. "Then just get it done. Conor and I are having a great vacation. He's doing well in school, and Emma's making sure he's having a good time. I think he's good for her, too. She's been struggling, and I know her dads have been worried about her settling in. So if you think of it that way, you're doing her a kindness by letting him stay with me."

Pawel lets out a rough laugh. "Okay, I get it. You keep my kid for a while."

"And you deal with those students you think are your kids, too," John says. "Mac, thanks for reaching out. Good to hear from you. You all keep each other safe."

"We will," Mac assures him. She touches the screen, then hands the phone back to Pawel. "There you go; decision made. We're going to Teas Please to eat, to help acclimate Nikolai and Seth, and to plan."

The tension breaks, and everyone cycles through the showers. The locals complain about having to put on the same clothes they were wearing, but Nikolai and Seth are so used to doing so that it seems to be the one normal thing right now.

Then they step outside, and his world abruptly turns upside down again.

Seth clutches at Nikolai's hand. Even having seen this world through Nikita's eyes and dreams, it's unsettling.

The neighborhood Pawel lives in makes Mikhail's street in Havenhill look abandoned. The cars parked along the street are new, bright and shining in the morning sun. More cars zip by along the road, and the sidewalk is neatly kept. The buildings are well maintained. Children play on lawns in the early spring warmth.

There are so many people. The festival was quiet by comparison, and this is only one small street. The noise is loud, with people calling out. Knots of strangers walk along the street, waving and talking. Many of them seem to be around Nikolai's and Seth's age, and when one group yells, Chris raises a hand and waves back.

"You can imagine how empty your world seemed to us," Nikita murmurs by his shoulder. "Come on. Let's get to Teas Please. It'll be crowded and noisy, but at least there will be food."

Nikolai allows himself to be nudged along, Seth staying tight by his side. "Our lives haven't been this way in a very long time," he replies. "It's like a memory. Or a dream."

"And in our minds, this is the equivalent of unsafe," Seth adds. "Cities are dangerous."

"They aren't dangerous here," Nikita says, "and we aren't going far. Pawel lives close to campus, and Teas Please is nearby. It's our favorite place to eat, and our friends work there."

They move slower than the others, and by the time they catch up, Chris stands before a shop set into the first floor of a line of buildings, one with a sign above the door that says "Teas Please." He holds the door open, and Nikolai trails after Nikita into the restaurant.

"Oh, hey, hello there new people." A pretty Asian girl smiles and waves as she gathers a stack of menus. "I've got your table in the back, but you'll be pretty squeezed in. I think Nate's right about someone having a Talent to get this table because seriously, a group left right before Heather called, and I got the reservation tag on it just in time."

"It's always a different group of us coming in," Alaric points out.

"Aren't you always involved?" Chris asks, and Mac snorts when Alaric growls at him.

" 'M not magical," Alaric mutters. "Not like that."

"Only where dragons are concerned," Mac says, patting his shoulder on the way by. "We get it."

There's an ease to the group as they shuffle around, trying to figure out how to squeeze into the U-shaped bench around a long table. Pawel and Mac grab another empty table and add it to the end, gathering chairs for the new-made spaces.

"Hi, I'm Serina, and I'll be your server." Serina hands Nikolai and Seth menus while they wait for the others to arrange themselves.

"Seth and Nikolai," Seth offers. He pulls out one of the chairs, and Nikolai takes it. He likes the idea of not being crushed in with everyone else.

Del slides into the end of the U, with Heather and Nikita on one side and Chris and Alaric on the other. Rory sits on one end of the bench, next to Seth's chair, and Pawel and Mac are on the bench opposite Seth. It's tight, but not too bad. Nikolai breathes more easily once the chaos is over.

He looks at the menu in his hands. "Wait. We have to pay for this."

"You don't have any money, so obviously we're paying," Nikita says. "It'll take time to get you settled into our world. Don't worry, we'll take care of you."

There are so many choices that Nikolai doesn't know where to start. Before he makes a decision, Mac gathers up the menus and orders a little of everything. Six pots of tea for the table, along with more coffee. Different kinds of crêpes and sandwiches, and she asks Serina to have everything cut into multiple pieces for sharing.

Serina collects the menus. "Of course!"

"Is Nate in today?" Mac asks. "I wanted to ask him something."

Serina shakes her head. "He's off. He'll be in tomorrow. He said he had a thing with his dad. I don't think it made him happy."

"Mm."

Serina hugs the menus to her chest, but she doesn't leave, her gaze dropping to Nikolai and Seth.

"Food?" Del calls out, and Serina startles.

"Oh. Yes. I'll put in your order; it'll be right out," she says. Instead of leaving, she leans down beside Nikolai and Seth. "My girlfriend, Carolyn—you know her, right? With the cards. She's really good at tarot. She did a reading before she disappeared—before she went to your world. And the last card in the reading was Death."

Nikolai's mouth drops open. "She's going to—"

"Oh, no, no!" Serina waves her hands, barely catching the menus before she drops them. "Nobody's going to die. Death means change. Carolyn's reading was about everything changing. And she told me about your home last night and what's happening there, and that…scares me. So, um, if you're here to help. Thank you."

Change. Like stepping neatly from one world to another. Nikolai can see in his mind the card from the reading Carolyn gave him, the way it lay on the table in front of him as if foretelling this moment. The way Serina emphasizes the Death card, and the way it was the final card for Carolyn, sounds like an even greater amount of change. When he considers how much change that might mean, and how that change relates to the Shadows—they are also called Deathstalkers, after all—it gives him chills.

“We’re here to help your world and ours,” Seth says, his hand on Nikolai’s back as he leans close. “And then we’re going home.”

“Of course,” Serina says quickly. “Carolyn told me.”

“Food!” Del calls again, more emphatically this time.

“Del,” Heather chides, but Serina straightens.

“Yes, it’ll be up soon. I’ll be out with tea as soon as we’ve got it steeping!” Serina turns on her heel, gone in a small whirlwind of motion.

“Refillable debit cards,” Pawel murmurs. “And Sera. We need Sera’s help, both to start a Technopath network in this world, and because she can get us some technology to help you two fit in. And Nikolai, you should work with Del and Nikita to form a Dreamwalker network within the Dreamscape.”

Nikolai glances at Seth. Everything’s moving too quickly around him, and Seth is the only thing familiar and stable. He reaches out, holding on, because he needs his anchor more than ever.

This is good. He’s uncomfortable, but they are safe and they have a plan. They’ll gather allies and reinforcements, and then they can heal the split.

24

The food is good and plentiful. Serina arrives with another server in tow and two overfull trays. She passes out plates. "Mallory picked them all, not me. That has nuts," she says, pointing to a plate Alaric's in the middle of picking up, and he passes it to Chris instead. "She said you guys needed more food."

There's something that smells like onions and garlic, and Nikolai steals it before anyone else can get their hands on it, splitting the half-sandwich with Seth. The onions are roasted and sweet, the garlic rubbed into a paste that complements the sweetness of the ham, and there's a hint of pineapple. He's never had anything like it.

Seth grabs for a salad piled high with vegetables and meat; he glares when Alaric reaches for it as well, and Chris takes Alaric's hand to move his attention elsewhere. The dressing is sharp, mixed sweet and sour, and Nikolai smiles at the taste of lemon bursting over his tongue. He and Seth devour their sandwiches and salad, and only then are they sated enough to look at any of the other options.

There is a surprising amount of food still on the table. Nikolai focuses on seeking out the sweets—a deeply chocolate slice of cake and a scone dotted with berries. He feeds a forkful of the cake to Seth and grins when Seth closes his eyes and makes a pleased sound.

"Hey." Carolyn arrives with two more guys—one who resembles her and is introduced as her twin Kit, and a grinning redhead, Rory's brother Thorne. They drag another table over and everyone rearranges so Kit can sit with Rory. Nikolai and Seth end up on the corner of the bench nearest the chairs, with Alaric and Chris pushed farther along the bench and Thorne on the chair. Serina comes back with even more food and pulls up a chair for herself, squeezing in next to Carolyn.

"I'm on my fifteen and I'm starving," she says, reaching to fill her plate.

This chaos of people makes their arrival in Havenhill seem quiet. Nikolai's stomach twists as he tries to find a way to connect to one of at least three different conversations. Del leans on the table to talk with Carolyn across everyone. Alaric and Chris are talking to Thorne around Nikolai and Seth. Pawel, Kit, and Rory are deep in a serious-sounding discussion. Nikolai is losing track of who is who, and the conversations shift as people change which they are involved in. He is confused and overwhelmed, but he can't escape. The warmth of Seth's body next to him is his only source of quiet and familiarity.

"Del." Pawel raps against the table, and conversations fade. Nikolai is reminded of when he first met the newcomers, how they all looked to Pawel as if awaiting his leadership.

"Mm?" She sits back, sipping at her tea. "Did I hear you say something earlier about some kind of Dreamwalker network? I think you might be nuts."

Pawel waves away her words. "We'll talk more about that later. I want to discuss Chelsea with you."

"Who?" Del looks around, frowning. "I thought I knew everyone here. I haven't met a Chelsea, have I?"

Silence.

Carolyn glances at Heather and Nikita, then back to Del. "You introduced us. Do you remember anything from the Dreamscape?"

"Any of the times you've talked to us?" Nikolai adds.

Del's brow furrows. "The Dreamscape and I have a loose relationship. Or more, I have a loose relationship with my mind when I'm there." She looks at Nikolai. "I remember talking to you."

"Chelsea is Conor's mother," Pawel says, tone flat. He corrects himself. "She was Conor's mother."

"You had her lead us back here?" Nikita's voice lilts up, questioning. "You said Mattie was broken and we needed someone who could lead us through the split to cross between the worlds, and she did. The method we used to return was very different than the way we got to Nikolai's world."

Del rubs at her face. "The way you got there left me unconscious on Pawel's living room floor for a few hours," she mumbles. "From my perspective, you were trying to look into his world so you could make sure he was okay. Carolyn brought up the illusion, and Nikita—you decided to walk into the middle of it, which felt…weird. There was a thunderclap, the room went pitch black, and I passed out. Your kid and neighbor found me." She glances at Pawel. "If he's scarred for life, sorry."

"I'm pretty sure nothing will scar Conor at this point," Pawel says dryly. "On the other hand, Chelsea's existence will definitely test that theory. Rory—" He cuts off, makes a face. "I'm sorry I called Mattie an 'it.' I was too self-involved to see her the way you were able to."

"Speaking of Mattie, where is she? I haven't heard from her since you came back," Rory says. "She did make it back, didn't she?"

"She did, but she disappeared with Chelsea." Pawel sits back. "I had no idea." He scrubs his hands through his hair, gripping as if he's trying to keep his brains inside his head. "I had no idea that Chelsea had…that she was…that she'd Emerged. I didn't even know then that was possible."

Nikolai wants Pawel to keep talking. As long as Pawel speaks, the focus is on him, and the table is silent. Nikolai can breathe more easily.

Seth squeezes Nikolai's hand and leans forward. "What happened?"

Pawel blinks at him, brow furrowing. He opens his mouth, then glances at the rest of the table. "I have a son. You heard me worrying about him—you heard him on the phone this morning. He's in third grade, just turned nine, and he was born when I was still in college. Chelsea was my best friend. We clicked immediately when we were freshmen. She was the first Mage I ever met, and she helped me through my own Emergence, which was…interesting, and a story for another time."

He picks up his mug, staring at it before taking a quick gulp. "We dated freshman year, then we stopped. We were both too busy to date. We loved each other, but we weren't in love, so we had an arrangement. When she got pregnant, she said she knew he was going to be a Mage. She could feel him and couldn't let him go even though neither of us was prepared to raise a child. We made plans to stay together in a partnership and raise him. Then she disappeared right after he was born. I assumed she'd panicked and run."

Pawel presses his lips together, expression pained, lines tight around his eyes. "I looked for her. Hell, my dad looked for her for me. He's the chief of police back home and he has some good connections and resources, but we never found her. I guess I know why, now."

"So that can happen?" Kit asks. "Someone who already has a Talent can just one day become a Shadow?"

"One day they become a creature who has no desires beyond eating other people's souls," Thorne points out.

"Beg to differ—Chelsea definitely recognized Pawel in the Dreamscape, and I think she was doing her best not to eat any of us," Mac says sharply. "They're still people."

"Look at how many people sitting at this table have Emerged with Talents other than the ones they were born with," Nikita says. "Me, Carolyn, Del, Alaric—having a Talent doesn't mean you're immune to Emerging."

"That implies that Emerging and being Talented are two different things," Carolyn mutters. She pulls out a notebook. "I'm adding that to my list of things to look into. It's possible that Emergence isn't an expression of a latent ability, but a layering of a new ability over the old."

"Like the Lince," Pawel says, leaning closer to her and tapping the notebook. "Talk to Ángel, if you haven't already. They're a unique Lineage of Clan with a singular cat form and the ability to call others to them, if they have any inclination to be a cat."

"Do you think there's a way to determine genetically if a person has a pre-disposition to Emerge?" Kit asks. "Either to predict what form that Emergence could take—will they be a Mage, or a unique Talent like a Teleporter—"

"I think traveling is a Lineage," Carolyn interrupts him.

It becomes impossible to follow the conversations again. Before, they had at least been speaking quietly. Now they're shouting. They're not angry, they're excited. Talking about topics that Nikolai has learned to keep quiet about, shouting loud enough to be heard. There are sparks and little pops, and he feels like everyone's Talents are simmering under their skin, just waiting to be let loose.

He can't figure out how to break into the conversation. He knows more about being a Dreamwalker than Nikita or Del, but they know more about this world. About being secure in sharing their Talent. About being loud. He knows how to stay quiet and avoid the Shadows. He can light up the sky and bring the Dreamscape into focus without endangering the world. He might be able to help with the Dreamwalker network, but he's not sure how.

He's awash in a sea of shouting, Seth his only anchor. His chest is tight, breaths sharp and quick.

The world moves abruptly as, beside Nikolai, Alaric stands up, pushing roughly. "Thorne, get up," Alaric growls. "Let them out."

Let who out?

Oh.

Himself. Seth.

Them.

Calm washes over him, sliding off his skin but unable to penetrate deep enough for Nikolai to truly feel it. He stands as soon as Thorne makes space, retreating from Seth and everyone else, his hands up as he tries to keep everyone away.

"Nik," Seth says quietly, and Nikolai shakes his head.

"No. I don't want—I just—" Words fail him. "Shit. Please."

"Do you need some time alone?" Alaric asks, and when Nikolai meets his eyes, he sees kindness and understanding.

"I need for my skin not to feel like it's peeling off," Nikolai says, crossing his arms, tucking his hands into his elbows. He tries not to see how Seth flinches. "I don't want to be touched. I'm sorry. It's too much. I'm going outside."

Thunder booms, echoed by the crash of a chair as Nikita gets up too quickly.

She's following him. Of course she is.

He pushes his way through the restaurant, the door banging open when he exits. Sleet bounces off the sidewalk, chill and brutal; he rocks to a stop just outside the door, hovering under the overhang. Thunder crashes again. He flinches.

The door opens again, but Nikolai doesn't bother to turn around.

"You can't get stormy every time I'm upset," he mumbles.

"I can't help it," Nikita says. "It's like we're…I think we're one person. Maybe it's because we're linked in the Dreamscape, I don't know. But you get upset, or I get upset on your behalf, and poof, weird weather. It's been an interesting time since I got to PHU."

Nikolai wraps his arms around himself, staring at the sleet rushing down. He wishes he'd thought to grab the jacket he left hanging over his chair. "So if I calm down, it'll stop."

"It'll stop when it stops," Nikita says. She steps closer, coming shoulder to shoulder with him. "You already seem less anxious but are still a lot angry. It's strange. I feel it, but I know the feelings aren't mine. It's like a layer of unreality surrounding me. It's disturbing, I'll admit. So." She nudges him. "Want to talk about it?"

He exhales roughly. "I'm struggling," he admits. "Where we come from, there was just the two of us. Crowds were dangerous. Now there are so many of you, and you keep bringing in new people. It's a confusing mess, Nikita. You keep talking about things I don't know anything about. You might as well be speaking another language half the time."

She doesn't respond, and Nikolai appreciates that. He wants her to listen, to try to understand where he's coming from and stop treating him as if his world is a movie.

"We need reinforcements," she says. "A lot of reinforcements, both here and in your world, so we can do…whatever it is we need to do to force the Shadows out. Because our world isn't as broken as yours, we are better able to communicate with people all over, although with Shamir and Amerika and the Technopaths, yours will get better. We need to find a way to communicate between our two worlds, and I think a Dreamwalker network will enable us to do that. But it'll take time to build, Nikolai. I know you don't believe me, but I swear to you that we'll get you home after. You can go back to your family and Havenhill."

His chest loosens, breath not nearly as raw. "What do you think the next step is? I want to know what you think, for both of us." Nikita's opinion matters to Nikolai. She is Nikolai's other self. Two people, two bodies, twinned across two worlds.

"Building the networks," she says. "We reach out to our allies and build a foundation. We need a Dreamwalker network, and to figure out how to make it safe. Sera can start on a Technopath network, a safe place for Talent online, in this world. Forging more relationships with other Talent will also help us learn where the Shadows came from and give us ideas for how to get rid of them." She holds out both hands, palms up, waiting until Nikolai places his own hands atop hers. "You and me and Del—the first Dreamwalkers in this world to be able to stand in a room together without triggering the apocalypse."

Nikolai glances down at the tiny balls of ice littered over the sidewalk. He snorts.

"This is only a tiny apocalypse," Nikita huffs. "At least weather is real and not part of a Dream. We've got this."

It won't be easy, Nikolai knows, but talking to Nikita makes him think it's possible. He can be part of the solution, not simply along for the ride. "I'm willing to do what it takes," he replies.

Nikita takes a step backward, and he follows, his hands still gripped in hers. "Just think"—she grins—"after dealing with my very loud friends, meeting up with a bunch of Dreamwalkers inside the Dreamscape will be easy, right?"

Nikolai isn't positive he agrees with that assessment. But when they return to the U-shaped table in the back corner and the loud din washes over him again, he has to admit that the Dreamscape is at least a known quantity of chaos.

Mac waves and is by their side in a blink. "Come back before Thorne tries to poach your boyfriend."

"I am not trying to poach his boyfriend," Thorne protests, one hand over his heart. "I'm hurt."

"That's because you never could." Seth reaches for Nikolai, taking him from Nikita's grasp and pulling him onto his lap. "Hey," he says softly, nuzzling Nikolai's cheek. "You okay?"

The crowd and noise are still a lot, but Nikolai has himself under control now. "Yeah. I'm totally fine."

Author unknown; reason for writing unknown.

My grandmother said once that we each have a shadow inside of us. That every person—Talented or otherwise—carries darkness in their heart. She taught us to use our Talents brightly. Strongly. She taught us that darkness doesn't have to mean evil; darkness can be used for good as well as ill.

I wonder, sometimes, if she knew another Shadowwalker, someone else who could slip between the worlds and walk from darkness to darkness and into the light.

She was almost 80 when I Emerged. She found it funny, so I did too. After all, my natural Talent has always been for light.

I remember playing tricks on our family. Nothing mean. I would hide in the shadows, meld with them, then call forth my innate Talent to let out sprays of light, like fireworks bursting from the night. My youngest cousins loved it, and when I grew older, I played with their children in the same way.

I never had children of my own. I wanted them, once, but no world I found felt quite right. I enjoyed my travels too much to be tied down in one place.

And circumstances changed, too.

The shadows grew darker, and the places between the worlds became a haven for fear. I no longer felt safe traveling through those places to find new worlds and new adventures. The creatures in the split seemed to be Shadowwalkers, but they weren't like me. They were mindless. Hungry. They reached toward me as they did toward anyone else.

They carried darkness upon their breath, and they also carried death. They had given in and thought themselves only evil.

I still carried my light.

It became too dangerous to slip between. I was forced to choose one world and make a new life for myself. Where I am now is different from where I was born. Lives are longer, and while I'm old by my birthplace's standards, I'm still young here. The blessing of a long life may be a curse as well; I remember my home and my family, and I wonder if they wonder what became of me.

Did they ever see the darkness I found? Did they ever learn to fear Shadowwalkers instead of rejoicing in the blessings of a new Talent?

My grandmother told me legends when I was a child. Stories of Talents I had never met. Deathstalkers. Soulstealers. Some confuse them with Shadowwalkers, but we are different.

I am not a stealer of souls.

But those creatures—those things that I hesitate to call people, whose minds seem to have been stolen—they reminded me of those legends. What happened to them? Why did they gravitate to the shadows and take our place? What changed?

This world I have chosen is free from the darkness of those Shadowwalkers. Here, it is safe.

I hope that is true of elsewhere.

I hope that is true for the family that I've left behind.

EVOLUTION

25

Being at PHU is fascinating and terrifying.

Everywhere they go is full of people going about their lives as if there isn't a crisis to be averted. Nikolai feels off-balance around them, resisting the lure of the safe life they enjoy. People smile and say hello to him and Seth, friendly and comfortable even though they know nothing about them. Nikolai isn't sure how to handle them. It's overwhelming.

The library is Nikolai's favorite place on campus. On their second day in this world, Pawel gave him and Seth small plastic university identification cards that can be used as money to obtain food at on-campus cafés. The card also allow them access to the library and, better yet, to the small special collections room focused on Talent.

Seth sometimes grabs Nikolai, clutching him tightly. Seth has told Nikolai that, to Seth's senses, campus is a riot of emotions: a rush of anxiety mixed with random notes of pleasure. They are thankful to have the special collections room to retreat to. Within that space Seth is centered, creating a soft blanket of calm to settle over them both.

This one room is a treasure trove. It's filled with books about Talent, old books and new, hand-written or printed in small runs. The door locks behind them; Pawel explained that only Magical Studies majors can access the room, and then only with his permission.

The books' content doesn't always match what Nikolai learned as a child, but they offer an interesting counterpoint.

They read voraciously while Nikolai drinks cocoa and Seth discovers a strong love of bitter coffee. At first, Nikolai dislikes the bitterness on Seth's tongue when they kiss, but it becomes part of kissing Seth, a part of his taste.

They adapt, slowly but surely.

Their ID cards show them as visiting scholars, and while the librarian on duty gave Pawel a dubious look when he introduced them, she is kind enough after that. It feels as if they have an ally in the library, someone who won't look strangely at them when they ask questions.

When Nikolai's stomach rumbles on Wednesday afternoon, they gather their few things, make their way to the front desk, and ask her for directions to Teas Please.

She smiles, prints out a map, and highlights the route. "Everyone loves Teas Please," she says. "If they aren't in the library's coffee shop, they go there for tea and crêpes."

"We've been, right after we arrived," Nikolai tells her. "It was good, so we figured we'd go back for dinner tonight."

"There are some other good places around campus; I can mark them off for you." The librarian holds out her hand, and Nikolai gives her back the printout so she can highlight and label several addresses.

The names of the restaurants go over his head, but they'll have time to investigate. Pawel gave them cards that function as money in this world and instructed them to buy what they need. One of these days, they need to explore. Even if they plan to leave, they should learn as much as they can and take that knowledge back with them. Use it to help rebuild in Havenhill once the Shadows are gone.

He and Seth link hands as they walk along the pathways that wind through campus, heading for one of the roads that leads out. It's a warm spring day, and there are people everywhere. The sun hangs low in the sky, there's a low breeze, and the lawn reminds Nikolai of a beach. There are knots of people sitting on blankets or towels. A few wear bathing suits, lying in the sun despite the coolness of the air. A Frisbee sails by, and a girl apologizes as she darts past them to grab it and throw it back to her friend.

The atmosphere is full of joy, in an entirely different way than the sugaring festival had been. Nikolai has heard the news of this world—killings and famine and poisonous water—but these students feel innocent.

They have no idea how different the world could be.

Seth squeezes his hand, and Nikolai squeezes back. Even if they stop the

Shadow invasion back home, they won't see their world become like this in their lifetimes. But they can help it start down that path.

When they reach Teas Please, they don't recognize the hostess who greets them. She has two menus in her hand and is about to mark something on a sheet in front of her when a waiter swoops in. He puts his hands on her shoulders and he leans in to whisper something in her ear; she looks at Nikolai and Seth, wide-eyed.

"Oh," she says, handing the menus off to the waiter, then marking a different spot on her sheet. "Nate will show you to your booth."

"I hear you've been here before," Nate says cheerfully as he leads them through the restaurant and into the back again. The U-shaped booth is empty and seems far too large for the two of them, but Nate drops the menus there anyway. He waves for them to sit. "You'll have company soon. Alaric asked me to keep an eye out for you, and if Alaric's coming by, there'll be a crowd before we know it. It usually works that way."

Seth slides in along the back wall, and Nikolai sits next to him. "Thanks," Nikolai says.

"He sent me pictures. That's how I recognized you." Nate shows them the image on his phone—they've been having lessons on how these phones work since they arrived, and they've posed for several pictures. "I'm Nate, and I'll be your waiter. Do you want any tea or water to get started? Any advice on the menu? Or"—he lowers his voice—"Mallory's in the kitchen, which means if you want a chef's special, today's the day to get it."

Seth's brow furrows as he closes the menu. "What's the chef's special?"

"I tell Mallory a little about you, and she makes whatever she thinks you'd like. She reminds me of the mother of a friend of mine. A teammate of Alaric's actually—the friend, not the mother." Nate slides onto the bench opposite them, leaning on the table. "Similar Talents, I think, although Mallory swears she's not Talented, just 'good at reading people.' So. Advice, time to look, or a Mallory special?"

"I want something I haven't had in a while," Nikolai says. "Something that reminds me of my childhood and doesn't have ingredients from cans or jars or anything else that was in a safehouse." He assumes Nate's heard their story.

"We'll share. You have those tiered things." Seth raises his hand above the table, then gestures at a couple at a smaller table with two of the three-tiered setups on their table.

"Afternoon tea, yes. You get a crêpe or a sandwich, a salad or a soup, and a dessert. Some options cost extra."

Nikolai digs into his pocket and pulls out the money card Pawel gave him. "This should be enough to afford that, right? Pawel said he put money on it and that we should use it."

"Should be good," Nate agrees. "So you guys want to share a—"

"Not sharing," Seth said. "Not like you're thinking. We each want one of those tea things, and we'll pick from the choices so there's no duplicates." He opens the menu and looks at it, frowning intently as he holds up his hand in a signal for everyone to pause.

Nikolai points at options, and Seth nods his responses. Nikolai doesn't mind letting Seth make the final decision, and he likes that they're getting lots to share.

In the end, they choose a savory crêpe, a bowl of lobster bisque, a simple green salad, a pilgrim sandwich, a sweet crêpe with raspberries, and a slice of marbled tea cake.

It sounds like a lot of food between the two of them.

It also sounds like bliss.

Alaric arrives before their food does, with a girl in tow. She has a silver bar in one eyebrow and a cluster of five silver rings at her temple. A nose ring peeks out, and when she reaches across the table with one hand to introduce herself as Sera, Nikolai stares at the intricate black ink decorating her hand and continuing up her wrist.

Alaric murmurs something, and Sera thwacks his chest with the back of her hand.

"We brought you phones," Sera says, sliding two devices across the table at them. "They're ready to run through a setup routine, and they're online, and you have email addresses and phone numbers." She gives them each envelopes. "Memorize all that and don't let anyone else have it. Security is everything, and if someone gets that information, they can essentially become another you. Technologically, not literal shapeshifting."

None of that makes sense, but Nikolai knows the polite response: "Thank you."

She walks them through answering questions on the phone screens by tapping, typing in the email addresses and passwords from the envelopes, then pressing their fingers to the little buttons to set a fingerprint scan, then finally letting the phones somehow recognize their faces. It's nonsense, but Nikolai follows the instructions, and when they're done, he can at least get into his phone and lock it when she tells him to do so.

"There are a lot of apps. You don't need anything complicated, but you do need to learn how to make a call, answer a call, and deal with texts," Sera says. "When we set up your accounts, we put most of the things you'd need in the cloud, so they'll load onto your phones automatically."

Nikolai stares at the thing in his hand. It's cold, and the text is weirdly small. He's not sure he likes it. "Okay," he agrees.

"Touch here," Alaric instructs, and both Nikolai and Seth touch the same place on their respective phones. It opens up a screen with a list of names, and Alaric shows them how to scroll through. Nikolai spots Seth on his list, and his own name on Seth's list. Several of the other given names are familiar, even if the surnames are not.

Seth mumbles something under his breath, and Alaric huffs. "Szczek," Alaric says. "It's Polish."

There are names Nikolai doesn't know—Drea Herne, and someone named Corbin. Dayton. Susan. Lucy. He thinks about getting rid of the strangers, but Alaric put them in there for a reason. Maybe Nikolai needs them. He can't think why.

Seth touches something on his screen; Nikolai's phone vibrates, then sings out with music Nikolai doesn't recognize. Seth's name flashes on his screen, and Sera reaches across to show Nikolai how to answer.

It's been a long time since he's used a phone, and he's never seen one like this. He remembers mobile phones as being more awkward. Clunky, something only his parents or older brothers had.

On the other hand, he's the same age his brothers were when they went to college, right before the Split.

That's a hell of a thought.

"Hey, everyone!" Nikita waves as she slides between two tables to reach them. She hip-checks Sera, encouraging her and Alaric to move down the bench. That leaves room for Nikita and Heather to join them.

Behind them are more familiar faces. Carolyn stands with Serina, the server from the other night. Serina has her palms on either side of Carolyn's face, thumbs light against her cheekbones as they rub their noses together. Carolyn tugs Serina in, arms wrapped around her for a long moment before Serina withdraws and presses a kiss to Carolyn's cheek.

"I've got to get to my shift," Serina says, waving with a flick of her fingers. "Nice to see you, Nik and Seth! Is Nate serving you? I'll make sure he brings your food out soon. Oh! Do the rest of you know what you want? I can bring your orders back and get them started."

Everyone shouts orders and Serina nods, then repeats it all back to them to confirm she's got everything right. She runs off, and the newcomers shrug out of their jackets.

"This happens all the time," Nikita says. "One person comes here, and then suddenly we have a crowd, and seriously, if we sit here long enough, half my floor will show up." She wrinkles her nose, then clarifies, "Half the people who live on the same floor of my dorm as I do."

Carolyn holds a small bundle of fabric. She unwraps her deck of cards, setting it on the table in front of Nikolai. "I was thinking, since we seem to have moved into and possibly through some of your last reading, a three-card reading might help us re-focus." There's a soft flush on her cheeks. "Serina said you were talking about the cards with her the other night?"

"No Death," Seth says firmly. "We've had enough change at this point."

"We're still in for a lot more change," Alaric rumbles. "I've been talking to Dayton—"

Nikolai remembers the name from their phones.

"Who?" Seth asks.

"One of my Clan allies. You have her number. Things are changing for Clan, at least in this area," Alaric explains. "We've always been traditional. What you saw in Havenhill isn't like my home now, but it's how I'd like us to become. More relationships with other Talents. Opening the community so we can grow. We can't stay the same."

Sera knocks into Alaric. "Look at you being all grown up and everything."

He bares his teeth and growls at her; she grins in response.

Carolyn idly shuffles the cards "We don't have to, if you don't want. Or we could do a general reading, for everyone. It might accidentally lock on to one person here, or it might give a general idea of the future we're all working toward. Because we are all working on something, right?"

"We need to build a Dreamwalker network and a Technopath network," Nikita says.

"I love that you have a name for me now," Sera murmurs. Her gaze has shifted, staring into the air somewhere over Carolyn's head. "I'm working on that, but it'll take time. I'm figuring out how to get the word out to the right people while keeping it a secret from non-Talented folk, because that could cause all kinds of entertaining trouble. Doesn't help that I don't know a single other Talent like me."

"Building a Dreamwalker network will be difficult; we can't bring them all to one location," Heather points out. "It'll have to start online."

Seth gestures from Nikita to Nikolai. "We can meet in the Dreamscape," he says, "and maybe in person. In case you haven't noticed, we have two of them right here. And didn't we have three the other day? Your Dreamwalkers need to learn control."

"We also had an ice storm that first day, and now we have 70-degree weather three days later." Heather leans forward, her hands clasped on the table. "Nikita and Nikolai are a special case; other Dreamwalkers from this world will be different. Right now, a meeting between more than just the two of you is asking for trouble."

"Pawel is working to set up an online Dreamwalker chat," Nikita says. "He knows a few Dreamwalkers, including the one I trained with. That'll get us started, and then we can use those contacts to set up a meeting in the Dreamscape."

"Where is our erstwhile leader?" Sera asks. "If we're talking about saving the world, shouldn't he be here?"

"He's in a weird position, socializing with his students," Carolyn says. "We've all spent a lot of time with him recently. The administration might say it's inappropriate."

"Mac told me that he had an appointment," Alaric says. When Carolyn makes a face, he adds, "Don't think we have typical student-professor relationships with him anymore."

"You're right. The line is blurred right now," Heather adds.

Nikolai and Seth's food arrives: two tiered cages, each three plates high. The scent of raspberry catches Nikolai first, followed by warm turkey and cranberry. Memories twist in his gut, and he reaches for the sandwich first. He breaks it, handing one half to Seth before taking a huge bite of his own.

Carolyn is still shuffling her cards, waiting for an answer. Nikolai ignores her, letting the conversation flow without him as he and Seth share first the sandwich, then the bowl of soup, alternating as they dip their spoons in and savor it.

Carolyn sets her deck aside when Nate brings the rest of the food, including a plate for himself. He pulls up a chair at the end of the table. "I've got a thirty-minute break," Nate says. "I've been going since the breakfast rush, and never took either of my fifteens. Serina will handle my tables while I hang out with you."

One of Nate's eyes drifts inward, and Nikolai finds himself staring at it, but when he apologizes, Nate waves him off. "I've had a lazy eye since I was a kid, and by the time anyone noticed, it was too late to fix it. Doesn't affect much. I don't need great hand-eye coordination. I only want to run a long way as fast as I can, and I can see the distance perfectly fine."

"You're a runner," Nikolai says. "My brother Mikhail was one in high school. He wasn't very good at it."

"I'm really good at it." Nate's gaze is far away, staring at an imaginary horizon in the distance. "When I'm running, it's me and the track or the road. I can feel the cadence in my feet; it mixes with my heartbeat. I've been doing it since I was a kid, and it got me a scholarship to PHU." He jerks his chin toward Alaric. "His teammate, Dax, started running this spring, and he looks like he might be pretty good once he finds his rhythm." Seth nudges a plate in front of Nikolai; it holds half the sweet crêpe and half the slice of tea cake, and both smell amazing. Nikolai nibbles while Nate keeps talking. "We started training together over spring break. He's used to running drills for football, but distance running is different from sprints.

It's impressive that he's as good as he is at both."

"When you talk about running, it sounds almost like fun," Nikolai says, "rather than a thing we had to do in order to survive."

"I don't think I'd enjoy it half as much if I were running from demons," Nate says. "The zombie apocalypse never sounds attractive."

Carolyn shuffles her cards again, the cardboard making a soft *zip* in her hand, claiming Nikolai's attention. She's not speaking, but the shuffling is a stronger hint than words would be.

Nikolai lowers his fork, watching the cards slip and slide together. "Okay," he says finally. "Last time, your cards warned me I was going to walk between worlds. Let's see what they say this time."

"Three-card reading," Carolyn explains. "I'll do a standard past-present-future layout." She stops shuffling and offers the deck to Nikolai. He waves it away, but Seth reaches out, takes off the top few cards, and sets them aside.

Carolyn nods and flips cards. The first card, on the left and upside down from Carolyn's perspective, is labeled "Temperance." A topless woman stands by a stream, pouring water from a cup into the stream without looking at either.

"This is your past," Carolyn says.

"I have never been a half-naked woman," Seth says dryly.

Carolyn continues as if he didn't speak. "It's a card of carelessness and indecision. It's about giving up rather than moving forward, or about spinning in place without making the decisions you need to make to stop going in circles. She's pouring the water into the stream and it's washing away. She's not even looking to see where it goes."

Seth's brow furrows. "Go on."

She lays down the second card, and Nikolai remembers it from the first reading she did for him. "This one is about balance," he says, and she smiles at him and taps it.

"The Six of Swords, and yes, it is. This card represented your thoughts about yourself last time," she says. "It refers to balance, but it's also about finding a new way to think that helps you achieve balance."

"Like coming here is a shift in how we think," Seth says slowly.

"Possibly," Carolyn says as she turns over the final card.

The man on the card is grinning, leaping across the sky with eight wands shooting through the air around him. He looks joyous.

Seth touches the cards. "Okay, so from the pictures alone, this looks like we go from wavering indecision, to balance, to leaping forward into the bright unknown."

"Pretty much," Carolyn agrees. She lifts the final card to show it to them more clearly. "This one isn't just about moving. It's about those big, sweeping changes that also result in big successes. If you weren't taking chances in the past, this recommends taking huge chances in the future."

"Like laying all our hope on things that have never been tried and might not work," Nikita says.

"Like doing something that might be risky because the reward will be worth it," Nikolai replies.

"This says you should take the chance," Carolyn says. She sweeps the cards back into her deck, glancing at Nate when he pauses, one hand raised in her direction. "Did you want a reading of your own?"

He retreats, pushing himself to his feet. "Maybe later. It's busy tonight, and Serina's on her own, so I should get back. Besides, I know I'm not leaping into the unknown. I'm running, steady and true and as fast as I can while keeping a good pace." Nate gathers up his empty plates, then stacks a few more on top of them. "I'll be back in a while to clear the table for you guys. Anyone want dessert while I'm heading to the kitchen?"

Everyone calls out at once, and Nate manages to sort the chaos into coherent orders. Nikolai's already had his dessert, so he takes out the phone Alaric gave him and looks through it. He scrolls through the contacts, understanding the phone part of it but still uncertain about this "online" that has been mentioned. The Dreamscape is easier for him to understand.

Balance.

He exhales, not seeing the phone in his hands as he considers Carolyn's reading. She's right. He's not in his own world, but he's still balanced in this moment. They're all balanced in this moment. It's precarious, and they need to pick the right direction.

Their next step will be a leap of faith.

26

When the doorbell rings during dinner, Nikolai jumps up. "I've got it." Maybe he should let Pawel get it—it's his house, after all—but sitting through meals with Pawel is a strange experience, like watching a child fidget, wanting to be anywhere but where he is. Nikolai can't figure out why Pawel is going through the motions of formal meals when it's obvious he has other things on his mind.

Nikolai pulls open the door, and Nikita shoves a pile of…bags?…at him. He isn't sure what he's holding, although he sees hangers poking out of one end.

He steps back to let Heather, Mac, and an unfamiliar girl into the house. Mac carries a similar large stack of bags. Nikita runs back to the bright-orange truck to grab one last stack before hip-checking the door closed.

"Mac," Pawel says.

"Pawel," Mac replies. "I warned you."

"See, there's a thing," Nikita says in a rush. She lays the bags on the couch, then grabs Nikolai and Seth by their wrists, pulling them close to her. "We're in a sorority. Or well. They're in a sorority, along with Carolyn, and a whole bunch of other people. I'm dating a girl in the sorority."

Nikolai follows that so far. Mostly. "You belong to an organization of women in school. Okay. So?"

"Heather does," Nikita corrects him. "I'm her date. It's an important distinction here because that's why we cannot possibly be your dates."

Nikolai looks at Seth; Seth blinks back at him and shrugs. "I don't get it," Seth says.

"The SigPsiEp formal is tomorrow night and it's a huge *thing*, and I know it isn't anything world-healing or earth-shattering, but it's really cool, and I'm going and it's not like you've got anything else to do, so Heather and I found dates for you so you can both go," Nikita blurts out.

Nikolai still doesn't get it.

"What?" Seth says.

"We're all going to a formal dance!" Nikita claps her hands, gesturing at the bags Nikolai holds. "Mac and Trish will be your dates in name only. We brought suits and dresses so we can figure out what you're each wearing and make sure you match!"

Nikolai suspects he should have a response to this other than the complete blankness inside his head.

Pawel presses his fingertips to the bridge of his nose. "Mac. I told you this would be a—"

"It's like prom for college," Seth says slowly.

Oh. That makes sense.

"Yes!" Nikita points both fingers at him. "If you remember what prom was like, it's exactly like that except it's college instead of high school and there may be drinking."

"We're going," Seth decides, tone firm enough that Nikolai won't argue with him. "As long as we can dance with each other." He points between himself and Nikolai.

Nikolai had written prom off along with the entire high school experience. This is a chance to make a memory he won't get back home in Havenhill. "You're going to make this into something ridiculously romantic," he murmurs, and he's not surprised when Seth answers with a kiss.

"See, I told you they'd do it!" Nikita says cheerfully. "Next step is getting everyone outfitted. We borrowed clothes from several people so we can find the best fit, and I'm hoping Nikolai isn't too skinny for everything we got that's tall. Nikolai, your date will be Trish." She indicates the girl he doesn't know, who wiggles her fingers in a small wave at him.

"Hey," Trish says in a soft drawl. "I've been friends with Heather and Mac here since our freshman year when we pledged together. I promise I don't bite unless someone asks me to."

"Don't scare the boys." Mac elbows her. "Trish is outgoing but harmless. She's also mostly out of the loop about the insanity going on around her and claims she's just happy to do something that lets her see we're still alive."

"You say that like I wasn't worried about you," Trish counters. When she turns, Nikolai catches a hint of ink on the back of her neck before her hair falls into place over it. "Y'all disappeared on me."

Mac sets a hand on her shoulder. "It wasn't intentional, and if we could've warned you, we would've. Believe me, gallivanting off to another world wasn't part of our project plan, either."

"They want to save the world, and me, I want to make music and fix engines," Trish says. She pushes her hair back from her face, and it falls in long waves. Her soft drawl sounds low and easy, but Seth tenses. Nikolai guesses from his body language that Trish is hiding a lot of tension. "The formal's a big party. Once we're there, you can dance with whoever you want. I'm figuring that I'm your date because you're the tall one, and Mac would need high heels to be in pictures with you."

"I'm glad you made a comment about Mac's height, not mine," Seth mutters dryly.

"It's not an actual date, so it doesn't matter. You and Nikolai look good together," Heather says. "Come on. We've got suits for you to try on; we want to do coordinating dresses for Mac and Trish." She glances over her shoulder. "Are you wearing a dress, Trish?"

Trish lifts one shoulder. "Usually do, for things like this. I did learn how to be a belle before I learned how to ride a motorcycle." She flashes a quick grin. "Had my arms up to the elbows in truck engines long before either of those things, though."

"The folks back home would like you," Nikolai comments. She'd get along great with Mikhail. Especially if she could help keep the Jeep running. "Everyone does something in Havenhill. We felt a little useless because we never learned practical skills like fixing engines."

"It's never too late."

Nikolai doesn't get the chance to respond as Nikita wraps an arm around his and nudges him toward the stairs. "Heather's bringing the suits. Let's get you changed."

They head upstairs and into Nikolai's and Seth's room. Heather spreads clothes across the bed, reminding Nikolai of when his father used to dress for work; when Seth holds a suit up in front of himself, Nikolai sees Seth's father as well.

Seth turns to look at himself in the mirror. His head tilts, and his brow furrows as he slowly lowers the suit, his fingers crumpling the fabric. "Do you have one that's lighter?"

"Fabric or color?" Nikita asks. She rifles through the piles and comes up with a suit in soft dove gray. "Try this one. It'll go with any dark and bold shirt, too, which gives us loads of options for matching you to Mac."

"What if I want to match Nikolai?" Seth asks.

"That'll be more of a challenge, but we're up to the task," Trish says. She leans in the doorway, motioning with a hand. "Don't mind me. I'm here for the suits, not to ogle the boys."

Nikolai looks to Nikita for help as he points at the door. "Out," he says. "We aren't dolls. You don't need to dress us. We can figure out how suits work."

They manage to get the girls out of the room and the door closed, only a muffled rumble of voices audible through the walls between them. Nikolai sifts through the piles of clothing, coming up with a pair of dark-gray slacks that seem long enough. They hang a little loose on his narrow hips, but they don't show his ankles and should stay up with a belt. Finding a jacket proves more difficult; all the options with long enough arms are too wide for his shoulders. He finally locates a lightweight one that fits across his shoulders even though the sleeves are too short for his arms; he can roll them to disguise the lack of length.

The light-gray suit, on the other hand, is a perfect fit for Seth. He's wearing it over a T-shirt, and even that looks amazing. Seth smooths it down, glancing at Nikolai worriedly. "I look ridiculous."

"You look like your father," Nikolai responds. There's a flash of pain in Seth's expression, his mouth pressed closed and lines tight around his eyes. Nikolai steps over the pairs of slacks that have slid off the bed and onto the floor to get to Seth and pulls him in for a warm hug, holding him against the painful memories. "And you look fantastic," he murmurs.

Seth goes lax slowly, releasing tight muscles by inches. When he pulls back, he shifts his grip so that they stand as if preparing to dance. Seth rests his arms over Nikolai's shoulders, and Nikolai holds his hands loosely at the small of Seth's back. Seth hums under his breath, and Nikolai sways with him in his arms.

It's nice.

Voices rise in the hall, and a sharp *rap* on the door interrupts them. "Are you decent?" Nikita calls out.

"It's safe," Seth calls back, not bothering to stop swaying to the music in their minds. He touches Nikolai's cheek, and Nikolai bends down so they can stand forehead to forehead.

"Awwww," Nikita says, and there's a *click* in the background. "You guys are so cute. We have to print out a bunch of pictures for you to take back with you. You should have these memories when you go home."

It's the first time she's referenced them leaving without Nikolai prompting her, and it makes his heart light to hear the words.

"We'll make a scrapbook, assuming we have enough time," Heather says. She moves into the room and collects scattered clothes, folding them neatly or placing them on hangers.

"Send them to me after the formal, and I'll make sure they get printed," Trish says. "Sera can send them off, or I'll have Soledad take them. Be prepared, right? In case y'all get whisked away again." She steps close to Nikolai and Seth; even in her sneakers she's taller than Seth. She tilts her head at them. "You both clean up pretty good. I'm guessing no one'll let me wear my favorite orange dress this time, huh?"

"We want to coordinate," Mac says. "Although I look damned good in yellow, so it's not entirely out as an option."

Pawel clears a space on the bed and sits down, distracted by the phone in his hand. He waves at the door. "Mac, Trish, use my room to pick out your dresses and find matching shirts for Nikolai and Seth. I want to talk to Nikolai and Nikita about the Dreamwalker network."

Heather helps Trish and Mac carry another stack of bags and clothes down the hall to Pawel's room, closing the door behind them. Pawel gestures at the bed. "Make a space. Sit and get comfortable."

Nikolai and Seth find a spot that isn't covered in suits and they sit. They lean back against the wall, shoulder to shoulder. Nikita crosses her arms and remains standing by the window.

"Don't," Pawel murmurs.

Nikita raises her hands, palms out and fingers spread. "I'm fine. Under control and not freaking out. I just don't feel like sitting." She lifts the curtain, then lets it fall. "I'm keeping an eye on the clouds."

Pawel lowers the phone, pulling his feet up to sit cross-legged. "The good news is, I've made several additional contacts with Dreamwalkers around the world."

"The bad news is, they all think a Dreamwalker network is an insanely bad idea," Nikita deadpans.

He looks at her, exhaling roughly. "Yes. Their gut instinct reaction is 'no,' which isn't surprising considering how Dreamwalker interactions in this world usually go. However, I have explained how Nikolai's world bonds Dreamwalkers with Empaths, and every single one of them was able to relate a story implying that may work here as well."

Seth gestures from Nikita to the door. "Nikita and Heather."

"Exactly. One noted that she's found she's less likely to Dream when she visits her brother, who married an Empath. Another remembered dating an Empath when he was first learning to deal with his Talent, but they lost track of each other. Many have been drawn to Empaths and found proximity to them calming. Thus, to gather Dreamwalkers in one place, we also need to find their Empaths. The eleven people to whom I've spoken are committed to finding those Empaths. And they'll also continue to reach out to other Dreamwalkers and bring them into the online space we have created."

"What about meeting in the Dreamscape?" Nikolai asks. He doesn't need to be an Empath to feel the way Seth goes tense next to him. He leans against Seth and stretches one leg out, tangling their ankles. "Del and I met there, and we may be able to reach Dreamwalkers from my world there. If everyone is anchored so that they can't disappear into a Dream, it might be the safest place for this world's Dreamwalkers to meet. We won't be going there physically; if we did, we'd be at risk for—" He cuts off because he's not actually sure what the risks are. "What matters most is making sure every Dreamwalker has someone with them to anchor them in reality."

"I'm sending you an invitation to the online space." Pawel taps on the screen of his phone. When he's done, Nikolai's phone—currently nearby on the bed—vibrates. "Begin there. Get to know the other Dreamwalkers from this world. Nikolai, you have more experience as a Dreamwalker than many here do. The Talent is pushed down here; few risk using it. Please help teach them."

Online. Nikolai knows now that online spaces are where Technopaths go—when Sera stares into space, that's what she sees. He imagines it's like a Dreamscape made of wires and machines. Speaking to Dreamwalkers in the Dreamscape sounds more productive to him; it's their natural space.

"Eventually we need to Dream," he says. "The Dreamwalkers from my world are hopefully also making a network in our absence, and we can't meet them online." Nikolai hopes the people of Havenhill are reaching out; after Alia's reaction to the proposition, he can't be sure.

The door down the hall slams open, footsteps and chatter approaching quickly. Nikita claps her hands as Trish appears in the doorway. Her dress is off one shoulder, the fabric crossing her chest like a bathing suit top, another strip going over the shoulder. The skirt clings until her hips, where the fit softens, becoming a long, flared skirt. And it is, indeed, orange—and black, in a tie-dye-like pattern that shimmers as she moves.

Mac squeezes into the room past Trish, her own dress closer to yellow than orange. It's a less striking design—a simple cut with a skirt that swirls mid-calf when she walks—but it looks good with her build. Mac holds out two ties that match the dresses. "We'll get dark-gray shirts for you," she says. "Let's get some pictures now so that our Sisters can approve."

"Your friends have to approve?"

"'Approve' isn't the right word." Heather spreads her hands. "The SigPsiEp formal tends to be a collective affair. It's very social."

Nikolai takes the tie from Trish and stares at it uncertainly. He has never worn one and barely remembers his father wearing one. It looks uncomfortable.

"Come here." Pawel gestures, and Nikolai hands him the tie. Pawel frowns, gesturing at the T-shirt, but Nikolai doesn't have anything else to wear, so Pawel puts the tie around his own neck, tying it with quick efficiency then loosening it to hand it to Nikolai. He does the same for Seth's.

Nikolai feels ridiculous in a T-shirt, suit, and tie, but Seth looks almost the same, which helps ease the embarrassment. Nikita places them in front of the window together; Mac stands on Seth's other side and Trish presses close to Nikolai. As Nikita takes pictures, Trish and Mac behave progressively sillier, until Nikolai can't help but laugh as well.

The last picture has Trish pretending to push him into Seth's arms, while Mac does the same with Seth. Nikolai doesn't want to resist, so he gathers Seth close and kisses him again.

"We're set for formal." Heather tucks her phone back into her pocket.

"Nikita, catch Heather up on what we discussed," Pawel says, and the atmosphere becomes immediately charged and serious. "Spend some time looking through the chat and getting to know the people I've pulled together. This requires a group effort. Nikolai, remember what I said about providing information from your experience."

There's a hint of concern in the air, masked as soon as Seth sidles close again.

"That's a problem for later." Mac pushes between them. "Heather, Nik, get these clothes back out to the truck. Seth and Nikolai, you hold on to your suits, and I'll have someone bring over shirts for you. Trish, let's change and get out of here. Pawel deserves a little peace and quiet." She gives him a stern look. "He should relax since he's obviously been working hard on world-saving problems all day."

"I'm not—" Pawel cuts off, his hands in the air. "Fine. We'll relax."

"Do I need to come back and make you watch movies after you call your son?" Mac asks.

Pawel wavers.

"He's going to disappear into his room and keep researching," Seth points out. "We're interested in the movies, if the offer is open."

"We'll *all* watch movies." Mac shoves a pile of clothes into Nikita's arms. "That includes you, Pawel. Go downstairs and call Conor, then order some Thai. I'm in the mood for noodles."

Nikolai likes that Mac is taking charge. He needs to talk to these

Dreamwalkers, and he needs to convince them that going into the Dreamscape is their best—and safest—option. But he also knows that there are risks, even if he's not able to quantify what those risks are.

He likes the idea of taking a night off, of being a teenager as he hasn't been before and that won't be possible when they return to Havenhill. The network will be there tomorrow.

27

The formal is held on Friday evening someplace off campus. Everything looks different in this world, the roads thick with cars zipping by. He likes the perspective Trish's truck allows, letting them look down on the other cars as they pass by. He also appreciates that Mac is in the front, letting Nikolai and Seth have the back seat together.

When Nikita had said "sorority" and "formal," Nikolai hadn't envisioned so many people crammed into a ballroom. There are large round tables scattered around the room and long, food-laden tables set up around the edges. Nikolai spots people he knows: Mac, Heather, Nikita, Carolyn, Trish, and Serina. The eight of them grab a table, leaving jackets and purses on the seats before they move out to be social. Trish keeps one hand on Nikolai's elbow, and Seth is carried along by Mac.

The photograph booth is the first stop, and Nikolai is charmed by how they print instantly, allowing him and Seth to carry them back to the table. They have pictures of the group divided into their couples for the formal; then they rearrange to put Seth and Nikolai together as a couple in the center, while Trish and Mac bookend the group. They do pictures of each couple alone, including Seth and Nikolai. Mac lifts Trish up and carries her, bridal style, in front of the camera; the images capture Trish pulling Mac down for a kiss, and Mac tossing Trish over her shoulder before blipping out of existence.

Nikita leans close to Nikolai to murmur, "Pretty sure Trish would be into that, but not Mac. I think Mac's straight, but mostly, Mac's heart was broken and she's not ready to deal with another relationship. Everyone is really respectful of that, and she and Trish are actually super close, enough so that Trish can get away with teasing her."

Seth leans around Nikolai to say, "Isn't some of that too personal to tell us?"

Nikita shakes her head. "They're both totally open about all of it. I'm only giving you context." She motions. "Come on. There won't be dancing until after we've eaten, maybe not even until the dessert tables are out. Nikolai, I want at least one dance with you, okay?"

"Okay," he agrees, letting her lead them to the buffet tables.

Nikolai hasn't starved for long enough, now, that he doesn't feel the need to take a little of everything. He picks and chooses from the available choices, taking what appeals. He'll still probably go back for seconds, and maybe thirds.

"Are you adding boys to the pledges now?" a voice calls out. The speaker isn't within Nikolai's personal space, but Nikolai still steps closer to Seth as he turns to face the man who stands two people behind Nikita in line. The stranger flashes a grin. "Looks like you two are here together, right?" He gestures between Nikolai and Seth.

Seth pushes his glasses up his nose, frowning at the newcomer. "Yes, but no. I'm here with Mac, and Nikolai is with Trish."

"Don't mind Corbin. He doesn't think until after he speaks, but we love him anyway." The girl looks familiar to Nikolai. He takes in the shape of her face and her height, and tries to match her appearance to someone he met at home. Maybe she's an echo of someone, like himself and Nikita.

Corbin stares at him in response, his gaze sharp, seeming to pick over every detail of Nikolai's clothes, until the girl elbows him and he looks at her. Corbin's expression softens. "Yes, I know who they are," he admits.

It clicks. Nikolai knows who the girl is. "You're Alaric's sister."

A shout from farther down the line encourages them to keep moving. Nikolai fills his plate while distracted by the newcomers.

"Yep. I'm Drea," she says, "and this is my boyfriend, Corbin. He's Alaric's best friend, so the longer you stay here, the more likely you are to have to deal with him. And me." She reaches out without looking, her hand thwacking against Corbin's chest. "So be nice," she says to him.

"I'm always nice," Corbin protests. "I'm just nicer some of the time." His sharp gaze falls to Nikolai again. "I'd like to talk later."

Nikolai can't think what they need to talk about, but it's easier to agree. That way, he can step away and eat. He heads to the table they'd claimed earlier, while Drea and Corbin head to a different table. Nikolai watches Corbin talk while gesturing enthusiastically and pointing at their table while other strangers look on.

"By the time this evening is over, everyone here will know we're visiting from another world," Nikolai mutters.

Nikita waves off his words. "They've already heard about you. Once secrets get told, they travel fast, like when we all found out about Mac's teleportation."

"That said, secrets that need to be kept get kept," Mac points out with a jab of her fork. "It took more than two years and a murder attempt before mine came out."

"Why is our presence the kind of secret that needs to be told?" Seth asks, his brow furrowed as he stares back at one girl who glares at them as if she can read their minds across the distance.

"We disappeared into thin air for two weeks and came back with the two of you," Mac says. "We're a close-knit group, and our friends and families were worried. Where we'd gone was not a secret that could be kept. I know you think that no one in this world is thinking about the Shadows and the danger they present, but those of us who have some idea what's going on? We're scared. Yes, we're here, and we're acting like everything's fine, but that's because we can't devote every second of every day to fighting this. So we take time out for things that were already planned, like this formal. We recuperate, revitalize, and re-evaluate, and we move on. It's strategic."

Nikolai can accept her explanation, but it doesn't make having a room full of strangers staring at him any easier to stomach.

Once they finish eating, Carolyn and Serina make their way to the dance floor; Nikita and Heather follow not long after. Nikolai lingers over his meal, and when Seth gets up to make another pass at the buffet, Nikolai chooses to stay where he is, listening to Trish talk about some music-related trip she's taking over the summer.

Nikita's chair pulls out, and Nikolai glances over as a tall, broad-shouldered man lowers himself to sit in it. His expression is pained, the tension lines easing around his eyes as soon as he meets Nikolai's gaze. "That's what I thought," he says.

"What's what you thought?" Nikolai replies. The girl with the hard stare from earlier sits in the chair beside the newcomer; her expression hasn't eased.

"I'm Dax. I'm on the football team with Alaric." Dax holds out his hand, and Nikolai takes it, brow furrowing when Dax holds on longer than seems necessary.

The girl's lips purse. "Well?"

"He's part of it," Dax says to her. To Nikolai he says, "This is Cass. My girlfriend. I wanted to talk to you because I had a sense you might be part of something I'm helping Alaric with. And while I can't say how or why exactly, if you need anything from me while you're here, just ask."

Nikolai thinks on why Dax seems familiar. He's tall, with short curls framing his face, and has a square jaw. It hits him, then, that he's heard the name before. "You're Nate's friend. The runner."

"Let me guess," Cass says dryly. "You've been to Teas Please. Because everyone's been to Teas Please, even people who've only been in this world for half a second."

"Cass," Dax murmurs.

She gestures. "Sorry, I'm interrupting. Go on. The world revolves around Nate and his scones and crêpes, I'm aware."

"I'm pretty sure that if the world revolves around anything, it's the back corner table that someone marked as 'reserved for the PHU magical troublemakers,'" Mac retorts with a grin. "Cass, you don't have to go there if you don't want."

There's an underlying current between them that makes Nikolai wish that Seth were there to smooth everyone's emotions out. "What are you doing for Alaric?" he asks instead, because that has to be a safer topic.

Or maybe not, from the way everyone goes silent and exchanges glances.

"Did I miss something?" Seth slides a plate of ravioli in front of Nikolai, then neatly cuts one with a fork, stabbing it to steal half. He puts his free hand on Nikolai's knee, and the tension melts away.

"Meet Dax and Cass," Nikolai says. He leaves it to Dax to explain anything else.

"I talk to ghosts," Dax mutters.

Cass glances sideways, lips pursed as she scans the space around their table, and Nikolai thinks maybe this is one of those secrets that isn't as widely known.

"Alaric and Drea's brother died," Dax continues. "I talked to him because I wanted to help figure out what happened and so he could settle and move on. And we found out that he was killed by a Shadow. Alaric even trapped that Shadow."

"Mattie," Mac adds. "You've met."

Nikolai nods; what they're saying explains a few things he'd wondered about.

"The thing is, solving the mystery of his death didn't settle Orson. There's something else I need to do before he can move on, and he can't tell me what it is. So I've been guessing, but then Alaric disappeared, and I was left in limbo. It's a constant itch in the back of my mind. When I saw the two of you, I knew that—whatever it is—involves you, too."

"How?" Seth asks.

Dax shrugs. "Not a clue. This Talent is like going on a scavenger hunt without a list of what I'm looking for. Sometimes it's easy: the ghost says they need a message delivered, or I have to find something they hid and bring it to a loved one. But this time—Orson's waiting for something, and I don't know what."

Mac leans forward, her voice low. "Best guess is that, until the risk of war is settled, Orson won't move on."

"War?" Nikolai has been worrying about a Shadow invasion, but he thinks Mac means something different.

"Alaric's community thinks Mages killed Orson, so they want to start a war with them," Cass says, her voice a soft lilt that sounds almost bored. She flicks her fingers. "They're Clan. No one listens."

"Alaric's trying to fix it," Mac says.

"And I guess so is Orson," Dax adds.

Someone taps Nikolai on the shoulder, and he glances up to see Nikita standing behind him. She holds out a hand, wiggling her fingers. "Come on," she says. "This isn't supposed to be a serious night. It's supposed to be fun."

Right. Nikolai had promised to dance.

As he rises, Cass stands as well, tugging at Dax. Nikolai takes Nikita's hand, letting her lead him to the dance floor. The music is quick, and most people seem to be doing something that involves waving their hands, swaying, and moving their feet. He can't figure out if they're following a pattern.

"I've never danced," he admits.

Nikita holds both his hands in hers, starts stepping side to side, swaying to the music. Nikolai sways with her. "Even when you were little?" she asks.

Nikolai tries to remember back when music came out of the radio, when his mother smiled and laughed and sang to him in the kitchen while she cooked. He has vague memories of waving his arms and shaking his backside while she cheered him on.

Doing that would be silly now.

"It's easy," Nikita says, her voice raised to be heard over the music. "There are two ways to dance. You can move however feels good and kind of fits the music, or you can slow-dance holding your partner and swaying and ignoring everyone around you." She lets go of one hand and points, and Nikolai can see people dancing both ways she's suggested.

Carolyn, Serina, Heather, and a bunch of girls and a few guys Nikolai doesn't recognize are in a group. They're laughing and moving, and it's a giant jumbled mess, but they seem to be having fun. At the same time, around the edges of the dance floor are couples, paired off and swaying close together.

Nikolai wants to do the same with Seth.

"Excuse me." Corbin sweeps between them, capturing one of Nikolai's hands and twirling him in place. Nikolai ends up closer to Corbin than he'd like to be, and Corbin plants a hand firmly against the small of Nikolai's back, keeping him there.

For a small man, he's a lot stronger than he looks.

"I want to talk to you," Corbin says, eyes sparking with mischief.

The music switches to a new song, and Corbin leads Nikolai slowly through a four-step pattern that includes occasional turns. It has a cadence that's easy to catch on to, and Corbin grins as Nikolai becomes more comfortable with it.

"Talk to me about what?" Nikolai prompts when Corbin doesn't continue.

"Life. Politics. The weirdness of being from another world." Corbin spins them, the steps carrying them closer to the edge of the dance floor. "I'm Alaric's second, and I know you know that Clan is teetering on the brink of war. Alaric doesn't want that to happen, but his father's an idiot who clings to the old ways."

"'The old ways,'" Nikolai echoes.

"The old ways," Corbin repeats. "We were raised to believe Clan's Clan. That Clan is who we are and what we are. It's how we live, and there is no other way. We are Clan and only Clan, not shapeshifters and not Talent. We do things our own way and we don't need help. But if Clan goes to war, it will affect the whole world."

"In my world, it's different. Alia married a Mage," Nikolai says.

"I heard that from Alaric." Corbin lifts one hand and waves to Drea as they pass by. "It's not that way here, and it's a problem. His father's coming around to the belief that the Shadows are the issue, not the Mages, but they're too hard to pursue to satisfy the bloodthirsty. Until you arrived. You stop the Shadows, and we stop a war."

"So you want to help heal the split. Or to do whatever it takes to push the Shadows out of both of our worlds," Nikolai says slowly, "because that's what's best for your world."

"I'll do whatever Alaric says is best for our community," Corbin says. "My allegiance is to him and Drea first, everyone else second. But yes, I'm in for helping heal the split. From what I've heard, if we fix our world and not yours—or vice versa—things will go to hell again in the future. Drea told me about the twin thing you've got going; the world's need to either un-twin completely or be in the same place properly."

Nikolai skids to a halt. "I'm already here."

"That's not what I meant." Corbin tugs, and Nikolai stumbles back into the dance, barely focused on the steps. "Either our worlds need to separate, so the Shadows can't go between them, or we need to merge into one world, because maybe we were never meant to be separate in the first place."

Nikolai's mouth opens. Closes. "That's impossible."

Corbin shrugs. "It's only my opinion, and I'm not Pawel-Szczek-who-knows-all. I'm just a bird who happens to pay attention."

"Are you causing trouble?" Drea slips between them, and Nikolai lets go of Corbin as she sweeps him away. "Ignore him," she calls out.

Nikolai thinks he hears Corbin say something about talking again in the future, but Drea has Corbin caught up in a kiss, so he can't be sure.

Seth clears his throat behind Nikolai. "Hey."

Nikolai places his hand over his heart, spins to look at him, and bows low, feeling ridiculous a moment later. He rises to meet Seth's gaze. "Hey." He holds out his hand, and Seth moves closer.

Nikolai wraps his arms around Seth and pulls him in, resting his head against Seth's as they slowly sway.

This kind of dancing is very nice.

They've been dancing a while, and Seth has one hand against Nikolai's heart, when Seth says, "You got along well with Corbin."

"He wanted to talk politics. And—" Nikolai frowns. "He wanted to talk about how fixing things might look. He has different ideas than Pawel."

"Good ideas?"

"I don't think so, but that doesn't mean he isn't right," Nikolai says. "It's beyond my experience as a Dreamwalker. He thinks we might need to combine the worlds. If we do that, I don't know what will happen to everyone. How will we combine? What will happen to the two Alias? To me and Nikita? You and Heather? It's uncomfortable to think about. I don't like it."

"It's not bad to look at all options," Seth reminds him, "Good and bad."

"We'll tell Pawel. Or Corbin will. He doesn't seem like the kind of person to stay quiet." Nikolai spots where Corbin and Drea have joined Alaric and Chris; Corbin is singing to Drea and Alaric.

"But not right now." Seth spins them, tugging Nikolai to face him. "We're taking a break from everything world-shattering."

"We are," Nikolai agrees. When he lets go of the dark thoughts that crowd his mind when he thinks about the Shadows, being here is…fun. "It's still dreamlike, but I'm glad we're here. And I'm very happy that you're here with me." A small smile slips loose as he whispers, "And that we can pretend the Split never happened. This is the prom we should have had. This is the college we might have gone to together."

Seth slides his hand up, cradles the back of Nikolai's head, and drags him down. "Normal is good," he says before he kisses him.

"We won't get this kind of future back home. Let's enjoy it while we get to borrow it."

The next kiss is slow and sweet, and the one after even sweeter. As they part, Nikolai cradles Seth close and hums under his breath, not quite in tune with the song, while they continue to sway. For a little while, it's nice to pretend that this is something they can keep.

28

The ballroom is hotter than Nikolai expected. Sweat plasters his hair to the back of his neck. He needs to get out of the crowd. He takes a bottle of water with him, leaving his jacket on the chair and Seth on the dance floor with Corbin and Drea. He follows the scent of fresh air to a propped-open door down the hall from the ballroom.

He emerges into the parking lot at the opposite end from the main entrance. Stone steps and an iron railing lead down, and at a landing below, a young woman sits facing the lot, her hair pulled back in waves that have gone limp, her shoulders slumped. Nikolai recognizes the blue of the dress spread across the stone. The door clicks as he almost closes it, and Nikita looks up at him, her phone a bright light cradled in her hand.

"Oh. Hi," she says. "Shouldn't you be inside having fun?"

"I overheated. Is it going to rain?" He joins her, waiting until she moves her skirt out of the way before he settles on to the step.

"If it does, it won't be my fault." She tilts the phone toward him so he can see the screen. The name at the top is Del. The message on the screen says, *I'm ready tonight, if you are.*

Oh.

Nikolai exhales. "Well. That's fast."

"It was your idea," Nikita points out. "I'm the messenger." She wiggles the phone in her hand. They'd spent an hour online that morning, Nikita showing Nikolai how the chat worked. He had elected to let her do the typing as they worked together to write up his experiences in his own world and his idea about meeting in the Dreamscape. "You have texts from Del."

"I thought tonight was about having fun and not thinking about saving the world."

Nikita leans into him, her weight unfamiliar but comforting. "I did say that. But you were right, we can't let this go on too long. We haven't heard from everyone Pawel reached out to, but the ones who are online did read what you had me write." She scrolls through too fast for Nikolai to read closely, but he sees images and text replies to their post. "They're listening to you, Nikolai. They've found anchors and are ready to meet in the Dreamscape."

Nikolai touches his pocket where his phone is tucked. "And Del?"

Nikita nudges him. "Look."

He exhales and pulls the phone out. He had been relaxed earlier. He'd had fun, and he wants to go back in and dance more. It was scarily easy to pretend that this was his life; he understands now why Dreamwalkers escape into Dreams.

Del has sent a wall of text to him and Nikita.

> *I did the thing. I went into the Dreamscape and I sent out a beacon. It's funny how I can feel it reverberating, dancing around the Dreams, calling people to me. To my meadow. To my own place where my mind lives. It's mine. Your space would be different. People will come, and until they do, I need to go back in and stay there. I told them to come soon. Tonight. I don't think I can stay longer. I don't know if that space exists without me, or if we can communicate if I'm not there.*
>
> *We need help. We need to talk to people from Nikolai's world. Maybe other worlds. He's right—this is the only place to do it, and my meadow is the only stable place I know. I'm the only one I know who Dreams like this. So I'm here. Come to me. They'll come too. Time is funny in Dreams but I'm sure it will work out somehow.*
>
> *Don't leave me alone for too long.*

There isn't a time included, but as Del said, time is strange in the Dreamscape. Del knows their schedule. "This isn't a lot of warning," Nikolai says. "I'll talk to Seth when we get home. I don't want to ruin his night."

"You think this will ruin his night?" Nikita pulls her heels in close to her body, knees bent and arms wrapped around to gather her skirt in.

"Did you tell Heather yet?"

Nikita wrinkles her nose. "You have a point. Do we think this'll work?"

"We're so far outside my comfort zone," Nikolai says, "that I can't tell for sure. You brought me here, and the most helpful thing I can offer is what I know about Dreamwalkers. If we want to have any kind of a concerted effort, the Dreamwalkers here need to get past their fear of working together."

"It's not paranoia if they're really out to get you," Nikita says. Nikolai gives her a blank look, and she explains, "It isn't an unfounded fear. Things get weird when Dreamwalkers are in the same physical place. You're banking on us being able to be in the same place in the Dreamscape without that happening."

"I met Del there and we were fine. More importantly, she was fine." Nikolai suspects he has had an easier time working with Del in the Dreamscape than Nikita has, but he doesn't think that's important enough to bring up. "What do we know about this beacon Del is talking about?"

"She reached us when we were in your world," Nikita says. "Me once. You twice. Right?"

"Right, but she knew you, and after that first time, she knew me. Who is she reaching out to now?"

"Anyone who's listening, I assume." Nikita worries at her lip, her shoulders hunching again. "She was on the phone with Carolyn while we were all getting ready in her and Heather's room."

"Hopefully the people who are listening are friendly," he says slowly. "Where is she sending it?"

Nikita shrugs. "Does she know? Del in the Dreamscape is so slippery. Like. I can imagine her spinning in that meadow of hers, sending thoughts out like a scattered flock of birds."

"That nest in trees that are gateways to other worlds," Nikolai finishes the thought. He can imagine it as well. "The trees closest to her meadow lead to my world and yours. We have to hope that whoever she reaches from my home has heard about the network. Someone who knows what's happening, who maybe has a Technopath with them, wherever they are."

The world is huge. There must be other places like Havenhill.

"Do you think about what life will be like after?" Nikita asks.

Nikolai pulls back, twisting on the step so he can look at her directly. "Are you going to try to convince us to stay again?"

For a moment, he thinks she will, but then she shakes her head once. "But we should think about what you should take back with you. Things from my world that can help you in Havenhill. Now that you've seen how the world can be, you must have some ideas on how you want to rebuild. So when you're in the library, or when you're exploring with Seth, think about that. Make lists. Buy things—Pawel will give you more money if you need it, I know he will. You were right. I can't save you. But you can get things to save yourself."

That's true. Nikolai isn't positive which resources he wants, or how he'll carry them between here and there, but she's right—he should take advantage of the bounty of this world. "I'll do that. But I still don't want to deal with this 'online' stuff. It's too much to learn when I'm not here for long."

"Deal," Nikita says, holding out her hand. Nikolai grips it, shaking once. "I'll be your voice online. You do the research in books. But electronic books are much lighter, you can carry a lot more information."

"Information I won't have any way of accessing at home," Nikolai points out. "Much less electricity. Don't even know if ours works the same as yours."

"You have a point." Nikita tilts her head into his shoulder again, sighing.

Nikolai's phone vibrates, and Nikita's makes a low *ping*.

This is Sam. Del's gone into the Dreamscape. Shawn and I are with her. Are you two going to meet her there tonight?

Nikolai holds the phone in his hands, Nikita's weight against his shoulder. He types carefully, the slick screen of the phone strange to his touch.

This is Nikolai. Hi. Yes. We are still at the formal, but we will Dream when we get home.

29

Nikolai sits on the edge of the bed, watching as Seth moves around the room. Seth's shirt is unbuttoned and untucked, hanging loose around his frame. His tie has been placed, neatly folded, on the dresser, his jacket hung in the closet next to Nikolai's.

Nikolai needs to change as well, but for the moment, watching Seth is a more enticing option. Nikolai considers assisting him—undressing him and tucking them both into bed. It's tempting.

His phone buzzes, and he exhales. He can't ignore it any longer.

Are you ready?

Nikita's words are stark on the screen. Nikolai carefully types out a reply, his fingers brushing the wrong letters several times; he keeps needing to back up and try again. *Getting ready now. You have Heather with you, right?*

Of course. Did you talk to Seth?

Nikolai's gaze strays from the screen to his boyfriend. *Not yet. I will. I'll see you there*, he responds.

Seth settles in next to him, hip to hip, his body warm. He touches the screen, Nikita's message lighting up for him to read. "Talk to me about what?"

A brisk knock at the door is all the warning they get. It squeaks open immediately and Pawel stands there, expression firm and set. "Nikolai, are you ready to—? Oh."

"The door was closed," Seth says blandly.

"Not quite. We're getting ready for bed," Nikolai says. He sets the phone down on the table and stands. He grabs T-shirts from the drawer for himself and Seth, tossing one and a pair of sleep pants to him. "We'll be ready soon. I need to talk to Seth."

"About?" Seth prompts, his voice lower and firmer. Tension settles around his eyes; the air is thick with Seth's wariness.

"The Dreamwalkers are meeting," Nikolai explains. "Del, Nikita, and I have organized the meeting in the Dreamscape that we'd talked about We've invited Dreamwalkers from our world, too. And Del sent out a call across the Dreamscape; whoever responds to that will also be there." He suppresses the concern over what that beacon could draw to them. As long as he believes everything *will* be fine, he can force the Dreamscape to respond to him and everything will be fine.

"Tonight?" Seth asks. He shrugs out of his button-down shirt and pulls on the T-shirt, words muffled as he continues to talk. "You waited until now to talk to me about it?"

"Del texted while we were at the formal. Nikita and I made plans with her while I was outside, getting some air." Nikolai grips the T-shirt in his hand. "I didn't want to ruin the party, so I waited to talk to you about it. Del's already in the Dreamscape, with Shawn and Sam watching over her. I didn't get a choice on the timing."

Seth's lips purse. He pushes his glasses up his nose—not with the middle finger, so at least it's not a subtle jab at Nikolai.

"I understand it's not the ideal end to your romantic evening, but Del's impetuousness aside, the sooner this is done, the better," Pawel says. "This meeting is a necessary first step in getting you home."

Nikolai is struck by the realization that when he leaves, he might miss this place. He will definitely miss these people.

"I'm not arguing about doing it; I'm angry about the lack of notice," Seth retorts. "I knew Nikolai and Nikita were working on this. I thought we would have time to prepare. We've spent so much of our lives being reactive, it'd be nice to have some notice for once."

"What do you need to plan?"

Nikolai looks between Pawel and Seth. "Seth needs to be aware that I'm Dreaming; he'll tether me so I don't lose my grip on reality or bring the Dreams here."

Nikita has said she's ready, so Heather will anchor her and the area will hopefully avoid a surprise storm. Nikolai hopes that the more accustomed

Nikita becomes to her Talent and her bond with Heather, the less likely she'll be to cause storms. On the other hand, she is also a Weather Witch, and Nikolai has no experience with that, and Dreamwalkers in this world are strangely broken.

"Will you be safe?" Pawel arches one eyebrow. "We're depending on the two of you. Out of all of us, you have the most experience as a stable Dreamwalker, and as a stable pair. I suspect that out of anyone here, Nikolai, you know the Dreamscape the best."

"Del knows it better," Nikolai counters. Del's comfortable in the Dreamscape to the point of becoming a part of it. "It's more dangerous to her than to me, but we need her. She's creating the meeting space, and she's bringing Dreamwalkers from other worlds to her. We hope."

Pawel stares at him, expression tired and drawn. He reaches for the door and grips the handle as he draws it almost closed. "Do you need anything?"

"Privacy," Seth says curtly.

Pawel closes the door as he goes.

Nikolai strips quickly, pulling on sleep clothes. "I was going to tell you."

"Why wouldn't I be rude? He knocked, sure, but he didn't wait for an answer before he walked in and—" Seth stops. "Oh. You wanted to have the other argument."

"You're right," Nikolai says. "This is our room, and he should have respected that. But we shouldn't be rude to the person who's given us a place to live." Seth's wariness lingers in the air, stronger than his anger at Pawel. "You want to yell at me more than him. I knew you'd be pissed off that I hadn't told you we're going into the Dreamscape tonight. I know you don't like the plan."

Seth finishes changing and climbs onto the bed, patting the space beside him. He waits until Nikolai lies next to him, both of them propped up by pillows against the wall. "I don't trust the plan, and yes, I think it's dangerous," he admits, "but I trust you, and I know you'll come back to me." He arranges them so that Nikolai is lying half on Seth, his head pillowed by the hair on Seth's chest.

Nikolai places a hand over Seth's heart, the beat strong and steady beneath his palm. "I'll always come back to you." He hesitates, then says,

"I'm not happy with how fast this is happening, either, but Pawel's right. This is a step toward healing the split, which means we can stop worrying about Shadows and live our lives, growing old together in Havenhill.

Seth closes his eyes, bending to brush a kiss against the top of Nikolai's head. "I know. I'll hold onto you so you don't get lost. I've got you."

"You always do." Nikolai exhales as he lets his body go loose and limp against Seth. The air in the room is cool, but Seth is warm beneath Nikolai. Seth pulls the covers around them both, the warmth echoing like they share a heated cocoon.

Nikolai inhales and exhales, letting his face go lax. His eyes relax. His mouth loses tension.

He knows how to seek sleep, even when his mind is racing.

On every exhale, he lets something else go. His forehead loosens, his chin drops, and his mouth opens slightly. His shoulders release, and his hand slides down Seth's body, no longer held by his will. He tilts into Seth, letting Seth be the one to hold him up, trusting in him. He sinks into Seth's warmth and floats.

There is no such thing as letting his mind go blank. It's impossible. The more he tries, the more stray thoughts intrude. So he does the opposite. He fills his mind with numbing words, the same phrase over and over, giving no space for other thoughts.

I'm going to the Dreamscape. I'm going to the Dreamscape. I'm going to the Dreamscape.

In a blink, he's there.

He stands on the edge of the meadow. Del is in the distance with her hands spread, her face tilted toward the sun as she spins slowly. Flowers fall around her, raining from the sky, and she laughs. With a sweep of her hands, the petals scatter and fall into the tall grass.

"She worries me sometimes." Nikita stands shoulder to shoulder with Nikolai. She reaches for him, taking his hand and squeezing as she speaks.

In this place, he and Nikita resonate on the same frequency. He hopes this doesn't mean they're combining in the real world, creating a Dreamscape across the campus of PHU.

"I think we're okay," Nikita answers his unvoiced concern.

He squeezes her hand once more, then lets go. “Del,” he calls out.

Del stops spinning, lowering her hands as she turns to face them. A slow smile spreads across her face, and when she raises her hands, butterflies lift from the grass and scatter. She wiggles her fingers. “Hi.”

“Hi,” Nikita calls back.

Time slips, and they stand in the middle of the meadow with Del. A child sits in the tall grass, braiding and twisting blades together in an elaborate decoration. The child looks up and blinks fair lashes. “You’re old,” they say.

“Not exactly,” Nikolai replies.

“You can’t call children for this,” Nikita protests. She reaches for Del, clasping at her hands to hold her still. “Del— Oh.”

The world shifts, and a teenager crouches in the grass instead, maybe a year or two younger than Nikolai and Nikita. Those same pale lashes blink over gray eyes. Their features are sharper now, elongated when the child grew. “If you didn’t have to be the you from the waking world, why would you be?” the teenager asks. “This is an escape.” A small pause, and they continue, “I’m Grace. They/them, please.”

Nikita’s mouth closes slowly. “I remember you from the online discussion.”

Nikolai remembers them as well, but this Grace seems different from the one in the chat. He wonders if coherence and attachment to reality is hard to come by in the Dreamscape, and if he’s been luckier than most. He’ll have to thank Seth again when he’s awake.

He needs to teach these Dreamwalkers how to stay sane. He hopes they’ll manage to long enough to do what needs to be done.

Dreamwalkers gather; Nikolai blinks, and there are more than stood with them seconds ago. Some drift in from the edges of the meadow, and some appear in that way that dreams can stutter and jump. Del snaps her fingers when there are nine newcomers, declaring, “An even dozen of us. That should do for now.”

“I have come a long way down the paths to find this place,” one man says. He’s taller than the others—easily a foot taller than Nikolai—and his skin has an unfamiliar grayish cast. When he gestures, Nikolai focuses on his hand—at first he thinks there are four fingers and a thumb, but one of the fingers seems to be a second opposable thumb. After watching Grace change their appearance, Nikolai isn't sure if this man's appearance is a reflection of the Dreamscape or of his reality.

"The Shadows are a problem in all worlds." Del touches a finger to her lips, voice lowering in a conspiratorial whisper. "Darkness is pervasive. They slip between the cracks, into the split and out again, and who knows where they go."

All save the gray-skinned man nod, exchanging glances. Nikolai wonders if he looks as haunted as these newcomers do.

"We should introduce ourselves." Nikolai speaks at the same moment Del opens her mouth. She closes it, gesturing to him and curtsying. She sinks down to sit cross-legged, braiding blades of grass. "We are Nikolai and Nikita." Nikolai gestures at himself and her. "We come from two different worlds that are so tightly twinned that we've been able to cross between them. Since we met..." And he launches into their story, with Nikita interjecting occasionally. It's the same story they posted to the online Dreamwalker forum. Only the gray-skinned man and one other seem surprised by what they say.

That man speaks next. "Brett," he says tightly. He's tall and slender, the lines around his eyes the only thing that betray his age. His gaze is fixed on Nikolai, understanding written in his expression. "I can't imagine anyone not understanding the need for an Empath to anchor us. I—" He hesitates. "I lost mine. My wife. San Francisco went dark, and we couldn't stay in that area, not with so many Shadows around, so we fled. We survived the darkness, but she died crossing the Sierra Nevadas. I made it to Utah with our children, to a tiny stronghold outside of where Salt Lake City used to be. It's safe for Talents here. It's...there are no cities in Utah. People either left or the Shadows took them. The foraging is good, and our community is growing as word gets out."

"Do you have any Technopaths?" Nikolai asks, and Brett gives him a startled, confused look.

"We might," Brett says uncertainly. "Do you mean people with an affinity for the tech from before the Split?"

That confirms that Brett is from Nikolai's world, and it gives Nikolai hope. “That’s my world,” he says. “I’m from Havenhill in New York, and we’re creating a network of Technopaths to establish communication between Talented communities. You’ve been called here to help establish a similar network of Dreamwalkers, so we can act inside the Dreamscape. We’re going to stop the Shadows’ progress and force them out of our world.”

Brett nods, his arms still wrapped tight around his center as if to hold himself in place. “We’ll look for you.”

It’s a start, at least.

A tall Asian woman stands to one side, her hands held by her side. “I am Ji-eun, and I prefer female pronouns. I am from Korea.” She nods shallowly but doesn’t move to join the larger circle. “Annyeong haseyo.”

“I am Amahle.” A small woman with dark skin and her hair cropped short steps forward, smiling as she offers Nikolai both her hands. “I am from Cape Town, and my family is quite large. We’re almost all Dreamwalkers, with few who are born without the Talent manifesting.” She leans in, speaking solemnly. “We also know the secret of the Empaths, but I have been unable to convince others of their help in stabilizing our Dreamers. Perhaps, with your help, we will be able to bring this knowledge to the world.” She steps back, spreading her hands to include everyone. “I am but one woman, but I bring the strength of my family to this effort. We will aid you.”

The others’ introductions are shorter. The gray-skinned man is Asahel. Jasmine lives in Vancouver, studying to become a nurse. Her family has had a few Dreamwalkers over the generations, although she’s the first in more than fifty years. Aaron, from Houston, speaks proudly of his great-grandson who will be a strong Dreamer someday. Tyler is homeless in Florida, living on the beach.

“How do you think we can help?” Tyler pulls fistfuls of grass free, scattering them. Del laughs when blades blow near her.

“Your world and mine are twinned. If mine falls to the Shadows, yours won’t be far behind,” Nikolai says. “You heard what Brett said about the West Coast; it’s the same on the East Coast where I live. From what our Technopaths have learned, the Shadows are pushing from the coasts inward.”

“The Shadows are killers,” Nikita emphasizes. “We need them gone.”

Asahel seems dubious. "Not all darkness means danger, and not all danger comes from places of darkness. Light can be as dangerous. The ones who slip between Shadows only cause trouble when they hunger."

Del scoffs. "They're all starving."

"Not all of them," Nikita reminds her. "Mattie isn't."

Asahel is silent, his brow furrowed, hands steepled in front of him, both thumbs splayed and pointing in opposite directions.

"Your Shadows don't consume entire cities?" Brett asks.

Asahel shakes his head. "There are those who hunger, yes, but they are not many. Certainly not an invasion. They stop when sated. They do not destroy indiscriminately. They are people, like any other."

"Carolyn says—" Del cuts off mid-sentence, her voice lilting up as if she's about to sing. She shakes her head, pointing to Nikolai. "Tell Carolyn what he said. She'll want to know."

Nikolai would have told her anyway. He wants to take Carolyn's notes about the intricate interweaving of Talent home to Havenhill.

"How do you think we can get rid of Shadowwalkers?" Grace picks at the cuticle of one finger, staring at it intently. "My friends and I ran into one when our friend Kimmie Emerged. She's dead now. The Shadow got her, the rest of us got away, and I can still remember her screaming. So. I'm in. But can we do this?"

"I did not see a plan in our discussions," Ji-eun replies. "I have also spoken privately to your Pawel, and he has goals but no path toward implementation that I am aware of."

"That's what we're here to figure out." Nikita chews on her lower lip, sitting with her knees up, her body hunched.

Nikolai sits next to her, trying to ignore how the waving, high grass casts shadows over them. The others sit as well, except for Tyler, who lies on his back with his braiding, and Del, who is back on her feet, spinning with her arms out, palms lifted toward the bright sun.

Nikolai can feel the real world dragging on him, the warmth of Seth's hold trying to pull him back. Staying in the Dreamscape and controlling the Dream is more difficult than when he lets it take him where it needs. He's the only one here who knows both the Shadows and what it truly means to be a Dreamwalker.

Proposing a path forward rests on his shoulders.

"I have an idea. When Seth and I need to escape Shadows, we push them away using a technique in which I pull a bit of the Dreamscape into the waking world," Nikolai explains. "Seth keeps me anchored and helps ensure I don't bring too much Dream into reality. It's bright, sparkling, and full of Dreaming potential. The Shadows hate it. Doing it is draining as hell, and obviously, I'm only one person. I've been thinking that if we create a cross-world network of Dreamwalkers, we could do a concerted push, hundreds of Dreamwalkers simultaneously doing what I usually do alone. Maybe we could shove the Shadows out of our worlds and back into the split."

"How do we keep them out afterward?" Brett asks.

"How do you know this will even work?" Jasmine adds.

"Won't this bring the Dreamscape into the real world on a global scale?" Amahle points out. "Even with Empaths to anchor us, that is as much of a danger as the Shadows are. We cannot be the ones to destroy our worlds. There are stories."

"There are stories," everyone echoes, the words sibilant as they drift across a dozen tongues.

There *are* stories. Nikolai has heard the warnings, couched as fairy tales. He's also read a few from Nikita's world during his time in the library.

"We don't know," he admits. "I've been researching, learning about how Talent works in Nikita's world. We need to share information—here or online. And the Dreamwalkers from your world need to understand the ones from mine, and vice versa. We have to teach each other."

"Help from other worlds is greatly appreciated, too," Nikita says, acknowledging Asahel. "We'll start with fixing our own worlds, but we want to protect others as well if we can."

"Perhaps you need to know more of Shadowwalkers like those of my world, as well as those of yours," Asahel suggests. "I would be willing to speak to the keepers of your knowledge."

"That's probably Pawel and Carolyn, but neither of them are Dreamwalkers, so getting them here will be difficult," Nikita says.

"I could." Del speaks to the sky, her eyes closed. "They won't enjoy it, but I could."

"We can talk about that later," Nikolai says. "Asahel, if we can bring them in, Del will call you."

"How do you know our world is linked with yours?" Grace asks. "I know what you two said about going between them"—they jab a finger toward Nikolai—"but why shouldn't we make sure our own world is safe before it becomes like yours?"

"Our worlds mirror each other; what has happened in mine is happening in yours. It's not a question of 'if,' it's a question of when," Nikolai explains again. Grace's skeptical look doesn't waver. Nikolai glances at Nikita, then pushes to his feet. "Del. Don't drift off," he orders. "Nikita and I are going to take everyone down our paths."

Del stops spinning, her hands floating back to her side. "Oh. A field trip. I'll go."

Nikolai reaches for Nikita, tugging her to her feet. They set off as one without talking to each other, hands clasped. Their paths run along one side of the meadow; they should be able to stay together until the path splits.

Shadows gather around the edges of the meadow, wreathed in darkness. Nikolai doesn't breathe easily until they set foot on the path and the safety of his space in the Dreamscape wraps around them.

"This is the way home," Brett says.

Grace gives him a sharp look as they retort, "Yes, it's the way to my home. Not yours."

"It's the way to both," Nikolai corrects them.

They set a brisk pace along the path. Nikolai refused to look into the distance; he doesn't want to see the Shadows waiting for one of them to misstep.

"Look at us," Nikita talks as she walks. She gestures with her free hand, inviting everyone to stare at her and Nikolai. "We look alike, right? Like we're twins, or maybe the same person from different worlds. When I traveled to his world, we found that some things were the same. There's one person there who Mattie—the non-starving Shadow we know—refers to as 'bedrock.' Someone who exists throughout multiple worlds. But others have their analogues. Similarities. Like me and Nikolai, and our Empaths."

The path narrows as they go, and after a time, Nikolai and Nikita barely fit side by side. "This isn't good," Nikolai murmurs.

"There are more of them," Del says lightly. "I could get a Shadow for you, if you need one to talk to." She turns as if to step off the path.

"Grab her," Nikita instructs, and Brett does so.

Del gives them a sour glare. "Spoilsports."

"She has no anchor here," Nikolai tells them. Apparently, Shawn and Sam don't anchor her as strongly as Seth does him. Her mind is slipping a little more every time she comes to the Dreamscape. "Del. Talk about the Shadows."

"Nik." Nikita touches his arm, then points ahead.

The fork in the road is there—three ways to go from a small clearing. One leads to Nikita's world, one to his own, and the last to somewhere he doesn't want to travel to. He can barely see that third one, the entrance to the path overgrown. When he looks at the path to his own, it's narrow, trees hanging in a heavy canopy overhead, and darker than other paths in the Dreamscape.

"There are more Shadows," Del points out. "I said that."

The group moves into the clearing, drifting into smaller groups. Brett gravitates with Nikolai toward their path, while Asahel and Del remain in the center. The others group around the almost-clear entrance to Nikita's pathway.

"What happens when it closes completely?" Brett asks.

Del blinks at him. "The Shadows win, of course." She points at all three paths. "There used to be three, but only two are left, and one of those is shutting down. When two are gone, the third will fall."

"That's why we care," Nikita says. "You can say it's their world or our world, but the truth is, it's all of us except Asahel. In this clearing, we have one shared path. We've already lost one fork, and Nikolai's world is falling. We need to stop this before we're overrun as well."

"Then we have much to learn, and very little time in which to learn it," Amahle says firmly. "We must make contact in the real world and build a network there as well. Reach out among your own worlds," she says to Brett and Asahel. "Bring others, as many as you can. More minds mean more conflict, yes, but also mean more thought and more resources. Learn. Explore. Experiment. We will find a way."

"We'll find a way," Ji-eun echoes, and everyone slowly agrees in turn.

Brett speaks last, his voice soft and pained. "We're going to stop the Shadows from taking over the worlds."

The weight on Nikolai's shoulders bears down on him, but it grows lighter as each person agrees. Sharing it makes it easier. He looks at Nikita, smiling slightly despite the grim darkness that lies ahead of them. "We're doing this," he agrees.

"We'll save the worlds," she replies.

30

Nikolai wakes when morning light spills through the curtains, turning the inside of his eyelids red. Seth is warm and lax beside him. Nikolai's limbs are heavy, and a weight presses down on his chest, making it hard to breathe. He blinks, opening his eyes to a blend of sunshine and a gathering of darkness thick above him. Chelsea's features are barely visible as she leans in, one hand on Nikolai's chest and the others on Seth's.

"Hey," Nikolai chokes out.

Chelsea slides back quickly. "I only took a little," she whispers, the sound shivering in the air.

It doesn't feel like a little. Nikolai feels as if he could be dragged back into sleep, the Dreamscape tickling at the back of his mind. His throat is raw and aching. "Hey!" he forces out, louder this time.

Chelsea flinches.

"What?" Seth rolls over, curling closer to Nikolai without opening his eyes.

A door slams down the hall.

"Are you okay?" Nikolai nudges Seth's hair back from his face, cradles his cheek. "How do you feel? Chelsea was—"

"I only took a little!" Her voice is firmer, shrill instead of sibilant.

The door to their room bangs open. "Chelsea was what?" Pawel asks, tone flat.

Chelsea looks down and away, her shadowed shoulders hunching until she is little more than unformed darkness in the corner of the room.

"Don't go," Pawel orders.

The Shadow shivers and remains where she is.

Each breath comes easier now, especially when Seth's eyes finally open, his brow furrowing in confusion as he looks at Nikolai. "What?" he asks again.

Nikolai touches Seth's chest, over his heart. "How do you feel?" he asks quietly.

"As if I slept like shit and had bad dreams," Seth admits. He shoves the sheets down so he can sit up and stretch. His arms lower slowly when he spots Chelsea and Pawel. "Why are you in our room?"

Nikolai sits up next to him, his arm behind Seth's back. "She was feeding on us while we slept."

"You were anxious," Chelsea whispers. "You Dreamed earlier, and it lingered, sweet and delicious."

"Fuck," Pawel mutters. He glances down the hall, shoulders relaxing. "Chelsea, you can't—"

"I only took a little." Shadowy hands rise from the darkness, pressing together until they almost meet. "Not enough to hurt. Not enough to notice. Just enough to keep me here and alive. They had so much. I could taste them on the air, and when they're together, these two are stronger than anyone else I've met." She hesitates, then adds, "Except for the tall skinny one who was here before. He'd be a gourmet meal. One sip could sustain me."

"Don't touch—" Pawel raises a hand, then lowers it again. "Hold that thought. We may be able to work something out. You're right: Rory is brimming with energy, much of it not his own. There may be a way to—"

"You can't let her feed from any of us," Nikolai protests. The bed shifts as Seth reaches for his glasses, and Nikolai slips from the bed, tugging up his sleep pants as he goes. "Pawel, she's dangerous."

"You need me." She goes to her knees at the end of the bed, peering up at him. Her body is bowed but her eyes raised, casting a soft light in the darkness. "I can take you home when you're done here. Without me, you can't go back to your own world."

Pawel pushes his hair back from his face with both hands, pressing his fingers against his scalp. He stares at her, expression raw.

"Mattie could—"

"Mattie can't." Pawel interrupts Nikolai.

"Mattie cannot, not anymore," Chelsea whispers. "It would be easier to be here, if I were like her. If my soul were restored and I didn't hunger. I feel it every moment. I feel you, your Talent whispering over my skin. It could be so good to suck you dry, but I won't. I will not let myself do that."

"What if we did restore your soul?" Nikolai asks, even though he has no idea how they would do that. What is a soul? How did they put Mattie's back into her? How do they find the right soul out of thousands—possibly millions—of Shadowwalkers who have lost theirs?

The darkness sways from side to side as Chelsea shakes her head. "If you do, I couldn't move between worlds. Not easily. Mattie can still go into the split, but not like she could. She doesn't belong there with the soulless ones."

This reminds Nikolai of Asahel's words. "We had our meeting in the Dreamscape last night," he says. He puts a hand up when Pawel looks about to interrupt. "One of the Dreamwalkers drawn to Del's beacon came from a world that wasn't mine or Nikita's. And he wasn't afraid of Shadows."

Pawel turns away from Chelsea. "Go on."

"From what Asahel said, where he comes from, Shadowwalkers rarely are starving," Nikolai explains. He sits on the bed again, next to Seth, and Pawel takes a spot at the other end of the bed. "He said only the ones who are starving are dangerous."

"There are three names for Shadowwalkers here," Pawel muses slowly, uncurling the fingers of one hand so he can touch the fingertips as he names them. "Shadowwalkers, Soulstealers, and Deathstalkers." Nikolai slips his hand into Seth's, holding his anchor as they both nod. The same names are used in his world. "So it's possible that at one time, they were different Lineages." Pawel stares at the wall, eyes unfocused. "It's possible there were three Lineages, and in our worlds, they somehow combined. And if that combination allowed them to spread—"

Seth nudges his glasses up his nose. "What if Shadowwalkers could always move between the worlds by using the split, but the other two couldn't. And when they combined—"

"—or Emerged as an entirely new Lineage," Pawel interrupts.

Seth nods and continues. "Or Emerged," he agrees. "And that allowed the ones that sound more dangerous—Deathstalkers and Soulstealers—to spread between the worlds as well."

He doesn't deliver it like a question. Seth makes it sounds as if all that's left is for them to accept this new understanding of Shadowwalkers.

"We need to bring in everyone else," Nikolai says slowly. "We don't know for certain yet. We have one perspective, you have another, and Carolyn will want to know about how Asahel's Shadows are different."

"Correct. There are more official Lineages than we knew of, and obviously those that we consider legendary are far more real than we thought. As for you..." Pawel's gaze refocuses, narrowing as he looks at Chelsea.

The darkness straightens, then slumps again. "I do not wish to hurt you."

Nikolai would like to think she means all of them, but he's fairly certain she's speaking specifically to Pawel.

"I know," Pawel says gently, "but you can't feed indiscriminately. You must ask permission and ensure that whoever you do feed from has the energy to give you. They need to be able to sustain you without you draining them, and they need to be able to stop you before you can take too much."

The darkness creeps forward, slipping to the end of the bed and settling there, a blot in the air next to Pawel. "I remember you," Chelsea whispers. "I do remember you."

Seth's hand goes tight on Nikolai's.

Pawel exhales. "I know, Chelsea." The name falls heavily, and she makes a strangled sound, like wind among the cliffs. Pawel gets his phone out. "I'll ask Mattie to come stay here for a while to help you. She's not like you anymore, but at least she understands."

And if Chelsea escapes into the shadows, maybe Mattie can follow her.

"When this is over..." Chelsea whispers.

Pawel taps at his phone, sends a message, then looks up. He blinks at her, and Seth's hand goes tight on Nikolai again. "When this is over...yes?"

"I would like my soul," Chelsea says. Her darkness drifts from the bed into the corner, where the Shadow slides tall and flat against the wall. "I'm not leaving for good"—her voice echoes in soft whispers around the room—"but I need to not taste you right now."

In the wake of her departure, sunlight floods into the room through the windows. Nikolai blinks, raising his free hand to shade his eyes.

Pawel lowers his hand, phone dropping from his fingers onto the bed.

"You truly believe she is your Chelsea," Seth says.

Pawel nods. "She's my Chelsea, yes."

"You believe that. I hope you're right." Seth huffs and carefully draws his hand from Nikolai's. He flexes his fingers, then pulls his knees up, hands over his face as he leans forward. "Fuck. Nik, we are so fucked."

Nikolai slides a hand up Seth's back, fingers splayed between his shoulder blades. "Get out of our room, Pawel. And I don't want her here again." Nikolai knows they can't keep Chelsea out of Pawel's house, but this room needs to be a safe space for him and Seth. He doesn't want to be reminded how she destroyed his life in Havenhill, nor that he still needs her to get home.

Pawel pushes to his feet, grabbing his phone with one hand, the other pushing through his hair again. "I'll take care of it," he mutters as he walks out, leaving the door open.

Nikolai sighs and pats Seth's shoulder, then he gets out of bed long enough to push the door closed with a soft *thunk*, twisting the lock after. When he returns, he curls up next to Seth, wrapping his long limbs around him. "We're safe here."

"I know," Seth says. "It's not only what happened this morning. I look at her, and I see everyone we've lost—everyone our whole world has lost—and it hurts so much. I want to be positive, Nik. But sometimes I wonder whether we can fix anything. Nikita seems so sure we can, but she doesn't know as much as we do about Shadowwalkers and Dreamwalkers. Pawel thinks he can learn enough, but we don't have time. I think of everything that needs to be done, and everything we don't know, and I think that we are well and truly fucked."

"Not a single one of them thinks before acting," Nikolai says.

"They say they do," Seth mutters, "but they don't." He exhales roughly, curling in so that his face is pressed into the hollow of Nikolai's collarbone, nuzzling in tight.

Nikolai threads his fingers through Seth's curls. He scratches at the base of Seth's skull, and Seth sighs, pressing into the touch with a pleased murmur.

"We need to talk to Nikita," Nikolai says. "Catch her and Heather up on what Chelsea did. Discuss what we're doing next. We'll ask them to take us shopping, too. Get things to bring home, and see if we can get you some new glasses. Practical things. But that's later. Right now..." His hand goes flat against the nape of Seth's neck.

"Mm?" Seth's voice is lazy, his eyes hooded when he looks at Nikolai. "Right now?"

"Right now, we don't need to go anywhere." Nikolai flips them so that he can straddle Seth, leaning in to kiss him. The door is locked. No one's going to barge in. And despite everything, they still have each other, and always will.

31

"'M GOING OUT," Alaric says, grabbing a jacket on his way out the door of his dorm room. "Chris and I are meeting Dax and Cass at the 'Skeller. Dax has some shit to go over. Cass is tagging along." From the way his voice gets a little sharper, Nikolai gets the feeling Alaric doesn't like Cass much. "Dax said something about Nate stopping by, too." Alaric shrugs. "Whatever. I think they've got new drill ideas for spring and summer training. Want me to bring you back a cookie?"

Nikolai has no idea what a Skeller, training drills, and a cookie have to do with each other. He glances at Seth, and they both shake their heads.

Kit sits cross-legged on the floor of the dorm room, digging through his bag and pulling out pencils one by one.

Rory settles next to Kit, his left thigh pressed against Kit's leg, a guitar balanced on his lap. "Bring back four," he says. "We'll probably need a snack by then."

"Hm?" Kit looks up.

"You'll be hungry after this," Rory says with a small, fond smile.

"Probably." Kit motions at Nikolai and Seth, using his hands to ask them to sit farther apart. Nikolai makes space between himself and Seth.

Alaric lingers in the doorway. "Kit, if you're staying here tonight—"

Kit continues to set pencils next to a notebook, organized in an order Nikolai doesn't understand. He glances at Rory, who shakes his head. "I'm heading back to my own room tonight. Rory'll be here."

"I've got that 8 a.m. tomorrow," Rory says.

Alaric grunts. "You don't have to—"

"We're fine." Rory cuts him off with a wave of his hand. "Go catch up with Chris. Get everything out of your system. Close the door when you go. That'll give us a chance of keeping most of the floor out. Except Nikita. Not much keeps her from barging in." He says it like it's a joke, and Kit mumbles a laugh in response as Alaric grumbles.

"Fine." He tugs the door shut with a soft *click* and *thunk.*

Kit looks at Nikolai, frowning deeply, then shifts to stare at Seth. He does nothing but watch them for several uncomfortable minutes while Rory plucks strings on his guitar.

Rory plays a few notes in succession, and Kit's posture eases.

"I was wrong," he said, holding his hands out toward each of them and bringing his palms together. "I need you together, at least to start. Your energies work better that way."

Seth shrugs, and they move together again; Nikolai raises one arm to drop it behind Seth, tucking him close. They lean against each other, finding a comfortable way to sit together.

Kit points at them with a pencil. "That's good. Don't move." He opens his notebook to a fresh page, props it on his knees, and hunches over as he works. The pencil scratches across paper, rough at times, smooth at others. Nikolai is afraid to break the silence; he doesn't want to disturb Kit's concentration.

Rory plays softly, his head tilted down and hair falling in his face, expression soft as he focuses on the music. He opens his mouth, and Nikolai half expects him to start singing. He's surprised when Rory speaks instead.

"You won't bother him," Rory says, his voice at normal volume. The music never stops, his fingers moving over the strings. "If he were doing a simple drawing, then noise would probably bug him, but when I'm boosting him like this, he's lost in the fugue."

"He can't hear us?" Seth asks.

Rory laughs, reaching up to push his bangs out of the way. "He can hear us. He's just…his Talent has him."

When it's phrased like that, it makes sense to Nikolai. He knows how easy it would be to slip into the Dream and never come back. He wonders if Kit feels that, too, teetering on the edge of madness. "That's a unique Talent?" He's not sure exactly what Kit's Talent is. He's drawing. Nikolai isn't even sure why, just that Pawel asked them to make sure they did this after the Coven meeting.

Coven. That was…something.

Nikolai exhales roughly and turns to press a kiss against the side of Seth's head. He hadn't let go of Seth's hand the entire time they attended the student ritual group, even when they were grabbing snacks.

"I'm surprised Pawel didn't ask us to speak in front of that Coven meeting," Seth mutters dryly. When Nikolai stiffens, Seth huffs. "Your tension rose. I figured you were thinking about it."

"Occasionally, Pawel has bursts of logic between his fits of mania," Rory says. He pauses, and when he starts playing again, the melody has shifted. It's faster now; Nikolai swears that Kit's pencil moves more quickly as well.

"Kit's from a Predictive Lineage," Rory says. Kit makes a disgruntled noise, and Rory presses his knee closer to Kit's. "It's along the female line, though, so Kit's not Predictive. He started exploring ritualistic magic, like my family does, which is how we met. Around that time, Carolyn discovered that she has a Talent for Traveling in addition to being Predictive. Her Traveling uses pictures."

"We've seen them," Seth says.

"My drawings," Kit mumbles. "They work best."

The lines of his art are already done, and even upside down, Nikolai recognizes the shapes of his and Seth's bodies. There's a soft energy to the image, as if Kit is drawing one person in two bodies. It's strange to see from the outside.

"Kit's art works really well for Carolyn. And when he's with me—" Rory slows his playing, turning the rollicking tune into a ballad. "My innate ability is that I can stop someone else's Talent when I touch them. When I first met Mattie, she told me I was absorbing their energy, not stopping it. So I've been learning to provide energy to others, and my Talent happens to work really well with Kit's."

Kit makes a soft noise, and Rory knocks against his knee gently.

"So I touch him to feed him energy, and he makes hyper-realistic drawings that Carolyn can use to Travel," Rory says.

"We're not a place," Seth says, gesturing from himself to Nikolai.

"She can go to you." Kit barely glances up before bending to grab a different pencil for shading. "I think you have to let her. She's used a picture of me to come across campus when she didn't want to walk in the rain. I'll do portraits of each of you as well. I needed to start this way, though. You've been together so long you're more like one person than two."

"Soulmates?" Rory murmurs.

Kit gives a shallow one-shouldered shrug. "Maybe. I don't know. I didn't meet Tony, so I haven't seen him with Ángel. I can't see us from the outside. And everything with Shane and Pels and—" Kit cuts off, making an irritable noise. "That's a mess."

"Pels is going through some shit," Rory says, the melody shifting to something capricious and strident. "She's not a Mage, and she's not the kind of person who likes to talk about her Talent. She's one of Nikita's roommates, but none of us have gotten to know her very well. She goes to Coven because she says she has to. We don't understand either."

Nikolai had met a lot of people at Coven, and he doesn't remember half of them. But it'd be impossible to forget Pels.

"She felt angry," Seth muses.

"Resentful," Kit mutters. "They'll figure it out eventually."

"So many Talents all in one place," Nikolai says. "It was strange to see everyone being so open."

"Four out of every five people at PHU are Talented," Rory says. "That's around five thousand students."

"No wonder you attract Shadows," Seth says, voice low and dark. "You gather openly. You're calling to them."

The strings go discordant under Rory's fingers. Kit stops drawing, sets down his pencil, rests his hand on Rory's knee, and slides his hand over Rory's leg until the music starts again. Then Kit picks up his pencil and resumes drawing.

Nikolai's face feels warm, and he stares at the wall to give them privacy.

"To be fair," Rory says slowly, notes underlining the cadence of his words, "we didn't have a problem with Shadows until recently. With your help, we're only figuring out now exactly how big a problem they are. We don't have your experience."

"You live openly, and the humans don't resent you," Seth says.

"We're all human," Rory counters. "And some do resent us, I'm sure, just like I'm envious of people with incredible musical talent. There are people who are afraid of what we can do. But we're here. We're a part of this world, and ever since Kenzie Davis Emerged, everyone knows we exist. In some cases, they suspected all along, like the people in the town around my grandparents' commune."

"Where are your grandparents from?"

Nikolai half expects to hear Havenhill in response to Seth's question, but he knows logically that can't be true. Not with what he knows of this world.

"Burlington." Rory bends his head, hair falling across his face as his brow furrows. His fingers slow; Nikolai wonders if he's picking out this slow melody for the first time. "Vermont. North of here." Rory glances up. "Alaric told me about Havenhill. And Alia. And him not being a part of it."

"We thought about going to Burlington," Seth says. "We'd heard about a group up there, but we weren't sure we could get there safely."

"Maybe there's a mirror of my home in your world." Rory falls silent when Kit sets his pencil down, then he leans in, lightly touching the paper. "That was quick."

"Mm, they're easy together. It'll be harder to draw them alone." Kit holds up the piece of paper. His art looks like a photograph imbued with their essence. Nikolai feels like if he reached out and touched it, it might come alive.

Seth whistles low under his breath. "You're good."

"I'm better with Rory." Kit motions for them to move, and Nikolai unwinds himself from Seth. It's cold as Nikolai finds himself a spot to lean against the wall. Kit points his pencil at Seth. "Hold still. Stop talking. Just be you." Seth makes a face, and Kit furrows his brow in return. "Okay, fine. Stare at Nikolai. That'll make you relax."

Seth snorts, but he turns to sit cross-legged, leaning back on his hands, head tilted as he looks at Nikolai. He licks his lips, and Nikolai's face warms.

"Tell me about Havenhill," Rory says when Kit bends back to his art.

"We have a house there." Nikolai smiles remembering it and the little touches that had started to make it feel like home. "It's on the edge of the first grove. Everyone thought it was haunted after the family who used to live there disappeared."

Rory blinks, mouth falling open as he startles. "The Berman house?"

"Benford," Nikolai corrects, "but we're not in the main house. There are two. Your friends took the big house while they were there, and we took the smaller one." He tilts his head back, exhaling softly as he relaxes. There's a small catch in Seth's breath, and Nikolai smiles, tilting his head farther to show off his neck. "Our world is a mess. We…we had a home, for a while, but then that was burnt down and I lost my family. After that, Seth and I started traveling to find Havenhill. They've hidden it, warded it against Shadows and humans both. There are five groves surrounding the main house where Alia and Val live."

He opens one eye to glance at Rory. The music hasn't changed, and Rory doesn't seem to be looking at him, but it feels like he has his attention.

"Val is Alia's wife," Nikolai says, and Rory makes a small noise of acknowledgment. "I don't think Alia has any children. Val has a son—Ethan—and she takes care of her… I think Marybelle is her niece. Alaric was surprised, both that his mother was married to a woman and that that woman was a Mage."

"Alia here is very different," Rory murmurs, "and Alaric's father hates Mages. Most Clan do. It sounds as if the Alia in your world became a very different person."

"It's a very different world," Nikolai agrees. "Our Alia has been trying to save her community from the Shadows for more than a decade She crafted Havenhill out of her home. Even if her life had been the same up to a point, the Shadows coming changed all our lives."

"It makes me wonder what our Alia would be like if not for Theobald." Rory pauses, shifting to a completely different melody, and Kit hums along under his breath.

"Carolyn told Alia to start a revolution," Kit says.

"What?" Rory pauses, hand flat against the strings.

"Drea brought her to Carolyn for a reading." Kit frowns at the paper, turning it before he starts shading with a different pencil. "The reading suggested she might start a revolution."

"Alia came to a Mage willingly for magic." Rory lowers the guitar and looks about to stand, but instead he glances at Kit and presses his knee closer to him.

"Maybe they're more similar than you think," Nikolai says. His gaze is on Seth, who still watches him, a small smile playing about his lips. "Magic is everywhere in Havenhill."

Kit sets the pencil down and lifts the pad of paper, looking at it before he flips to a clean sheet. He changes his angle so he's looking at Nikolai. "Maybe the people who went there needed to see how everyone had cooperated to build someplace safe. Even after the Emergence here, our communities are all still separate. We're still sorted neatly by Talent."

"You think they went—" Nikolai quiets when Kit raises a hand and mimes cutting him off.

"Stay still," Kit orders.

Seth stretches, finally released from staying in one position. "And us coming here lets us see what our world could've been like, and we can bring back things to help us rebuild after we get rid of the Shadows. Even the humans—"

"Maybe stop thinking of it as Talent versus humans," Kit says.

"They want to kill us as much as the Shadows do," Seth shoots back. He props his elbows on his knees and hunches forward. "But they've forgotten what life can be like, too. None of us remember what it's like to live together, intermingled and safe. Maybe seeing how people in this world manage can help us rebuild."

Rory's phone buzzes. "Hang on, it's Alaric."

Kit stops drawing; the image-in-progress of Nikolai is only an outline on the page.

Rory leans forward to place the phone in the middle of the floor. "You're on speaker," he says. "What's up? I thought you were doing football things."

"We were." Alaric's voice rumbles through the phone, other voices in the background. "Drea's here. My mom called to talk to us."

"Oh?" Rory asks warily. He rests one hand on Kit's knee, and Kit goes back to working on the art, pencil scratching hurriedly across the paper.

"She's called a Gather," Alaric says. "We're going. This weekend. Be ready to leave Friday right after classes. Dax and Nate are trying to figure things out; they've got a track meet Saturday."

Nikolai frowns at the phone until Kit makes a small noise; Nikolai tries to relax his expression.

"Who is included in the 'we' that is going?" Seth asks.

"All of us," Alaric says. "Mages. Clan. Emergent and Lineage. My allies are coming in from other Clan communities. Everyone needs to be there. We need to make a plan, and we're hosting the Gather at Haverhill."

Nikolai's mind replaces "Haverhill" with *Havenhill.*

"Your mother is opening up the house to everyone," Rory says slowly.

"She's asked me for your family's contact information," Alaric replies.

Rory blinks, and Seth makes a small sound of surprise. Rory's hand goes tight on Kit's knee. Kit pauses long enough to cover Rory's hand with his own until his grip eases.

"And your father?" Rory asks, his voice tight. Even Nikolai can hear the wariness in his tone, see it in the stiffness of his body.

"Don't know," Alaric says quietly, "and don't really care. This is the best thing for us. My mother agrees, so we're doing it. Be ready to go on Friday."

The phone goes silent.

Rory picks up the phone, fingers sliding over the screen. "This is going to be a mess," he says. "But hopefully it'll be a good mess."

"We're going back to Havenhill," Seth says, his eyes crinkling as he grins.

Nikolai wants to kiss him, but when he moves, Kit holds up a finger to keep him in place. Nikolai holds still as Kit draws, letting Seth crawl across the small space between them and brush a kiss against his lips.

They're going back to Havenhill. It feels like a step in the right direction.

Letters written by Alia Davis and Valentine Munroe.

Alia,

I made it home safely. Honestly, I think you'd like it here. Yes, I know, you're reading this and objecting and complaining about not wanting to be surrounded by Mages. You don't mind me, do you? Think about how utterly bored you'd have been if we hadn't lived on the same floor this year. Admit it, you were glad when you smelled me out. You walked into my room growling and wrinkling your nose, but then you sat down and stayed, even though Megan thought you were nuts.

I wonder what it would be like if the rest of our floor had any idea what we are, that we're here living among them. Mages. Clan. Every Talent. I just wonder—how can they have no idea?

Anyway. I've got three months of farming, cooking, planning, and everything else I'm expected to do for summer work. It's a good thing I've got a scholarship because kids in my community don't get outside jobs to pay for school. But home is a commune, so it works out. They say it takes a village to raise a kid, and in our case, the whole village sends that kid to college, too.

Say you'll come visit.

Peace and magic,
Val

Val,

You do realize that I am just as busy as you are over the summer, yes? I'm expected to work in the fields and care for the little ones, particularly those who are having difficulty shifting to different forms. I also work with the textiles. I knit and weave, and I am learning dyeing, although I hate the stench. The dyes reek, and I can't get it out of my clothes.

I've had time to go swimming in the river, though. I think you'd like it. There's a place where it opens up and the current moves swiftly down one side, while it's lazy on the other side. We take inner tubes out there and rest and laugh and bask in the sun.

Your commune is as small as mine, isn't it? There are a few others here close to my age, three who have come back from school in the years ahead of me, and more who stayed out. I don't have to come back until I graduate. It's not required, but I like it here. Out there is interesting, and yes, I met you, but here... this is home.

There are only two others from my school year here, and both of them went much farther for their schooling. Eddie is happy to be back and isn't sure he wants to leave again in the fall when his next semester begins. Mary thinks she wants to be a veterinarian and is petitioning to stay at school longer to bring those skills back to our community. She's smart; I think she'll be able to do it.

I'll see if I can visit. If I'm visiting Mages, I can't easily explain to my family where I'm going.

- Alia

Alia,

Okay, so, I know you just left and I'm already writing a letter. You won't get it for a few days anyway, with the way mail travels from VT to rural NY, right? But the point is: it was awesome to see you. I'm so glad you were able to come, and thank you for visiting. I'm glad we'll be going back to school soon, because I miss you already.

Jack's been asking about you. Yes, already. I think he was flirting with you. Did you notice? He's kind of cute, I guess, if you didn't have to grow up with him. You could do worse. Well. Except that he's a Mage and I'm sure your family would have a fit about it.

Have you told them who you're rooming with next year? I don't want to have my throat ripped out before fall semester starts.

This world needs something better than letters and carriers that move at a snail's pace for communication. Yes, I could call, but if I call your house, I might have to talk to your parents. I have a feeling that wouldn't go well. You didn't even tell them the truth about who you were visiting.

I miss you already.

Peace & magic,
Val

Val,

I told them I was going to Burlington, which was not a lie. I brought them back information from the school of agriculture, so the trip was considered productive. They fully expect me to visit again in the future.

Tell Jack I'm not interested. Thank you.

I miss you, too. It won't be long before we're back.

And no, I haven't told my parents anything other than the truth: I have an apartment with three other girls from school. They won't be with me when I return in the fall. I've spent part of the summer working with my Uncle Danny on a car. We've gotten parts from the local junkyards to rebuild the engine. I was going to keep it secret as a surprise, but well, you asked, and the truth is, I'll be driving out on my own. My parents don't like leaving Haverhill and I don't like having them at school. They think letting me have a car means I'll be home more often, or that I'll be able to drive up to Burlington to meet with the school of agriculture again.

They're sort of right, I suppose. I'm sure we'll think of plenty of other things we can do with a car at our disposal.

That reminds me. I've never seen New York City. Maybe we could go down for a weekend during the fall. If you want to.

I've heard it smells terrible, but I'd like to see it with you.

- Alia

Alia,

In case you haven't noticed, I'm sticking to you through thick and thin. I will go to the ends of the earth with you, whether that means disappointing Jack (he's so sad now) or driving into the den of iniquity that is the City. I'm with you.

We should see a play while we're there. Are your tender senses up for it? I'll protect you. I've heard we can get cheap tickets through some booth in Times Square if we don't care what we see.

It'll be our adventure. Clan and Mage together, exploring the world. Wherever you want to go, I'll be by your side.

Peace & magic,
Val

Val,

Congratulations on your engagement. I know you will be happy.

- Alia

Alia,

Seriously, that's all you say? I suppose I should be glad you wrote back. I miss you, you asshole. Why did you stop writing to me?

We should start talking on email. It's a thing now, if you've got a good phone line and a dial-up system. Well, and a computer—do your parents have a computer? Email's faster and more reliable than letters. You won't even have to go to the post office.

I mean it, though. I miss you.

Tell me you'll be here for the wedding.

Peace & magic,
Val

Val,

I'll be there for the wedding.

Email, however, is not going to happen here. We do not have a good way to do so.

In the wake of my father's passing, things have been difficult here. The Council wants someone else to take over, but I'm strong enough to hold my position for now. I'm good for our community, and my mother continues to support me, as does my uncle. The problem is, they're old. One day they'll be gone, and everyone is waiting for that day.

They want me to make a mistake.

They might think traveling to a community of Mages is that mistake.

In case you're wondering, I don't agree.

School seems so long ago, doesn't it? It wasn't, really. Ten years since we first met, and an entire world has come and gone it feels like.

Tell me about him, Valentine. Tell me he makes your heart sing. Tell me about his magic, and about his courtship. Tell me that he worships the ground you walk on.

Tell me that he is good for you.

I miss you as well.

- Alia

Alia,

Enclosed please find one (1) dress and a pleading, begging entreaty for you to stand by my side when I make my vows. I can't do this without you.

He's good, Alia. We started dating a year ago. The time's gone by quick, but when he asked, it felt right. I'm here, he's here, and I think I want to have kids. I never really thought about that before. It seemed like such a faraway idea, but now sometimes when I sit and think, I see a small boy with his eyes and my smile, and it seems like it's supposed to happen.

I wonder, sometimes, what it would be like to be Predictive and have glimpses into the future. How far do they see? I think about this child, but that's only a few years down the road. Who knows, in ten or twenty years everything could be completely different.

Like you said, it's not that long and forever, all at once.

I need you here, Alia. Can you come before the wedding? Can you be with me for this?

I could sneak away. We could go to the City.

Would you come with me?

Peace & magic,
Val

Val,

I am extremely sorry to send this at this late date, but we have an issue here, and if I leave now, I may never be able to return.

Haverhill is my home, and I must keep it safe from those who would try to change it for the worse.

I am sure you are beautiful as a bride, and I hope you send pictures.

The dress you sent is very nice. It looks strange on me, but you know I don't dress up often. I think you made my mother cry.

She knows who you are. What you are. She still thinks you are good for me, and that gives me hope that someday my community can be better than we are now. That's why I have to stay here. I want my home to be a haven for anyone who needs it.

Love him with your whole heart, Valentine. And he'd best love you.

- Alia

Val,

I need your help. I can't trust anyone else.

- Alia

Alia,

I promised you once that I would stick to you like glue, so yes, I'll be there as soon as I can. Things seem dire, but we'll make it through. I am by your side, no matter what, through thick and thin.

Love, peace, and magic,
Val

Reinforcements

32

Pawel is still inside the house, on the phone, when the rest of the caravan leaves for Alaric's home. Two cars, a truck, and a minivan roll out—more vehicles than Nikolai thinks are necessary—and Nikolai and Seth are left waiting on the steps of Pawel's house with Mac nearby on the sidewalk.

The door is cracked open, and they can hear the murmur of Pawel's voice.

Mac paces back and forth, her arms tightly crossed. "I know," she says, even though no one's said a word. "He's talking to his dad. I think he said Conor's at a friend's house, and he—" Mac pauses, turning back toward the house. "I'll get him. We need to get on the road."

She disappears.

"I think we're supposed to get there in time for dinner," Seth says. He holds Nikolai's hand in his and draws with a fingertip against his palm. "Do you think it'll be like Havenhill?"

"It has to be something like Havenhill," Nikolai says. "They're the same place, in the end. Alaric said Haverhill was similar but more disconnected from the outside world. And Havenhill has Mages." He has the impression that the people in the five cars heading to Alaric's home may not all be welcome there, despite Alaric's invitation.

"Then use hands-free!" Mac says, loud enough to be heard from inside. Pawel's response is muffled; her groan after is clearly audible.

Mac reappears, crossing her arms again. "Five more minutes," she mutters, dangling the keys from her fingertips. "Let's get the car warmed up and we'll be ready to go when he is."

They toss their bags into the trunk, and Mac gets in the driver's seat while Nikolai and Seth take the back. She adjusts the mirror and seat while the car rumbles, warmth blowing around them and taking chill from the air.

When Pawel finally emerges and locks the house behind him, he pauses halfway down the walk, then resumes and stows his bag in the trunk, feet moving as though in slow motion. He pauses again by the passenger door, then opens it and stiffly slides into the seat. He slams the door with more force than seems necessary.

"I'm worried about Alaric," Mac says curtly. As soon as Pawel fastens his seat belt, she pulls out of the driveway. "And his father. The idea was for all of us to get there at the same time to back him up."

Nikolai remembers Alaric's shock that his father didn't exist in the other world and his confusion at Alia's marital status. He's seen Alaric's temper in action, and it's hard to imagine him butting heads with someone who sounds even worse.

Or rather, it's easy to imagine, but difficult to think of a positive outcome.

They've never ridden in a car with Mac driving before. They crowd the car ahead of them, shifting lanes and passing quickly when they can. On the long rural road, as soon as there's an open stretch with no one around, Mac presses the gas down and they leap forward, Pawel's car roaring as they speed along the pavement. Is she always like this, or is it because of the traffic around them or the urgency of the current situation?

Nikolai squeezes Seth's hand, needing reassurance. He is not at all comfortable with this.

They pass through a small town, and as they turn onto another long, narrow road on the other side, Mac slows down behind a line of cars that includes a minivan and a familiar bright-orange truck.

"We've caught up," she mutters.

It's not as bad after that.

They pass through one more small town that's oddly familiar. The school looks exactly like the one in Havenhill, only newer, with lights over the playground on one side and families gathered there. They pass by, then go down the long street that Nikolai remembers from learning to drive, and eventually turn onto the tree-lined road that leads to the main house.

Mac grips the wheel tightly, her knuckles white.

"Alia invited us," Pawel says.

"Unless someone's locked Theobald up, I don't think Alia's invitation changes anything," Mac replies.

"He hasn't met us at the end of the road, so it's already an improvement from what I've experienced in the past." Pawel leans back, fiddling with his phone. "Take it one move at a time, Mac. Be ready to stop a fight. We won't start anything, but we can finish it if need be."

Mac nods once.

The road opens into a clearing in front of a large house. It's reminiscent of Havenhill. The cars are newer, and there are no horses, but there are still animals everywhere. A sleepy lion lies off to one side, fur streaked with gray. A mixed flock of birds chitters in branches overhead, more kinds than Nikolai's ever seen in one place. A small pack of puppies plays nearby; they halt as the cars stop.

One puppy lowers his head to the ground, eyes wide and hopeful as he wags his tail.

Alia stands in front of the house, her hands held loose at her sides, her hair pulled back from her face. Nikolai can see the resemblance to the Alia in his world, but there are differences in her stance and demeanor. He can't quite put his finger on how, exactly, she's different, though. The Alia from his home is harder, but there's a sharpness to this one as well. The man next to her must be Theobald. If he were a Weather Witch, clouds would be gathered and the storm already begun. His expression holds hurricanes.

Alia's expression warms when Alaric and Drea emerge from Chris's car and Dax's minivan.

Theobald takes a step forward, and Alia touches his arm to halt him. His gaze is fixed on Alaric, no attention spared for the crowd emerging from the cars.

"Are my allies here?" Alaric asks.

Theobald huffs. "You brought them all."

Alaric glances at them. "Not all. These are my friends from PHU. Allies, yes, but not the Clan allies. Mom—"

"Dayton made arrangements, yes," she replies. "We've readied a wing for our guests, Clan and otherwise. Baths are fresh, kitchens are stocked, and your cousins have been warned that mice and other unexpected vermin are not welcome."

Drea snorts, and Corbin says idly, "Hawks are always hungry and in need of rodents for snacks." He makes a face at some of the animals lounging about, and the smaller ones scatter.

"Don't eat our Clan," Drea chides gently, but she's laughing.

Nikolai suspects the threat was only for show and holds no weight. He can't imagine Corbin eating a mouse that was actually a person. He can, however, imagine Corbin having a fun time putting a good scare into someone.

Theobald shakes off Alia's touch and steps forward. In a blink, he's a wolf, huge and growling, feet splayed and body tense with anger.

A bear stands in Alaric's place, roaring loudly and standing tall before he lands on all four feet and lumbers to meet the wolf.

"Theobald," Alia calls.

"Alaric!" Drea shouts at the same time.

Their yells make no difference.

Mac throws the car into park and pulls the emergency brake. It's still running when she climbs out, her hands up as if that's going to make a difference. She disappears and reappears next to Drea and Corbin.

The wolf snarls, baring its teeth.

"We're not afraid of you," Mac says. "We stand with Alaric, and we stand with Alia."

Alia has yet to move. She slowly brings her arms up, crossing them over her chest, her stance steady as she refuses to intervene. "I will not forgive you if you kill him," she says. Nikolai has no idea which one she's speaking to.

The wolf and bear seem to take her words as permission to fight.

Space is cleared quickly, some of the nearby animals resolving into humans, forming a wide circle around Alaric and Theobald. Mac teleports to move the new arrivals, arranging them in a human wall. Nikolai climbs out of the car, joining Seth to take a place in front of Pawel's car.

No one joins hands, but they nevertheless stand in solidarity, Mages and Clan.

Alaric and Theobald circle each other, the bear huffing as the wolf snarls, snaps his teeth, and barks loudly. The slow and steady lumbering of the bear belies a surprising speed; he's ready when the wolf leaps at him, mouth wide and aiming for his throat. Alaric falls backward, rolling with the impact to throw Theobald off and send him tumbling. It takes Theobald longer to regain his feet, but his snarl is deeper than the before, his teeth bared in fury.

Alaric circles again. Waiting.

"There will be blood," Alia murmurs. "We will heal from this, as we always do. But there will be blood."

There's a sharp whine from the wolf, then Alaric attacks, mouth open and front paws out. Alaric grabs the wolf around the shoulders as if to hug him, teeth closing on Theobald's cheek. The wolf is huge, but Alaric is larger, stronger, and younger. He bites down—first blood drawn—and Theobald howls as Alaric pushes him back, taking him down and pinning him with his greater weight. Alaric's teeth sink into Theobald's shoulder for second blood.

Wriggling enables Theobald to get out from under him; he circles behind Alaric, then attacks his back and sinks teeth into his shoulder. With a roar, Alaric throws him off. Theobald lands on his flank with a *thump* and a whine. He rolls to a crouch by Alia's feet, breathing labored, then pushes up; one leg is splayed and shaking.

Alia puts her hand on his shoulder, and Theobald stays down. "Alaric claims first blood, and first pin, and you attacked his back," she says. "Finish this as men, with your words. You know what you need to do."

Theobald melts into humanity on his hands and knees, head bowed, body shuddering with every breath. Blood drips from the side of his face and his shoulder, and his shirt is frayed. He gets one leg under him and tries to stand; he falls back to his knees immediately.

Alaric stands over him, one hand on the top of Theobald's head. "I don't want to fight you for this," Alaric says. "You can't keep the world from changing. If you hadn't forced us to live apart from other Talents, Orson might be alive. He might have been here, with his Mage friends, living amongst us, and he might have survived. We will never know for sure. If you want to grow our community, and if you want to continue to thrive, we need to change."

Theobald continues to breathe, loud and raw, but says nothing as he stares at the ground. One hand curls against his chest; the other is on the ground, his nails in the dirt, clawing at it.

"Either you change, or we do," Alaric tells him. "Mom and I are willing to do what needs to be done to ally ourselves and force the Shadows out. We don't want war with the Mages. We want to keep our home safe."

"I want to keep our home safe," Theobald snarls. He looks up, chin tucked and neck protected. "Clan's Clan."

"Clan's Clan," Alaric agrees. He drops into a crouch, meeting Theobald's gaze at eye level. "That doesn't mean we can't make connections. You chose me to lead, and I'm going to do that while we still have a Clan left for me to do it with."

Alaric drops his hand from Theobald's head, both arms loose as they rest on his bent knees, and he stays crouched and balanced on his toes. "Do you cede?"

A soft rumble echoes among the Clan watching.

Alia lowers herself slowly, her forehead pressed to the side of Theobald's head as her fingers curl around the nape of his neck. Nikolai can hear a rustling, as if she's whispering to him. Alaric's expression doesn't shift, but Theobald's shoulders slump and his eyes close.

"I cede." His words are clear and sharp.

Alia rises, her arm around Theobald's back to bring him with her.

Alaric stays where he is a heartbeat longer, giving Theobald that moment to look down on him before Theobald's back straightens and he looks at the Mages and Clan gathered around him.

As Alaric comes to his feet, he stretches out his hand, and Theobald takes it, jaw locked tight. He meets Alaric's gaze. "From this day forward, Alaric will lead," Theobald says, each word steady and controlled. "In his stead, while he has his years apart, Alia will be his hands, his ears, and his voice here in our community. If anyone has anything to say against this, say it now or be done."

There are more people standing in human form than in animal now, more than Nikolai had realized were there. Adults, teens, children—people of every age from toddlers to elders. There are no birds in the trees, no creatures scurrying along the ground save for the small group of puppies still playing to one side. A cat leaps into the fray, and Nikolai wonders if any of them are actual animals, or if they are all Clan children.

No one says a word.

"More guests and allies will arrive tonight and tomorrow," Alia says. She points to the sides of the large lot in front of the house, then to the cars that have been left haphazardly in the drive leading in. "Please park carefully and allow everyone room. There will be a meal in the main room. For tonight, the Gather will be open; all from our community are welcome to greet the newcomers. If you wish to be involved in discussions of our involvement going forward, petition Alaric or myself tonight. Tomorrow's discussions will begin at breakfast and will be open to only those invited."

She turns, Theobald walking by her side as they head into the house.

Drea and Corbin stand to either side of Alaric, leaving space for Chris by his side. Mac appears nearby, joining the group. Alaric stands tall, speaking quietly with them as the crowd disperses. Nikolai doesn't see the Clan change forms, but birds fly up into the trees and cats chase down the pathway as the place empties of humans.

Pawel pulls open the door of his car, sliding into the driver's seat and adjusting it so it's comfortable for him. Nikolai and Seth move out of the way so Pawel can park between Trish's orange truck and Dax's minivan.

Nikolai doesn't know what to do next. His skin itches and he feels as though he's witnessed something monumental that he doesn't quite understand. He drops an arm over Seth's shoulder and tucks him close so they can lean on each other.

"What next?" Trish calls out. She has a soft case with her guitar in it slung across her back, and she carries a bag loosely in one hand. Seeing her reminds Nikolai to get his things out of the trunk of Pawel's car, and her words seem to mobilize everyone else as well.

"Come with me," Alaric says, motioning to lead the way. "Welcome to my home."

33

Dinner is a long affair. The big room at the center of the house reminds Nikolai vividly of the same room in Havenhill; he can understand why Alaric was off-balance there. For the Gather, food is set up along the outer edges, and tables with seating have been placed in the center. People take what they want and drift from place to place, either standing and talking or settling in at a table for a time.

It's easy to get lost and overwhelmed.

Every time Nikolai blinks, it seems as if someone new arrives. Rory introduces him to his mother and fathers, and later to his grandparents. Alaric is in the middle of introducing several Clan from other communities when one loud girl arrives and brashly interrupts to pounce on the back of another girl in Alaric's group. At the sound of a shriek, Nikolai looks to the door and spots a small child—the youngest he's seen at the Gather—barreling across the room. She throws her arms around Alaric's legs, then lifts her arms high and demands to be picked up. He does so, fitting her on his hip and spinning around so that her brightly colored knit cape swings out.

Across the room, Val stands with a skinny teen. She smiles fondly as she watches.

Nikolai reaches for Seth as his mind spins with the disconcerting sensation of two realities overlapping. "Alaric," Nikolai says, "I thought you didn't know Val."

"Hm?" Alaric's gaze follows where Nikolai points.

The small girl in his arms waves wildly. "Mama! Elijah! Come meet Alaric! He's a dog!"

She slips down as Alaric's hold loosens, his fingers momentarily slack. He grabs on, hoisting her up again. "Only sometimes, Miranda," he says, hand steady on her back.

"Only sometimes," she agrees. "You haven't met my mama."

"I haven't." Alaric carefully lowers Miranda to the ground, making sure she's settled. His expression is closed and tight. "You're right. I should."

"Maybe they're both bedrock," Nikolai murmurs. Maybe this is when Val and Alia meet in this world. Maybe them not being together is how the worlds diverged. Would that be a good thing or a bad thing? In many ways, Havenhill is far ahead of the Haverhill community. But Nikolai's world is in much more dire straights.

Val approaches, her hand out and a steady smile in her expression. "You're Alaric. I'm Valentine, and this is Miranda's older brother Elijah. I'm glad we finally get to meet. When I heard that Susan, Allison, and David were planning to come, I asked if my family could join. Miranda is excited to visit your home."

Alaric takes her hand, shaking it and not letting go. "Do you know my mother?" he asks, a soft growl under his words.

"I—" Valentine tugs her hand free and takes a step back. "We may have crossed paths in the past. Did she attend PHU?"

"Most of us do."

Her smile is thinner, stretched a little too wide. "Then it's a possibility. You'll have to introduce us when you get a chance. All I know so far is that her son is excellent with fiber work and good with small children. She obviously raised you well."

Miranda tugs at Alaric, and he picks her up again while distracted. His skin is pale, and it's a moment before he replies, "Thank you. I'll take you to her."

"This would be a good time for us to step out," Seth murmurs.

Alaric turns around, and Nikolai remembers then that he has great hearing. "You can go anywhere in the community you'd like, although I don't recommend driving," Alaric says. "Not everywhere has roads. Don't go into people's personal homes or gardens."

"The house where we stayed in Havenhill?" Seth asks.

Alaric expression twists with distaste. "If you want. It's worse here than there. No one considers it habitable. Ignore the mess. My father wrecked part of it when he lost his mind briefly."

That statement makes Nikolai curious, but Alaric is already turning away, Miranda in his arms as he stiffly heads toward Alia with Valentine and Elijah in his wake.

Seth squeezes Nikolai's fingers, and Nikolai nods. He's right. It's time to take a break. There are too many people here.

Nikolai breathes more easily after they emerge from the house. The small parking lot is as crowded as ones he saw on the PHU campus, and the license plates seem similarly varied: New York, of course, but also Ohio, Massachusetts, Maine, Rhode Island, Connecticut, Maryland, Pennsylvania…

"I take it we're not the only ones getting claustrophobic?" Nate's voice is cheery. He waves from where he crouches off to one side, lacing up his sneakers. "Dax and I are heading that way. We're going to do something he doesn't want to do, if you want to come along."

Nikolai is surprised to see the two of them alone. "Where's Cass?"

"Inside with the rest of the SigPsiEp contingent. I think Drea's claimed sisterly rights or something in order to introduce them to her Clan friends." Nate straightens up, arching his back as he stretches. "We'd planned to run to where we're heading, but we can walk if you want to join us."

"We're going to the place where we stayed in our world's community." Seth asks. His gaze shifts to where Dax stands on the road that leads toward the Benford house. Nikolai can see that he's stiff before Seth comments, "He's apprehensive."

"We're going to talk to a ghost." Nate gestures, and they walk together to join Dax. "We've got company."

"I'm sure Orson will be thrilled," Dax mutters. "Running?" He has on sneakers as well, bouncing lightly on his toes. He's graceful for someone so broad and tall, whereas Nate looks like an antelope, all arms and legs.

"Unless something's chasing us, I'd rather not," Seth replies.

Dax shrugs and starts walking. This way between the big house and the Benford house in Havenhill had been clearer, with many small houses and outbuildings along the path. This road is open for a ways, then it narrows to a path between the trees, as if it's traveled only rarely.

Nikolai doesn't remember seeing a cemetery in Havenhill, but there's one here, off the path and farther away than he'd expected. Dax leads them there with ease. There are footsteps in the mud outside and paths worn through the grass above the graves. Some are marked by flowers or plants, others plain aside from the headstones. Dax hesitates, eyes closed and hands clenched.

" 'We' are not going to talk to a ghost," he says. "I am. And I'm going to do my best to talk to only the one ghost. Something's riled up the spirits here. They're much chattier than before. Would've been nice for Alex to warn me."

"Do Alex's warnings actually make sense?" Nate asks.

Dax huffs. "You have a point. C'mon. Orson's over here."

The grave is newer than the others, the grass still sparse, fresh growth. Ivy climbs the stone, and hostas are coming up around the base. The writing on the stone is bright and still sharp.

Orson Herne. Beloved Son and Brother.

He was only twenty-two when he died.

Dax crouches on the grass, his fingers skimming the tops of the tiny blades. "Hey," he says, looking at the stone. "Long walk to get here, but you know that. Like Alaric said, this place wasn't built for people like us. You Clan can all run on four legs or fly."

He smiles slightly. "You have a point. It's tough on the lizards and bugs."

The smile falls away, his brow furrowing. "Slow down. Please."

Seth takes a step closer to Nikolai.

Nate moves to stand behind Dax, his hand hovering over Dax's shoulder. "Do you—?"

Dax cuts him off by bringing one hand up. Then he presses the heels of his palms to his eyes. "I get it," he mutters. "You said that. I'm trying to protect him. I'm trying to finish this. Why the hell is everyone else so angry about it now? Is it because of the Mages—" He stops, hands falling from his face as his mouth opens slowly. "Oh."

Dax rocks back on his heels, then rises. He brushes against Nate before he pulls away. He opens his mouth, drawing in a breath. It looks as if he's about to launch into a speech, the words hanging heavy in the air, waiting. Then he says, "Okay." He takes another step back and nods. "Okay."

"Okay?" Nate asks.

Dax shakes his head, exhales roughly. "I'm not, but they—it will be. I need to put some distance between me and this place. You said we're going…where?"

"The old Benford—"

"Berman," Seth corrects him.

"The Berman house," Nikolai says. "It's where we stayed in our own world, and where Mattie came back from being a Shadow. It's down that same path, if we keep going."

"Sometimes it's weird being the one non-Talented person hanging out with you guys," Nate muses. "You all have so much going on, and I just tag along for moral support."

Seth nudges his glasses up his nose. "Never underestimate the value of moral support."

Dax turns and heads back the way they came. Nate falls into step beside him, and Nikolai and Seth follow.

Nate glances back at them. "Yeah, but your moral support is more like—" He lifts his fingers and wiggles them at Dax. "Mine's being present and talking."

"He talks a lot," Dax confirms.

"Some people would find that a more comforting method of providing empathy than the Talented version," Seth argues. "Some people don't like Talent. There's a reason humans fear us."

"Plus Shadows," Nikolai reminds him.

"There's that."

Nikolai reaches out to catch Seth's hand, and they slow down, letting Dax and Nate move ahead. There's no reason to hurry; they aren't running from anything.

Nate's hands lift and move as he speaks, but Dax and he are far enough ahead that Nikolai can't overhear them. The distance stretches as they move along the narrow path.

"They're going somewhere. We're out for a relaxing stroll," Nikolai observes.

Seth's gaze is narrowed as he watches them, too. "Mm," he agrees. Nate reaches out, grabs Dax's shoulder, and points at something in the distance. "We just happen to be going in the same direction."

The distance between them steadies eventually, which is good, because Nikolai's hard-pressed to see the difference between the small path they follow through the trees and the turn-off toward the Berman place. These are places where wolves run and birds fly. There's no need for human pathways.

He can feel the house before they arrive. It pricks at his senses even more than the Benford house did, tingling across his skin.

Nikolai pauses as the house comes into view. "You feel that?"

Seth nods. "I feel something. Not sure if it's the same thing you feel, but this is worse than home. This place has an active 'stay out' feel. I'm uncomfortable getting close. I'm not sure how they walked up so easily."

Nate waves for them to come forward. He waits at the base of the steps, and Dax is standing at the doorway and looking inside. The door has been ripped apart by something with claws and hangs awkwardly on the hinges, partly open.

"There aren't any ghosts here," Dax says over his shoulder. "It feels dead."

"That's because Mattie's already gone," Nate guesses. "I wonder if you would've been able to talk to her before she was pulled out?" He crosses his arms, shuddering theatrically. "This place gives me the heebie-jeebies. I can't imagine how bad it feels to you."

"It feels like the Dreamscape is already here," Nikolai replies. He lifts a hand, staring at his fingers as they move through the air. He's watching for that moment when he slips, when the Dreamscape comes out into the real world. It doesn't happen, but it feels like it could if he breathes wrong. "This place is dangerous."

"It was." Mattie stands in front of Dax, Chelsea a column of darkness behind her. Maybe she's not entirely gone after all. She's certainly here, now, suddenly. "I Emerged here, and my family died. This place ate my soul."

"Feels like it could do it again," Seth says dryly.

"Probably," Mattie agrees. She pulls what's left of the door open wide. "Why don't you come in?"

Dax walks past her, circling around Chelsea. They stare at each other as the rest move in; Chelsea slides forward, one hand out and reaching for Dax's face.

"Not for eating," Mattie says.

Chelsea pulls back, shadowed hand falling. "I wasn't going to. He feels different. I want to know why."

"It's all right." Dax closes the distance between them, reaching for Chelsea's hands and wrapping his fingers around her dark wrists. He lifts her hand, offering his face for her to touch.

"Are you sure you should—?"

"I've been thrown across rooms by ghosts." Dax interrupts Nate, holding still while Chelsea spreads tendrils of darkness across his skin.

"She also drinks souls," Seth reminds him. "We woke up one morning to find her feeding on us."

Nikolai can't see her features clearly, but he suspects the look Chelsea throws Seth's way is both hurt and indignant.

"I apologized," she says. "And I'm not doing that now. I'm not hungry. Much." Her attention returns to Dax, her darkness almost hiding his face as she leans in close. Her hands curl around the nape of his neck, and he stands quietly. "What are you?"

"Descendant of the Oracle of Delphi and an Empathic line. I talk to ghosts."

"You aren't like the skinny one, but you are still brimming. Your energy is not for me." Chelsea slips backwards, light spilling into the space around Dax as she goes. "You carry the weight of others."

"Hundreds of ghosts over the years," Dax agrees. He shudders, seeming to shake something off.

Nikolai tunes them out. He wants to see more of this place, and he lets the tingling on his skin draw him through the living room and into the kitchen. The floor is covered in dirt. Windows are broken, wind whistling in. Old pans lie on the stove and dishes on the table, immortalizing the moment when the family disappeared.

The kitchen is where the sensation is strongest, as if he could step from reality into the Dreamscape. He draws in a deep breath and lets it out slowly, centering himself. He feels Seth's calm from the other room; even from a distance, his anchor is stable.

"There," Mattie whispers.

Nikolai turns, startled. "I didn't hear you following me."

She moves past him, touching the stool that stands by the stove. "I was right here," she says. "You can feel it, can't you? How thin the barrier remains. I wonder if there are other places like this in the world, if every time a Shadow Emerges it leaves a rift behind. I wonder if that is how other Shadows slip into the world, if places like this give them access. It didn't feel this thin in Havenhill, did it?"

Nikolai shakes his head. "No." He presses his hand next to hers on the stool, and for a moment the kitchen is in color, macaroni and cheese bubbling on the stove, the scent rich in his nose. He steps back, and everything returns to darkness, dust, and dirt. "Is this where you were were trapped?"

Mattie crosses her arms, sinking to sit on the stool with her back to the stove. She nods. "My soul was waiting. It never went far."

"Do you think it'll be the same for Chelsea?" Nikolai has a feeling there will be a lot of faith involved in the process of returning a soul to a Shadowwalker, but from Carolyn's description, he can see how they slipped into the Dreamscape and found Mattie to bring her back. "Do we need to go where she Emerged? Do you think she'll be waiting there?"

Mattie presses her lips together and shakes her head. "I don't think it will be the same. I didn't have anywhere else to go. Chelsea's linked to Pawel. She keeps drifting back to him."

Nikolai's gaze goes to the doorway. Seth, Nate, Dax, and Chelsea are talking, voices slipping over each other, Chelsea's more sibilant than the others but no less strong. "So you think that, if she's waiting anywhere, it's near Pawel," he says. "That's where we'll find her."

"If she's anywhere," Mattie agrees. "Are you going to restore her soul to her before the ritual to heal the split? I know they want to stop the Shadows; depending how you do it, it might kill her."

"She'll be around after whatever we do," he says as if stating it confidently will make actually doing it that simple. "She needs to help us get home, since you can't."

"I can't," Mattie confirms. "I can't easily get into the split now. It feels as if I should be able to, but something makes it only for those without souls, only for those who hunger and have needs that go beyond sanity. Perhaps after the ritual, that will change." A small, wistful sound escapes before she smiles. "I'd like to travel."

Nikolai closes his eyes and relaxes, letting the sensation of the Dreamscape wash over him. It's so close that he could mold it here, bring it into being. He accustoms himself to the sensation and does his best to keep it under control. He'll save this for later.

34

Nikolai wakes when he hears voices in the hall: Dax laughing and Nate shushing him as they pass. The voices recede, and there are no more house noises or steps after. The bed is warm, and Seth is asleep, so Nikolai rolls over and tugs Seth closer so he can drift in almost-sleep.

He's not sure how much time passes before there's a knock on the door, but the room is brighter, more sun spilling around the window shade.

"Drea says breakfast is in the big hall downstairs," Mac calls out. "You can come down with us in a few, or you can come down later on your own."

Seth rolls over, burying his face in the pillow.

Nikolai doesn't remember exactly how to get to breakfast from here, but… "We'll be down later," he says.

"Gotcha." Mac's steps recede, more voices joining hers in the hall.

Seth rolls onto his back, reaching up to frame Nikolai's face with his hands and drawing him down. "Much later," Seth mutters.

That sounds like a great plan to Nikolai, and he wastes little time in putting it to action.

The delay in getting out of bed means that by the time they have towels wrapped around their waists as they go looking for the shower down the hall, no one else is there to interrupt them. There is a long row of shower heads on one side of the room, and a selection of soaps and scrubbers to use. The bath is heated and the size of half a swimming pool, with a sign that says "Please cleanse before you bathe" hanging on the wall above it.

As tempting as it is to shower together, it's easier to shower separately and wash quickly. By the time they're finally done, dried, and dressed, at least an hour has passed since the rest of their group went downstairs.

They make their way carefully, taking direction from teens who wait at two of the intersections, pointing their fingers without looking up from their phones. Nikolai imagines that sitting around waiting for people to get lost is boring. One of the teens peeks at Nikolai and Seth as they go by; as soon as she realizes she's been caught, she looks away quickly.

The room at the center of the house is full of people, even more so than the night before. The seats around the tables are mostly full, and other people linger near the buffets around the room's edges. Motion catches Nikolai's eye, and he spots Corbin waving and pointing at a small cluster of tables where most of the people from PHU are. When Nikolai nods, Corbin gestures toward the laden tables against the wall.

Drea leans in to say something to Corbin and lightly smacks the back of his head; Corbin flies up as a crow, staying close to the ceiling before he drops down, in human form, to land in front of Nikolai and Seth.

"I've been sent to make sure you eat," he says.

Nikolai's suspects that's not what Drea said, but he won't correct him. "Thanks. Is there space for us?"

"Alaric and Chris said something about heading upstairs." Corbin makes a face somewhere between a smirk and a wince. "Drea and I were thinking about heading to the apple grove to see how the trees are doing. It's been warm, so they're probably close to blooming."

"There's an apple grove?"

Corbin nods at Seth. "We have about a dozen varieties. Plus peaches, plums, and pears. We have strawberries, blueberries, blackberries, raspberries, and black caps. There's farmland for vegetables and other kinds of fruit, and there's also livestock. We're fully self-sufficient when it comes to food."

"Maples, too, I assume." Nikolai thinks he spotted some while they were walking yesterday.

"Sugaring season recently passed, and I was so glad not to be here for it." Corbin exaggeratedly wipes a hand across his forehead. "Sugaring is hard work, and I'm happy to leave it to everyone else for a few years." When they reach the table, Corbin points to a silvered pot sitting over a warmer. "But if you want to taste it, that's the good stuff. The jams and preserves are better, though."

They load up their plates, moving slowly through the line. Nikolai spots Pawel ahead, talking to a man who reminds him of Thorne and a woman who has strikingly striped red and black hair. They are vaguely familiar, but Nikolai can't place names to faces.

"...finding them was a godsend," the woman says. "They've taken in five kids already. And Pawel, I know you have Conor, and with your schedule, it might be difficult to officially place anyone with you, but if you ever think you might be able to—"

The man puts a hand over hers as she reaches for Pawel. "Luce. Give him a chance to think. Don't worry, Pawel, she understands that not every Talented adult out there is a great candidate to foster Talented kids who need homes. She gets enthusiastic."

"And you don't, Rowan?"

"I don't mind," Pawel says, with a small, tired smile. "Lucy, I appreciate what you are trying to say, and what you need, but unfortunately I already find myself acting as a parent to young adults who are barely younger than myself. In fact, I have two living with me right now." He gestures, motioning for Nikolai and Seth to approach.

"I'm going to let you two field this on your own," Corbin whispers. "Those are two of Rory's parents, in case Pawel forgets to mention." He disappears with a flutter of wings and a breeze.

Right, they met the night before. Rory introduced them.

Lucy smiles, turning to face them with her hand extended. "I'm Lucy Wilson, and this is Rowan Baker, one of my partners."

Rowan grins, and he's eerily like Thorne aside from having more smile lines around the eyes. "It's good to see you again. World travelers aren't the usual kind of Talent we get to meet."

"Just an Empath and a Dreamwalker," Seth replies, nudging his glasses up his nose after he shakes hands. "The world-walking wasn't planned."

"We run a program to help rescue Talented children who have either already dropped into the foster system or who are endangered in their homes," Lucy explains. "We'd love to have Pawel involved, even if only in the outreach to help Emergent children who have parents who aren't as familiar with what being Talented involves. There's so often a sense of fear, and children try to hide—" She stops when Rowan puts a hand over her mouth.

"Lucy rescued our Daniel, and she hasn't stopped rescuing people since," Rowan stagewhispers with a fond smile. "She forgets that sometimes she needs to stop being an advocate and simply be a Mage who happens to sniff out Talents in an alarmingly accurate way."

Lucy wiggles out from under his hand. "I also fly. On a broom. Like a witch." She grins, the corners of her eyes crinkling. "Because it's fun."

Her enthusiasm is infectious; Nikolai finds himself smiling back. "We live in a community at home that is a haven for all Talent. Our world isn't friendly to us. You would love it. You should talk to Pawel about that; he was with us for a while. It's built in the same place as this Clan community is here."

"For all Talent?"

"A cooperative community for Emergent and Lineage Talents, from Clan to Mage and beyond," Pawel confirms. His expression relaxes, and he gestures for Lucy and Rowan to move. "Why don't we sit down and I can tell you about it. Your experience growing up in Burlington might be similar, Rowan. I know there's another group in New Hampshire that has combined communities as well; they are part of the alliance that Alaric has been forging. This needs to be more common on our world. It is absolutely vital to survival in Nikolai and Seth's."

Nikolai breathes more easily as Pawel, Lucy, and Rowan drift toward one of the tables. He nudges Seth, and they move on; they finish filling their plates, then look to see if there's space with their friends so they can sit and eat.

When Nikolai takes a step, another vaguely familiar woman blocks him. Her gaze is narrowed, amber eyes focused intently on Nikolai first, then Seth. She doesn't have a tray or plate; her hands are clasped behind her back. When Nikolai meets her gaze, she moves carefully, reaching up to tuck wavy strands of her tawny hair behind one ear as her head cocks, neck protected when her chin lowers.

"Dayton!" someone calls.

"I'm not going to eat them," she replies loudly, her gaze never wavering.

"I want to meet them." Her voice lowers as she leans in, nostrils flaring. "So. You two are the catalysts. Do we blame you, or give you acclaim? Likely both. I think more good than bad will come of this; it's what we wanted, after all. Cooperation."

Nikolai has been hunted by humans and Shadows alike, but this sense of being prey is entirely different. He remembers her now—the girl that Stormy had leapt onto. She hadn't seemed so predatory last night.

Seth pushes forward, putting himself between Nikolai and Dayton. "I don't think we're at fault for anything."

Nikolai consciously relaxes, wrapping one arm around Seth's shoulders and kissing the side of his head. "We'll help as much as we can, but I don't think we're any kind of catalyst unless you blame the Dreams that Nikita and I shared. It sounds like the Emergence is the real cause, given everything we've heard about your world."

"You didn't have an Emergence?" Dayton's expression softens enough to unpin them; Seth untenses in Nikolai's arms, leaning back against him. "What happened in your world?"

"Shadows," Seth says bluntly. "We were outed by Shadows destroying everything they could. We'd like to keep that from continuing to happen before our world falls into darkness."

Dayton's smile is swift and sharp. "And so would we. You'll be useful allies. Alaric's community is becoming wide and varied, and that can only be good. We need diversity and Talents of all kinds. The world is changing." She turns and stalks away, her movements long and lithe like an animal's.

Definitely a predator. Definitely Clan.

Nikolai steps back, still balancing his plate in his other hand. "Let's eat."

They grab the nearest table with people they know. Del kicks out a free chair for Nikolai, and Heather gets up to offer hers to Seth, switching to share with Nikita. They squeeze in around the table as Del introduces Sam and Shawn.

Nikolai tries to eat quickly. This small peace won't last.

"How long before you have to go back into the Dreamscape?" Shawn asks.

Nikolai lowers his gaze, chewing on a piece of bacon. Not even five minutes before attention is back on him.

Seth leans close, shoulder to shoulder. "Do you ever miss being on our own?"

Nikolai nods and offers him a strawberry. At least the company comes with plenty of good food.

"Me?" Del taps her chest. "Or us?" Her gestures encompasses Nikolai and Nikita. "The answer's different depending on which you're asking about."

Sam raises both eyebrows as he looks at her; even Nikolai senses the silent judgment.

"You," Shawn says curtly. "You've spent too much time there. It feels like it's getting more and more difficult for you to come back."

Nikolai remembers Del in the meadow and the paths, looking like she could easily skip into the Dream and lose herself. "We won't let her go," he says.

"Of course we won't!" Nikita agrees. "Del, you have anchors."

"I have two of them." She pats Shawn's hand where it lies clenched on the table, but she doesn't meet his eyes. "And the answer is, I'll be going soon. I need to go in before we start meeting officially this morning. And I'll be going again tonight. I need to keep checking to see who's responded to our call. It's not like we can talk to Dreamwalkers from other worlds on our own internet; I'll leave the online communication to the two of you."

"You've been going in alone." Normally, for a Dreamwalker with an anchor, Nikolai wouldn't think going alone a bad idea, but he has a feeling that repeated trips into the Dreamscape aren't good for Del. "Do you need us with you? How have you been—?"

"I'm fine," Del brushes him off with a wave of her hand. Shawn inches closer to her, his hand across the back of her chair. Del leans her elbows on the table, intertwines her fingers, and rests her chin on her hands. "You don't have to worry about me, Nikolai. I'm not going skip off into the distance."

"I disbelieve," Nikita counters. Her weak smile attempts to soften the worry that suffuses the rest of her expression. "Pretty sure we've seen you do that."

"It's easier with these two holding me back. We're learning, even if they aren't Empaths. We've got our own way of doing things, though we could use some advice from someone with experience," Del admits, her attention shifting to Seth. "I don't know if you can extrapolate from the Empath point of view, but anything you can suggest to help us out would be good."

"I'd also be interested in the Empath way of looking at things," Heather says. "The thicker the Shadows get, the harder it will be to keep the Dreamscape out of reality."

"We're fine," Nikita says, gesturing between herself and Del. "Not even a flurry outside."

"We should still pick Seth's brain," Heather says.

"That makes it sound like you're planning on eating my mind," Seth mumbles around his food.

"You don't need me for this, do you?" Nikolai's not entirely satisfied with the conversation he had with Valentine. He can't stop thinking about what the Shadows mean when they say "bedrock." If Valentine is also whatever that is, it's important to fully understand how that affects their twinned worlds. He pushes back from the table, pausing when Seth catches his hand, dragging him back down for a kiss. "I'm not going far," Nikolai assures him. "I can't add anything to the conversation about how you anchor me in reality; I only know you do."

"And I always will," he says, letting go of Nikolai's hand. "I'll be here when you're done."

Nikolai grabs a chair on his way to where Valentine sits, surprisingly alone, at a table; all the other seats have been stolen, leaving her with a quiet space. Her plate is empty, and she holds a mug of something steaming that rests on the table as she looks across the room.

Nikolai follows her gaze to where Alaric sits at the table with Corbin and Drea. Miranda is perched on his lap, her brother on the next chair. She speaks excitedly, and Alaric dodges every time she gestures and almost hits him in the nose.

Nikolai slides his chair next to Valentine's so he can look in the same direction. She has her back to the wall with a good view of everything but one part of the buffet. In this corner, everything smells like coffee from the drink table, but the view is worth it.

"He really is good with kids. I saw it in Havenhill, too."

Valentine flinches. "Miranda adores him." Her arms are crossed, her toes pressed against the floor as she rocks back on the rear two legs of her chair. "Elijah hasn't decided yet. He seems torn between looking up to Alaric, since he's older, and resenting that his little sister likes Alaric better. I should have made more of an effort to meet him before now. He's been out to Burlington twice. David's told me he's a good kid." She hesitates, then laughs. "Young man. You all are in that awkward age of being adults, but you still seem like kids."

"I've been on my own for a few years," Nikolai points out. "We grew up quick."

"I suppose you would," Valentine says. She licks her lips, tension rolling through her. "Alaric told me a little about your background. Pawel told me more."

Nikolai glances at her, mirroring the way she leans back in the chair, his own chair creaking.

She glances at him, her smile wry. She pulls one hand free, lifts it up, and spreads her fingers. She curls her fingers into a fist, then tucks her hand back in to cross her arms again. "What?"

"Did you lie about knowing Alia?" he asks quietly. He doesn't know who might be listening, and if she lied, she probably doesn't want to talk in public.

"I thought that might be what you wanted to know." Her gaze rests on Alaric, half smiling as Miranda finally catches him in the nose with one hand. "Don't worry about eavesdroppers; they can't hear us. Manipulating sound is my natural ability. I can be really loud, or completely inconspicuous. It's handy as a parent."

"I never asked what Val's innate ability was." Nikolai watches Alaric and Miranda, wondering if it makes it easier for Valentine not to have to look him in the eye. "So, then."

"I lied." Valentine lets her chair fall with a soft *thump*. "We knew each other when we were students at PHU. There was a large community of Talent at the school even then. It was a safe place. The people who weren't Talented didn't make a fuss when they found out about us, and they weren't afraid of us. Talent was an open secret, although not everyone was in on it. We found each other our freshman year, and we even lived on the same floor of the same dorm two years in a row. But Clan hated Mages, so we never got along."

"How much did Pawel tell you about Havenhill?"

Valentine huffs. "He started with how Havenhill is led by a married couple—Mage and Clan—myself and Alia. I could see how that could happen. She's gorgeous. Strong. Driven. Loyal. She's the kind of woman who wants what's best for her people. So am I, which is why I'm here. I didn't only come because Miranda wanted to see Alaric again."

For a moment, Nikolai thinks she means that she's here for Alia. But no, she means she's here for the war, such as it is, against the Shadows. "You intend to join forces with the Clan."

Valentine nods. "We need to move past old prejudices. My community doesn't hold those beliefs, but it's been impossible to move past her hating me. There we were, in the same place, and when I extended an olive branch, she rejected it."

"So you rejected her," Nikolai says, and Valentine nods.

One thing could make a difference between the two worlds. One tiny change: an overture accepted. A friendship created instead of enmity.

"So we'll try again," Valentine says. "I'm positive she remembers me. We haven't talked about it, and I don't think we will. It's simplest to ignore it and move forward for the best of our communities. I've already made plans to work with the group from New Hampshire." She gestures at another table, where a pregnant woman speaks excitedly with a group that includes Dayton. "They've had tragedy strike down two Clan communities and one Mage community, and they're rebuilding together. They could use the support."

"The Shadows refer to Alia as 'bedrock,' " Nikolai says. He feels Valentine's attention shift to him, so he finally looks at her full-on, giving her the weight of his regard. "She's in all worlds. Or most worlds. Everywhere, she's exactly who she is with only minor differences. Unlike people like me and Nikita, who are similar people across the worlds, but not the same."

"You want to know if I'm bedrock as well?" Valentine scrubs a hand across her face. "I wouldn't know."

"You fit the description. Val has a son—Ethan. He's a little older than your Elijah. She's also the foster mother for her niece Marybelle," Nikolai says. "She's close to Alia, of course. I have to think that having anchors on both sides of the split is a good thing. Whatever ritual we're going to do—or rather, that you'll be doing while we Dreamwalkers do our part inside the Dreamscape—would benefit by having bedrock on both sides. So you should think about that when you're planning the ritual with Pawel. He's probably thought of it; the similarities are too strong not to. But there's a chance he won't remember to say anything, so you should know. It might impact how you handle the ritual. Pawel is a strong Mage, and a good person, but he's also exhausted and running ragged. I have the bad feeling he's out of energy and doing his best to fake being okay."

Valentine's chair scrapes when she pushes it back. She holds out a hand to stop Nikolai from rising. "You're fine," she says. "If you're right, we need to build a foundation on this side, which means it's time for me to extend an olive branch again. This won't work if the bedrock is cracked."

Nikolai watches her leave. He hopes that Alia doesn't reject her overture. It was Alia and Alaric who called this Gather, after all. They opened their community to all Talents. That's how Havenhill started, too. Different types of Talent cooperating is how they'll make sure the Shadows can't win.

35

By the time breakfast is over, the room is overfull. Cats, dogs, mice, birds, lizards, and any number of other animals are everywhere. Dayton has transformed into a tawny lion, curled on the floor at the foot of the chair occupied by one of Rory's bandmates. Nikolai only recognizes some of the people in the room, although he suspects he has been introduced to others. He hopes it doesn't matter that he can't put names to most of these faces.

Nikolai sits at the long table at the front of the room, sharing a seat with Seth. Nikita and Heather sit next to them; Del is on his other side. Alia sits at one end with Pawel and Alaric. Sera fills in the space between the two groups.

When Alia stands, much of the room falls silent, the rest following in a wave of murmurs that fall away to nothing. She smiles tightly. "We shall begin. I thank all of you for taking the time to travel here, to come together in a meeting of Talent. I hope that in the future we will continue to work together to achieve a peace our world has not yet seen." She glances at Pawel.

He rises quickly enough to knock his own chair over. While Alaric reaches to right it, Pawel moves out from behind the table. "I've knocked my computer off the podium while teaching. Probably better for me to get some distance," he says, voice raised and clear, easy to hear throughout the room. His hands move as he speaks. "Everyone here has heard some part of this story, but I want to make sure that we begin from a clear starting line today, and that we can easily map out where we are going. I don't want to bury us in detail, but rather, I want to give an overview of the facts. We are working together—Clan and Mage, Lineage and Emergent—to eliminate the Shadows that threaten all Talented people."

On one side of the room, Mattie coughs loudly.

Pawel ignores her. "We have determined that our world is not the only world, and that there is one other world that is tightly connected to our own and may share a fate with ours. That world has been overrun by Shadows, threatening Talented and non-Talented people alike."

"There was a third one," Del interjects, leaning forward on the table where she still sits. "It collapsed."

Pawel's attention shifts abruptly as he gives her a sharp look. "What?"

Del gestures at the rest of the room. "Do you want us to talk about the Dreamscape now, or do you want to keep explaining?" she asks. "Because it sounds like you're enjoying the explaining. You like teaching." She flinches, and Nikolai suspects that Sera kicked her under the table. Her gaze doesn't waver from Pawel.

Nikolai leans closer to Del, murmuring, "You're right. It's important. We'll talk about it when it's our turn."

Pawel turns his back on them. "We have determined that the Talents of traveling and Dreamwalking are related, and both share aspects with Shadowwalking. The Dreamscape lies between and connects worlds, and Dreamwalkers all pass through the same Dreamscape. But they are not able to exit it into other worlds, except in unique situations. Within the Dreamscape, we were able to identify our correlation to another world."

"Two worlds," Seth says, voice low but carrying.

Pawel turns to look at the cluster of Dreamwalkers. Nikita raises one hand. Pawel gestures, his expression tight.

"There are three paths," Del says. "There's a point where they diverge. When I visited with my Predictive friend Carolyn and her brother, they said that one was correct, one was almost correct, and one was very, very wrong."

"The one that's 'almost correct' is my world," Nikolai says. "Carolyn, Pawel, Alaric, and others were able to travel to it, and Seth and I were able to travel here. When you had the Emergence, we had the Split—Shadowwalkers invaded. Now, they actively hunt us. Our world is falling to them. That third path leads to a third world that's been almost completely overrun."

"It's gone now," Del says flatly. "The Shadows are creeping closer to the paths, and I'm worried we won't be able to get to your world, either, soon. The path is getting narrower."

The way home is growing blocked. Nikolai's fingers curl against Seth's stomach, and Seth covers his hand, squeezing lightly. Nikolai exhales, trying to center himself.

"We've been creating a network," Del explains. "We started with a dozen Dreamwalkers, and now we've connected to over a hundred. We intend to work together to create a ritual in the Dreamscape that will affect both worlds."

"Dreamwalkers can't work together," someone says from the far side of the room.

"There are three at this table," Nikolai replies sharply. He feels the weight of the attention this draws to him. "Dreamwalking requires education. Training. I've had Seth with me since we were kids, and he's my anchor. Look at us: me, Del, and Nikita. We can work together, so you know it's possible for others to do so as well, if we teach them. Just because Dreamwalkers haven't worked together in your world doesn't mean they can't."

He does his best not to shrink at the sudden buzz of sound. Seth's calm washes over him, envelopes them both in warmth, and Nikolai focuses on that rather than the regard of too many strangers.

"If you know any Dreamwalkers, give me their information," Nikita says. "I'm handling the online parts of this effort, and Nikolai, Del, and I will work with them in the Dreamscape."

"Let's move on," Pawel says, silencing the murmur passing through the room. "Sera, please."

"Yeah, sure." Sera pats Pawel on the shoulder, then climbs up to stand on the table. The ink on her hands crawls up her arms, creating new designs. "I'm Sera, and I'm a Technopath, which is a fancy name for a technology-related Emergent Talent. Some of us interface with technology natively; some of us have it inside of us. Me, I absorb it, and thanks to that I'm always online, like a human interface to the internet at large. Pawel put me in charge of creating a space for Talented people to gather safely online and bring together information in secure databases." She makes a face, nose wrinkling. "We've also been working to hack into some secure databases that do not belong to us."

She hops forward and sits on the edge of the table, her feet kicking. "We've established our own network. We're encrypted and secure, and we're hosting the Dreamwalker spaces online. Carolyn and Pawel are also curating a ton of information about Talent. But security is a huge thing because, turns out, we aren't the only secure repository of data about Talent out there. The other one is owned by the US government."

Silence.

Sera raises her hands. "So. If you've ever thought 'hey, there's a government conspiracy about us,' you were right! There is an organization within the government named Sigma Delta—'the sum of change.' They've been gathering information on us for decades. Lineage information. The percentage of normal people who Emerged in an average year prior to the Emergence, and the same information for the years since. And rituals. They have databanks of information about rituals. We haven't managed to crack all the files we've found. We're trying not to let them know that we're rooting around in their data."

"They know." Mac blinks into existence as she speaks. She touches Pawel's shoulder, grabs him, and yanks him close enough for her to be able to whisper in his ear. Pawel holds up a finger, and Sera stays silent while Pawel and Mac confer. When they separate, Mac takes a step closer to Sera and stands, legs slightly spread, hands clasped behind herself.

"Sigma Delta is a military training program for Talent," Mac says. "I began training with them as a teen, right after the Emergence. They also had a lot of people in the program prior to the Emergence. I heard a bit about it before I was formally involved, back when my dad started to date my mom." She hesitates, then adds, "My stepfather—Senator Delwin Palmer. He's involved in the project. It's a top-security, eyes-only kind of thing, and I'm breaking a lot of oaths by talking about it here." Her head turns, and Nikolai follows the path of her gaze to where Cass sits. "But given what I've managed to put together, and what Sera's said, we need to talk about it."

Cass stands up, her chair falling down behind her. If looks could kill, her expression would spell Mac's death. She turns and pushes through the crowd, heading for the door.

"The government's been involved in our lives since before the Emergence," Mac says, her gaze tracking Cass's path. "They're still trying to find more of us. Trying to make us do their—" Her expression falls, worried, when the door slams behind Cass. "They want to use Talent to gain power," she says. "I need to talk to Cass. Sera, you're up." She disappears.

"Well, then," Sera says. "That wasn't part of my speech, but what I have to add is even worse. We believe Sigma Delta researchers may have caused the Emergence. Probably accidentally, but what they were trying to do wasn't any better."

Her feet kick slowly as she holds one hand out, three fingers raised. "Once upon a time there were three separate Lineages: Soulstealers, Deathstalkers, and Shadowwalkers. We've found evidence that Sigma Delta wanted to create a heavy-duty government-controlled weapon. They collected a group of latent Deathstalkers and Shadowwalkers—people who were of both Lineages but had never manifested either Talent. Then they set up a ritual, unleashed the few Soulstealers the had managed to find, and allowed them to feed on the group they'd collected. The ritual was meant to force any latent Talent to Emerge, but from what we can read, the ritual wasn't focused properly. We don't have proof this caused the Emergence, but the timing is…suggestive. Damning, in my opinion.

"So there's something different about our world now, and people are more likely to Emerge. And it created the new kind of Shadowwalkers that killed Alaric's brother and many others. Ones who are starving. Soulless. Split between the Dreaming and the darkness." She glances at Mattie. "Able to be healed and become Shadowwalkers of the traditional, legendary variety, if they're reunited with their souls."

Conversation erupts throughout the room. Nikolai can't sort through it; too many voices are saying too many different things.

"So," Seth murmurs, twisting so that they face each other, forehead to forehead, cocooning them in their own quieter space, "when they did the ritual here, it affected us as well."

"Maybe because our worlds are so close together," Nikolai muses. "Because of people like Alia and Valentine, Nikita and me, and you and Heather."

He wonders what happened in that third world. He wonders why they died so quickly, and where the Shadows from that world are going now.

It's not a good thought.

"Can we reverse this ritual?" someone asks. "Can we undo what the Mages did to us?"

"It's the Mages fault," someone else says.

Alia slips into the form of a lion and roars, the sound echoing off the walls, and then she returns to human form. "This is not about Clan versus Mage," she says sharply.

"Clan were there, too," Sera says. "There are Clan in the government organization, and there are Mages, and there are a host of other specialized Talents. This isn't about what kind of Talent anyone has. This is about how *some people*"—she emphasizes the words, hard and sharp—"decided to gain power through any means possible. And their actions created the potential for whole worlds to be destroyed."

"It's already happened in the third world," Nikolai says. "The path is gone. It fell, or it's close to it. The path to my world has been getting darker; it's close to falling as well. Where do you think the Shadows will go when there's no more food to be found on our world, and yours is so close by?"

"It wasn't bad in our world, at first," Seth says. "Then more and more people started dying, and fear is an amazing thing: it changes the world overnight. As soon as our world made the battle about humans versus Talent, the Shadows had the upper hand."

Alaric stands abruptly, shoulder to shoulder with Alia, looming despite not being the bear. "This is not about Clan versus Mage," he repeats in a growl, the words resonating throughout the room. "This is not about Talented or non-Talented people. This is about making sure that the Shadows cannot have our world. This is about undoing the damage that has been done, here and elsewhere."

A woman takes a step forward, hands on her hips. "Can we reverse the ritual?" she asks again. "Can we undo it? Make the Shadows go back to being whatever they were before, and keep them from hunting us?"

"We don't know," Pawel admits, "but we're damn well going to try. The problem is, we don't know how they did the ritual, just that it happened. And the things we don't know could kill us if we rush to action without more information. When a ritual is cast, the energy has to come from somewhere, and I suspect that when the original ritual was created, that wasn't accounted for."

"And that's why it went horrifyingly wrong." Sera hops down from the table. "We're working on identifying the cabal behind that original ritual. The Technopaths are having a blast trying to see how deep they can get before they're discovered." She holds up her hands. "Not me, of course. I'm keeping my Talents in totally legal places."

"All ideas are welcome," Alia says. "Please, share those you have. No one community can do this alone."

Alia's words seem to signal to the assembly that the meeting is over. People move between tables, and some leave. Nikolai stays where he is, with Seth close by. He can stay right here and speak with anyone who is willing to talk. They need to cooperate and find a way through the darkness.

36

The post-meeting discussions go on longer than Nikolai expected, and he's hoarse from long conversations to forge connections. He believes that they are making headway, but he's exhausted by mid-afternoon. He and Seth retreat to their room to rest and enjoy some alone time. It's dark when there's a sharp rap on the door and then Corbin pokes his head in. "Thorne's going to light things on fire. We have beer."

"I locked that door," Nikolai says, emerging from the blankets to glare at him.

Corbin twists the knob, and it turns easily. "Guess not," he replies. "My point is, we're having a bonfire, and if you don't want to be left behind when we head to the place, get your asses outside. It's maybe a mile walk." He starts to close the door, then pushes it back open again. "It's a chance to get away from the crowds and hang out with a smaller group of people."

He closes the door with a *thunk*, but his footsteps don't go far. A moment later, there's another rap farther down the hall, and Corbin starts talking again.

"I can be ready to rejoin the world." Seth pushes the blankets down, untangling them from his feet. He rolls over and plucks his shirt from the floor, dragging it over his head. His hair is a mess, sticking out in every direction; Nikolai's not sure it can be tamed. And it's not the only part of him, or of Nikolai, that's a mess.

"We need showers," he says, grabbing for the hem of Seth's shirt.

There's another knock against the door, but it stays closed this time. "If you're planning on showering, make it quick," Drea calls out. "We'll wait."

Seth rolls out of bed, grabbing their towels from the back of a chair. He tosses one to Nikolai before wrapping one around his own waist. "Give us five minutes," he says to Drea as he opens the door.

Drea wrinkles her nose, huffing an almost silent laugh. "We'll give you fifteen," she says. "Get cleaned up."

When they make it downstairs, the rest of the group has already gathered. Dax and Nate are back from wherever they'd gone, hair as wet as if they've freshly showered, although Nikolai didn't see them in the baths upstairs. Alaric seems more relaxed than earlier, glancing up from his conversation with Corbin when they emerge, then returning to it earnestly. Maybe a half-dozen others are there, people from the university and Alaric's friends from the Gather. There are more people than Nikolai is comfortable with, but he'll manage.

They meander down a pathway behind the house that Nikolai thinks might lead to the river. They've already been walking a while when Nikolai realizes someone's missing. "Where's Thorne? You said he was going to light a fire."

Rory makes a noise. "Doing something."

"Or someone," Stormy says cheerfully.

"Not this time. He's part of the ritual discussion group," Rory says, brow furrowed. He holds tightly to Kit's hand as they walk.

That might be where Nikita, Heather, and Del are. Nikolai wonders if he and Seth should be with them. He fishes his phone out of his pocket, unlocks it, checks his messages—none—and sends one to Nikita.

Are you making a ritual that Seth and I need to be there for?

His phone stays stubbornly silent, so he pockets it in time to see Stormy pat Rory's back, her soft expression matching his worried one rather than her words. "I have a lighter, so we don't need his Talent for making flames. We'll handle it old school, and if anything gets out of hand, I'll rain on it to put it out."

"We will still have a bonfire, never fear," Corbin assures them, ducking between Nikolai and Seth, sliding his arms through theirs. "I promised everyone a quiet night and relaxation, and I will deliver."

"How's it going to be quiet with you there?" Alaric rumbles.

Corbin squawks and lets go, disappearing in a flurry of feathers as he flies up and lands on Alaric's head in raven form. He pecks at Alaric's scalp while Drea laughs.

The mood is lighter, the air is easier to breathe, and Nikolai is thankful for this break.

The walk takes longer than Corbin implied, but it's worth it when they emerge at the top of a small cliff with a waterfall cascading into the small river, flowing toward the house. It creates a natural background noise, and it sets Nikolai at ease.

True to her word, Stormy sets up the fire and gets it roaring. Bags are unpacked, bringing out chairs, blankets, pillows, small tables, and food. Seth claims one of the oversized chairs, pulling Nikolai to sit with him in it. They're squeezed in, but it's not uncomfortable.

When someone presses a red cup into his hand, filled with liquid that smells yeasty and bitter, Nikolai accepts it and takes a cautious sip. He wrinkles his nose; it's…darker…than he expects. He can't think of a word for it, but the second sip isn't as bad as the first. Bitter, definitely. A little fruity, too. He passes it to Seth, who takes a long gulp, obviously liking it better than Nikolai does.

"We have hotdogs, and s'mores for later," Drea announces. "Tonight, cook your own food over the fire, grab yourself a bun, and feel free to drink and eat as much as you want."

Nikolai remembers s'mores from his childhood, and he'd rather have those than beer. But the hotdogs are out first, and he joins the group crouching around the edge of the fire to toast two of them over the flames—one for him and one for Seth.

Stormy sits cross-legged on the ground, drumsticks in her hand as she taps a rhythm against a flat rock. Dayton leans back-to-back with her, her head tipped back and eyes closed. There's a low rumble as if she's purring to the rhythm of Stormy's improvised beat.

Drea sits with Corbin's head in her lap, combing through his hair with her fingers. Sera has a skateboard that she balances on, shifting back and forth easily as she talks, hands moving. Her gaze is fixed, as if she's reading something Nikolai can't see at the same time as she's speaking.

"Should've brought my guitar," Trish comments idly from where she sits on the ground, leaning back on her hands. She glances toward Rory, who is curled in a double chair with Kit.

Rory laughs. "I'm trying to learn how to be social without a guitar in my hands," he admits.

Kit pats Rory's chest. "We can leave any time you want," he assures him.

Nikolai's phone vibrates, and he pulls it out find that Nikita finally responded to his earlier message. *All good. We're talking and brainstorming and Del and I have the Dreamwalker part under control. You focus on feeling better. I know it's been a lot for you. Anything you want us to bring up that I might forget?*

Nikolai can't think of anything, so he holds the phone loose in his hand, looking at the others. Seth slides a hand over his shoulder, and the flicker of calm over Nikolai's skin is pure bliss. Nikolai closes his eyes, luxuriating in the sensation, only opening them again when he catches Rory's words.

"I'm worried that Thorne and Mom are going to leap without looking." Rory covers Kit's hand with his own, fingers curling as he holds him still. "Dad usually keeps Mom and Dad from jumping in the deep end, but sometimes that turns into Dad trying to catch them after they've already leapt."

"They must've been fun when they were our age," Trish observes.

"Dad started the band when he was still in college, and that gave Mom and Dad plenty to focus on, which kept them out of trouble." Rory slumps in his chair, curling closer to Kit. "Thorne, Carolyn, and the others need someone to be the voice of reason or else they're going to end up world jumping again."

"Not without us," Seth says.

Nikolai looks back at his phone. *Don't go anywhere without us,* he sends. *No going into the Dreamscape unless I'm with you, and definitely no attempts at world walking without me and Seth.*

Nikita sends back three thumbs-up emojis and a string of hearts in different colors.

Nikolai has to admit he likes the convenience of this device. He'll miss it when he returns home; they'll need to have their Technopaths recreate the technology.

"'M fine if I don't have to go back to the other world," Alaric rumbles.

Chris makes a soft sound. "I'd prefer you don't disappear again," he agrees.

"They're doing what you want, though, right?" Cass asks. She sits on the ground, her head tilted against Dax's shoulder and her feet over Nate's outstretched legs. "All these Talented people getting along and making plans instead of starting a war. This is exactly what you wanted."

"It's what needs to happen for our future," Dayton replies. "Particularly if we want to fight against your child armies."

"My what?" Cass sits upright, Dax grunting as she elbows him in the chest.

Dayton levels a look at her, unblinking.

Cass pushes to her feet, hands in fists as she looks down at Dayton. Dax rubs his chest, but it's Nate who stands and touches Cass's hand silently.

"What?" she snaps, glaring at him. A moment of silence, and she spots Dax. "Shit. I'm sorry. I just—"

"—overreacted. I know." Dax pushes to his feet, offers a hand. "C'mon, let's take a walk."

"Which is code for don't anyone else take a walk," Chris murmurs.

"Or pick a different direction," Cass retorts. "Honestly, there's a lot of forest out here. I'm sure you can find your own little hookup corner and leave us to ourselves." She tangles her fingers with Dax's, and they slip through the trees, disappearing into the woods.

Alaric tilts his head back. "They always stink," he mumbles. "Always."

Seth passes the beer cup back to Nikolai, and the next sip isn't as bad as the first. Nikolai has food in his stomach, and he feels a little warm and kind of relaxed. He takes a longer gulp before handing the cup back to Seth so he can finish it.

Someone refills it after that, and it's comfortable enough that Nikolai loses track of how many times it empties and seems to be magically refilled. Time passes quickly, yet the night stretches out, time elongating in the flicker of the firelight and the ease of slow conversation spilling around them.

He doesn't understand a lot of what they talk about. The conversation has left the current problems of the world behind and moved on to movies and television and books and sports. Cass comes back and chats about clothes with Trish, while Alaric and Chris disappear. At some point, Drea and Corbin drift away. Nikolai thinks Dayton is gone, but he spots her again by the food, talking to Stormy as they pile chocolate onto peanut-butter cookies.

Peanut-butter s'mores are new to him; they're not using marshmallows, but Nikolai would never skip those. The first taste of sweet after the bitterness of the beer makes his nose wrinkle, and he can't help the full-body shudder that passes through him. Someone hands him a bottle of water, and he drinks it, cleansing his palette for more dessert.

They had four bags of marshmallows when the night began. Nikolai thinks he and Seth ate half a bag of crisp, warm, slightly burnt sweetness on their own.

His phone buzzes in his pocket, and he peeks at it to see a text from Nikita: *Mac's had enough. She's coming out to where you are.*

Moments later, Mac appears by the food, pours herself a beer, then joins the group. She steps over Trish and lowers herself to sit next to Cass, her feet drawn in and knees bent. She exchanges a look with Cass that makes Nikolai wonder what they talked about when Mac disappeared from the meeting earlier, but Mac doesn't address it. "They're discussing how they can replicate the ritual, or undo it, or find a way to heal the Shadows so they stop threatening our worlds."

"Knowing what happened to them at least gives us somewhere to start," Sera volunteers.

Mac raises her beer in acknowledgment. "True. But I'm not sure this is reversible. And if they do reverse it, how far does that go? Does that fundamentally change our world and lower the number of Emergences again? Does it force the Shadows out of Nikolai's world, or will they be trapped there? Does it heal the Shadows or only make it so more of them can't Emerge and eat people?"

"It sounds like a bad zombie movie," Nate muses.

"More like vampires," Dax says.

"The point is—" Mac raises her beer, then stops. "Hell if I know what the point is. I'm not sure they do, either."

"Shadows can travel." Nikolai remembers that much. "Chelsea can move between the worlds through the split. If we heal them, will they still be able to travel?" He doesn't voice his fear that this could close his way home.

"Actually…" Sera's gaze drifts after she speaks the one word. Trish elbows her, and Sera refocuses, one hand in the air. "Hang on, let me find— Okay, here it is. According to the Sigma Delta files, Shadows used to be able to move freely outside of this realm. The government didn't know where they went, and Shadowwalkers didn't like to talk about it. Those were normal, pre-Emergence Shadowwalkers. Whatever happened in that ritual perverted their traveling Talent. It's possible that after this ritual, normal Shadowwalkers—like Mattie—will be able to move between the worlds without needing to go through the split."

"But we won't know until we try," Nikolai says.

"We definitely won't know until we try." Mac glances toward the trees as Corbin and Drea walk back into the circle around the fire. "Rituals like this involve levels of power like I've never seen used. I don't know how we'll do it. I don't know how the government did it originally."

"But you were involved with the project."

Mac cranes her head to look at Trish. "I was involved because they trained me to join the military before I even knew that's what I was being trained to do," she says. "I was a teleporting soldier whose partner was an assassin. So. No. I don't know anything about what happened before I Emerged. And I don't think my dad's going to answer questions if I ask. I also don't want to let him know how much we've learned."

Cass exhales roughly. "My dad already knows I'm upset about something. He's not suspicious; he thinks it's about my sister. He's not entirely wrong."

"Why don't we want them to know we're coming for them?" Corbin asks.

Mac shakes her head. "That's bigger than we can deal with right now. We need to fix the problem of the Shadowwalkers. Fixing the government will be harder, but we can stop helping them, and that'll at least make a start." She and Cass exchange another look; Cass nods in response.

"What about the twinned worlds?" Nikolai asks. "Something must have happened in my world, and in the one that's already gone." He refuses to let the pit of fear about that missing path devour him; the same thing won't happen to his home. "If it happened in all three worlds, it needs to involve all three again. Or at least the two that are left."

Seth knocks into him. "That's what we're trying to do with the Dreamscape, right?"

"Right." The Dreamscape is critical to whatever they're doing. Trying to coordinate Dreamwalkers from both worlds—one where they are spread out and terrified, and another where they are too afraid to use their abilities to work together—will make executing this ritual much harder.

Is Del going back to the Dreamscape tonight? Should we go with her? Nikolai asks Nikita.

Hang on. Dots appear and disappear before Nikita's response comes. *Yes, and yes. I don't think we need to spend the whole night with her, but we should be there. We need to talk to the Dreamwalkers who are coming to terms with what we can do.*

I'll talk to Seth. We're with you, Nikolai replies.

"I have an idea." Trish reaches into her pocket and drags out a piece of paper. She reads it, makes a face, and puts it away again. "Not that piece of paper. We need blank paper, and something to write with."

"For what?" Sera's gaze shifts from unfocused to curious, watching Trish.

"Everyone write a wish down, then toss it in the fire. Whatever deity you believe in, think of it being sent to them when it burns," Trish says. "Momma's a Baptist through and through, but we used to do this even though it's not exactly a Christian rite. I think we could all do with a little magic."

"We'll fetch supplies," Corbin says, then he flies up in a flurry of black feathers. Alaric's eagle follows him, racing through the sky.

More marshmallows disappear while they're gone, the group silent in the wake of the serious discussions. Minutes later, Corbin drops out of the sky with Alaric. Both transform back into humans, with bags clutched in their hands. Alaric distributes the paper while Corbin hands out pens.

Nikolai stares at the blank sheet, uncertain what to write.

Seth slips from the chair and leans against a rock, writing something that looks more like a long letter than a simple wish.

Kit writes with his paper against Rory's back, while Stormy kneels across the way, her paper pressed against the hard ground. Dayton walks away, tapping the pen against her thigh.

Trish scribbles quickly, crumpling her paper when she's done. She's the first to throw her wish in the fire, and she crouches close to the flames as it burns, ashes drifting into the sky. She rolls back on her heels when it's gone, offering a hand to draw Sera forward.

They go alone and in pairs: Sera, Kit and Rory, Cass, then Dax. Nate is still writing when Alaric and Chris put their papers in. As soon as Nate's done, he crumples up his sheet and throws it in from a distance, flinching when it lands in the flames. Mac pops in next to the fire to set hers carefully among the embers. They flare up, and she teleports to a safe distance to watch it burn.

Seth stands up and turns away from Nikolai, the paper hidden as he folds it neatly then drops it into the fire.

Nikolai hasn't set a single word to paper yet.

He writes while Dayton returns and squats next to Stormy, whispering, and then they go to throw their papers in together.

> *I want to be able to go home and live with my family and grow old with Seth.*
> *I want this world to be safe from Shadows.*
> *I want my own world to be safe from Shadows.*
> *I want my friends and family and myself and Seth to be happy.*
> *I want to live in a world where we don't just survive, we thrive.*

Nikolai sets the pen aside and crumples the page roughly. He grabs one of the sticky, abandoned marshmallow sticks and uses it to stab the paper, then holds it in the fire, keeping it in view while it crumbles to ash and flame.

He doesn't know if the words go anywhere, but it lightens the mood. It's time to make their wishes reality.

From the journal of [REDACTED].

According to history as recorded by Sigma Delta, the first known Talent in the military enlisted in 1911 and flew for the Air Force during World War I. He was a Weather Witch; fog rolled in to cover his flights and lightning cracked to foil his enemies. He didn't tell his commanders about his Talent; he was discovered when he took a young Clan soldier (the second known Talent in the military) under his wing. The two were overheard discussing their respective abilities.

The government was curious, wary, and delighted to discover this untold wealth, and they put great effort into combing through the ranks and unearthing Talented people, pulling them together as special forces units within the different branches of the military.

In 1963, Sigma Delta was formed, and the active recruitment of Talent began. I joined in 1985, fresh out of high school after having been encouraged to join JROTC during my teenage years. I could have gone to college with an ROTC scholarship, but I was starry-eyed, hopeful that we could bring Talent to bear to end the Cold War and create a new, safer world. I wanted to do that by being an active-duty soldier. I wanted to make a world that would be a safe haven for my eventual children and grandchildren.

SD is a strong effort that works within the US and forges relationships and alliances around the world. We bring together Talent in a way that the world has failed to bring together its citizens. We rise above prejudice. We are the protectors. We want a world where no one goes hungry, where war doesn't destroy our lands and our people. We want to unite and move forward together, as one humankind.

We studied the history of Talent, gathering stories from around the world, from all eras. We know that the Oracle of Greece was a true Predictive Talent. We know that Saint George was an allegory for a Church that strove to drive Clan out and thus slay the dragons. We know that where there is myth, there is Talent.

I teethed on stories of the deadly ones. Popular imagery personified Death as a wraith in a cloak and cowl, bearing a scythe. I knew that a Deathstalker could creep from the shadows, cover the mouth of a man in his bed, and steal his last breath.

We found our first Deathstalker in 1993 and trapped her in a room from which she couldn't slip into the darkness and escape.

Her name was Marion. She was surprisingly normal, for all that she fed on the dying breaths of those who were leaving the world. She couldn't explain how she knew, only that she was drawn to them in those last moments, and that she was a necessary part of the world.

She was not alone; death would still walk without her. But she fed on the fear, and the acceptance, of what might come. She fed on the final acquiescence as the soul slipped into darkness.

Then she'd return to her job in the daylight, and her small children and husband who had no idea that she was Talented.

She chose to join SD, to help us in our efforts. Her Talent was as natural as breathing, a part of life and death.

We met our first Shadowwalker not long after. She was a friend of Marion's, walking into SD through the darkness. Rebecca also seemed like any other of our ranks, for all that she could become a shadow and then slide through the darkness to anywhere she could imagine.

Anywhere. Truly anywhere. Rebecca told tales of visiting other worlds. For all I know, she may have come from one, but she chose to settle here.

I liked them both.

One day, Marion went stiff in the middle of a conversation, rose, and turned, one hand out. On the other side of the room, one of our group stood abruptly with a strangled noise. She was at his side in an instant, following him down to the floor, her hand on his chest as she shushed him.

"It's okay," she whispered. "I'm with you. I'll make it easy."

He was dead in moments.

Some said we might have saved him, but the coroner said his heart could not have been restarted. She eased his way into a painful death.

There were those who recognized what Marion had done, and how we could use it.

In 1998, we began a new effort: to understand how the Deathstalkers led people into death, and to learn how the Shadows traveled in the darkness. We sought to combine their abilities so we could leverage them to bring peace to our world.

In 1999 we met out first Soulstealer, and a new plan was born.

It took almost a decade, and the combined forces of Talents around the world, to create this ritual. In controlled conditions, Mages worked to enhance the abilities of our Talented guinea pigs. Our goal was to merge Soulstealers, Deathstalkers, and Shadowwalkers into one Talent—as many throughout history had already assumed they were—to create a weapon no one could fight against.

We failed.

None of these Talents were dangerous on their own, but the newly created Soulless are dire creatures with no intellect and no remorse. They are shameless killers, starving and desperate. The energy used to create them was magnified, pushed throughout the world through our network of Talent, reverberating in unexpected ways.

The Emergence means there will be more soldiers for SD—more people to fight for good in the world.

But the Soulless continue to multiply. To Emerge, and to kill.

We have made a grave mistake, and we will go to our graves in payment.

REVOLUTION

37

THE NEXT MORNING, Nikolai views the world through a bleary lens. He and Nikita spent much of the night in the Dreamscape with Del, speaking with and coordinating the Dreamwalkers interested in helping with the ritual. It took longer than intended, and despite solid sleep with Seth afterward, he still feels the after-effects.

Del is sitting on top of a table on the other side of the room, gaze unfocused as she toys with the braid trailing down the side of her face. Shawn and Sam sit, each with a hand on her knee and a palm at the small of her back. She seems both more awake than Nikolai feels and less, as if she's dreaming while awake.

If anyone could, it would be Del.

This should be their final meeting in Haverhill, although it could have waited until later in the morning in Nikolai's opinion. At least the tables are groaning with the weight of breakfast offerings, but no one looks awake enough to enjoy the feast. Pawel is the worst of all. He wavers as he stands next to a table, one hand out, fingers spread against the wood to balance himself. His scruff is thick and ragged, his hair unkempt. Dark circles beneath his eyes stand out against the paleness of his skin, and the moles on his face are stark circles. A faint scatter of freckles is visible between the moles. Nikolai has never seen those before; he supposes they're too faint to be seen when Pawel's skin has a healthy color.

Pawel inhales, then closes his eyes. His free hand clenches by his side.

Mac is abruptly there, leaning her shoulder against him to prop him up.

Pawel pushes his hand through his hair, shoving his bangs back from his face. "It's been a long twenty-four hours," he says. "Carolyn's returned to PHU, along with Lily from the New Hampshire combined community and David Pierson from the Burlington community. They'll comb through the archives to find every bit of historical information we can obtain about Shadowwalkers, Deathstalkers, and Soulstealers. Sera is working online with researchers around the world, looking for the same information. Del, Nikolai, and Nikita spent the night working with those in the Dreamscape to gather what they can from the other worlds, to better understand how we are tied together."

Nikolai exhales. "We spent more time trying to convince the Dreamwalkers from your world that nothing was going to explode, and from mine that it was safe to use their Talent despite the humans and Shadows hunting them."

"But we did learn something," Nikita says. "Before the Emergence here, and your Split, our histories were very similar. Different people, subtly different events, but over all, events unfolded essentially identically."

"Our worlds were on the same cusp prior to the Emergence and the Split," Pawel says flatly, "implying that a similar cause was at the root of both events."

"Three events," Del says idly, picking at the seam of her jeans. "Don't forget, there were three worlds once, not just the two. One's already dead."

"There were three worlds," Pawel agrees. "I believe the rituals shattered the close connection between the worlds, and now they have drifted apart at the same time as Shadows have invaded. I don't think the split existed, such as it is, prior to the ritual. Nikolai, do you know?"

"I don't remember it being in the Dreamscape before the Split, but I was young," Nikolai replies. "I was eight years old when the Split happened, and I tried not to go into the Dreamscape. But the older Dreamwalkers we've talked to have confirmed that the shadows in the Dreamscape weren't the same back then. There were dark spaces between the paths, but there weren't soul-stealing Shadows hiding in them."

"So you think that this ritual created the split." Seth leans forward, brows furrowed and expression intense. He folds his hands together, fingers linked tightly. "When you say 'the split,' do you mean the darkness inside the Dreamscape, or the Split that happened to our world? Or both?"

"Both." Pawel's tone is definitive, strong despite his exhausted and weak appearance. "I think the ritual—and the likelihood that it was cast on all three worlds, in parallel, simultaneously—broke the connection between them. It created a space that opened up and has become a yawning abyss."

"It's spreading," Nikolai says. "It might have started here, but even Dreamwalkers from worlds far away from ours have seen changes to Shadowwalkers in their worlds. No one outside of our two worlds reports anything as drastic as it is here, but the split is bringing the soul-stealing Shadows to other worlds."

"So you're saying the government created a multiverse pandemic?" Corbin asks.

"That's one way of thinking about it." A chair appears behind Pawel, and he sits in it. Mac leans on the chair; she whispers something to him, and he brushes her away. "The wider the split grows, the more Shadows emerge, and the more they invade other worlds to feed. I don't know what happened to the world that's gone, but I suspect it has been absorbed into the split. And I suspect that will be the fate of Nikolai's world, and eventually our own, if we cannot stop them."

"So what you're saying is that if we destroy the split, we can destroy the way the Shadows breed," Seth says slowly. He glances at Nikolai, and Nikolai can't read his expression.

"'Breed' isn't the best word," Pawel acknowledges, "but yes. I believe that if we destroy the split, where the Shadows congregate, we will slow the Emergence of new Shadowwalkers of the destructive, soul-devouring kind. Of course, this is only a theory. The only way to prove it is to succeed."

"Do you have a plan?" Alia asks. She sits to one side, near Pawel but not at the same table. She remains seated, ceding control of this breakfast meeting to him. A cat lies on her lap, a small smoky-white tabby curled upon a pile of something knit in lavender and gray. Alia's fingers comb gently through the fur behind its ears as she speaks.

"We don't have all of the explicit details hammered out, but we will." Pawel's tone is decisive.

"And when it's done?" Nikolai speaks before thinking. Seth's grip on him tightens, and Nikita exhales softly. "When you've…" He struggles for how to word this. "When the split is gone, and no new bad Shadowwalkers are being made, what's left? How will Chelsea get us home? What will even happen to Chelsea when this happens?"

Silence has weight, and this one rests heavily on their shoulders. Low breaths scrape; somewhere in the room, someone moves their chair.

Pawel slumps, gaze dropping. "I don't know. I haven't talked to her, and I need to. And to Maggie. They are our only contacts for learning about modern Shadowwalkers."

"We can find out about old-school Shadowwalkers from the Dreamwalkers we met from other worlds," Nikita says. "Right, Nikolai?"

Nikolai nods. "I haven't heard of anyone knowing any Shadowwalkers exactly like Maggie and Chelsea, but there were people who once knew some who weren't trying to devour everything in sight. If that helps you."

Pawel raises a hand over his face; it muffles his voice. "We are so far past what I know that I can't predict the outcomes of our actions. Based on what we've learned, I do believe that once the split is gone, Shadowwalkers who have their soul will be able to travel between worlds. With luck"—the word falls flat—"that's the multiverse we'll restore."

Nikolai's gut clenches. Seth rises abruptly, waiting, balanced on the balls of his feet, for Nikolai to stand. He grabs Nikolai's hand and pulls him from the room, then through the halls.

"I'm okay," he says.

"You're not," Seth argues. "I'm not, either."

They pass through the warm kitchens and out the back, into the grassy courtyard formed between the wings of the huge house. Seth veers toward a bench and collapses onto it, slumped forward. "Fuck."

Nikolai sits next to him, curls over his slumped back, and places one hand on the nape of his neck. He leans in close and tries to press their knees and thighs together, as much contact as he can manage.

"I want to go home," Seth mumbles. "I want to do this, yes, but when it's finished, I want to go where we have our family and our own place. It looks so much like Havenhill here that I'm homesick for a place I barely had a chance to get to know."

"I want that, too." Nikolai presses cheek to cheek, then kisses him lightly. "We need to believe it's going to work out."

"That when it's over, either Mattie or Chelsea can work with your Dreamwalker abilities to get us home," Seth says.

"Yes." Nikolai can't suppress his worries completely; he knows Seth feels his anxiety. But he is determined to believe. They sit there quietly while birds chirp somewhere above them in the warm spring morning.

"And if it doesn't work that way?" Seth asks.

Nikolai doesn't want to think about it.

He inhales, then lets the breath out slowly rather than speaking. He needs time to wrangle the words properly. "Then we stay," he says finally, and the words are heavy in his heart. "We stay, and our friends help make identities for us, and we find a way to fit in here. Maybe we go to school. Maybe Pawel adopts us, or we find a place in that program Lucy has for wayward lost Talented kids. But if we can't go home, then we have to move forward and live our lives." He squeezes Seth's hand tightly. "Together. No matter what, it's you and me. Okay?"

"I'd rather go home," Seth huffs. "But fine. Whatever happens next, we're in it together."

38

Monday dawns with perfect spring weather.

It's warm enough that Nikolai doesn't need more than a T-shirt, and as he and Seth walk to Teas Please, they see several PHU students in shorts, sundresses, and sandals. Apparently, this week is an annual Spring Festival that the university holds; it reminds Nikolai of movies about life before the Split. Nikita told them that most classes on these days have been canceled, which has made all their planning easier to schedule. The loose academic schedule combined with the good weather lends an air of celebration to campus and the surrounding homes. Towels are spread on lawns, music plays loudly, and people are everywhere outside, tossing footballs or basking in the sun while studying.

Nobody cares that Nikolai and Seth walk hand in hand down the street. Some kids wave cheerfully, and one apologizes after diving in front of them to capture an errant ball.

"I'll miss this place when we go," Seth says. "Not enough that I want to stay, but there's something about this—"

"It's innocent," Nikolai agrees. "Freeing. It's easy to live here."

"That's it, yes." Seth slides his thumb along the edge of Nikolai's hand. "We can go get food. We don't have to scramble for a place to sleep. If we were staying longer, we'd have to work, but right now, we're able to enjoy ourselves. I'll miss that part."

Nikolai grabs the door to Teas Please and pulls it open for Seth. Nate spots them and waves, calling out "I've got them" as the hostess at the front pulls two menus from a stack.

"Nate will be with you shortly," she says, handing them the menus.

They follow Nate into the back of the restaurant. A group of strangers is at the U-shaped table, but Cass sits at a table for two next to it, and the table beside hers is empty. She looks up as they approach and sighs heavily, standing to help push the two smaller tables together.

"I've got lunch break coming up," Nate says. "Give me your order, and I'll get everything in at once and bring it out, or—" He breaks off, frowning as he leans in close to Cass. "Hey. Want a Mallory special?"

She rolls her eyes and sits back, arms crossed over her chest. "Whatever. It was good before."

Nate hesitates, then nods. "Okay, fine," he says, then walks away.

Nikolai takes the chair opposite Cass, and Seth sits next to him. She's piled a light sweater and purse on the bench beside her, making it so no one can sit there. "Are you all right with us joining you?" he asks.

She looks at the ceiling and shakes her head. "No. But it's fine. I knew when I came here that I'd probably end up with half my sorority or some other random group of people I know coming in eventually."

"Then why did you come?" Seth looks like he's going to continue, but his expression gentles instead.

Cass shrugs. "Nate's here. The food's decent. I don't have most of my classes this week because the professors know no one'll show up anyway, except for this one stupid exam I have on Thursday. That professor's a total dick; he made the exam this week because it's the Festival and he knows people will be hungover after going out drinking on Wednesday." She tilts her head to look at them more directly. "That's Election Day."

None of what she's said makes sense to Nikolai, but he nods as if he understands.

"Would it help if I—?" Seth cuts off, his hand in the air when Cass glares at him.

"Don't," she says curtly. "I don't need a Talent-induced high, or the equivalent of an emotional back rub. My emotions are fine the way they are, and I will deal with them, thank you very much."

"Noted," Seth says, his hand falling back to the table.

It occurs to Nikolai that Nate never asked him and Seth what they wanted to eat. He supposes they're getting Mallory specials as well.

"Do you want to talk about it?" Seth offers. He doesn't shrink away from

Cass's continued glare, watching her with the same quiet consideration he's given Nikolai his whole life.

Cass blinks first. She picks up the napkin-wrapped silverware and carefully unwraps the fork and knife. She lays them on the table, flattening out the napkin then putting it on her lap. "I'm fine."

Even Nikolai can tell she's lying. "You don't sound it."

"This semester—this whole school year—has been a lot," Cass says, her voice tight and words careful. "This"—she gestures at Nikolai and Seth—"is the end of several months' worth of dealing with too much."

"And you're the kind of person who would rather bottle up being overwhelmed than rely on anyone else," Seth says. When she tries to skewer him with yet another glare, he spreads his hands, palm down, on the table. "It's an observation, not a judgment. You have your reasons. I don't know what they are, so I can't judge. But you seem pretty miserable. I'd know even if I couldn't feel it radiating off of you. Not that I'm listening on purpose. I can't help it—you're doing the emotional equivalent of empathic screaming. I'm surprised that Heather hasn't tried to hold you down and smother you in happy. She seems like the type who'd do that."

"Heather isn't good with negative emotions." Cass has a small smile. "She likes being our social director because it means she gets to work hard at making people happy. But she's also very easy to fool. A thin layer of pleasure over everything, and she won't dig any deeper. I love Dax. I love sex with Dax. And I generally have fun at house events. Just the Dax parts are enough to keep her at bay." Her head tilts as she considers him more closely. "Yet you can tell easily. Is it because you haven't seen me as much with Dax? Or am I slipping?"

Seth nudges his glasses up his nose. "I think it's the first. I don't have that formed opinion of you as a part of you-and-Dax. If you asked me, I'd say your closest friends are…hm." He leans back in his chair, tapping his chin with one finger. "You rely on Dax, but in a 'seeking comfort' way. He's a blanket you take everywhere, and he treats you the same way. Not a bad thing, but it's like you both take each other for granted in a common way people who've been together forever do. Then there are Mac and Carolyn; you have this weird love-hate thing going with them. And you're afraid of

Heather, which is how I know you don't like Empaths."

"Or Telepaths," Cass admits, "but I've only ever met one person who could get inside my head telepathically."

Nikolai's surprised. It's a fairly common Talent. "You may not know you've met them. Most Telepaths are instinctive, like Empaths."

Cass's expression twists into something vaguely constipated. "Lovely."

"Then there's Nate," Seth continues as if they hadn't interrupted him. "You're comfortable with him, but it's also like you're afraid of him. Sometimes you look at him like you have no idea what he's even doing there. But you trust him, and I think you hate yourself a little bit for that."

"Cass hates herself for trusting someone?" Nate nudges her sweater and purse out of the way so he can drop into the empty spot on the bench next to her. He pushes a plate in front of her, piled high with salad and a thinly toasted sandwich cut into four wedges decorating the rim interspersed with potato chips. "One Mallory special. Kim's bringing out a shared meal for the two of you," he tells Nikolai and Seth.

Nate's own plate is a three-tiered sandwich made of thick, dark bread. Nikolai can smell peanut butter, and the strong scents of smoke and maple. "What is that?"

"Bacon peanut-butter club," Nate says. "Take a peanut-butter sandwich, slather the top of it with mayo and cranberry sauce, add lettuce and bacon and a third slice of bread, and there you go. It's disturbingly good."

"Ew," Cass says, but she holds out one small triangle of her toasted sandwich and accepts a quarter of Nate's sandwich in return.

A girl who must be Kim arrives with one of the three-tiered contraptions, but instead of small bites on each plate, each one is overflowing, and she carries another plate in her hand. "Mallory apparently thinks you're starving," she says as she sets it between Nikolai and Seth. "I hope you're in the mood for some citrus. You've got a carrot-and-leek non-dairy creamed soup with fresh lemon and ginger, and a spring salad with candied orange peel and walnuts. The sandwich is a chicken-and-brie panini with apple slices. I've had that one; it's really good, and I wish we'd put it on the menu. For dessert, a lemon-berry crêpe with a dark-chocolate drizzle."

Kim straightens up, glancing at the booth next to them where the patrons are filing out in a burst of noise. She lowers her voice and nods at it. "It'll take me five to get it cleaned up, okay?"

Nate grins. "You know us so well. I don't think we're expecting anyone else, but I wasn't expecting anyone in the first place. If that booth's emptying out, I figure there are more of us incoming."

Cass rolls her eyes but doesn't speak, her mouth full of Nate's peanut-butter club sandwich.

As soon as Kim finishes cleaning the table, Nate nudges Cass, and they all pick up their things to move into the booth. There's plenty of room to spread out, and Cass slides down to the end, leaving space between her and Nate.

"So," Nate asks. "Who do you hate yourself for trusting?"

Cass holds out another of her toasted sandwich triangles, and Nate silently passes her another quarter of his club in return. "You, obviously," she says. "I don't trust people easily."

"But you do trust me," Nates says. One hand over his heart, he smiles at her. "I'm honored."

"I'm going to throw chips at you." Cass brandishes her piece of sandwich, and Nate laughs.

He stops mid-motion as he turns away, then lifts a hand, waving at Mac, Serina, and Carolyn as he slides farther down the bench and closer to Cass. He makes enough room for Mac to sit, but Carolyn lingers to kiss Serina.

"I'll come by later or, if you're still here when my shift ends, we can, I don't know, go somewhere else then," Serina says. She stretches up on her toes and kisses Carolyn's forehead. "Eat some real food. You've been buried in the library so much you're going to turn into a book."

"I've been eating," Carolyn protests. "I swear I have, but Pawel—" She glances at Mac. "We should bring home something for Pawel. He's—"

"He ate an apple at breakfast," Seth comments.

Nikolai thinks that was his whole breakfast. Sort of. "He ate a bowl of cereal a while after that. He's drinking a lot of coffee. He eats granola bars. If we put something next to him, it's gone when we come back. What he's not doing is sleeping."

"I tried to stop in, and he threw me out of the house and told me you were here," Mac grumbles. "I bumped into Carolyn on the way over. He needs to take care of himself. He's no good if he's so worn out he collapses."

"I think he's too grouchy to let go," Seth says.

"Like a toddler," Mac insists. "He's a child who doesn't want to miss anything and won't nap."

Serina gently pushes Carolyn onto the bench. "I have to work." She wiggles her fingers at Nate. "See you when your break is over," she calls out to him, and he lifts a hand to wave back.

Nikolai watches Cass as Mac and Carolyn settle in. She doesn't tell them to leave, but she doesn't seem welcoming either, focusing instead on her salad and her remaining toasted sandwich triangles. Mac reaches past Nate to steal a chip from Cass's plate. Carolyn pulls a laptop and a notebook from her bag and opens them both.

"I have information," Carolyn says. She looks up, frowning. "Not that we came here to meet. We need to order food. But since some of us are together, I thought I could catch you up."

"We live in the same house as Pawel, but he hasn't told us anything. So yes, please, talk to us." Seth makes a *go on* motion. "Have you made any progress on the ritual?"

"Pawel's still looking into it, but I don't think the original ritual can be reversed." Carolyn's fingers move quickly over her keyboard, then slow. "If we try to reverse it directly, we might destroy the split, but that could backfire by either destroying all the Shadows—effectively committing genocide against an entire Lineage of Talent—or it could cause another global Emergence and push more Talents with vestigial Shadowwalker blood into the Dreamscape."

"Neither of those are ideal solutions," Cass mutters dryly.

"Exactly," Mac replies. She steals another chip, dodging as Cass swats at her hand. "So reversing the ritual is off the table for now. Pawel's researching a different ritual and making plans that don't involve sleep."

Carolyn scrolls through her document, frowning.

"I'm half afraid to ask, but what kind of ritual is he considering?" Cass asks.

"We need several places where the liminal spaces between reality and the Dreamscape are weak." Carolyn touches her screen as she reads from it. "The idea is to create a ritual that transcends this one world. If we have the worlds in contact when we perform the ritual, that should protect us. Them." She motions as if to indicate unseen Shadowwalkers.

"What about the Benford house?" Nikolai asks. "The Berman place here. We could feel the connection to the Dreamscape in our world, before you guys cleansed it with a ritual, and here it hasn't been touched."

"Would trying to contact another world from there end with you dragging us all into the Dreamscape?" Cass asks. Nate gives her a confused look, and Cass points at Carolyn. "When she brought that Shadowwalker back, she dragged everyone into the Dreamscape with her somehow."

"That was Mattie's crossover and has nothing to do with this," Carolyn replies. She closes her laptop with a soft *thunk* and crosses her hands on top of it. "That was a unique situation caused by her soul being so close to this reality, my own Talent still being in the process of Emerging, and Del's presence and our history."

"If you're looking for somewhere that blurs the line, that's probably a good place." Mac's words nudge the conversation away from Cass and Carolyn glaring at each other. "You think it's a liminal space?"

"It's close to the Dreamscape," Carolyn agrees. "It was close enough that Del and I were able to travel to the Dreamscape from there accidentally. Do you think the cleansing of the Benford place would mean it's not as close now?"

"No, even after cleansing I think it's exactly the kind of place Pawel's looking for. I've been to the Berman house here—"

"So have I," Carolyn says softly.

"Then you've been to both, too. You know what I mean. They aren't the same, but they correlate," Nikolai says. "Alia won't like the risk, but I think Val could be persuaded. The Alia and Val of our world," he amends, because now he knows there's a Valentine here, too. "I don't know what the Alia here would think about it, and it's probably not something Valentine really gets a say in. It's not her home."

"The Alia of this world isn't a fan of magic," Mac admits.

"She's getting better." Carolyn closes her laptop and turns to the notebook. She shows a page with cards drawn on it, with neat writing beneath them. "She came to me for a reading a couple of months ago, and I told her to start a revolution. That's exactly what seems to be happening."

Mac makes a *hmm* noise and steals another of Cass's chips.

"I need to get back to work." Nate slides his plate in front of Mac, the sandwich gone but a pile of crispy chips still remaining. "Let me out, then you can finish my chips. Leave Cass's alone."

Mac and Carolyn slide out, but Carolyn doesn't manage to sit down again before her phone sings out. She looks at the number, lips pressed together as she silences it. "I've got to go," she says, shoving her laptop and notebook back in the bag. "I'll get something to eat later."

"Want me to bring something back to the house for you?" Mac offers; Carolyn is already walking away.

"Actually, yeah, that'd be great. I need to—" She stops several steps from the table, turning back to say, "Make Nikolai and Seth take something home for Pawel. And tell Serina that I—"

"—had to go. She's right there." Cass points. "Kiss her on your way out. I'm sure she gets it."

"She probably doesn't entirely get it," Mac murmurs as Carolyn catches Serina and kisses her cheek on the way by. "Serina's swept up in this because people around her are. Alaric and Nikita are on her floor. She's dating Carolyn. But she's not Talented, nor involved with what we're trying to do now."

"She's there for Carolyn," Seth says. "Right? Sometimes when one person's the raging river of chaos, it's good that the other one's the stable rock."

Nikolai reaches under the table to slide his hand over Seth's knee in silent thanks. "Are you saying I dragged you into this?"

"You are the Dreamwalker who dismantled wards so badly that you not only got us thrown out of Havenhill, we left the world entirely," Seth says. The sharp words are softened by a fond smile, and Nikolai can't resist stealing a kiss.

"Is that how Dax and I look?" Cass mutters.

"All the time," Mac whispers back. "Only you usually look even more like you're going to jump Dax any second. What I'd like to know, though, is when you and Nate started trading food like an old married couple?"

Cass blinks. "You stole my chips, not him."

They're distracted, and it's a perfect time to steal another kiss that tastes of blueberry crêpe and bittersweet chocolate.

39

Nikolai doesn't know when Pawel last slept. They left Haverhill on Sunday; Pawel was still up that night when Nikolai went to bed, still sitting at the same spot at the kitchen table on Monday morning. He's eaten whatever they set near him, including the food they brought from Teas Please Monday night, but Nikolai isn't sure he's doing any other forms of self-care.

He's positive that Pawel hasn't taken a shower. When he suggests one on Tuesday, Pawel picks up his things and moves into an office at the back of the house.

"Now we can't see him and make sure he eats," Nikolai mutters. Seth touches his shoulder, then searches through the fridge and makes eggs and frozen hash browns, handing a plate to Nikolai and pointing down the hall.

Nikolai delivers it while Pawel continues writing notes in shaky handwriting, scrolling through pages on his laptop.

"I'll pick up the plate later and bring you something else," Nikolai says.

Pawel says nothing.

"You should take a shower and get some sleep," Nikolai says. "Speaking as someone who was on the run for literal years, rest and cleanliness are two of the best things for your Talent. You'll be able to do more and faster if—"

"I'm fine," Pawel mutters. He waves at the door. "Close it when you go out. Carolyn said she's coming over. Help her with whatever she needs. And tell Mac to stop mothering me."

Nikolai retreats and pulls the door shut behind him.

"He's not going to be reasonable," he says when he returns to the kitchen. He wraps his arms around Seth from behind, resting his forehead against the back of Seth's head. His voice is muffled by Seth's long curls, and they tickle Nikolai's face. "The only way to get him to sleep is to knock him out."

"You're probably right," Nikita says.

Nikolai goes stiff, stopping with one hand under the hem of Seth's shirt. "When did more people get here?"

Nikita giggles. "While you were bringing food to Pawel. We didn't bother with the doorbell. Maybe you should save snuggling with Seth for later."

Nikolai's cheeks heat. He pats Seth's stomach, then disengages and steps back, running fingers through his own unruly hair in an attempt to make himself vaguely presentable. When he turns, Carolyn, Nikita, and Heather are at the table, and there are three laptops and several notebooks laid out before them.

"Pawel and the others aren't ready, but we've set a date anyway," Carolyn says. She smiles slightly when she looks up, then touches the chair next to her. "We've got some work to do in the meantime."

"We brought muffins," Heather comments.

Seth replies, "Let me finish making these eggs."

Nikolai settles into the chair, wincing when he recognizes the screen on Carolyn's computer. He's had a crash course in computers the last few weeks, learning to use the forums on both his phone and on Pawel's computer. Using them to talk to people all over the world is overwhelming. Overwhelming, but necessary. So he does it. It's better than having to slip into the Dreamscape every time he needs to explain again that yes, Dreamwalkers can work together without exploding the world.

Carolyn nudges the laptop closer to Nikolai, and he carefully sets his fingers on the keyboard and trackpad. "We'll do the ritual tomorrow," Carolyn says. "This week is the PHU Spring Festival, so classes have been light. And tomorrow is Election Day, and there are no classes at all. There's a picnic, and everyone will vote on school officers and enjoy the good weather, if we have it."

"We'll have it," Nikita says cheerfully. "The Weather Witches will make sure."

"You're involved in this ritual—that could lead to some unexpected changes to that weather," Heather points out. "You might want to let the folks you know who are working on the weather aware of that."

Nikita makes a small, displeased whine, and nods. "Point taken."

"Tomorrow," Nikolai says. There are hundreds of new posts on the forum since he went to sleep last night. Many are marked with names he recognizes from meeting Dreamwalkers in the Dreamscape. "You think we'll be ready to do whatever it is we're going to do by tomorrow, simply because it happens to be a perfect day for you to take off?"

He opens a message from Ji-eun: *I have found a place that I believe touches both worlds. Upon speaking to Brett within the Dreamscape, his Technopaths assured him that there is a similar location in Korea. He has found Dreamwalkers in Korea who claim they will be there, as will I, late in the day on the 26th of April—morning for you.*

"Pawel has this sense of urgency, and it's affecting everyone," Carolyn says. "He's not sleeping, but Del is, almost constantly—much more than you and Nikita are. She's terrified about the darkness encroaching on her meadow. She's scared about how it's affecting both your world and ours, and she's afraid that your path will disappear. She's anxious, so he's anxious, so he's pushing the timeline."

"Pushing the timeline" seems to a gentle way of putting it. "He needs to sleep before this happens," Nikolai says stubbornly. "Even if someone has to make him sleep. He can't lead if he isn't rested."

Seth turns from the stove, a pan of scrambled eggs held out, and nods. "I agree," he says, setting the pan in the center of the table.

Nikita jumps up to grab plates, and they all take food.

"It might take both of us," Heather says, glancing at the hall to Pawel's office. "But if we work together, we should be able to make it an environment where everyone rests easy tonight. I agree with Nikolai: we need to be at our best before doing this. Whatever 'this' turns out to be."

There's a message in the Forum from Grace as well. It includes a picture with a label stamped across it from two years prior. Grace is in the center, with their arms around two other people. Their message is blunt: *That's Kimmie on the left with the long hair. Kimmie Emerged, and died, and yes, I'm going to help you get those fuckers. I'm meeting two other Dreamwalkers at an old tree in the middle of the woods three towns over. There are massive numbers of legends about it. We're hoping it's what we're looking for. Those fuckers are going to wish they'd never Emerged.*

"Dreamwalkers are finding places, and they're also finding more Dreamwalkers," Nikolai says. There's a lot of information here, and he's having trouble parsing it. When Carolyn hands him a pad of paper and a pen, he makes two columns and takes notes to try to organize his thinking. "These places with thin barriers might be like the people who are bedrock. Or they might be more like me and Nikita—similar but not the same. I wish we had more people like us, or even better, more bedrock people like Alia and Val. It has to mean something that they—"

"—are getting along really well here, now, too?" Carolyn finishes the sentence, and that's not quite what Nikolai was going to say, but it's close enough.

Heather's expression twists. "Um. How well?"

"They're talking, according to Drea," Carolyn says. "And Valentine returned to Burlington late Saturday night, but she came back to Haverhill on Sunday with Miranda and Elijah. Valentine and Alia are planning together, and Valentine may be heading the group of Burlington mages who are helping in Haverhill."

"But they aren't so close that Alaric's going to freak out at a key moment, right?" Heather's brow furrows, concerned. "And how's Drea doing?"

"Drea's here, not there; she has someone in Haverhill feeding her information. She doesn't sound upset, but she handles things differently than Alaric does."

"It's good to have anchors," Seth says firmly. "If we have people we know are bedrock between the two places, that should make it easier to either bring the worlds together or, if necessary, push them apart."

"Which are we trying to do?" Nikita asks. She reaches across the table, her hand next to the laptop in front of Nikolai. It takes him a moment to realize what she's doing, but when he does, he covers her hand with his as she squeezes.

"Both options are on the table," Carolyn says. "Are you done with this?" She tugs on the laptop, and Nikolai pushes it and a pad of paper toward her.

"Please take over," he says. "You'll be faster."

Nikita's fingers flex, and Nikolai loosens his grip. She doesn't let go, just resettles her hand and tugs until he looks at her. "You okay?" she asks.

"With the computer? No. I could be here another month and I'd still be struggling with your technology," Nikolai says. She cocks her head, and he makes a face. He doesn't want to talk about what's actually worrying him, but he will. "Whatever happens tomorrow will happen. We'll do everything we can to fix the problem, and after it's fixed, we'll figure out how to get home. If we can still get home."

They've made peace with the idea that this may be their new home, but acceptance hasn't stolen their hope. As comfortable as this visit has been, Nikolai wants to go home to his family.

"What can we do to help you feel better?" Heather asks.

"That's a good question," Seth replies, his voice careful. He looks calm, but Nikolai can feel Seth's uncertainty pricking at his skin. He hears the way Seth's voice shakes, quietly underlining every word. "I don't know if there's a way to best make sure we can get home when this is done, unless there's a way to send us home while we're in the middle of it."

Carolyn closes the laptop lid, setting the pad of paper and notebook on top of it. "That's an interesting idea."

Nikolai thinks he knows where Seth is going with this. "If we're doing a Ritual in a place where the barriers between the Dreamscape and the real world are thin, it might be a place where we could enter the Dreamscape on one side and go out the other. Even though that's not what Dreamwalkers do."

"Do Dreamwalkers ever go into the Dreams of people from other worlds?" Nikita asks. When Heather moves closer, touching her leg under the table, Nikita adds quickly, "Just curious, since I'm still new to the 'acting like an actual Dreamwalker' part of this."

"I don't know," Nikolai says.

"They don't travel," Carolyn adds. She flips through her notebook, opening it to a page. "Standard Dreamwalkers can enter Dreams with their minds. Some people have the ability to go into Dreams physically, like Del. Some people travel using the Dreamscape but don't land there, only pass through. That's what I do. And I suspect that other Talent with traveling abilities may move through something similar, but they have no idea they're doing so. It's complicated, and I'm figuring out how the different Talents fit together."

"But some Dreamwalkers can bring people physically into the Dreamscape with them," Seth says. His gaze is fixed on Carolyn. "I heard the story of how you and others went into the Dreamscape at the Berman house, and that's where we will be."

"That may have been because Mattie was there," Carolyn says. She sits back as Seth waits for her to say more, acquiescing with, "But yes. We did. That's why we chose that location. We've had this discussion already. However." She raises one hand to forestall anyone else speaking. Nikita closes her mouth and slides her chair closer to Heather's. "It's dangerous for people who aren't Dreamwalkers to be in the Dreamscape. We didn't know what we were doing when we did it, and it's lucky we got out. We can't keep relying on miracles. Everything we've done so far has either been a mistake or has made things worse. The Shadowwalkers may have gained a better foothold because we enlarged the split when we bulled our way through it to get to your world. Or they may have done so when we brought Mattie's soul out of the Dreamscape." She pauses, slowing down in way that lends weight to her words. "It's possible we've caused more problems than we've solved."

Seth glances at Nikolai, and Nikolai nods. It's a risk, yes, but… "If there's a possibility we can be in the Dreamscape for the ritual, we need to be there," Nikolai says firmly. "Even if it's a risk. It might be a way for us to get home, if the barriers are thin enough for us to walk through to our world. I know it might unbalance things, but we're owed that much. You said we could go home. We have to try."

"Agreed." Carolyn speaks before anyone else can, and she holds out one hand. "If there's anything I can do to help, I'll do it. I think that'd be a fitting end to this, if we're able to put everything back the way it belongs in one massive move."

40

Nikita and Nikolai spend the day online coordinating Dreamwalkers, then taking turns slipping into the Dreamscape to pass information to Del. Nikolai naps in the early part of the evening, curled together with Seth in their bed.

Nikita and Heather sleep, too, across the end of the same bed, Nikita's fingers resting on Nikolai's ankle.

They awaken right before midnight to the sound of an alarm, and Heather and Seth begin trying to get Pawel to rest.

Nikolai heads downstairs to work with Nikita and Carolyn and the other Mages who have arrived while they were napping.

When Pawel returns to the kitchen, he's slept for only a couple hours and is wavering on his feet. Mac hands him a coffee and says gently, "You're not driving to Haverhill. Conserve your energy. You'll need it."

Pawel blinks at the gathered group. "Is Rory here?"

Rory raises his hand; he's sitting next to Kit at the table. "I'm as ready as I can be," he says.

"Everyone has transportation," Mac says. "We have a caravan readied. We've ensured everyone is synchronized to start the ritual at the same moment. We've chosen locations around the world—there are hundreds of them. Every single place selected has a history with the Dreamscape either through Emergent Shadowwalkers or through Dreamwalkers. As far as we know, they also all exist in both our world and Nikolai's. We can't say for sure about the third world."

She's answered with silence. Nikolai's thoughts dwell unpleasantly on the world that has already fallen.

It takes Mac's quiet efficiency to get them all cleaned, dressed, fed, and out the door. No one packs a bag that isn't related to the ritual. "We'll be back tonight," she says when Pawel brings it up.

He starts to say raise another concern, and she puts a hand over his mouth. "We will be back tonight," she says firmly. "You'll call Conor and tell him that the world has been saved. We'll have pizza and beer to celebrate, and you'll panic about how there are only two weeks left of class and you somehow still have to write a final exam for a class you've barely taught, not to mention grading final projects. You should think about great gifts to buy for your TAs once we're out of this hell; they deserve them. Oh, and either give Carolyn and Kit a high grade for saving the world, or an extension on the final project for their independent study."

Pawel wraps his fingers around Mac's wrist, carefully moving her hand. "Do you have a preferred rank, or should we address you as the captain of this sinking ship?"

"Not sinking, not captain. I happen to be the most organized person here. It's nice getting to plan an op where no one's going to die." Mac holds up both hands before anyone can say a word. "This is an op where *no one is going to die*," she repeats slowly. "Pizza and beer to celebrate when we're done. Now. Let's go heal the split."

Nikolai lets himself doze on the way to Haverhill. He's tucked into the back seat of a minivan, squeezed between Nate and Seth. The drone of conversation between Alaric, Chris, Dax, and Nate eases his mind. They're talking about running and football; it's nice to hear them discuss a topic that, at least for them, is normal. He feels the Dreamscape nearby, called by his recent frequent visits there, but Seth's hand on his knee keeps him anchored in simple sleep.

By the time he wakes, the van is bouncing along the long road that leads to the big house in Haverhill. They don't stop there, driving as far as they can toward the Berman house before they have to get out and walk. Mac disappears with Pawel; the two are sitting on the cracked step when Nikolai and the others arrive.

It takes time to gather everyone, and Nikolai notes significant faces that are missing. The Mage from the New Hampshire Clan isn't there, nor is Thorne, nor are several Mages from the Burlington community.

Valentine stands near Alia, fiddling with her phone. "Elijah talked David into letting him help today." She sounds resigned as she scrolls. "They drove to the site in Maine last night, and they've promised me they'll get here as soon as they can after everything's done. They have more people than we do. That site was the location of a significant Emergence, more than a dozen Shadowwalkers at once, around a decade ago. Elijah says it feels icky." Valentine's mouth twists as she surveys the space around the Berman house. "I understand what he means."

"Until recently, no one disturbed this place aside from teenagers trying to prove they weren't afraid of ghosts," Alia says dryly. "You can blame the claw marks on my husband, but the aura is what was left after Mattie Emerged. We had no idea at the time; we blamed her family's disappearance on magic."

Valentine glances sideways at Alia. "I get the feeling that a lot of things we've blamed on each other over the years may have been misunderstandings," she says.

Alaric growls low in his throat, and Corbin wraps an arm around him, dragging him down so he can rub his cheek against Alaric's head. The noise shifts to something disgruntled as Alaric tries to wrestle himself free.

"We are on a tight timeframe," Pawel says, voice tight, "if you wouldn't mind getting started."

Quickly, they arrange themselves, starting with Nikolai, Nikita, Carolyn, Del, Mattie, and Chelsea in a loose circle. Chelsea curls in on herself, a slender column of darkness that Nikolai can feel as much as see standing next to him, as if she matches the air around them in ways that no one else does. The other Mages encircle them, with Rory positioned as a bridge between the circle's center and its outer ring; he lays his hands on Carolyn's shoulders and touches Kit, who stands in the outer circle.

"This will work," Rory mutters. It sounds as if he's trying to convince himself, and that's not exactly comforting.

Carolyn looks down at the sketch she's holding, bright and fresh new artwork of Del's meadow drawn the day before by Kit. Nikolai's Talent isn't the same as Carolyn's, but he still focuses on that image as he reaches inside for his abilities. He leans back into Seth's anchoring touch, feeling the real world in Seth's fingertips and the earth below his feet as the Dreamscape tickles over his skin.

Nikolai inhales, and on the exhale, he lets the Dream come closer to him.

"Now," Pawel whispers, and the sound echoes around them. Nikolai can see that one word in the air, a soft, silvered blue that infuses with light.

Everything feels unreal and all too real. Nikolai slowly turns toward the house and slips his hand into Seth's. He focuses on the way their fingers curl together as the group moves toward the door that lies open and waiting. He hopes this is working as planned, but they are mid-ritual, and while Nikolai has no idea what the Mages are doing, he knows they don't have time to check their phones; they have to trust that, all over the world at this exact moment, groups of Dreamwalkers are approaching their own liminal spaces in attempts to simultaneously enter the Dreamscape.

They will do this together.

The way ahead is made up of dual images: the scratched and scraped door that hangs open, and a brightly colored front door that is cracked ajar and waiting. Nikolai crosses the threshold after Carolyn, Mattie, and Del and stops inside the door as he realizes that his hand is empty.

"Seth?" He turns to look behind himself, and only Nikita stands there. No Heather. Nikolai takes a step toward her, but Nikita's expression hardens with resolve, and she puts her hands on his shoulders.

"They couldn't come with us here," she says. "You knew that might happen." She nudges him, and he turns to walk with her.

It seems natural to take her hand, for them to each anchor their other self from a different world. Nikita squeezes his hand as they stop in the living room.

"This was my home," Mattie says, turning as she looks around. "As it was then, and as it still is in the Dreamscape."

"This is where we came to find you," Carolyn agrees. She glances at Del before crossing her arms, shoulders hunched. "I'd hoped that, with Del's help, we'd be able to do now what we did then, and bring the others with us."

"There are too many of them," Del says. She shrugs, then moves to the nearest window, looking through what seems to simultaneously be bright glass with freshly painted sills and cracked and dirty glass. "Or maybe there are too many of us, and the Dreamscape wants us for itself. Who knows?"

Nikita and Nikolai.

Carolyn.

Del.

Mattie.

And the darkness that is Chelsea, hovering near a corner as if she might melt into it. She looks uncomfortable in the light.

"We have to assume that it went like this for the Dreamwalkers around the world," Carolyn says.

"Worlds," Nikita corrects, emphasizing the plural.

"Worlds," Carolyn agrees.

"My meadow is outside," Del comments. She goes to open the window, making a disappointed sound as the sash doesn't lift. "Door it is." She skips across the floor, pausing when she reaches the door that lies open, light spilling in around it. "There are so many of us," she whispers. "The Dreamscape can barely contain us all. It wants to spill out. But the darkness is pushing in. It's almost too late."

She pulls the door wide, and for a moment, the light is blinding enough that Nikolai brings his free hand up to shade his eyes. The smell of flowers is overwhelming; Nikita sneezes three times, her entire body shaking.

"Let's go," Carolyn says, and follows Del through the door.

Nikolai goes too.

The Dreamwalkers stand in knots—in pairs, in groups of a dozen or more. They are all ages, all races. And there are more of them than Nikolai can count.

Surrounding the meadow are the liminal locations. The Berman place/Benford home overlap behind him; he turns back briefly. Maybe he could walk into the Benford home from here. But he stops after a step. Not without Seth.

There's a pond in one direction, a cliff seemingly jutting out of nowhere in another. He swears he sees Stonehenge, which makes sense when he thinks about it, and before the standing stones is the largest gathering of

Dreamwalkers. Some of the liminal places, he feels he recognizes dimly; others are familiar landmarks. Still others are strangely simple, like the truck stop with a flashing neon sign, or the Berman/Benford house behind him, or the big tree that Grace stands beneath.

Nikolai exhales and tries to wrap his head around the entire world being here in Del's meadow. Two entire worlds, condensed down to entry points in a microcosm that they've brought together.

It feels too big yet too small.

And it begs the question: what next?

"There are more people here than in our entire community."

Nikolai recognizes Brett from his world, his eyes wide as he looks around the meadow.

"We have come together, across two worlds, and we are many," Amahle says with a gentle smile. "We are well met, and we will persevere."

"Why is she here?" Grace is angry, jabbing a finger at where Chelsea crouches behind Mattie, as if to hide in her non-existent shadow under the bright overhead sun of the meadow.

"I want to help," Chelsea whispers.

"The darkness is crowding in, and you bring more?" Grace's throws their hands wide, and Nikolai looks toward where they gesture. He can see the cracks around every place they've brought together. The darkness threatens to split them apart. It moves, undulating and alive, and Nikolai imagines he can see faces and hands grasping and grabbing at their homes.

He imagines he can see them crumbling.

"Can't you feel it?" Grace asks.

Nikolai can. It crawls over his skin, pricking and pulling at him. It wants to tear him apart or shove him back to reality. It wants to claim him and suck him dry.

Chelsea takes a step back. "I want to help," she whispers again. "I don't want to be part of them. I'm not here to—"

If they are distracted by this argument, the Shadowwalkers will win.

They have to act now.

"We have two choices," Nikolai shouts, and the slow-building murmur falls silent, cutting the argument short. "We have Dreamwalkers and travelers here, and we need to do one of two things before we run out of time."

Ji-eun and Amahle step forward from their groups. Nikita tugs, and Nikolai stands tall, creating a central point in the meadow with her. The people Nikolai has come to know best from their Dreamwalker network gather around him slowly. Even Grace grudgingly joins them, a scowl still twisting their face as they sigh dramatically.

In the distance, Nikolai sees something on the edge of the meadow: a third version of some of their selected places flickers in and out of view. The house that looms in the place of the Benford and Berman homes is larger, a third floor added on, the exterior dark with paint and fallen into disrepair.

"Our third is here," he murmurs. "Barely, but there's still something of it out there."

"It feels hopeless," Nikita whispers back. "It's waiting for us to fall, too."

"We have two choices," Nikolai repeats, voice carrying across the meadow. "We can either pull our two worlds together, squeezing out the split. Or we can push our worlds apart completely. However, if we do that, the split might become too large and the Shadows might overwhelm us, and it's possible our worlds will disconnect completely. I don't know what that would mean for us."

"You think we should tie our worlds together," Ji-eun says.

"What would happen to us? Would all the people of both end up in one single world? That seems like a bad idea," Brett says, glancing around the group. "Either we'll be overrun with Shadows, or we'll face massive over-population. And what happens to the people who are bedrock or who have analogs?"

Nikolai tries to imagine a world with two of Alia. No one is ready for that.

"Pawel thinks we might have been one world, once upon a time, and that our worlds diverged over time when small events had minorly different outcomes," Carolyn says. Nikolai remembers this discussion, vaguely, and it feels right when she says it.

"We're too different," Nikolai says. "In the modern day, your world and mine are completely different places. There are similarities, but they're not the same anymore. If we pull them closer together, I don't think we'll merge. I'm not sure anything would change, other than making it so that there's no room for the split."

"No split means no Shadowwalkers," Ji-eun says thoughtfully. "Yes, this is our best solution."

"No split means no walking death destroying the population of my home." Brett is emphatic. "I'm in."

"But what if—?" Grace cuts off when everyone looks at them. They cross their arms, cheeks pulled in as if they're biting their tongue. "Fine," they say sharply. "But if we cause a cataclysm because we try to squish two realities into one—"

"Three," Del calls out cheerily.

"—I've read enough science fiction to know this is a bad idea!" Grace mutters loudly.

"It's worth the risk," Nikolai says. He tries to return the smile Carolyn offers, but his feels weak. "There's a risk, yes, but the reward is higher. We need to end this, not just put a bandage on it or make it worse by doing too little."

"This could still make it worse," Grace points out.

"How will we do this?" Amahle asks.

"We all came from places twinned across the two worlds." Nikolai gestures at the overlapping places around them. "If we can bring our reflections—the two or three versions of our spaces—into alignment, then maybe that'll do it."

"But what about the Shadowwalkers and the split? How do we push them away?" Brett asks.

Nikolai is glad to finally be able to speak about a topic he's the expert in. "I don't know if it'll work in the Dreamscape, but I know how to push Shadows away."

"That light thing you do." Nikita's mouth is open in a small "O."

It sounds too easy.

Nikolai takes a deep breath. He doesn't have Seth to anchor him here, but he has Nikita's hand in his, holding on tight. "I pull the Dreamscape into the physical world, forming it into small bundles of light." He shows them, capturing Dream with his free hand. It fills him abruptly, his skin vibrating with the direct connection to his Talent. "We all need to do it at the same time."

Around the circle, other Dreamwalkers try it, their Talent sparkling, visible to the naked eye.

Del sighs. "I have a really bad feeling about what this means for my meadow." She crouches down, running her fingers through the grass. "Just in case," she whispers. "Goodbye."

Something flickers at the edge of Nikolai's vision. He turns to look at the Berman house; it's wreathed in Shadows, the darkness licking around the edges of it, encroaching on the meadow. "I don't think we have a lot of time," he says. "They're drawn to the power we've gathered here. They want it."

"It's time," Del whispers. She dances to the center of the meadow, her hands out, butterflies flapping around her and rising into the sky as she slowly spins.

The Benford/Berman house is dark. Nikolai hopes that Seth is still in Haverhill waiting for him, that time is passing differently here than there, and that Seth isn't panicking.

He feels like if it were him, he'd be panicking.

Nikita holds out both of her hands, and Nikolai takes them. The light of her Talent flickers over him, sparking against his skin, calling to his own. Carolyn stands nearby, and Mattie and Chelsea watch. Nikolai is aware of other groups of Dreamwalkers echoing their motion, of light building. Some of the groups themselves seem to have a mirror, as the Benford/Berman place mirrors—there are two groups in those places, one from Nikita's world and one from his own.

Their numbers and Talent give him hope that this will be enough. That they can be enough.

"This is going to hurt," Chelsea murmurs.

That may be the only thing Nikolai regrets: whatever they are now, the Shadowwalkers were people once. Pawel loved Chelsea, and if this works, chances are he'll never see her again.

Nikolai exhales roughly, closing his eyes and extending his senses into the Dreamscape. He sinks into it easily, feels it rise around him. There's Nikita's world and his own, and that faint hint of someplace beyond. He feels the Dreamscape, and the worlds, and the Shadows, and he clings to the edges of the twinned realities, pulling them toward each other.

The darkness tries to slip between, tries to pull back, and it's a tug of war, a war he knows how to win.

All he has to do is twist the Dreamscape into bright, sparkling particles of unreality and push those into the darkness.

Magic builds under his skin until he glows with the effort of keeping it contained. He waits until all he can see is that glow vibrating around the edges of Del's meadow, obscuring the darkness beyond.

"Now!" he shouts.

It's a relief to let that much power go. To open his eyes to the bright diamonds that flash in the sky, illuminating the entire Dreamscape until his vision is filled with dazzling white light, overloading his mind, painful and sharp like daggers in his skull.

Everything goes incredibly, intensely bright.

And just as abruptly, everything goes very, very dark.

Narration by Seth (last name withheld).

We were eight years old the first time it happened.

Nikolai was bored; I could feel it as clearly as if he'd said it aloud. He fidgeted at his desk in our classroom, his feet dragging along the tiled floor as he kicked back and forth. I knew it would get him in trouble, so I poked him across the aisle between our desks. His toes made a scraping sound when he tucked them under his chair, and he sighed at our teacher's reprimand.

It wouldn't be long before he started again, so I tried to distract him. Afterward I wondered for a long time if what happened was my fault, because I was the one who directed his attention outside.

He stared as soon as I pointed, and I watched him watching the spring sun sparkle along melting piles of snow. The remaining drifts were pure white, the pristine snow revealed when the dirty exterior had melted.

His shoulders relaxed, and I felt him ease. I breathed in sync with him.

I had no warning that he'd slipped until he raised his hand and the sparkling light from the sun was echoed in our classroom, dancing to the choreography set by his fingertips. I felt the Dreamscape then, rising around us.

"Nikolai!" I whispered as loudly as I dared.

Our teacher snapped "Mr. Petersen!" at the same time as a girl across the room shouted.

Nikolai shuddered, his hand pausing mid-air. For a moment, shards of light hung suspended, then they burst out, sparkling through the room as if fireworks had rained down on us. Nikolai slid off his chair, hunched over, his hands pressed to eyes that were tightly shut.

He was in pain.

I knelt next to him, one hand on his shoulder. I couldn't ease physical pain, but instinct told me to give him as much calm as I could. "We should go to the nurse," I said. Nikolai murmured something indistinct, and I helped him stand, my arm around his back to guide him.

His eyes remained tightly closed.

The teacher opened the door for us as our classmates chattered. The girl who had shouted watched Nikolai, awe written into her expression. She leaned closer to her friend, seeming to respond to something I hadn't heard. "I don't know," she said, "but it was beautiful, wasn't it?"

"I made dreams real," Nikolai murmured.

He had done exactly that, and even that young, I knew it was something so dangerous that he could never do it again.

The world changed not long after that. The Split made it dangerous to be Talented. Our families left our home to find a new one, and years later, that safe space was set on fire.

Nikolai and I escaped and ran, alone.

It was exhausting, and after the first few days, neither of us had any energy left.

"I don't know if we can do this alone," Nikolai said hoarsely.

It was a sunny day, the bright warmth the polar opposite of the emotional chill we both felt. We leaned against a tree and I wrapped an arm around Nikolai, taking his weight as much as I could. "We can do this," I said, trying to make it sound as if I believed it. "We have to do this."

We needed a safe place to rest. Every night I worried that the Shadows would catch us. We barely slept. We had no food.

I stroked a hand over Nikolai's back, sending warmth and ease while I looked around us. We were off the road, but there was a path through the trees to a house with broken windows, the interior dark. "I see a house," I said, pointing when Nikolai opened his eyes. "It looks abandoned. We could give it a try."

It wasn't like we had another choice.

He didn't say anything, simply took my hand, and we walked together to the house. It was silent inside; it felt as if the world was holding its breath. Maybe that was because it still seemed lived in, with pillows tossed carelessly on the couch and a blanket lying crumpled after someone had gotten up.

We searched the entire house, but found no other people. Maybe they'd left recently. They'd been gone long enough that I didn't think they'd be coming back.

"We'll be okay here for the night. I'll go see if they left a flashlight behind."

I left Nikolai in the living room, the darkness already closing in with the sun sinking outside. I needed to find that light fast. I could hear him moving the couch, and I imagined he moved it closer to the window to take advantage of the fading light. That's what I would have done.

I found the flashlight in the drawer of a nightstand in an upstairs bedroom. "Got one!" I called out, and hurried to the stairs.

"They're here!" Nikolai shouted, his voice hoarse and rasping. "Shadows!"

Fuck.

I raced down the stairs, screaming his name as light bloomed sharply around me. Dancing shards, like falling crystals: the Dreamscape made solid, whole, and bright. He cut a path for me, and I pushed through it to reach him, throwing my arms around him and toppling both of us onto the couch.

He stiffened, then went limp beneath me, the blizzard of light flaring so bright that I couldn't see, then abruptly fading.

I held him, whispering nonsense words, trying to keep him in reality with me. I didn't want to lose him to the Dreamscape.

Nikolai blinked up at me, exhaustion lining his face.

Distraction was always a good thing with him. I held up the flashlight and flicked it on, smiling at the beam of light it emitted. "Still works."

He exhaled and closed his eyes, wrapping his arms around me. I let him pull me closer, holding me like a stuffed animal.

"I've got you," I told him. "You can rest."

"It's still beautiful," he mumbled.

I remembered then, what he'd done when we were children. And I realized that he'd said there were Shadows here, but after the light, there were none.

He'd saved us.

"We'll have to work on that trick again," I said slowly. "It's amazing."

"I could break things with it."

He could; we both knew that. "You won't," I said firmly. I patted his chest with a light touch, then rested my head there, listening to his heart. "I've got you, and I trust you. We won't break the world."

We were alone, and this trick of Nikolai's was the only weapon in our arsenal. And I would anchor him, no matter what, because he was going to need to use it, even though doing so was also a huge risk.

RECONSTRUCTION

41

Nikolai is far too warm.

There is heat beneath him, strong and solid. Nikolai's fingers press against the hair on Seth's chest, his hand trapped under Seth's shirt, Seth's heart beating strong beneath Nikolai's palm. Nikolai is lying face down, his cheek pressed to Seth's shoulder, his leg thrown over Seth's, and a body presses in behind him, trapping him there.

He has no idea why someone else would be in his bed.

He rouses slowly, inhaling deeply then exhaling for several long counts as Seth's hand twitches against the back of his head. The body behind Nikolai rolls away, and while it's not cold, he feels the chill of open air in their absence.

"Some of them are waking up." A low whisper, and when Nikolai carefully opens his eyes, Drea is bent over them, her face too close. She straightens up, turning to speak to someone behind her. "Nikolai's awake. They'll probably all start waking up soon."

Seth stretches beneath him, making a small sound of irritation.

Nikolai sits up, taking stock. Aside from his shoes, he's still dressed. The sun is out, visible despite drawn curtains, although it might be low enough to be later in the afternoon. For all he knows, it could be a completely different day.

The bed is full.

The person at Nikolai's back had been Mattie, and it's strange to see her lying there, so still with sleep. She looks like any other exhausted person, her face as relaxed as Heather's and Nikita's. Del might be dreaming, her expression tight and twisted; she clings to Carolyn, who has one arm around Del's shoulders, the other thrown wide and hanging off the bed.

They are all slowly waking.

The room is also full.

Alaric sits in a rocking chair, a basket by his side and knitting in his hands. The needles slide and click as he works, his gaze watchful. He nods when Nikolai meets his eyes, then drops his gaze back to his work. Corbin stands behind Drea, his hand on her shoulder. Shawn and Sam are both nearby, too large for the space where they've squeezed between wall and bed, within reach of Del if they push past where Carolyn half falls off the bed. Chris is near Alaric, and Dax and Nate are deeply involved in a quiet conversation on the far side of the room, sitting on the floor while Cass lies next to them, her head in Dax's lap, her mouth open and lax with sleep.

Drea straightens up, hands on her hips. "Mac's gone to get Pawel and the others," she says. "We should get you all something to eat. You expended a lot of energy."

They'd been promised beer and pizza after the ritual, then a return to home. That obviously hasn't happened yet. Nikolai's can't figure out what has happened, other than that he and Seth ended up in bed with several other exhausted people.

"Corbin, get them something to eat," Alaric replies, never looking up.

"Fine, fine, I'll do your bidding." Corbin catches Drea's hand as he walks away. "Come with me and help. This room's crowded, and I hear more people coming."

"Kit's on his way with Rory," Drea adds, waving as she's pulled out the door.

Alaric lowers his needles. He makes a low grumbling noise, pointing one needle at the bed. "Don't start talking until you're all awake and everyone's here."

Nikolai pushes the blankets back and carefully untangles himself to swing his legs out of the bed. He aches from head to toe, and the room wavers until he manages to get it to stay still. "I need to pee," he says firmly.

He's thankful that they let him go alone.

On his way back, he meets Seth in the hall. Seth grabs him, turns him, pushes him against the wall, and grabs Nikolai's face, gently cradling his head before he pats across his shoulders, across his chest.

Nikolai catches his hands and presses them to him. "I'm fine," he says.

"You weren't," Seth replies. His voice is tight. Hurt. "You were inside a building that disappeared, and you were unconscious. Valentine thought you'd be fine, but we had no idea if you'd wake up today."

"It's today. That's good." Nikolai's sleep had been dreamless, the kind of deep sleep that made it feel like no time had passed. "I did…we all did the thing with the light."

Seth blinks. "You brought the Dreamscape…into the Dreamscape?"

"Something like that. We used it to push everything dark away while we made our worlds close." Nikolai can say the words—he knows what they did and how it felt—but it feels impossible to describe it any more than that. "I'm pretty sure we did what we needed to do."

A rough cough catches his attention. Alia and Valentine stand at the door to Alaric's room. Carolyn and Del emerge from the bathroom, passing by Nikolai and Seth in the hall. Nikolai tangles his fingers with Seth's, and together they make their way back in, taking a seat on one side of the bed.

It takes a while for the rest of the group to freshen up, and by that time, Pawel has arrived and Corbin and Drea have returned with a cart of food.

The large room feels very small with everyone crammed in.

"The Berman house is gone." Alia opens the conversation, ignoring that the people she's speaking to have their mouths full with sandwiches or sweet fruit.

"Collapsed?" Carolyn asks around a mouthful of ham. "Like the Tower crumbling down."

Pawel shakes his head. "Gone," he corrects. "As if it never existed. The foundations are clean. You were all lying on the ground where it used to be."

"It no longer reeks," Alia adds. "The scent of death and darkness is gone."

"If houses grew like trees, a sapling would be sprouting there right now," Valentine comments. She grins. "It's not simply cleansed, it's aching to be built. Magically provident. If you're thinking of opening this community to Mages, that would be an excellent place for one to build a home."

"Are you planning on staying?" Alia asks sharply.

Alaric makes a choked-off sound.

"We watched from outside," Pawel interjects before Valentine can respond. "The Berman house…imploded, for lack of a better term. It disappeared, it's cleansed, and the Shadow remnants have also disappeared. From our perspective, the ritual was completed. Can you tell us what happened from your perspective?"

Seth's hand tightens on Nikolai's.

Nikolai glances at Nikita, who looks to Del, who looks to Carolyn, who makes a soft huffing sound.

Mattie mutters, "Don't expect me to explain it. I don't know what happened or how. It hurt, and I have a headache. I haven't had a headache in more years than I can think about, and it feels unfair."

"I think 'cleansing' is a great word for it," Nikita says cheerfully. "Nikolai showed us how to make the Dreamscape into light, and we pushed the darkness away. It felt like we were scrubbing the Shadows out of the Dreamscape."

Del flicks fingers next to her own head, almost hitting Shawn in the face. "I feel it," she says, and when Shawn tries to capture her hand, she pushes him back. "More than before. It's a constant presence now."

"Is that a good thing?" Nikolai asks dubiously. "As far as I'm concerned, the Dreamscape is safely back where it belongs." He can't feel the itch of it in his mind and has no need to call to it. He glances at Nikita, and she nods: they're on the same wavelength.

"It's brighter there. I looked around while we were sleeping, and everything's as it should be." Del looks at Nikolai. "I was alone, so I couldn't check in with anyone to confirm, but I think your world will be in better shape than when you left, and that your invasion will be gone."

"We'll find out when we get home," Seth comments.

"The question is, how do we get there?" Nikolai asks. "We have two immediate problems—if the split is gone, how has that changed the path between here and there? And what happened to Chelsea? She was with us in the Dreamscape, but she's not here now."

"She wasn't there when the house disappeared, either." Pawel's voice is flat, carefully neutral. "It's possible that, depending on how the ritual affected the Shadowwalkers, she can no longer enter this world."

"I don't think what we did destroyed existing Shadowwalkers. I'm hopeful that, by removing the split as an influence, we've stopped the Emergence of any more…" Carolyn hesitates. "I don't want to say they were 'broken' Shadowwalkers. Mutated, perhaps. I think that if Shadowwalkers Emerge now, they will be true Shadowwalkers."

"Something changed," Mattie mutters. She lies curled on her side, a pillow over her head. "I haven't been this exhausted since before I changed. You sucked my soul out. Y'know how I say some souls taste like eating good chocolate? Well, I feel like I was the chocolate."

Pawel turns away, his arms crossed. "Excuse me," he says tightly. The door creaks when he yanks it open, thumps as it drops closed behind him.

Carolyn pats Mattie on the head. "I think we may have removed the remains of the Soulstealer influence from you, so you won't miss feeding anymore. You're more human. You'll adjust, and you'll be fine. It may have affected Chelsea similarly. Wherever she is, she's probably fine." She glances at Mac, who disappears from the room. "I think this is it. We're done. As done as we can be."

Valentine turns to Alia. "So we ally instead of making war."

Alaric slowly bundles his knitting into a bag, setting it in the basket by his feet. "There are people here who need to talk about Clan and Mage business. Let's make arrangements for our communities and plan for the future." As he stands, he adds gruffly, "Corbin, Drea, stand with me for this. Mom…" His voice gentles. "You'll be my voice for the near future."

"I'll be your voice," Alia agrees. She tilts her head, a small smile gracing her expression. "And?"

"See if Dad would like to be there for the talks," Alaric says. Drea exhales roughly, and Corbin makes a small squawk that sounds like protest. Alaric continues speaking before Corbin can comment. "I want to give him one more chance to be involved. I'd rather have him work with us than have him work against us or do nothing. He has experience that would help, but he needs to be open to these alliances. He needs to be ready to move forward."

"I'll speak with him." Alia's smile is wider than any Nikolai has seen from her—either this Alia or the one in Havenhill. She is pleased with Alaric's decision in a way that has Seth squeezing Nikolai's hand in response to her emotions spilling over.

"Valentine." Alia takes a step toward the door, then halts.

"Yes?" Valentine asks.

"Please join me as an emissary from the Burlington community," Alia says. "If Theobald is to work with this alliance, I would like to see him begin immediately. You represent a large community of Mages, one connected to the first Mage my son has allied himself with." She gestures to where Rory sits with Kit on the floor. "Our extended families are already bound through them, and Theobald needs to recognize that."

"And if, instead of opening his heart, he decides to open my chest, you'll protect me?" Valentine quips with a wry smile. "Can't raise my kids if I'm mauled."

"He will do you no harm," Alia says solemnly. "Come."

"I'm not sure if I should say 'welcome to the family' or if you should, or if it's a mutual merging." Rory's fingers move along Kit's hand as if he's playing the guitar instead of holding hands. "We might want to run interference, Alaric?"

"I don't think I want to be anywhere near that," Corbin says dryly.

"Rory's right." Alaric doesn't look thrilled, but Chris steps close to him, one hand on Alaric's back as they head for the door with Rory and Kit close behind. "Corbin, Drea—please make sure that everyone here is settled and has what they need. Then join us. I still want you both by my side for negotiations, but you're also right—it's best if few people are there to witness Theobald's acquiescence or refusal."

Corbin pulls out plastic containers with lids and more plates from the bottom of the food-laden cart he and Drea have wheeled in. "Some of you look ready to fall over," he says, holding up a container in one hand and a plate in the other. "If you want to head to your own room, we can make you a plate to take with you. Food and rest—you need both."

Mattie makes a noise and yanks the blankets over her head, becoming a lump under the covers.

"Or stay right there, in Alaric's bed," Corbin says. "That's fine, too."

Seth wraps his arms around Nikolai's middle, his chin resting on

Nikolai's shoulder. "I want to go back to our room," Seth whispers, "and reassure myself that you are here, anchored in reality, and that everything is fine."

Nikolai is definitely not thinking about food. He pushes to his feet, tugging Seth with him. When Corbin gets between them and the door, Nikolai protests, "I know where we're going, and we're not hungry."

Drea snorts. "For food."

"Take a care package for later." Corbin shoves one of the plastic containers at Nikolai's chest and shoves another to Nikita before she can slip past hand in hand with Heather. "We know how to take care of energy expenditures here. Shifting shape uses a lot of energy, and whatever you all did made you sleep for a full day. You're running on reserves. What's on your mind—that takes energy, too, and I'm pretty sure you don't want to pass out in the middle. So pack a box before you go."

He has a point. Nikolai just wants to crawl into bed with Seth and curl around him, but he can feel exhaustion pulling at his bones. "Fine," he agrees. They fill a box with fruits and cheeses and breads and let Drea show them the way back to the guest wing.

Nikolai hears Pawel's voice when they approach their rooms, and he exchanges a glance with Nikita at how loud he sounds. The words are muffled, but the tone is anxious, followed by Mac's placating, quiet reply.

"Let him work through whatever he's working through," Heather says. "Pawel's so wound up right now; he's the only one who can decide if we've done enough for him to relax." She raises her voice. "We saved the world, Pawel. Go to bed."

"That's what I've been telling him," Mac calls back.

Heather spreads her hands. "See?" Then she yanks open the door to her own room, and she and Nikita disappear inside.

"Go," Seth urges, and he pushes Nikolai into their room, the door slamming closed with a *thunk* once they're inside. Seth has Nikolai up against the wall again, but this time he strips him out of his shirt, tossing it to one side, then leans in, hands pressed to Nikolai's chest, fingers spread. He kisses just above his heart, his breath broken as he leans his head down. "Please tell me we're done trying to save the world. Either world. Any world."

"All that's left is to figure out how to get home, or how to live here," Nikolai assures him. He touches the side of Seth's face, waiting until Seth looks up so he can bend to meet him, lightly brushing their lips together.

Seth makes a broken sound, and Nikolai swallows it, chasing him and pulling him close for another kiss. Seth pushes him back, and the wall is solid. Nikolai lets it hold him, yanking Seth close enough to lie against him as they kiss. Small nips, then slower and deeper, exploring each other, lingering over the taste.

Nikolai slips his hands under the edge of Seth's shirt, tugging at it to get it over his head and off. He wants to feel him close, to remind himself that yes, this is his reality. "This is better than any dream," he mumbles, tilting his head back as Seth kisses his jawline. "So much better."

A sharp rap on the door interrupts them, and Seth jerks back, his head clipping the underside of Nikolai's chin.

"Ow," Nikolai mutters. "In my dream we would not be interrupted."

Seth waves at the door and heads for the opposite side of the room, standing behind the bed as he looks through their bags for something.

Nikolai shifts, trying to make himself more comfortable before he yanks open the door. "Yes?"

"I'm going to find Chelsea," Pawel announces.

At least Pawel knocked. Nikolai needs to remember to lock the door. "Okay," he agrees.

"And we'll figure out how to get you two home," Pawel continues. Each word is cut off and abrupt, tight in his throat.

Behind Pawel, Mac reaches for him, trepidation twisting her expression. She pulls back before touching Pawel's shoulder. *Sorry,* she mouths.

"If we have to live here, we'll need help making ourselves 'real,' in a legal sense, in your world," Nikolai says. He's not certain what Pawel needs to hear, but he can tell that there's something that he's waiting for. Maybe some kind of absolution for dragging Nikolai and Seth into this.

Pawel nods once, quickly. He brings up both hands, heels pressed to the bridge of his nose before he runs his fingers through his hair. As his face emerges from under his too-long bangs, he stares at Nikolai.

Nikolai stares back, fingers curled around the door. He resists the urge to close it and go back to what he and Seth were doing.

"Are you all right?" Pawel asks abruptly.

"I think they're going to be fine," Mac says.

Pawel ignores her, watching Nikolai closely.

"I'm okay," Nikolai says. It's mostly the truth. "Give me some time—give both of us some time—and we'll be even better."

The tension in Pawel's shoulders loosens, and he rocks backward. "Good," he says roughly. "That's good. I'll find Chelsea, and when I do—"

Nikolai doesn't know if Pawel wants to find Chelsea for himself or because they need her help to get Nikolai and Seth home. He has a feeling it's more the former than the latter. "Find her first," he says. "Find her and make sure she's safe, then we'll figure out the rest. You don't need to rush."

"For the first time in a really long time, none of us need to rush," Seth points out. "And I, for one, would like to take my time reassuring myself that Nikolai is as okay as he says he is. I plan to do a thorough job."

Nikolai's cheeks go hot. There is absolutely nothing he can think of to say.

Behind Pawel, Mac covers her mouth with one hand, humor dancing in her eyes. She wiggles her fingers as if to say *no, that's fine, go on and say nothing*. "Come on, Pawel," she says, dropping her hand. "We should let them get back to that reassurance."

"We should check in on Nikita and Heather," Pawel suggests.

Nikolai shakes his head quickly, and Mac giggles.

"Maybe not. Pretty sure they're fine, too. Come on."

Nikolai closes the door and twists the lock. When he turns around, Seth is on the bed, lying back with his arm stretched toward Nikolai.

"C'mere," Seth says. "Reassure me."

So Nikolai does.

42

Nikolai expects there to be a celebration in Haverhill, but there isn't one. Instead, an air of calm replaces the anxious expectation that had suffused everyone in recent weeks. In many ways, this is easier. Nikolai can finally relax, even if there are still things that he needs to do. The worst is over; they have time for the rest.

Most of the older delegates and Clan leave, while many of the Mages linger. Rory says goodbye to his parents and grandparents, but Valentine stays, her daughter trailing after Alaric like a brightly caped duckling and her son hanging around the edges of the PHU crowd, listening intently.

At one point Cass turns to Elijah, her lips pursed. He blinks as if surprised to gain the regard of one of the older crowd. "You're staring," she says curtly.

"So?" he retorts. "I might go to PHU someday. I'm studying you."

"Hmph." Cass crosses her arms, turns her back on Elijah, and takes a step closer to Nate, making space for Elijah in the circle.

He hesitates before stepping in and allowing them to include him.

Dayton makes a late entrance, moving as if she doesn't have a care in the world while the rest of her community's contingent waits impatiently to start the long drive home. Stormy trails behind her, barefoot and still in a rumpled sleep shirt and shorts. Stormy rubs at her eyes, yawning and stretching as Dayton turns around and reaches for her. Stormy falls against her with a small noise that turns to a low rumble when Dayton kisses her and rubs her cheek against Stormy's. Dayton sets her back on her feet, and Stormy sways, her cheeks flushed.

"I knew you were flirting when you met her," Rory mutters.

"I wasn't, not then, but oh man, she is fun," Stormy admits. "I doubt it'll be a long-term thing, but it'll be a good time every time we meet up. When are you planning on staging another crisis? I'll pencil in another round of crisis-survival sex."

Mac coughs around a laugh while Rory looks pained. "I don't need the details," he mumbles, and Stormy nudges him with her shoulder.

"You're still taking me back to PHU for the Festival this weekend, right?" she says. "I promise to behave better than Thorne. Let me go shower and pack up, and I'll be ready to go."

"It's not hard to behave better than Thorne!" Rory grumbles.

Stormy laughs and blows him a kiss before walking away.

Heather's phone pings, and she checks it, frowning. "I'm missing an exam. I don't even remember one being scheduled; who does that during election week? It's the Spring Festival."

"The professor's a dick, remember?" Cass mutters. "I'm pretty sure he scheduled it on purpose because everyone still on campus got drunk last night."

"Your absences are excused," Pawel says. "I spoke to administration. You have all been noted as working on a special project for me, details to be provided upon my return to the school. You'll be able to make up the exam next week, just in time for finals."

"Lovely," Heather mutters. "I didn't have enough work to do in the next two weeks. Is there any chance they'll drop our lowest exam score? We did save the world."

"There's no magic you can work for that one," Nikita murmurs, her arm around Heather's back. "But that's okay. We'll get through finals with a lot of screaming during primal scream time, then we get a whole summer off."

"Some of us have to work for the summer," Rory points out.

"You're touring," Nikita counters.

"That's work! Have you ever set up heavy equipment, then spent an hour performing on a hot stage, then lugged that heavy equipment off stage again so you could pack it up before getting stuck in a small, stinky, beat-up van for hours on the road? It's hard work," Rory grumbles. "Plus we have an album to record. That we need to write songs for."

Seth wraps his arms around Nikolai, whispering, "I'm looking forward to getting back to Havenhill and getting jobs. It'll be hard, but it'll be safe. Imagine what it'll be like when nothing's chasing us and the world isn't falling into darkness."

It sounds like bliss.

"Dax!" Cass's voice breaks through the low chatter as Dax comes into the room. His light jacket is unzipped, hanging open, and his curly hair is windswept. He smiles, and his expression is lighter as he approaches Cass, wrapping his arms around her and kissing her quickly.

"Well?" Alaric asks.

"It's done," Dax says, his smile infusing his tone. "Orson's settled, finally. He might still be here; I get the impression he wants to stick around for you and Drea. But he's not worried about war anymore. If you go there to talk, he'll listen."

Alaric's expression shifts from pleased to pinched, hands flexing by his sides.

"Let's take a walk," Chris offers. "We don't have to leave this second, and I don't mind heading out there." He slides his hand into Alaric's and waits.

Alaric huffs. "Thanks," he mumbles, meeting Dax's eyes, then turning to leave with Chris.

"Hey." Carolyn touches Nikolai's arm. "Can we talk? Before we split into different cars and things get even more chaotic."

Nikolai glances at Seth; with his tacit approval, they both head for the back of the house, and Carolyn follows them. They sit on the bench that says "For Cats."

"Del left early," Carolyn says. "She woke me up before she went. Sam and Shawn wanted to get home, and I think they were worried that if she stayed, she'd go back into the Dreamscape."

"They think she won't want to if they take her home?" Nikolai knows Carolyn understands from the way she smiles. "I don't think anything will keep Del out of the Dreamscape."

"She wasn't always like this," Carolyn explains. "We're still trying to catch up with who we are now. She said to tell you that she'll stay in touch with you, and that she promises not to get lost."

Nikolai isn't sure he believes her. Usually, Dreamwalkers want to pull the Dreamscape into the real world. But the Dreamscape is a siren's song to Del, pulling her in. "You can tell her I'll come find her after I'm home," he promises. "But first Seth and I have to figure out how to leave."

"Actually"—Carolyn twists her hands together—"I have a favor to ask you. Before you go."

Nikolai can't think why she's nervous, unless… "Does it involve staying? Because we really don't want to," he admits. "You've got a lot of good things here, but home has Josef and Mikhail."

A soft, rough laugh. "No, I know you want to go, and I don't blame you. I can't imagine being separated from Kit, and yes, we're twins, so maybe it's different, and actually that—" She looks at him sideways. "Have you thought about what it'll be like to be apart from Nikita?"

"We aren't that kind of close." The words come easily, because they're true. He and Nikita aren't like twins who were raised together. Their relationship isn't even like the one Nikolai has with his brothers, despite the years when Nikolai thought they were dead. "We're not siblings. It's more like we're the same person. Besides, we can also meet in the Dreamscape, possibly." He likes Nikita, but he can handle the idea of being in a different world again. That feels more right than how they are now.

"I'd like to take a look at your relationship with Nikita scientifically, as well as considering your personal histories," Carolyn says, her fingers tangled tightly in her lap. "In this world, Talent has always kept records for ourselves—we didn't start sharing them until after the Emergence. Sera and other Technopaths have started making a safe space to keep our records online, and we can find Talented scientists to work on private studies. I'd be happy to share what we learn…"

"Nikita or Del could tell me," Nikolai suggests. "You've already said Del and I have a date to lie around in the meadow and watch butterflies, right?"

Carolyn's shoulders soften as she laughs. "Right. I guess you do. I think—this might tell us something more about Talent. We can say 'it's magic,' but if we know the science beneath it… The more we know about these twinned worlds—"

"—the more of them you can go save?" Nikolai asks.

Carolyn gives him a startled look. "That's not—"

"You said your traveling is linked to the same kind of Talent that Dreamwalkers and Shadowwalkers have, right? Now that the split isn't a pit of darkness, you might be able to use it too. Maybe you're more like a traditional Shadowwalker than the corrupted kind that had been Emerging, and that's why you couldn't figure out how you fit in."

"I—" Carolyn stops talking, her mouth slightly open.

He reaches over, covers her tightly clasped hands with his own, and squeezes. "Maybe I'll see you again someday. I'm glad we met, and I'm happy we were able to help each other."

He rises, and Seth follows his lead. When Nikolai reaches out, Seth's hand is there. Their fingers tangle together like they've always fit.

Carolyn stays on the bench, head bowed and brow furrowed.

"Do you want us to tell someone—?"

Carolyn shakes her head. "Kit won't let them leave without me," she says. "I'm going to sit here and think for a bit."

"That was a hell of a theory to drop on her," Seth whispers as they walk toward the front of the house. "I didn't even think of it."

"I might be wrong," Nikolai says. He doesn't think he is, though. The more he rolls it over in his head, the more sense it makes. And he suspects that's how they made it from one world to another in the first place. She might not be able to control it yet, but with time she'll likely learn how.

Valentine meets them in the hall.

"I spent some time talking to Alaric," she says.

"About Havenhill?" Seth asks, then nods. "Okay, yes, about Havenhill."

"Empaths are honestly a bit disturbing," Valentine replies. She looks down the hall, then motions for them to move into the great hall. Aside from some tables around the room's edges and a few chairs, it's empty and echoing.

Nikolai isn't in the mood to sit down for another serious conversation. "He told you about Val?"

"My counterpart that's married to Alia's counterpart? Yes," Valentine confirms. "And that I apparently helped create that safe haven, and that I'm Alia's right hand there, and that I help her handle things calmly and reasonably. And that I told you to leave."

"It was a group decision," Nikolai says. "We didn't argue against it. We broke the wards and let the Shadows in. We broke the rules."

"Do you get to go back?" Valentine asks.

Seth laughs dryly.

"If we can figure out how," Nikolai says. "Why?"

Valentine stands with her arms akimbo, hands resting on her hips and her elbows out. She turns on her heels, looking over the large room. As she exhales, tight shoulders lower and loosen although her stance remains stiff. "Do you think you can carry anything back with you? I'd like to send you some research to give to the me of your world. They're things that she might not have thought of because we're different enough people, but that she'll understand if she's like me."

"If we can carry it, of course," Seth says. "Or if we read it, we might remember enough."

Valentine makes a small, displeased noise. "It'll be more than you'll want to memorize. You aren't traditional Mages. You don't know ritual, and if you make mistakes, it won't go well when Val tries to use it. I'll email Pawel. He can print it, and if you can carry it, fine. If not, well, I tried."

"And what about here?" Seth asks.

Valentine turns back slowly. "What about here?"

"You're going to work toward forging a relationship with Alia, right?" Seth says. "We pushed out the darkness created by the Shadows, but you still have a government out there that created them in the first place. You need each other."

"What kind of relationship do you mean?" Valentine says curtly.

Seth raises his eyebrows. "The alliance kind. She's married. I'm guessing you have a husband somewhere—"

"We're divorced," Valentine interrupts.

Seth makes a motion with his hand as if that isn't important. "I'm not saying to get involved with her romantically. Befriend her. Build on what Alaric's started. Forge the alliance between here and Burlington."

Valentine rocks backward, turning away again as her hands fall from her hips to hang by her sides. "We've started doing that, too. I met with Theobald and Alaric yesterday, and our communities will not remain separate. You're right: we need each other. The world needs to change, and I'm ready for it to. From what I've heard of your world, it sounds like that change was pivotal in keeping Talented people safe. We aren't endangered here, but there are still dangers. Like the virus that broke out in New Hampshire. Like the Shadows. Like the bad blood that could still result in war if we don't watch out. So yes"—she turns back—"we've made our alliance. This isn't your Havenhill, but we will work on creating a haven, both here and in Burlington, and with other communities as well. We will bring our world together."

Seth hesitates, his expression intent as if he's trying to read her. He finally nods, then reaches back to tug Nikolai forward. "I think we're set, then. I'm glad things are in good hands here."

Valentine doesn't ask before stepping forward, her arms wrapping around both of them as she tugs them in for a hug. It's awkward and strange as she kisses first Seth's cheek, then Nikolai's. This Valentine is much more open—much less hardened—than their Val.

"Don't look so surprised," Valentine says. "You don't know me that well. You don't know the other me that well, either. I bet she and I aren't as different as you think. Give her time to warm up to you."

"You should see Alia," Nikolai mutters.

Valentine laughs. She keeps her arms around them as they move to the front of the house. Most of the cars have gone. Pawel stands with Alia, his hand out and clasped in hers, her shoulders relaxed and loose as they speak. Finally, Pawel draws back. He looks up and waves when he spots Nikolai and Seth. "I'd wondered if I was going to have to go find you. Mac's already in the car. Ready?"

Pawel still seems half a ghost. His skin is pale, his eyes darkly rimmed in shadows. But there's a life to his step that's been missing, and Nikolai suspects that he's slept more than anyone else. Good; he needed it.

Nikolai pauses by the car to take one last look at the big house. Alia stands on the steps, holding the door open for Valentine. It's familiar, but not. Nikolai hopes the next time he sees something similar, he'll be home.

43

For a few days, there is nothing Nikolai and Seth can do other than live their lives in this new place. Chelsea hasn't reappeared, and neither Del nor Mattie know where she is. He and Seth relax, spending time together enjoying the sheer luxury afforded by the world. They get new clothes and new glasses for Seth. Two pairs, in case one breaks.

The days are lazy, and the nights are joyful. The peacefulness would be bliss if Nikolai weren't waiting to find out if they will be able to go home.

It's hard to let go of hope.

Mid-morning on Saturday, someone rings the doorbell of Pawel's house, then knocks for good measure. Seth answers because, with sweatpants on, he's more dressed than Nikolai, who has to drag on a pair of jeans before he can leave the bedroom.

Nikolai makes it to the stairs as Nikita and Heather come inside.

Seth scratches at the hair on his chest. "We were asleep," he says.

"Dozing," Nikolai corrects. They'd gotten up earlier, had some breakfast, then climbed back into bed. It seems decadent to lie around and do nothing, but eventually they won't have this luxury. He wants to enjoy it while he can. "Pawel is still asleep."

"Was," Pawel calls from upstairs. "Waking up now. Who's here?"

"We've come to take Nikolai and Seth to campus," Heather yells back. "OPT and SigPsiEp are running the barbecue at the Spring Festival lawn party, so we'll be grilling and eating from now until after sundown. Phoenix Rising has a set as part of the live music during the afternoon."

"This is the big spring weekend at PHU, and I'm excited that we get to enjoy it without the end of the world hanging over us." Nikita mimes something dropping down on her own head. "You'll love it. Be ready for crowds, though. This makes the sugaring festival look poorly attended."

Heather makes a shooing motion with her hands. "Go. Get ready. Let's get out of here so Pawel can spend his day catching up on the grading he hasn't made his TAs do. Or maybe meet with his TAs so he can figure out how to finish up his classes."

"I heard that." Pawel makes his way past Nikolai down the stairs. "She's right, though. Go. I have work to do, and you deserve to have a little fun." His hair sticks up in different directions, but his skin has more color than Nikolai has seen in a while and the bags under his eyes are less pronounced. "I promise I will eat and take care of myself."

Heather shoos them again. "Get dressed. Come on."

It doesn't take long before they're on their way to campus. The music is audible even at Pawel's house a few blocks away, and it gets louder the closer they get. The band playing as they walk has a heavy fiddle component and strong drums.

Nikita and Heather walk hand in hand. As Nikita starts swinging their joined hands to the lively beat, Heather laughs and lifts her arm, twirling Nikita. Nikita swings back toward Heather, captures her, and skips down the sidewalk, dancing along.

They wait at the corner, laughing.

Nikolai feels the light, airy sensation of being free in his heart.

It's weird.

Seth catches his hand, twining their fingers together. "I could live here, if I had to," he murmurs.

"Me too." Every day that passes makes Nikolai think that this is what there is for them. It wouldn't be so bad, staying in Unity, maybe attending PHU, particularly on a beautiful spring day like this one. The sky overhead is blue, and the air is warm enough that Nikolai is comfortable in a T-shirt and jeans. Nikolai's hair, a little longer than he'd prefer, blows in his face. He huffs to blow it away, then reaches up and threads his fingers through it, pushing it back.

"Want a ponytail holder?" Nikita stops dancing and offers a purple band held between pinched fingertips. She motions, and Nikolai turns so that he can pull his hair back into a twist at the back of his neck. Some of his bangs aren't quite long enough and fall forward as he tilts his head. She pats the back of his shoulders. "Everyone's going to love that bun."

Seth leans close. "You know how you like it when my hair gets long, even though I hate the curls?" he whispers. When Nikolai nods, Seth grins. "I like that I can play with your hair. It looks good on you."

Heat suffuses Nikolai's cheeks. Maybe he won't cut it right away.

Even before they reach the Quad where the stage and barbecue are, there are people everywhere. It's as if the entire population of the campus is out. People lie out on blankets, bathing in the warmth of the spring sun. It's lazy and loud and different from anything he's used to.

"They're all so happy," Seth says.

Heather's cheeks are flushed a warm rose. "They always are during Festival week," she says. "They have no idea what we've done. This is when we celebrate that spring is finally warming up and that we're close to the end of the school year. It's a weekend to let cares fall away. It feels so, so good."

Nikolai suspects that Heather might be high on the leaked positive emotions surrounding them.

The music ends and the singer talks to the audience. Nikolai can't hear everything, but he thinks it's a farewell and thank you and announcement that the next band is coming up. The name of the band is swallowed by the roar of voices responding, and Nikita shouts, grabbing Nikolai's hand.

"Rory's up," she says, running. Nikolai catches Seth, and they follow her as she rushes through the crowds.

The brick path widens into an empty space ringed by at least eight buildings. The Quad consists of several grassy stretches split by walkways going every which direction. A stage has been built in front of one building, and as musicians carry instruments off, Nikolai recognizes some of the people waiting to carry their own gear up.

"Rory!" Nikita yells, and he turns, raising a hand in their direction with a confused expression that eases when Nikita waves wildly. He smiles and waves back.

Once the other band has cleared the stage, Alaric and Chris help carry up a drum kit, placing it according to Stormy's directions. She's barefoot, wearing only shorts and a tank top that doesn't hide the sports bra under it. She orders them around, arranging things the way she likes, then pulls up a stool and settles in, playing a tripping beat with her drumsticks while the others finish up.

Kit sits on one back corner of the stage with a woman Nikolai doesn't recognize. There's another man on stage, as well, tuning his instrument with Rory and Thorne until Thorne goes to adjust mic stands: one down to his own height, one higher for Rory.

"I'm hungry," Heather says. "We should eat while we listen, because we'll be working after this."

As they head over to the grills manned by OPT and SigPsiEp, Thorne's voice rings out. "Hey, PHU! I know you already know half of us, but we're Phoenix Rising, and we're really glad to be here today. Rory and I are a captive audience of course—"

He cuts off as the crowd yells out "Hi Thorne!" He pauses long enough to blow kisses.

"Thanks, everyone. We've got the rest of our band here with us today. Andy"—he points to the guy at the back, who raises one hand—"and Stormy." She runs a long riff that settles into a low, rolling beat in the background while Thorne continues to speak. "We've only got a half hour, so I'll stop talking—" Again he cuts off as the crowd yells. Behind him, the band shifts into the intro of something that sounds quick and rambunctious. Thorne backs up, raising one hand as he yells, "Let's make some noise!"

Nikolai doesn't know the music, but he gets the sense of it despite it being nearly drowned out by the crowd singing along with Throne. It's loud and fun and the beat gets under his skin. He eats while Heather and Seth talk, trading Empathic and Dreamwalking tips in too-loud voices, shouting over the music to hear each other. Nikita gives Nikolai a small, fond smile, and he nods. He can't help but love Seth when he's intense like this, earnest about his abilities and protective of Nikolai, and he knows Nikita feels exactly the same about Heather.

"Here." Nikita takes the empty plate from Nikolai's hand and gives him another laden with potato salad, hot corn on the cob with a stick shoved into it, and a steaming sausage. A fork sticks straight up from the potatoes, and he starts with them. It's all good. The sausage has a smoky, spicy bite to it, and the corn is sprinkled with a sweet-salty-spicy seasoning that sticks to the butter and char from the grill. Nikolai can't quite finish the sausage, so he holds it out; Seth turns to him and takes a bite.

When Seth kisses him, he tastes of smoke and sunshine, and Nikolai's heart thumps loudly. There are times and places for hiding, but this doesn't feel like one of them. They are finally getting their celebration, so he frames Seth's face with his hands and leans in, presses their foreheads together, then kisses him several more times.

He hears shouts and his name being called, but no one sounds angry. Everything about this day is full of joy.

Nikolai wonders if this is what it's like to be an Empath, to feel the emotion rolling off of everyone around them as if they're shouting pleasure to the wind. Seth's cheeks are flushed, his smile wide enough to crinkle his eyes.

"I need to help out here," Heather says, pointing to the grills where OPT Brothers and SigPsiEp Sisters are busy cooking and handing out food. Manning the grill with a pair of tongs in one hand, Carolyn gives her an urgent wave with the other; Heather turns back to Nikolai. "However, Nikita's not actually a Sister—"

"She lives in our room! She could still help," Carolyn interrupts.

Heather gives her a dirty look. "Nikita's not actually a Sister," she emphasizes, speaking to Nikolai and Seth, "so go have fun with her. There are games, and drinks, and Thorne and Rory will be finishing up soon if you want to see them."

"Oooh, Twister!" Nikita grips Nikolai's arm and pulls. "Come on! Lawn Twister is fun!"

"Lawn Twister?" Seth asks, letting her pull them along in her wake.

The path twists and turns, taking them to the far side of the Quad under a circle of trees where several mats decorated with brightly colored dots have been set up. Groups of four people surround each of the mats but one, where a single woman waits. As they approach, Nikita waves to the man standing off to the side, running the game. "Can we join in?"

He gestures in assent, and Nikita runs up. "Hi, I'm Nik, and I'll be your partner."

"Be my guest," the other girl says.

Nikita goes over the rules quickly, and Nikolai vaguely remembers having a game like this when he was young. It sounds easy enough.

Nikolai sheds his shoes and socks and steps onto the mat. The referee calls out, "Right hand red!" and Seth crouches down to put his right hand directly in front of his right foot. Nikolai has to twist across Seth to reach a red dot, but his height helps.

The game goes quickly after that.

Nikita's partner is twisty, and Nikita's height gives her an advantage. Nikolai and Seth end up hopelessly tangled, but the game is easier for them because neither of them care where they touch each other. They press together closely, and they don't fall until Nikita's foot slips and she pushes against Nikolai's foot on her way down.

All four of them end up in a heap, laughing as the referee yells out that they've been eliminated. Of the ten mats laid out, they are the eighth to fall, so they have a short chance to rest before the final team is declared the winner of the round.

Apparently the winner gets a tiny pair of stuffed animals, which the winning team raises high while everyone cheers.

They play another few rounds before Nikolai is feeling overstretched and achy and his ribs hurt from laughing. They don't win, but that's okay. The last round, he ends up in a heap with Seth straddling him, and he reaches up to pull Seth into a kiss while people cheer and egg them on.

It's very much worth it.

Music continues to play in the background, changing every half hour or so as one band shuffles off and another on. At one point Trish takes the stage—just her and a guitar—but it's no less rollicking and fun once she starts to sing.

When someone presses a bucket of water into Nikolai's hands and points him toward Nikita, he doesn't ask questions. She turns to face him with some kind of plastic gun in her hands, and a memory of backyard water fights surfaces from his childhood. He manages to upend most of the bucket over her head while she sprays him in the face. She has better range, and he's soaked by the time he reaches Seth; he tries to hide behind him, laughing.

They end up with their chests bare and their shirts over their shoulders to dry while they soak up the warm spring sun.

"I wouldn't mind walking miles on a day like today," Nikolai comments as he stands to one side, breathing in deeply and resting finally. The water war rages on, but they've managed to get out of the way.

"We've eaten. We'll eat again. We have a bed. A nomadic life's easy with help like that," Seth notes. He squeezes Nikolai's hand and presses against him shoulder to shoulder.

"We know it's not always like this here, but right now it's full of joy," Nikolai replies. He soaks in the ambient happiness like it's sunlight.

"Not for everyone," Seth observes. He shoulders Nikolai, then looks off to one side. Nikolai follows his gaze and spots a short, skinny girl under a tree, her arms crossed tightly and her head tilted as if she looks at an invisible person nearby. She speaks in hushed tones, dark brows furrowed and her expression angry.

"She is not full of joy," Seth says. "Hey," he calls out, approaching her. Nikolai sticks close by.

She silences abruptly and turns to face them. "Hey…" She draws the word out uncertainly.

"Seth. Nikolai." Seth taps his own chest, then nudges Nikolai. "We met at your Coven thing." Right—Nikolai thought she looked familiar. That explains why Seth wanted to talk to her, considering they already kind of know her. "You seemed pretty angry then, too."

"I'm Pels." Her gaze narrows. "Empath?"

Seth nods.

Pels rolls her eyes, making a dismissive gesture. "Stay out of my head. I don't need your help."

"Why are you here if you don't want to be?" he asks.

"I'm not into crowds," Pels mutters. She glares and gestures to the space beside her. "I'm here because I have to be."

Nikolai furrows his brow, trying to see what she pointed at. There's nothing there. "We don't like crowds much either," Nikolai admits. He's finally reached the point where the number of people around him doesn't leave him watching the shadows for movement, but it's still difficult. "We were on our own for long enough that having this many people around is unsettling. We're still enjoying it, though."

"Good for you," Pels mutters.

"Is it that you won't enjoy it, or that you don't want to enjoy it?" Seth asks. "Or is the risk that you might enjoy it, and that would change how you see yourself?"

"What the hell?" Pels asks.

Seth's pushing too hard, even if he might have a point. When Pels flinches, stepping away from the empty space, though, Nikolai has to wonder what other influences are going on in her life. She seems to be running from something other than them. One thing Nikolai definitely understands is how hard it is to let go and relax.

"You could seize the day," he offers. "It doesn't mean you have to—"

"Maybe I don't want to seize anything, and maybe I'm tired of people telling me how to live my life because they think I need things I don't necessarily need," Pels spits out, looking at the empty space rather than at Nikolai.

"Well, you never know when you're going to be whisked away to another world entirely," he says ruefully. "So if there's ever anything you might regret, deal with it first. Things can change fast."

"Don't I know it." She throws her arms up, and Nikolai gets a glimpse of darkness on her wrist. She moves too fast for him to see what it is, and she crosses her arms again quickly as if to hide it. "It's well-meaning advice, fine, but sometimes, I've got to—" She cuts off, swiveling to face the space on her other side. She jabs a finger into the air. "And you can shut up, too," she grumbles. "Look, I've got to…" Her voice trails off, hands uncrossing to hang loose by her side.

Nikolai follows her gaze across the Quad. She's staring at the barbecue, where Alaric is standing with Mac, handing out plates of food.

"If you're hungry, you should eat," Seth says.

Pels jerks back, blinking as if she forgot they were there. She sighs and bows her head, hair falling into her face. "Maybe I could eat," she decides.

Her shoulders hunch, her hands shoved into the pockets of a light jacket she probably doesn't need in this weather. She makes a beeline toward the barbecue.

Seth's brow is furrowed. "I can't figure her out. I hope that wasn't too pushy."

"I get the feeling that no matter what anyone says to her, it's too pushy," Nikolai observes. "Rory said she was working some things out, and I think some of that has to do with whatever—or whoever—she was yelling at."

"Weird Talent," Seth says, and Nikolai has to agree.

The afternoon passes in a haze of more spring sun and more food. There's a break in the music as dusk falls, and Nikolai and Seth are pressed into helping OPT and SigPsiEp at the grills. Everyone seems to want dinner served at the same time. They work while dusk slips into darkness, until everyone is sated and the grill is shutting down while the headliners of the day take the stage. Nikolai has no idea who they are, but the energy in the Quad rises to an even higher level. The crowd screams, calling out names, and on the stage, the band setting up chats back. Nikolai gets the impression they're famous, not a local group like Rory and Thorne.

They play, and the excitement reaches a crescendo, the screams almost deafening. Seth's expression is alight with pleasure, and he sways as Nikolai wraps his arms around him, moving to the music.

Nikolai and Seth are cast in shadows, only the lights from the stage illuminating the Quad, and it's strange not to be afraid of the darkness. They can enjoy the intimacy and the pleasure of being out in public with a crowd while cocooned in their own space.

"Nikolai." The voice is a soft whisper from the darkness.

Seth goes stiff in Nikolai's arms, and they turn as one.

"Nikolai," the voice comes again, and a figure steps out of the deepest darkness and into the faint light. She's person-shaped, but still shadowy, her form more cohesive than a Shadow's usually is. She reaches out, then drops her hand. "I'm not starving," she says softly. "I haven't killed anyone. I promise."

"Chelsea," Nikolai says, and the shadowy head nods.

She's alive. Great news for Pawel, and possibly for them as well. Nikolai swallows hard. Where his hands wrap around Seth, he can feel Seth's heartbeat ratchet faster.

"Are you here for—?"

"I've figured out how to take you home," she says. "It's not the same as before, but I can do it. If you help me, then I can help you."

Nikolai's heart stutters. They can go home. "Of course," he says quickly. He holds his hand out to her and doesn't flinch when her shadowed fingers drift over his skin. "Whatever you need."

From the journal of Valentine Munroe.

It's been ten years since the Shadows first came.

Ethan just turned 18. As we celebrated last night, I remembered it was barely a few days after his eighth birthday when Miriam and Jack died. Marybelle was six years old when she became a part of our small family. I lost Edward not long after.

It's been a long, strange road since then, but it's been worth it.

When Alia first asked me to come to Havenhill, I didn't stop to think about it. I packed our things, put us in a car with everything I could carry, and hit the road. I knew how to get here—it was still Haverhill then—from Burlington without worrying about prying human eyes. We arrived to find the town in chaos, as Alia tried to build a community that was safe for Clan and Mages, and all Lineage and Emergent Talents.

Long ago, I had told her that should she ever need me, I would be by her side, and I was.

We worked hard together for those first years. It took time to bring in the Mages who had the Talents we needed and to lay down those first borders.

Those years were difficult. Marybelle missed her parents. She woke crying in the night, and that would set off Ethan, and he'd scream for his father. Alia carried the weight of the world during the daylight hours, but in the darkness of night, she would care for my children as if they were her own. She opened her house to us.

She opened her heart more slowly.

I knew, of course.

I knew long ago, the same as I knew that Alia was in a place where there was too much expected of her for her to be able to do what she wished. I loved her to distraction, but she could never let herself have the luxury of admitting she loved me back.

Once the world ended, Alia had no one left to answer to. Her parents were gone. The Clan elders who had controlled her life stepped back, allowing her to take actions that previously would have been considered taboo. She used Mages and magic to protect Clan, and she integrated our worlds. All Talent is welcome in Havenhill.

It took two years, but she welcomed me to her bed.

We have built this place together, and when I look at Havenhill, I see our hearts laid bare. We share our children—Ethan and Marybelle call her Alia, but she's a mother to them. Everyone here is family. All of them, no matter when they arrived, no matter their Talent. Each and every person in Havenhill is a part of this community that we've built, and Alia is our matriarch.

I suppose that makes me the consort.

It's been difficult watching my son and niece grow to adulthood in this world. They were supposed to have simple and predictable lives. They would grow up in Burlington, then leave for school. If the world were the one we'd expected, I would be dropping Ethan off at PHU in the fall. I went there. Most of us do. Did. It's gone now, and that makes me sad.

Pine Hills University is where I first met Alia.

I'm not sure why we—Clan, Mage, Talents from the surrounding area—were drawn to PHU. It was safe, like neutral ground. I moved into my dorm freshman year, and there she was, this huge new part of my life. I never looked back.

I trusted the road she set me on, and my heart broke when she retreated from me. I healed, yes. I fell in love again. I married. I had Ethan. But I never forgot Alia, and when the world fell apart and she needed me, I went to her.

There is a point when you move forward, one day after another, because it is the only direction in which you can go. We had to move forward after the Shadows came, or we wouldn't have moved at all. But somewhere along the way, which direction was "forward" changed. We no longer had to devote our all to surviving; we had a path to new beginnings in front of us, new choices we could make.

Now that we are here, I can't imagine there ever having been another direction we could have gone.

Home

44

Pawel stands talking to two nurses at the station in the maternity ward of Unity Central Hospital. Chelsea lingers in the shadows in one corner, hovering near a young couple sitting on a couch, an infant cradled in their arms. She reaches out, then pulls her hand back while glancing at Nikolai.

She doesn't look guilty, but she does seem upset, though Nikolai can't see her features well.

Seth shifts his stance, makes a face. "This is not somewhere I ever expected to find ourselves," he mutters.

Nikolai has to agree. Hospitals are alien to him, and the maternity ward was never on his radar. "She led us here," he says, "and we made a promise to her. The question is, how are we even going to get on the floor?"

They'd been stopped the second they got off the elevator, and Nikolai still isn't sure how Pawel convinced the nurses to listen rather than simply making them leave.

Given that it's been a good ten minutes and they're still arguing while Nikolai, Seth, and Chelsea wait, it doesn't look promising.

"We can't have people doing rituals in the hospital," one of the nurses says firmly. "I'm sorry, Professor Szczek, but that's a hard rule."

Pawel rocks back on his heels, his hands shoved into his pockets. "Is there still a nurse named Jackie Ellenwood working here?"

The two nurses look at each other. "She's moved to a different department. Why?"

"Could you let her know I'm here? And that this has to do with the birth of my son Conor and the disappearance of my girlfriend Chelsea." Pawel leans on the counter, his attention fully on the two nurses even when Chelsea makes a soft, sibilant noise. He smiles, and now that the bags have eased under his eyes, they crinkle attractively. "Please."

The younger of the two picks up the phone; Nikolai can't hear her low conversation.

Soon, another nurse approaches from down a hallway and joins them. Her badge has a stripe of color on it, and her scrubs have purple pants instead of green. Her gray hair is pulled back sharply into a bun, but smile lines appear around her eyes when she spots Pawel. "It's good to see you. How is Conor?"

"In for a hell of a surprise whenever I get around to filling him in on everything that's happened," Pawel says dryly. "Thank you, Jackie, for taking care of us."

"You looked so lost." Jackie shakes her head, spreading her hands for a hug that Pawel accepts. She's taller than he is, and she tucks him in close, patting the back of his head. "I'm sure you've done fine in the years since. You've grown a bit. Don't look quite so much like you're barely out of high school."

"I was barely out of high school," Pawel admits with a rueful smile. He gestures, and Nikolai and Seth approach carefully while Chelsea drifts closer on the other side. "We need your help."

"I heard you've been pestering Naomi and Beryl," Jackie says. She crosses her arms, looking down at him. "What is it you expect me to—?" She cuts off, attention shifting sharply to where Chelsea hovers near Pawel's shoulders. "What is—?"

"Short version: Chelsea didn't run away, she Emerged as a Shadowwalker," Pawel says. "She won't hurt anyone."

"A Deathstalker?" Jackie takes a step back, her hands up.

"Not exactly," Chelsea whispers. "It's complicated. I only want my soul back, and I think I left it here."

"She's not a danger to the parents or infants," Pawel adds. "None of us are. When Chelsea Emerged as a Shadowwalker, the part of her you see now was split from her soul. Since that happened here, this is the most likely place for us to be able to reach her soul and restore it to her. She feels a pull to the hospital."

Chelsea smiles slightly and makes a soft sound. It's weird and eerie and makes Nikolai's skin crawl.

Jackie looks past Pawel to Nikolai and Seth, her gaze skirting away from Chelsea. Nikolai tries to appear as unassuming and harmless as possible. Jackie's lips purse, discomfort evident in the way she moves stiffly past them with long strides. "I'll take them back. It's on me."

"Thank you," Pawel murmurs.

"I owed you for…you know," Jackie replies, just as softly. "It doesn't bear talking about now. But if you need anything more than this, it's your turn to owe me."

"Understood."

Nikolai trails behind them, Seth by his side, their fingers almost tangling but not quite. Chelsea leads the way, unbothered by the bright lights as she floats through the hall. She rounds a corner, then pulls up sharply with a loud inhalation. She presses her hands in twin blots of darkness against the window. "Here," she whispers. "I know this place."

In the room on the other side of the window are neat lines of bassinets, most with a small child nestled within. Some of the infants sleep; others are fussing and crying. One is empty, and a nurse sits in a rocking chair off to one side, giving an infant a bottle.

"I have never seen so many babies in one place," Seth murmurs. "Hell, I haven't seen this many babies ever, not since the Split."

Jackie gives him a look, frowning.

"The nursery, of course." Pawel rubs his face with his hand. "This is the busiest place, and the one place I can almost guarantee they won't let us do a ritual. Chelsea, are you sure?"

Her shadowed head nods; she doesn't look away from the infants.

Nikolai closes his eyes and reaches for the Dreamscape. This isn't like the Berman house. The Dreamscape doesn't linger close. But as soon as he reaches for it, it's within his grasp. It shimmers like an illusion at the edges of his sight, yet it's also wrapped around Pawel, Chelsea, and this spot.

Pawel draws Jackie away; the shimmer thins, falling away.

"Pawel," Nikolai says.

Pawel stops and turns, taking a few steps back. The sense strengthens again when he draws closer.

That gives Nikolai an idea. "Chelsea, can you go with Pawel?" Nikolai waves them both off. Pawel steps away first; Chelsea takes time to pull herself from the glass. Once she's with Pawel again, the liminal lines return. They aren't as strong as before, but they are visible when they are together.

"We can use a different room, as long as its near here," Nikolai suggests, "and as long as the two of you are together."

"Do you know what to do?" Chelsea asks.

Only vaguely, based on what he's heard about when Carolyn retrieved Mattie's soul. But he's relatively sure it will work, and that it will be safe. And that it absolutely depends on— "Yes," he says. "If we have a space where we can do a ritual, and if Carolyn is here, we can do it."

Jackie's mouth is pinched, her expression tight.

"Is there an available room?" Pawel asks. His tone is careful, as if he's trying not to poke too hard.

"What, exactly, are you planning to do?" Jackie replies. She leads them down the hall, stopping at the only closed door. Upon opening it, there is one bed inside and far too many machines. "For cases when we have someone we want to keep a close eye on," she says. "Luckily, we don't any patients like that right now. Even if I say yes, you'll need to be quick. There's always someone giving birth in labor and delivery, and we are always bringing new people onto the floor. We have a quick turnaround here. So what, exactly, are you planning to do?"

"Seth and I will call Carolyn," Nikolai says. Pawel moves closer to the window with Jackie and Chelsea, already explaining, while Nikolai and Seth remain close to the door. Nikolai puts his phone on speaker, reduces the volume, then presses Carolyn's name.

"Hello?" she answers. "Nikolai. You left the Festival early last night. Is everything okay with Pawel? Am I on speaker?"

"You are." Nikolai takes a deep breath. He should have planned ahead and reached out to Carolyn before now. "Chelsea showed up and said she's ready to take us back, but she needs her soul first. We need your help."

"My help?"

"You worked with Del to bring Mattie back, right?" Seth asks. "That means you can work with Nikolai to do the same thing for Chelsea. The split changed after we fixed things, so we need to do this before we can go home. Please, Carolyn."

He makes it sound so simple. Nikolai hopes it's anywhere near that simple when they actually do it.

"I have no idea how I did it before—"

"We need to try," Seth interrupts her. "We're at the maternity ward at Unity Central Hospital. Chelsea says her soul is here. Nikolai says—"

"The Dreamscape shimmers here. There's a liminal space around where Chelsea thinks her soul is, and around Chelsea and Pawel when they're together. She's linked to him, and as long as we're close to where she was split from her soul, I think we can step into the Dreamscape. The tough part will be getting back out," Nikolai says. He's heard the story of how Mattie's soul was re-fused to her Shadow; he knows how it worked before. He suspects he even understands why the other people present at the Berman house that day went with them physically to the liminal space where Mattie's soul was.

If he's right, Seth and Pawel might travel into the Dreamscape this time, too.

"I'll be there." There's a rustling sound in the background, then the call abruptly drops silent.

When Nikolai looks up from the phone, Jackie is staring at him from the other side of the room.

"Are you absolutely positive that this will not affect the people on this floor—adults and children alike?" Jackie asks.

"As sure as I can be," Nikolai replies. There are risks, of course. But from what he understands and what he can see here, he suspects that once the ritual is invoked, they won't be in the hospital any longer.

Pawel's head snaps up, his mouth open. "Jackie, step back," he instructs, and waits for her to do so. Nikolai sees an image of Carolyn's room, like a dream superimposed against the backdrop of the hospital room, then the illusion falls away and Carolyn is standing beside Pawel.

She tucks a piece of paper into the small purse she wears slung across her body and withdraws another paper and unfolds it. "Okay," she says. "I'm ready when you are."

Jackie's eyes are wide. She looks from Pawel to Carolyn and back again.

"It's for the best if you wait outside the room," Pawel says to Jackie. "Any idea how far?" He directs this question to Nikolai.

"The liminal space is pretty tight around the two of you," Nikolai gestures to Chelsea and Pawel. "So Jackie could probably stay in the room if she needs to. However, she should be as far from us as possible because opening the Dreamscape won't be as exact as what Carolyn did to travel. The closer we are to the door, the better, so maybe over there, by the window?" He points, eyeballing the distance. The door will be a barrier for anyone in the hall outside, and the length of the room will be enough to keep Jackie out of the Dreamscape bubble he expects Chealsea and Pawel's liminal space to open into.

"I'd rather be in the room." Jackie relocates to where Nikolai pointed, leaning against the window ledge. She crosses her arms and jerks her chin toward where Carolyn waits at the door. "Go on then. Let's get this done."

"I'll let you know the outcome," Pawel promises.

"You think you're leaving," Jackie says, her tone flat.

"I think we're all leaving," Pawel responds. "The last time we did this ritual, we went into the Dreamscape in one place and came out in another."

Carolyn waves the piece of paper in her hand. "I've warned everyone in at SigPsiEp. This is assuming we can repeat what we did before."

Seth's touch to his back grounds Nikolai. "I'm ready," he says.

Nikolai reaches for the liminal outline of the Dreamscape that surrounds Pawel and Chelsea. Once he gets hold of it, he traces a trail it makes that leads out of the room and down the hall to the room with all the infants. The center is fixed on Pawel and Chelsea, which gives Nikolai the anchor he needs. Pawel reaches for Chelsea's hand, and the Dreamscape blooms into a bright shimmer that Nikolai suspects only he can see. He grabs it and snaps it into place.

The room changes.

Chelsea stands by the door, her hand on the knob and the door half open. She is wholly human, no longer wreathed in shadows. Her hospital gown gaps in the back, showing serviceable underwear that she doesn't appear to care is visible. She holds a pole on wheels in her other hand, a bag hanging from it, a slender tube leading to an IV on her arm. Her hair is pulled back, wisps escaping in tangles around her face, and her skin is pale.

"Come on," she says. "I want to see our son."

Pawel stands there, mouth open slightly. "Chelsea," he whispers.

"That's who I am. Hasn't changed, even though I suppose someone is going to be calling me 'Mommy' soon enough. When he can talk. Not you." Chelsea lets go of the door to stab a finger in Pawel's direction.

When he doesn't budge, she lets go of the door and it bangs shut. She grabs her IV stand and moves closer to him. "What is it? Are you afraid of being a father?"

"Look at me," Pawel whispers. "Look at them, Chelsea."

Her brow furrows, and she slowly reaches up to thread her fingers through his bangs. She pinches a hair and plucks it, grinning when he makes a face. "Gray hair," she announces. "You'd think you were the one giving birth, not me."

She spares a brief glance for Nikolai, gaze drifting to Seth and Carolyn. Her mouth parts, as though she's about to say something, but the door swings open behind her, and she turns, hands reaching out for the bassinet on wheels being brought in by a nurse. "Here he is!"

"Do you think she realizes?" Seth murmurs.

Nikolai shakes his head. "Was it like this with Mattie?"

Carolyn lowers the piece of paper in her hand. "A little. Her trapped soul was stuck at the time when she Emerged. Mattie was a little girl. This is the Chelsea who just gave birth. But Mattie cared that the people she recognized were older. Chelsea doesn't seem to care that there are strangers here with Pawel."

"Maybe her soul's entire focus was on how much she missed Pawel," Seth suggests.

Chelsea grabs Pawel's hand and pulls him to where the bassinet sits, a ghostly nurse nearby.

"We need to go." They are all in the Dreamscape. The longer they stay here, the more Nikolai worries how it will affect Seth and Pawel. "We need to take her with us and go." He looks to Carolyn; this is her part of the ritual.

"You'll see my room in a minute, and when you see it, you have to go into it. And take her with you," she says to Pawel, waiting for him to acknowledge her words. She looks at Nikolai. "You and I will leave last, since I have to keep the door open and you're in charge of the Dreamscape."

She focuses on the piece of paper in her hand, and the image of Carolyn's room blooms to their right, her bed visible with books scattered across it. The pictures on the wall are crisp and clear, as solid as the Dreamscape around them.

Pawel touches Chelsea's arm, sliding his fingers down to take her hand. "I need you to come with me."

"But what about—?"

"He's fine. I promise you'll see him again." Pawel's voice is choked. "Chelsea. Please."

Her smile is wide and trusting. She touches his cheek lightly. "You're my best friend," she says. "I'd follow you anywhere." She lets him lead the way, stepping into the image of Carolyn's room, with Seth close behind.

Carolyn holds out one hand, and Nikolai clasps it. For a moment, he sees the Dreamscape, her room, and the window of the hospital room with Jackie staring at them. He raises his free hand to Jackie in a shallow wave by way of saying goodbye, then follows Carolyn through the illusion and into her room.

Pawel clasps Chelsea to him, one hand cradling the back of her head, his forehead bent to touch hers. He murmurs something Nikolai can't hear, and Chelsea's shoulders shake with tears. She's no longer the pale girl in a hospital gown, nor the woman made of shadows. Instead she's wearing jeans and a T-shirt that seem all too normal, despite her bare feet and tangled hair.

"We did it," Seth says, and Pawel glances up, eyes wide to see them there.

"We did it," he confirms. He steps back, his hands on Chelsea's shoulders. She lowers both hands to press against her stomach, bending forward but not quite doubling over. "Chelsea." She lifts red-rimmed eyes to look at him, her shoulders still shaking. "It's been about nine years."

With a low cry, she pushes close to him again; he wraps his arms around her and holds on tight.

Nikolai doesn't think they'll be doing anything other than this any time soon. "We should give them some privacy."

They step into the hall, though they leave the door open. Chatter echoes from other spaces in the house. With Pawel and Chelsea still in view and the Dreamscape not far from Nikolai's mind, it feels like standing between two worlds.

"Why can't you do that for us?" Seth says, gesturing at the door. "Use one of your images and open up a portal back to our house. Our home."

"I can't reach your world," Carolyn reminds him. "I tried to get home that way when we first arrived there, remember? I couldn't reach here. I couldn't even reach Kit or Serina. That's not how my Talent works. Maybe if I'm physically in the Dreamscape, like we were—"

"We could try," Seth says. "As soon as we're ready, you could—"

"It doesn't work like that," Nikolai says. "Remember, when we went into the Dreamscape during the ritual to fix the split, you couldn't come with us. I fully intended for you to be there as my anchor, and you weren't."

"Then why—?"

"Because of Chelsea's soul," Nikolai says. "That's been the difference both times that non-Dreamwalkers have gone into the Dreamscape. They've been pulled in because there was a Shadowwalker accompanying them. That must be part of their Talent. I think the only way for us to go home is for Mattie or Chelsea to take us. And I don't think Mattie knows how, so we need Chelsea's help."

Nikolai and Carolyn share a knowing glance. Maybe someday she'll have that ability, too, but she doesn't know how yet.

He glances toward Pawel, still wrapped around Chelsea like a comforting blanket.

"I don't think Pawel's going to give Jackie an update any time soon, so we should contact her." Nikolai hesitates, not sure how to best do that.

"We'll look up the phone number and call," Carolyn offers. She pushes the door mostly closed, giving Pawel and Chelsea a little privacy.

"We can't do this ritual for every Shadowwalker," Seth murmurs. They follow Carolyn down the stairs.

"We can't, but we can try to publicize the information on how to reunite the Shadows with their souls. There will be others who can help." Nikolai thinks of Grace, who also lost a friend after they Emerged as a Shadowwalker. "We know they can be healed. We'll make sure other Dreamwalkers know as well."

45

Nikolai and Seth spend Sunday night on the floor of Rory and Alaric's room. Alaric stays with Chris, and Rory stays with Kit, so they have a tiny measure of privacy that lasts until Nikita realizes they're there. She helps them collect and print as many photos of their visit as they can, placing them in a photo album over the course of the evening. When they're done, she lingers as if afraid they'll disappear when she isn't looking.

"We won't leave without saying goodbye," Nikolai promises, hugging her. She clings to him, and his shoulder is wet when she finally steps back.

Nikita pats his shoulders, then turns and hugs Seth just as hard. "You'd better not," she mumbles. "I'll see you tomorrow, then."

Seth locks the door when she leaves, and Nikolai draws him down, into their nest on the floor.

Monday morning when they awaken, they have texts that Pawel sent hours before: *Come home for breakfast. Chelsea is here to discuss the details of your crossing.*

Chelsea waits for them in Pawel's foyer and greets them by sliding in close, one hand raised toward Seth. She yanks it back when he flinches. "I won't hurt you," she protests. "I can't, now. I promise. I had eggs for breakfast."

"No offense, but since the last time you touched me, you were feeding, I think I'd rather—" Seth cuts off, making a shooing motion.

"Understood." Chelsea backs away, hands behind her back and head tilted down. Long curly hair falls in her face, hiding rosy cheeks. She looks healthy and very, very alive. Unlike Mattie, the shadows don't seem to cling to her; she appears wholly human, though Nikolai knows she isn't. "I'm sorry. I was starving. That doesn't make it right but might make it understandable."

"I understand and I still don't like it," Seth says curtly.

"I have bagels." Pawel moves between them, one hand on Chelsea's shoulder to nudge her farther from Seth and Nikolai. "Bagels, cream cheese, smoked salmon, and eggs. I'm guessing no one thought to feed you before they scattered for their classes."

Nikolai raises both eyebrows. "Now that you're not stressing, you're a mother hen?"

"I'm a single dad. I'm always like this," Pawel says as he ushers them into the kitchen. "I was distracted. And when I stop sleeping—"

"He's always been like that, too," Chelsea says with a small smile. "When we were freshmen, he pulled two all-nighters in a row because of a report he'd put off until the end of the semester. Somewhere around the thirty-six-hour mark, he stopped eating. His roommate realized that if we put something next to him, he'd try to eat it. He had a lot of interesting ideas of things to try. Luckily Pawel isn't allergic to anything."

"Do you remember the time since—?" Seth cuts off as Chelsea's expression clouds and she takes another step away from them. "That's a yes. I can feel it."

"I remember everything," she says. "Some things better than others. But yes, I know what it feels like to suck a person's soul out, to feel the moment that they take their last breath. I will never be able to forget that. I think Mattie both regrets and misses it. I regret it so damned much. I'm thankful that I didn't hurt anyone I loved."

"It isn't unusual for an Emergent Shadowwalker to devour their family," Pawel murmurs. "We were very lucky."

"I couldn't," Chelsea says. "So I ran." She moves into the kitchen, standing on the far side to give them space. She crosses her arms, hunching around herself. "I know how to take you home, Nikolai and Seth. It isn't the same as it was, but I can get there."

Nikolai takes the plate Pawel hands him, sitting when Pawel motions toward the table. Once he and Seth are seated, Pawel pulls out the fourth chair. Chelsea takes it cautiously and sits as well.

Nikolai ignores her as best he can and eats.

"Tell them what you told me this morning," Pawel directs.

"I spent the night going in and out of the Dreamscape," she says. She folds her hands on the table, fingers entwined. "The split is no longer a danger, as far as I can tell. It is…healed, a place through which normal Shadowwalkers can slip between the worlds. I practiced going between this world and the others I could reach. I think I can take you with me." She looks at them, her eyes wide. "After you all healed it, I couldn't get into it, not without my soul. The soulless ones are kept out."

"That's good news." Nikolai can't assume that the Shadows are gone from his world. It can't be that simple. But there won't be growing numbers of them, and if others Emerge, they should be like Chelsea and Mattie are now, not like how they were. They have a chance.

"What about the other—?" Seth is gripping his fork so tightly that his fingers are white. Nikolai feels the worry coming from him, uncontrolled and almost angry. "Our third twin?"

"It's there. I found it." She whispers it like a secret, a soft laugh at the end. "There are people there. I might visit someday, to see if we can help them heal."

"Tell them to meet us in the Dreamscape," Nikolai says. "We should continue to grow the alliance, to reach out to and learn about the different worlds. We need to keep this from happening again."

Pawel sips his coffee, eyes alight with pride. He nods at Nikolai's words.

"I will," Chelsea promises. "I don't think I can stay there long. I feel tied to this world." She glances at Pawel.

Nikolai opens himself to the Dreamscape, and he can see the shimmering light around them, binding them. She's not wrong.

"So I need to take you soon, and I don't think I can be gone long," she says. "I need to figure out how to fit back into this world now, and how connected I am to it."

Seth lowers the fork. "So what you're saying is we go now, or not at all."

Chelsea blinks. "You can finish breakfast."

Nikolai holds back a snort of laughter. After all this time waiting, suddenly they're supposed to hurry up. "We don't want to delay long."

Something knocks into his foot under the table, and when he glances over, Seth is looking at him.

Nikolai isn't lying. He wants to go home. He wants to get back to Mikhail, Josef, and the new family he and Seth have found in Havenhill. He wants to settle in to his house and his future with Seth. He wants to create his space and move forward without feeling like there's something holding him back.

Seth places his hand on the table, palm up, and Nikolai takes it. He can't help but reflect that they've been in this world for three weeks. They've met dozens of people and made new friends. The only ones he's certain he'll see again are Nikita and Del. Once he and Seth leave this world, they won't be coming back. He'll miss the people he's met.

It's always been so easy to think about going home.

It's strangely hard to think about leaving here.

"Oh," Nikolai says under his breath as he sets down the remainder of his bagel.

"Go pack," Pawel says. "Finish breakfast when your appetite returns. Focus on making sure you don't forget anything, and I'll get in touch with people and ask them to come over. Is there anyone in particular—?"

"We promised Nikita we wouldn't leave without saying goodbye," Seth says.

"Everyone." As soon as Nikolai says it, he knows it isn't possible. It's Monday. They have classes. Some of them aren't even at Pine Hills University, like Del. Some of them he barely knows, and some he's closer to. But he's afraid that if he starts naming names, he'll forget someone important.

Seth squeezes Nikolai's hand. "It would be nice to see as many of them as possible, but if they can't get here, we understand."

They have so much to carry home. Pawel brings in a large duffel, and Seth and Nikolai stuff it full of clothes for all seasons. Nikolai lingers over the photo album before carefully sliding it into the duffel next to a copy of Carolyn's notes on Talent and a notebook he'd started when they were spending time in the special collections room of the library.

Knowledge is one way to bring light into the darkness. Nikolai wants to bring back as much as he can.

Once their bag is packed, Pawel adds a rolling case with the zipper stretched tight to their luggage. The books inside are dusty, and Valentine's printed notes for Val take up a significant amount of space. Nikolai's glad the case has wheels; he wouldn't want to carry that much weight.

He pulls out his phone and sends a quick text to Valentine. *Thank you for the books and notes. I'll make sure Val gets them. I'm sure she'll appreciate them.*

Their old, beat-up backpacks hold novels, games, and snacks they've come to enjoy.

With everything else full, Pawel gives them another, empty, rolling case. "People will bring gifts," he says.

"I hope we're able to carry all this," Nikolai mutters. "In theory it sounds good, but—"

"If I can go, the rest can go," Seth tells him, nudging his shoulder. "We didn't come through naked."

"The clothes we're wearing and the several bags of luggage we're carrying are very different," Nikolai mutters. "This is magic, not logic. Dreams are never logical."

"But they are usually either nightmares or wish fulfillment, and right now, this has to be the latter," Seth says firmly. "We're going home."

People drift over to Pawel's house during the next several hours. Pawel stays with them. Nikolai wonders if he's supposed to be somewhere else, but he doesn't tell him to leave.

Alaric drops off a bag with skeins of yarn and instructions to give them to Alia when they reach Havenhill.

Trish brings a bottle of whiskey. "As a homecoming gift for whoever you think needs it most," she says. Nikolai resolves to save it for when Josef and Amaranth get married; it'll be good for celebration. He also takes the tool bag she hands him, filled with various kinds of tape and other useful consumables. He's sure it'll be appreciated.

Nate brings a takeout box filled with scones and muffins, while Dax carries a plastic box of homemade cookies. When he cracks it open, the rich scents of peanut butter and chocolate invade the room. He closes it again and sets it into the suitcase with a small smile.

"According to my mom, someone's been craving those," Dax says. "Not a clue who, so it's up to you to distribute them."

Cass doesn't bring a gift, but she surprises Nikolai by stalking up to him and staring at him, head cocked and ponytail swinging, then throwing her arms around him and hugging him hard. He slowly puts his hands on her back, holding on as she whispers, "Do not get eaten by a Shadow. Apparently people would miss you if you do."

He has no idea how he made this impression on Cass, but she moves from him to Seth, whispering something in his ear as well before she finally steps away. Her chin lifts and her eyes shine with unshed tears as she tucks her hand into Dax's before they head out.

Mac arrives with Nikita and Heather in tow. "Carolyn is with Kit, Serina, and Rory," she says. "Something they couldn't get out of; I don't know what. But we wanted to be here when you go."

"You've got the album, right?" Nikita reaches for Nikolai; he cracks the duffel open to show it to her before he wrestles the zipper closed again. "You won't forget us."

"I don't think we could forget this if we tried," Seth points out. "It's been the weirdest adventure of a lifetime."

"It'll feel like a dream someday," Nikita says. "Maybe even more for you than for me and Nikolai. We'll see each other again, but in ten or twenty years, you'll be like 'did that really happen?' when you think of us. You'll know it did, because life will get better in your world. But it'll seem soft and in the distance."

"She's not wrong." Mac's voice is gentle, her smile wry. "But that's true of anything that happens before a major change. My life before the Emergence seems like a faraway dream sometimes, and that was only eleven years ago."

Nikolai thinks back on his own world before the Split, how distant those memories feel. Seth nudges him, and Nikolai nods. "I know what you mean," he agrees. "It may eventually feel far away, but we won't forget."

There's a soft knock on the door; it opens, and Chelsea lifts a hand in greeting as she enters. "Are you ready?"

They have more luggage than it seems possible to carry; it feels more like moving day than moving on. He considers asking Chelsea to carry something, but she stands with her arms wrapped around her center, looking uncertain, and he realizes that she probably won't even leave the Dreamscape with them. They shoulder their backpacks, then Seth grabs the large duffel and a suitcase, leaving the last bag for Nikolai.

"I think we're ready," Nikolai says.

Nikita throws her arms around him, and Nikolai rocks under the additional weight. "I'll see you in our Dreams," she says.

He lets her hold on as long as she wants. When she finally disengages, he promises, "We'll be fine. Life will be good."

"Better be."

"I'll take these guys and get far enough away that we don't have to worry about being swept up in your wake," Mac says. She shoos Nikita and Heather out of the room, and as they pass Pawel, she grips his shoulder. "You, too. We don't want you leaving again."

"Go into the kitchen. I'll be down soon," Pawel agrees. "You're right, it's wisest to be at some distance. Everyone who falls on the Dreamwalker and traveler axis has the potential to get caught in magic like this."

Pawel and Chelsea's goodbye is intimate. There are no pronouncements of love, but they're still sweet and emotional as he holds her and kisses the top of her head. "Be safe," he says.

"I have to haunt you," she whispers, patting his chest as she steps away. "Don't worry, Pawel. I'll be back. We have unfinished business."

Her words seem like a strange way to discuss leaving a lover, but Pawel leaves the room without looking back.

Seth grabs Nikolai's hand and holds on tight; Nikolai clings back, unwilling to risk leaving him behind. "How do we make sure that I go into the Dreamscape?" Seth asks.

"We'll travel through the healed split," Chelsea says.

She holds out her hands, and they shuffle their bags so they can grasp her as she steps backward, taking them with her.

The transition is quick. One step they're in the spare bedroom, the next they stand on the Dreamscape path where it diverges into three. The breath between steps seems an instant and forever, and Nikolai is glad he didn't have to witness the actual trip this time.

Seth exhales roughly. "Okay, I'm here. I'm actually here."

They both are, and they still have all of their gear. It's working so far.

Chelsea lets go of them, stepping away and circling behind them so they have to move toward one of the paths. She points to the one Nikolai knows leads home. "I'll walk with you as far as I can," she says. "The Dreamscape knows where you belong. All you have to do is be close enough to wake up."

"Wait." Nikolai pauses because he needs to look at the third path. The two leading to his own and Nikita's worlds look the same, but the other is brighter than he remembers. Light filters through the leaves, and the branches no longer hang low enough to block the pathway. Along the forest floor, small dots of greenery have sprung up as if the path is regrowing. "It's healing."

Chelsea grins. "I told you it was. I'll give them your message, I promise."

Someday Nikolai might meet people from that world—might meet the person who is him and Nikita, whatever they are like. "Thank you. I'm looking forward to meeting people from that world. I'm glad it didn't die."

They set out walking, moving as briskly as they can with their heavy baggage. Chelsea moves behind them, almost skipping. She periodically looks off the path and delves into the foliage. She reminds Nikolai of Del.

They reach the tree marking the entrance to his and Seth's world more quickly, and far more easily, than he expects. Nikolai can feel the draw of his own world here, pulling him back. Sunshine gleams amidst the leaves; the dappling shadows flicker without malice. He could relax here and enjoy the Dreamscape. He doesn't feel the fear of darkness closing in on him.

Chelsea's expression sobers. "Hold on to him, Seth," she murmurs, crowding close to Nikolai.

Seth's hands rest on Nikolai's waist as he presses close from behind.

Chelsea frames Nikolai's face with her hands, drawing him down so she can gently press her lips to his forehead. "Wake up," she whispers.

And he does.

46

Sun spills across the room, filtering past the half-open curtains. Nikolai rolls over, and dust motes float up, sparkling in the sunbeam.

Seth groans, shoving a hand out. "Stop."

The backpacks and bags lie on the floor; they must have managed to drop them before collapsing on the bed. They're still dressed but lie tangled as if they've just woken on a regular morning. Nikolai sits up and counts the bags—they're all there.

More importantly, they're here—in their room, in the smaller of the two Benford houses. In Havenhill. "We're home," he says.

"Mm." Seth rubs at his eyes as he sits up. "My brain says I just woke up, but it looks like it's—" He hesitates. Nikolai walks to the window to pull the curtains wide.

"Late afternoon," Nikolai says. "About the same time as when we left Pawel's house." He assumes they have Chelsea to thank for them being in Havenhill instead of still in Unity. He doesn't know exactly how her traveling works, but it got them home.

He lifts the sash of the window, and sound filters in. Music plays somewhere in the distance, and the shouts remind him of the sugaring festival. When he leans out, he can't see any people, but there is a lazy column of smoke swirling into the sky. Maybe a bonfire was lit near Alia and Val's house.

He pulls his head back in and leaves the window open to let fresh air into the room. "Something's going on." He holds out his hand, and Seth takes it as Nikolai tugs him from the bed.

They take a moment to stand there, arms around each other, foreheads resting together. Nikolai draws Seth into a slow kiss; after, Seth pushes his glasses back up his nose.

Nikolai grabs a hoodie out of his backpack, and Seth finds a light jacket. By the time they've changed, there's a rumble of an engine outside, then someone bangs on the front door.

They exchange a look.

"The wards," Seth says.

"Probably." Their abrupt arrival from the Dreamscape most likely tripped some kind of alarm. He hurries out of the room, heads downstairs, and pulls the door open as the banging starts again.

Ethan stands there with his hand raised, mid-knock. Marybelle is behind him, and in the distance, the Jeep is rumbling down the dirt road.

Ethan lowers his hand slowly.

"We're back." Nikolai barely gets the words out before Ethan is hugging him, Marybelle crowding close too. They drag Seth in as well, but the embrace only lasts as long as it takes for Mikhail to park the Jeep and get up the front steps.

Nikolai and Seth are pulled out of the house, passed from Mikhail to Josef and Amaranth, and when Nikolai realizes his face is wet, he's not sure if he's crying or if his brothers are.

"We heard from a Dreamwalker in Utah," Ethan tells them. "Our Technopaths created—well, helped create—a network. And he said he had a message from you."

"Brett."

"Yes." Ethan grins. "He said you'd done it. That the world has been changed. There's news coming in from all over about it."

"I wasn't sure you'd be able to come back," Mikhail admits. "I'm glad you're here."

Seth tilts his head, pushing his glasses up his nose again. "Of course we came back," he tells them. "Our family is here. All we had to do was figure out how."

Nikolai laughs. It's not funny, but also, it is. He's a little afraid that if he gives in to all the complicated emotions rolling through him, he'll never come back from the laughter and tears.

Seth grabs his hand and holds on tight, always knowing when Nikolai needs an anchor, and Nikolai is thankful for him.

"Chelsea brought us back. The same Shadowwalker who got us thrown out in the first place," Nikolai explains. "After we healed the split, we needed to help her become…" He trails off, not sure how sum things up. "It's a long story, but she's like Mattie now. She knows how to travel and was able to bring us back. So we're here."

"You're here." Josef leans on his cane, his smile bright.

Amaranth hugs Nikolai again, her long hair tickling his cheek. "God, I'm glad you're back. You're just in time for May Day. We're all about new beginnings right now."

"Speaking of—" Josef cuts off, glancing at Amaranth. She steps back, moving into his space, her hand behind his back as she leans in close. "We set a date to kick Mikhail out of the house."

"You've got a spare room for your brother, right?" Mikhail asks. "I don't want to encroach on the honeymoon once these two are married in June."

"No," Seth says, ducking when Mikhail makes a mock grab for him. "We want our honeymoon phase, too."

"Are you getting married?" Mikhail points out.

"God no," Nikolai says, trying to school his expression to something less horrified when Seth laughs. "We're young. I mean, maybe, yes, someday, but honestly, I want to live in a house, just Seth and I, for a while. Without needing to worry that the darkness will eat us—and believe me, it's tried. I want to live a normal life."

"What passes for normal," Seth allows.

"The new normal," Ethan tells them. "Because what used to be 'normal' is changing."

Joyful shouts ring out from far away, and Nikolai wants to join in the celebration. But if he gets in the Jeep now, he can't hear Ethan's news. On the other hand, he doubts Josef'll want to walk all the way to the big house.

He turns in place, looking between the path and the road.

Josef catches the motion. "We can meet you there, if you want to walk," he offers.

"I'll walk with them," Mikhail says. "You and Amaranth take your time. I still need to convince them to give me that spare room."

"No," Seth says again, a little flatter than before, although he smiles when Mikhail does, as if they're both just teasing.

Nikolai wants to say that the path feels lighter than before, as if the wards don't weigh as heavily on Havenhill. He doubts that's true; it has to be his own perception, the knowledge that every shadow isn't going to whisper and move. Still, he can feel new beginnings in the air, like the warmth of the spring air.

"The cities that were gone are still gone," Ethan says soberly. "We've been sending people to investigate the ones we can. Our communication network is better than what the humans have right now."

"We're all human." At Ethan's sharp look, Nikolai tries to explain. "We're Talented. They're…not. But maybe some of them are and are haven't Emerged yet. We're all still human, it's just that some of us are also magical."

"He has a point," Mikhail murmurs, and Nikolai is glad for the backup.

Marybelle circles in front of them, walking backward as she speaks. "There's a community outside Portland, Maine. Two Technopaths and a Dreamwalker from there were part of the efforts on our side for your ritual. Friday morning, they woke up to find hu—" She stops, frowning. "There were newcomers from Portland outside their wards. They said the Shadows were mostly gone. They'd seen a few, but not crowds of them, and that they weren't as brave as before. So a few of the"—she hesitates, then tries—"non-Talented city people and some of the Talented community decided to take a trip down to Boston. There's no one alive there. But there are no Shadowwalkers there, either. It might be safe."

"I'm guessing if they made it there in just a couple days, they drove," Mikhail says dryly.

"They made it there in *hours*," Marybelle says, her voice hushed like that's a miracle. Maybe it is. Talent and those without together, on the road, in public.

"What about the government?" Nikolai asks.

Marybelle's gaze drops, and Ethan makes a face. "DC is dark," Ethan admits. "We don't know who's left. They don't have a network like ours. At this point, it looks like the Talented communities will be spearheading rebuilding efforts."

"So we have a chance to make it work for us and stop the persecution of people with Talent," Mikhail says firmly. "We need to make a better world."

"We should reach out to Albany and Bennington," Ethan suggests. "I've tried talking to Mom and Alia—"

"We'll help," Nikolai tells him. Seth tightens his grip in approval. "We learned where magical communities are located in the other world. We're different, but what we found out will help us make connections here."

"Mom mentioned going to Burlington," Ethan says. "Some of the folks from Utah are trying to figure out if they can cross the country to get here. We've talked to communities in Chicago and Detroit. Getting in touch with the magical communities is easy—it's outreaching to the walled cities that's difficult."

"It's only been five days, and so much has happened already," Nikolai murmurs.

"The first five days of the new world," Marybelle says happily. "Imagine what'll happen next."

The sun peeks through the canopy of trees as they walk down the path, leaving the walkway dappled with spots of bright light that chase the shadows away. As Nikolai walks along, Seth's hand in his, he hears singing in the distance, voices raised in cheer and happiness to greet the spring.

Seth lifts their joined hands and presses a kiss to Nikolai's fingertips.

Nikolai feels the warmth of that touch spread through him like dawn after the longest night. "It's a new world," he agrees softly. "And we're going to make sure it's a better one for everyone."

47

"I WANT TO know everything," Val says.

Nikolai shifts on the loveseat, his leg pressed against Seth's, their hands locked together. They're in a small sitting room he hasn't been in before, bright with sunshine streaming through large windows that stretch from barely a foot above the floor almost to the ceiling. Sheer curtains are drawn back, leaving plenty of space for hanging plants to spill from their pots, vines dangling down. The furniture is plush and comfortable, although worn—a loveseat, a couch, and two oversized chairs. Val sits on the edge of the couch, while Alia leans back, her spine straight and one arm stretched over the back behind Val.

Val's eyes are wide with excitement.

Alia's lips are pressed thin.

Nikolai can't stop watching Alia, feeling her disapproval.

Ethan lounges in one of the chairs, feet drawn up as he slouches. "I'm interested in hearing the story too. There's another me! And the other Marybelle is a kid."

"It's not exactly like that," Seth says. "Things happened differently there."

"But she's essentially me." Val picks up one of the books Valentine had sent with Nikolai and Seth. "This is what I would have done, if I could have. Or had thought of it. We think enough alike that I'll find something useful in these materials. Please find a way to give her my thanks. And I want to hear—"

"It's not our world." Alia cuts her off. Her touch against Val's cheek is gentle, unlike her curt tone. "What the Valentine and Alia of another world do has nothing to do with us."

"They've become friends, at least in part due to the two of you," Nikolai says. "I think their world needed that. Thank you for inspiring them."

"We're inspiring." Val grins, leaning into Alia's touch. "Well, tell other-me that I appreciate the gift, and say the same to Carolyn. Her notes will be useful. Not to mention what Pawel's sent. We lost our archives. Fleeing for our lives didn't allow for carrying libraries with us. Hopefully we'll be able to reclaim some of our history now that we can reach other communities. The Technopaths say they're building a space online."

"I'd like to be involved in that," Nikolai says, amending it as Seth squeezes his hand: "Both of us would."

Val opens her mouth, then closes it again when Alia lowers her hand. Alia leans forward, both hands clasped as her elbows rest on her knees. Alia's lips are still pursed, lines drawn around her eyes.

"Is this when we get thrown out of Havenhill?" Seth asks.

Alia blinks, her expression relaxing abruptly. "Of course not."

Nikolai flashes back to Alia's snap and snarl over the broken wards. "We weren't sure we'd be welcome back," he admits. "We didn't leave on good terms."

Alia's expression goes sour. "No. You did not. However."

Nikolai waits through the silence, focused on the way Seth's thumb slides over the side of his hand.

"They were impulsive," Alia says. "They did not care about the dangers that we took very seriously. However, they were instrumental in forging a new path forward for our world, one without Shadows lurking in the darkness. You aided that, and we are thankful. With the Shadows no longer so great a danger, Havenhill can be more welcoming than before, and we can rebuild."

"I heard her say 'heroes,' " Ethan says.

"You did not," Alia snaps.

Val snickers. "She didn't say 'heroes,' but she was thankful in the aftermath. We have had a lot of chaos in the last several days, but it's the good kind of chaos. The world is better now."

Alia stands, her hand resting atop Val's head. "You are welcome here for as long as you wish to stay. I'm sorry that the larger Benford house is no longer available for your family."

It had disappeared at the same time as the Berman house, when they had merged the worlds in the Dreamscape. Nikolai is thankful that the smaller house is still there for him and Seth to come home to. "If Mikhail wants to be near us, he can build a cabin. We're fine," he says. He exhales and stands as well, Seth tight by his side. "Thank you. We've been looking forward to being a part of Havenhill."

The tension around her mouth eases. Nikolai wouldn't say Alia smiles, but her compressed frown is gone. "We look forward to that as well," she murmurs. She slides her hand down Val's head, lingering for a moment on the back of her neck. "Welcome home."

As soon as she departs, Val slides forward another inch. "I'm still waiting. Tell me everything about the other world."

It takes hours. They pore over the books Nikolai and Seth brought back, Val asking constant questions. She grabs paper and takes meticulous, tiny notes, asking them to repeat things until she's certain she's understood. She scrawls thoughts in the margins. Nikolai suspects that Val is most fascinated by hers and Alia's counterparts; he lingers over those details as much as he can. It's a pity that they'll never meet, although he can't imagine a world with two Vals in it, let alone two Alias.

When they're finally finished, Val promises to have someone drive over to pick up the fiber Alaric sent, and Seth and Nikolai promise Ethan that he's welcome to look through the photo album they brought with them.

By the time they walk down the road toward their home, the celebration for May Day has wound down to a few bonfires and some excited chatter. Nikolai catches the bitter scent of beer on the wind, but he has no interest in tasting it again. He has something else in mind, and his steps speed as they draw closer to home.

"We don't need to run," Seth points out.

"I have something I want to do Do you remember the night in Haverhill when we burned our wishes?"

Seth nods. "I don't know if that was magic or not, but my wishes have been coming true."

Nikolai remembers the words he wrote that night.

I want to be able to go home and live with my family and grow old with Seth.
I want this world to be safe from Shadows.
I want my own world to be safe from Shadows.
I want my friends and family and myself and Seth to be happy.
I want to live in a world where we don't just survive, we can thrive.

He won't know how all of his wishes turn out for a long time, but so far, the future looks bright. "Mine too," he says. "I was thinking about that, and the way that Dax was able to talk to ghosts, and how he said that Alaric's brother was sticking around. Even though Alaric couldn't see him, he'd be listening, if Alaric wanted to talk to him."

The corners of Seth's eyes are bright and damp. "And?"

"I want closure," Nikolai says. He pauses on the path, their house visible in the distance. He takes both of Seth's hands in his. "We spent the day celebrating spring and new beginnings, which seems more than appropriate this year. I'm ready to move forward, and while we'll never forget, I want to say goodbye to our past." He lifts both of Seth's hands, kissing his knuckles. "I want to tell our parents everything we've done. I want their blessings on the future. I want them to know that we'll be fine now, that we're in Havenhill, and that we're safe. That the world has changed, and that the Dreamscape is safe."

"Is it?"

Nikolai thinks about how different the Dreamscape felt when they passed through it with Chelsea. "It is," he says firmly, "and the Dreamwalker alliance will make sure it stays that way. We can learn and better understand how the Dreamscape works and study how people with traveling Talent move through it. Even without the split, there were still places off the beaten paths, places we can explore safely now that they aren't filled with Shadows. And I know that you'll always be here to draw me back."

Seth moves forward, wrapping his arms around Nikolai. "I am not letting you go," he mutters against his chest.

That's more than fine with Nikolai.

"So, let's go inside and write letters to our parents, then burn them to send them," Nikolai says. "We can tell them everything we want them to know about our lives."

They have paper packed in with the things brought back from the other world. Nikita had insisted. They settle at the table across from each other, Nikolai holding the pen he's carried carefully for the past year, making sure it stayed dry while they traveled. The ink is starting to fade—it'll run out soon. It seems right to use it to write this particular letter.

Mom & Dad—

Hello from Havenhill. Seth and I made it here, finally, and we found Josef and Mikhail. I wish you were able to be here with us. Josef is getting married. I've got whiskey as a gift for him from Trish.

Who Trish is, and how I met her and a whole bunch of other people, is such a long story. I don't even know where to begin.

Nikolai stops, the tip of the pen between his teeth as he thinks through his words. Seth writes continuously, his penmanship small and cramped, conserving paper the way they learned to once the world collapsed around them. Nikolai knows he should be writing as well. He has so much to say, and this was his own idea.

He puts the pen back to the paper, the letters showing bits of white among the black as the ink runs low.

I love you. I miss you more than I can say, and I always will. But I know that you loved us, and you protected us, and you taught us well. And somewhere out there is a world where there is someone similar to you, because I met another version of myself from a world that never had the Shadowwalkers invade.

Our worlds are twinned. On similar paths, but not exactly the same. I think you'd like her, if you were able to meet her.

He writes until he runs out of room, cramming as much of the story onto the page as he can. When he finally finishes, Seth sits quietly across from him, elbows on the table and chin propped on his hands.

Seth smiles, the corners of his eyes crinkling. "You mentioned a bonfire."

"It doesn't have to be that big," Nikolai says.

They investigate their own backyard for the first time, finding a small bricked space scarred with old char and smoke. They gather sticks from the ground, piling them up. The fire isn't big once they get it burning, but it's warm and the flames licks toward the sky.

Nikolai sits on the ground, his letter in one hand, crumpled from his grip.

Seth looks at his own paper. "It felt good to talk to them," he says.

"We can do that any time," Nikolai replies. "And maybe we should. Who knows what happens when people die? They might be listening. Magic's magic, after all."

"Dax could've told us for certain."

"True." Nikolai carefully smooths the paper of his letter, looking it over one more time. Then he balls it up and tosses it on the fire. Flames curl around it, catching the edges first, tiny pieces flaking off as ash, floating up in the hot air.

Seth kneels to do the same, watching for a long moment before he settles back to the ground, closer to Nikolai. "I love you," he says.

Nikolai can see the shine in his eyes, can feel the dampness in his own. He puts an arm around Seth's shoulder, pulling him close and pressing a kiss to his temple. "I love you, too," he murmurs. "Welcome home."

About the Author

Tris Lawrence has been writing since she was a child, filling notebooks with the worlds, dreams, and voices from inside her head. She declared in sixth grade that she wanted to be a writer, started drafting her first novel in seventh grade, and never looked back.

Tris has always been fascinated by the way people work: how their relationships fit together, how they interact socially, and how they learn and discover. She has read avidly her entire life, devouring mysteries, romances, science fiction, and fantasy novels, and as an adult still loves all of these genres. Her favorite stories center on people who are learning or discovering new things, and coming-of-age stories top that list, which is how Pine Hills University came to be. She wants to share stories of people who are learning how to relate to each other, how to adult, how to college, and how to just be. She hopes to share stories about diverse characters with representation of everything she wishes she could have read growing up, and she hopes that these stories will touch the lives and hearts of those who read them.

When not writing, Tris is a wife, a mother (to two children, two cats, and a dog), a knitter, a system administrator, a black belt in taekwondo, an avid reader, and a music aficionado. Sleep, she claims, is optional.

Links

Author site: trislawrence.com
Bluesky: tryslora.bsky.social
Dreamwidth: tryslora
Facebook: trislawrencewrites
Mastodon: wandering.shop/@tryslora
Patreon: tryslora
Pillowfort: tryslora
Tumblr: welcometophu

Titles by Tris Lawrence

Warm Anything You Want

Welcome to PHU

Twinned Trilogy

Book 1: Commit to the Kick
Book 2: Missed Fortunes
Book 3: Into the Split

Side Stories

Best Friends AND...
if it's meant to be
Just Let Me Lose Control
Live Like There's No Tomorrow
so he won't fly away

Books and short stories in the Welcome to PHU 'verse available at

- https://duckprintspress.com/about-duck-prints-press/creators-we-work-with/authortrislawrence/
- https://welcometophu.tumblr.com/
- https://www.pillowfort.social/community/WelcomeToPHU/

Anthologies including Tris Lawrence

Add Magic to Taste (author contributor)
He Bears the Cape of Stars (author contributor)

About Duck Prints Press LLC

Duck Prints Press LLC is an independent publisher based in New York State. Our founding vision is to help fanwork creators navigate the complex process of bringing their original works from first draft to print, culminating in publishing their work under our imprint. We are particularly dedicated to working with queer creators and publishing stories and artwork featuring characters from across the LGBTQIA+ spectrum.

Support Duck Prints Press on Patreon!

Find us online at our website https://duckprintspress.com/ or on social media:

Bluesky: duckprintspress.com
Bookshop.org: duckprintspress
Instagram: duckprintspress
itch.io: duckprintspress
Patreon: duckprintspress
Pillowfort: duckprintspress
TikTok: @duckprintspress
Tumblr: duckprintspress

Goodreads: https://www.goodreads.com/user/show/129902473-duck-prints-press-llc
Storygraph: https://app.thestorygraph.com/profile/unforth_duckprintspress

If you enjoyed this story, don't forget to leave us a review!

www.ingramcontent.com/pod-product-compliance
Lightning Source LLC
LaVergne TN
LVHW020648110826
845149LV00012B/1951